The Healing

By Lynda Faye Schmidt

The Healing

First published in 2021 by

Halifax, NS, Canada
www.ocpublishing.ca

Cover design and original cover illustration by Krista Wells
Interior book layout and design by Grace Laemmler

ISBN - 978-1-989833-06-3 (Paperback Edition)
ISBN - 978-1-989833-07-0 (eBook Edition)

DISCLAIMER
This novel is based on true events and therefore may closely resemble
the people and places depicted. Characters and events are a complex
interweaving of imagination and reality, the lines between them blurred
by the creative force and the personal experiences of the author. No two
realities are the same. *The Healing* is the author's adaptation of hers.

*I dedicate this work with limitless love, appreciation,
and gratitude to my beloved, David.*

Chapter 1

*C*ATE'S APPLE-RED MAZDA IS PACKED to the
ceiling with suitcases, Rubbermaid containers, and
boxes bulging with the entire contents of her life. In the
spirit of her new-found freedom, she's committed to
downsize and de-clutter. Dana's artwork is stacked and
wrapped in Cate's favourite African, handwoven, wool
blanket. Candles, sage, framed meditations—the artifacts
that create sacred space—are stored carefully in a wooden
trunk that was carved and hand-painted in Thailand.
Fredrick's kennel, which becomes a clothes-drying rack,
rattles on top. It's close to ten o'clock in the morning
when Cate is finally ready to hit the road.

"Goodbye Taylor," Cate says to her son as she embraces
him on the front doorstep one last time. Her eyes, emerald-
green with specks of amber-brown, are bright with tears that
escape onto her cheeks as she reaches up to run her hand
through her son's thick, chestnut-brown hair. She rests her
hands on his shoulders.

"I'm going to miss you like crazy," Cate says.

Cate prays her son will be alright, but she knows she no longer needs to sacrifice herself for him, or her girls, or anyone else. She is grateful that Celeste and Dana have moved out and on with their lives, and consoles herself with the knowledge that her son is eighteen, a man really. She wipes her eyes with the back of her sleeve and stands on tiptoes to kiss Taylor's eyelids—their private ritual since birth—one more time.

"Take care of yourself," Cate says.

"I will, Momma," Taylor says. "Try not to worry so much. I'll be fine."

Cate calls to her bichon-shiatzu, Fredrick, who has been busy rolling in the dry autumn grass of the front lawn. She gets in the car and scoops him up to sit on her lap. She picks off some dry leaves that cling to Fredrick's paws and tosses them out before closing the door and starting the car. She continues waving back at Taylor until the house disappears from the rear-view mirror.

Cate drives to her friend Amy's, who has agreed to accompany her on the first leg of her odyssey westward. Along the way, Cate's mind races.

The weight of the unknown presses down on me. Now that I'm free, I'm scared as hell. I haven't been on my own for over twenty years, since I moved in with John. Will I find work? Will I make new friends? Will Celeste return, well and ready to resume her life, pick up where she left off? And then, where will I go?

Cate pulls into Amy's driveway and files her worries in the back of her mind. She honks the horn. Amy waves from the window. She has a Calgary Flames cap on her head, her long auburn hair pulled back in a ponytail that sticks out through the cap's opening. Seconds later, Amy comes out of her house and around the passenger side, dressed for the outback in a pair of khakis, a loose-fitting T-shirt, and sport sandals.

"Are you sure you have room for me?" Amy laughs as she climbs in. She wedges herself in-between the cooler and dog dishes and tucks her backpack between her feet. Fredrick jumps from Cate's lap to Amy's and barks a friendly greeting.

On the road to Amy's family cabin in Revelstoke, Cate and Amy engage in open and honest conversations about love and loss.

"I can't believe you're leaving," Amy says. "It won't be the same at the school without you to vent and share strategies with."

"Well, don't forget, this is all a trial," Cate says. "I have a year of leave to sort things out, but who knows, I might be back."

"I'd love that," says Amy. "But I want whatever is best for you."

The four-and-a-half-hour drive whizzes by, and as luck would have it, they make it just in time for the last afternoon ferry across the lake.

"Turn right here," Amy says following a short drive from the ferry. She points toward a back road that is more like a rough clearing. Cate grits her teeth as her sort-of-new car bounces noisily over the potholes, belly scraping on fallen branches and protruding rocks, until they arrive at the edge of the lake. Cate parks the car. Amy hops outs and Cate follows in her high-heeled boots down the rocky incline, purse and overnight bag slung over her shoulder. Inside there's a bottle of wine, still in the liquor store brown paper bag. Fredrick waddles along beside them, sniffing his way to the boat that is idling at the shore. Amy's father welcomes Cate like family and tosses her belongings onto the deck of the boat.

"Hop in," Amy's dad says as he reaches for Cate's hand. "Grab a seat; there's a life jacket under the bench," he says as he puts the boat in gear and eases the bow forward.

Minutes later they pull up alongside a rickety dock, several planks missing and paint peeling. Cate's face says it all. She stifles a gasp as she looks across to the cabin.

"I told you we'd be roughing it," Amy laughs.

Cate recalls Amy mentioning that the cabin isn't accessible by road, but somehow she's not prepared for things like outhouses. The cabin looks more like a shack.

As evening falls and Cate settles in by the fire with a glass of wine in hand, she manages to distract herself. She chats it up with Amy's eighty-year-old family friend, Luke, about the good old days. His mind is still as sharp as ever, and he looks physically fit too. Cate feels inspired and happy in a way she doesn't quite understand. The unlikely assembly sits around the fire, drinking wine and smoking pot and telling stories. Soon Cate is laughing so hard her cheeks hurt. She feels incredibly funny herself. It is late when she passes out in the trailer, the stickiness of the outback rendered irrelevant in slumber.

Cate rises early, as the first rays of sun filter through the tiny window. Amy snores, sound asleep. Cate retrieves her journal and pen and bundles up in a heavy sweater.

She ditches her boots for her running shoes and wanders down to the lake, Fredrick on her heels. Rocks crunch under her feet.

The boys are up and at 'em. Cate waves at them. A fire crackles warmly in the pit. It is still and peaceful. The air is brisk and oh so sweet. Tarps are tightened and tied over the picnic table. Empty cans and bottles are strewn about, evidence of last night's carefree abandon. Juno and Joe, the two border collies, frisk playfully along the water's edge, but Fredrick chooses to curl up in a ball by her feet once Cate settles into a lawn chair. The sun is still climbing, lazily burning off the night's clouds. For Cate, the pace feels like freedom. She gets out her journal and begins writing.

> *Dirt under my nails. Reminders. The muckiness that I was trying to escape. For so long I'd felt dirty, or should I say ashamed? I'd felt responsible for being abused, and stupid for staying in an unhappy, unhealthy marriage. But things are about to change.*

Cate stops to brush away a fly that has landed on the stark blankness of her page with a swipe of her hand.

> *Cups are overflowing and spilling in this land of plenty. The goose calls its mate earnestly. Chit chat, chit chat; noises in my head. The open road is just over the lake, and I'll be driving it. Road trips are so epic. Like* Summer of My Amazing Luck, Ulysses, *and the first Vancouver Island. I'm coming back. Same, same, different; things like that, as they said in Thailand.*

Cate stops to look out at the rocky beach. She feels heavy with the weight of her uncertain future. Her heart beats, thump, thump, as though a captive inside her ribcage.

*Little pinpricks of ice are dancing along the surface
of my so-called reality. Here at the lake, at Chug-a-Lug
cabin, where dreams unfurl and secrets are revealed,
I feel alive and present, attuned with my own body.
The stillness is deafening. Like when a butterfly causes
an earthquake. Butterflies in my stomach.*

Cate is distracted, this time by her feet, ice-cold
despite the heavy socks and sleeping bag thrown over them.
She shivers and rubs them together.

*Fredrick is basking in the multitude of stinky
scents. Letting go of his once-leashed fears. Fish are
practically jumping out of the lake into nets, onto
fishing lines. Gutted, then fried. Life ebbs and flows.
Why are some more, some less? The impact of a dead
fish, a smacked mosquito, a father lying in a hospital
bed, wheezing his last breath from his tired lungs.
Choices, thoughts, meanderings, musings. Some
answers, but mostly questions.*

Cate closes her journal and heads back to the trailer.
She rolls her dirty clothes up neatly and packs them
carefully into her bag. Amy wakes up.

"You're up early," Amy says with a yawn and a stretch.
"It looks like you're getting ready to go. Can I offer you some
breakfast? We've got eggs in the cabin."

"Thanks," says Cate, "but I'm not hungry; I had an apple
and your dad brought me a coffee. I'm anxious to head out."

"I wish you luck, then," Amy says, getting out from the
covers to give Cate a hug.

"Stay in touch," Cate says, then calls to Fredrick and
heads down to the dock.

Amy's dad lifts Fredrick into the boat as Cate climbs in,
and he takes them across the lake to where Cate left the car.

Cate waves as Amy's dad turns the boat around. She searches her purse for her keys and calls Fredrick, ready to get back on the open road.

On the drive down a sparkling black highway, through a tunnel of nature, Cate thinks of how, in her married life, she'd always been in the passenger seat. This time it's going to be different. It's all up to her and it isn't a one-month adventure; it's her new life.

In Vernon, Cate stops for lunch and a stretch, picking up a sandwich and a bottle of water from Subway before walking through the city centre park. The weather is perfect, sunny and warm. Ducks and geese waddle along beside the pond. Cate stops to watch the families picnicking and a ball game going on in the field. Fredrick rolls in the grass, his caramel-coloured fur turning a dirty grey. Soon it's time to get back behind the wheel.

True to form, Cate gets lost in Peachland. She calls her Aunt Winfred, who sorts her out. Cate drives through the orchards, heavy with apples, through the tiny town, and onto her aunt's familiar driveway. She wonders how many times, in how many different vehicles, she has made this trip. As she ascends the cement stairs, memories of sugar cookie dough, skinny-dipping, and apple raiding filter into her consciousness.

"Thank goodness you found us," Winfred remarks with relief as she opens the screen, her stocky frame filling the doorway. "Henry, go on now and help Cate with that giant suitcase. And who is this now?" Winfred laughs as Fredrick jumps up on her calf and barks.

"Down, Fredrick," Cate says. "Did I not mention I was bringing him? I hope it's okay." She starts to flounder.

"Oh, now I do remember you saying you were bringing your dog, dear, and of course it's no problem." Winfred stops to give Fredrick a pat.

Henry returns, just slightly out of breath. Cate thinks he is starting to look his age, despite his still-thick, salt and pepper hair.

"Thank you, Henry, and you too, Winfred," Cate says. "I so appreciate you having me. It's good to see you. It's been too long."

Cate knows her way around the house like the back of her hand. She stashes her insulin in the fridge and digs out the bottle of wine she picked up in Vernon, handing it to Henry who thanks her and places it on the kitchen table before disappearing out into the garden. Winfred and Cate sit down in the living room to talk about everything under the sun.

"So, you've finally made the big decision to leave," Winfred says. "I'm so proud of you. I never thought much of John. Your mom told me all kinds of horrible stories. Still, I know better than anyone the ties that bind."

Cate knows that Winfred separated from Henry more than once over the years. But she always went back.

"I don't think it's ever easy," Cate agrees. "Despite everything, John has his good points. I took my marriage vows seriously, the whole 'in sickness and in health' thing. And having kids complicates things."

"Yes, but your kids are all adults now," says Winfred. "How old is Celeste?"

"She just turned twenty-eight last week," Cate says.

"My goodness, doesn't time fly?" Winfred touches her hand to her ample bosom. "I've always had a special place in my heart for that girl."

The past is resurrected, briefly, in the sharing of their memories.

It's Thanksgiving weekend and Winfred has been slaving in the kitchen all day to prepare a traditional turkey dinner.

"I'll set the table," Cate says while Winfred whisks the gravy. The meal is soon ready.

"Henry, it's time to come in and carve the turkey," Winfred calls out the kitchen window.

Winfred's forgotten that Cate is a pescatarian, and Cate doesn't have the heart to remind her, so she just digs in and eats turkey with all the fixings. The meal is delicious, and the traditional dishes bring forth their own nostalgic whisperings.

As Winfred whips up thick cream for the pumpkin pie, Henry finds a casserole in the oven and tut-tuts at her absent-mindedness, but Winfred laughs off her failing memory.

"The casserole will be perfect for tomorrow's lunch," Winfred says.

After dinner, Cate and Henry clear the table and Winfred makes a pot of tea. Henry chooses to stay and be a part of the conversation, totally out of character. After dinner he normally disappears downstairs to his study.

"Remember that time Henry came to pick up you and Sally from the beach early and caught you skinny-dipping?" Winfred laughs.

"Do I?" Cate laughs along with her. "Only like it was yesterday! I've never dressed so quickly in my life, and I was treading water!"

It isn't long before Henry is tired of socializing. He grabs the remote and turns on the TV. Cate notices his hands have aged too, become gnarled with arthritis and spattered with age spots.

"Oh Henry, must you turn that dratted thing on?"

Winfred complains as she rolls her expressive eyes. Winfred and Cate sigh in unison, then find themselves drawn in by the drama unfolding on the screen. They watch the news but before long, all three of them are yawning.

Cate takes Fredrick out for a pee, comes back in, and says goodnight with two quick pecks on her aunt and uncle's cheeks. She retires to her room and tucks herself in. Fredrick curls up in a ball by her feet, and soon they are in a deep sleep.

Cate wakes up early and patters out to the kitchen. She lets Fredrick out and puts on a pot of coffee. There is no sign of her aunt and uncle, so she decides to get out her journal and settle on the couch to write.

> *Yesterday I was on the road, feeling the lightness of freedom, but today I'm fearful, questioning the enormity of what I've done. Yet, I know there is no turning back. Watching Winfred and Henry together after all of these years and all their challenges, I started to wonder. Hearing the two of them squabble about something or other in the kitchen gave me pause. But what I left wasn't squabbles. It wasn't a case of irreconcilable differences. It was deeper and darker. I can't let myself forget.*
>
> *I feel a shift deepening, a widening. I'm shedding a skin, and someone I don't quite recognize anymore is emerging. She's been hidden in the darkness for so long. I'm curious and excited to rediscover her.*

Winfred comes in, dressed in her velvety robe, and spots Cate on the couch.

"I'm sorry I overslept," Winfred says. "I'll make up for it with a pot of my infamous porridge."

"It's no problem," Cate laughs, tucking her journal away. "I'll come help."

Soon the aroma of cinnamon fills the house, and Winfred calls Henry, who is reading the newspaper in the living room, to breakfast. They share the morning meal and clear up the dishes.

"Thank you so much, for everything," Cate announces, as she puts away the last bowl in the cupboard, "but it's time for me to go."

Cate retrieves her things from the spare bedroom, wheels her suitcase down the hall, and calls Fredrick.

"Drive safe," Winfred says, a tear in her eye as she hugs her niece goodbye on the front step.

Henry just grunts, but the twinkle in his eye gives him away and he gives her a sort-of hug too. As she pulls out of their driveway, back out onto the open road, Cate feels the call of the wild and answers with a full-on, from-the-belly howl.

It is a long drive through the winding highways of British Columbia that weave in and out of tree-lined forests and craggy mountainsides. Autumn is radiant in all its glorious colour: green pines surrounded by rusty oranges, burnt yellows, burnished reds, soft pinks, and deep burgundy leaves.

The wind blows through Cate's open sunroof, tousling her fine, cotton-candy-blonde hair. Cate has her iPad hooked up to the car stereo, and Michael Buble's "Feeling Good" blares out while Cate sings along at the top of her lungs and drums the steering wheel in rhythm.

When she passes through the sleepy town of Hope, she knows she's almost there and her heart starts to beat a little faster, a little louder. The worry of what lies ahead returns, but Cate silences her fears, repeating the affirmation in her head, "*I am safe, I am protected.*"

Cate arrives on Vancouver Island in the pitch-black dark of night. There are no street lights, only the moon and stars to guide her. She drives right past the turnoff twice, but eventually she spots Celeste's bright yellow jeep. She pulls into the driveway. The car tires crunch over the gravel, the only sound in the silence.

Fredrick jumps out of the car and scampers about. He sniffs the heady air that is thick with damp forest and ocean breeze. Cate soon realizes she has forgotten the instructions of where to locate the key. Her cellphone is dead. She takes a deep breath. Her heart beats loudly as she creeps about the property in the dark, looking for a likely key-hiding receptacle. On the large covered deck there is a table. She lifts each jar of half-melted candles, feeling underneath, and finds the keys.

Cate lets herself in and turns on the lights. She feels the chill of the empty house, and after storing her suitcases in the master bedroom, she looks about for the thermostat. She turns it up to 22°C. She is too exhausted to do much more than rummage through her things for her toothbrush. She gives her teeth a half-hearted swipe and falls into bed.

Morning blazes through the still wide open, forgotten curtains. Cate wanders into the kitchen, where she is delighted to discover a bag of Drumroasters coffee and a carton of Silk creamer in the fridge. There is a note on the counter from Celeste: "I recall you loved this locally roasted coffee last time you were here, enjoy!"

Cate smiles, thinking of her daughter, then brews a pot of coffee. She sits on the couch in Celeste's living room with the sun pouring in the huge windows. She pinches herself in disbelief. Her decision to take a year's leave from teaching in Calgary and sublet Celeste's rental seems outlandish. But Celeste asked for her support, and in the end, her children still meant everything to her and it was exactly the excuse she needed to push herself into making the leap.

Cate and Fredrick go out to scout the property. It is massive, with an overgrown garden in the back and caterpillar infested apple trees in the front, all surrounded by forest. The air is fresh, and it is like her own little garden of Eden.

Back in the house, Cate looks around for a suitable spot to set up her sacred space. There is a wall hanging of the Buddha in the corner of the living room, next to the fireplace, and being somewhat of an eclectic spiritualist, Cate decides it is the perfect place. She finds a plank of wood in the basement and sets it on an old cardboard box, then covers it with flowing purple and scarlet silk scarves. On it, she sets her framed Vision Board, along with her Goddess cards, a statue of the Buddha, some candles, crystals, and incense. She finishes by taking a cushion from the couch to place on the floor. She lights incense and sits in meditation. Cate closes her eyes and takes a few deep, calming breaths. She repeats an affirmation inside her head, *"I love and approve of myself."* She takes another deep breath, inhaling peace. She bundles up all her worries and anxieties and exhales them.

Feeling centred again, Cate returns to the task of unpacking her suitcases and boxes. When she finishes, it is close to noon. Cate hitches Fredrick on his leash, and they walk down the hill to the pier. It is a bustling centre of local businesses along the fishermen's wharf. Cate chooses a patio at a small café where a sign informs that dogs are welcome. She sits down at a wooden picnic table and ties Fredrick to the table leg. She orders fish and chips and a glass of pinot noir. The simple meal is greasy, salty deliciousness. When she finishes, they walk back up the steep hill to their new home, that is really Celeste's, and settle in for the rest of the day.

Later that afternoon, Cate runs a bubble bath and lights candles. She takes off the chill of the autumn day, of the ocean damp, her petite frame easily immersed in the sudsy, warm water.

After a good soak, she dries off and gets dressed in cozy clothes before setting her computer up in the office to work. She leans back in the big black leather chair and notices for the first time a message in giant lettering across the office wall: "You will be published!" She smiles and gets out her journal to work on the activities for week one of the writing course she just started, The Artist's Way, by Julia Cameron. The affirmation this week is, "I am a gifted and talented writer with a voice that deserves to be heard."

> *Looking. Looking out the window and at my reflection and inside myself.*
>
> *Hearing. Hearing the sound of the crows cawing, a plane in the sky, the heater coming on, Fredrick's tags clinking together as he rolls on the carpet.*
>
> *Tasting. Tasting strong, bitter coffee smoothed out with milk.*
>
> *Thinking. Thinking about options.*
>
> *Writing. Time to work on my book.*

Before long Cate's brain is drained, the words turning to drivel in front of her eyes. She takes a break. She heads outside with Fredrick to investigate. The misty mountains poke through the clouds in the distance. She feels God's presence. She prays that following her heart will lead her on the right path, that God has the keys for the cupboard labelled "Cate's Life."

Seemingly out of nowhere, it begins to rain intensely, yet still the sun's rays pierce through the clouds. Cate and Fredrick run through the deluge with gleeful abandon. The rain soaks her clothes to the skin, but she doesn't mind. Surrounded by the abundance of nature, she embraces the chance to heal.

The next day, Cate and Fredrick head out for yet another adventure. They take the path at the end of the lane that leads to the ocean. It is slippery with felled fall foliage and dew. Cate moves cautiously while Fredrick runs off ahead, oblivious. Cate starts to think about bears foraging for food, preparing for hibernation, and her heart beats faster, but then she is through the forest and standing on the rocky beach looking out at the vast ocean and forgets to be afraid. Woman and dog walk and run, taking in the sights and scents of nature with no sense of time, following their own internal rhythms.

Back home, Cate spots three deer in the yard. It feels like a sign of good fortune to come. Fredrick starts to bark and goes a little crazy. Lucky for him, the deer run away.

Inside the house, Cate makes tea. She drinks out of a blue ceramic mug with an eagle embossed on it. It is so quiet. The fridge rumbles and the dryer squeaks. Cate retrieves her journal.

*The sound of silence creates space for me to feel
my fears. My choice feels crazy, and I'm scared. I know
I need to push through it, embrace the silence, and
open my heart. I'm looking for the courage I know
resides inside of me. I'm summoning my faith that,
in this space I have created, inside of the fabrication
of my life, God will show up with possibilities that feel
like coincidences but are of the Divine.*

Cate sets her journal on the table and stares out the
huge bay window into the forest. The sun filters through
the tree branches. Cate longs for a soft touch, for hands
caressing her. She closes her eyes and imagines soft lips
kissing her. She pictures herself lying naked and completely
at ease with her body, without judgment. She thinks of her
pregnancy stretch marks and diabetic needle scars. She tells
the critic inside her head to shut up and chooses to notice
her strong, lean legs instead. She looks in the mirror over
the fireplace at her dreamer eyes and full mouth. She smiles
at her reflection.

Cate decides to go to a restaurant by herself for the second
time in two days. The writing course is having her stretch
herself out of her comfort zone. She calls herself names
inside her head, like loser and geek, but stops herself.
She takes a deep breath. She makes a conscious decision
to quit criticizing herself and wondering what other people
think of her. It's none of her business. She looks around
the restaurant, observing. She pulls out her Out and About
journal and starts writing. Not long after, a handsome,
young, Indigenous man approaches.

"Excuse me, but do you mind me asking what you're
writing?" he asks.

"I don't mind at all," Cate says with a smile. "Would you like to join me?" she asks, pointing to the empty chair.

K'esu sits down and within minutes they are engaged in conversation about magic and the spiritual world. They talk for over an hour.

"Wow," K'esu says, as he glances at the clock on the wall. "I really enjoyed our connection, but I need to get going."

"I did too," says Cate. "Maybe I'll see you around some time."

When K'esu leaves, Cate lets her mind drift. She starts thinking about sex again. She was in the same relationship for twenty-six years and is excited about being with different men. She thinks about the guy from the local repair store with his grey hair and icy blue eyes. She thinks about the human resources fellow with the Cowichan school board. She thinks about strangers she hasn't yet met.

As part of her new life, Cate decides to try a new style of yoga at a studio in Duncan. She's been practicing yoga for a few years, but Bikram yoga is all new. She rolls out her mat on the foam floor. The heat is so intense, she's sweating, full-body, within five minutes of the practice. The instructor barks out, "straighten your knee, reach further, work harder!" He tells the class to look at themselves in the mirror. Cate looks at her body and the criticism immediately sets in. She doesn't feel like the image staring back at her belongs to her. But the heat and the difficulty of the poses distract her from her judgment, and soon she is present only to the physical sensations.

Life on the island continues to pick Cate up and hurl her out of her comfort zone. *But that's what adventures are for,* she tells herself.

Part of her weekly tasks with the writing course require her to take herself on an artist's date. This week she decides to go to the pub on the wharf. She chooses an empty stool at the bar, one seat over from a man sitting by himself.

"Excuse me, do you feel like company?" he asks.

"Sure, why not?" Cate answers.

"I'm Bruce, and you are?" Bruce says as he pulls back the stool beside her.

"I'm Cate." Cate smiles. She shakes Bruce's hand, which is large and deeply calloused.

"Are you new to the area?" Bruce asks, sitting on his stool. "I don't remember seeing you around before."

Cate proceeds to tell him the framework of her story. They talk about the weather. Cate discovers that Bruce is an automotive repair man. He has a boat and likes to fish.

"You can walk down to the wharf and buy fresh fish right from the fishermen," Bruce says.

Cate finds Bruce attractive, although he is much younger than her. After a while, some of Bruce's buddies come into the pub, and he introduces them to Cate. They are surprised when Cate reveals she is forty-five. She tells them stories about Celeste, Dana, and Taylor, getting a bit carried away with the details of her children's lives. She's clearly a bit rusty with the flirting routine.

When Cate gets back home, she is feeling the wine and wants sex. She regrets not making a move with Bruce but decides to have a bath with bubbles and candles and put on sexy red lingerie, just for her. She tries touching herself, but it doesn't do anything for her so she lets it go. She reads her book until her eyes are heavy.

Cate wakes up to the kind of day Islanders talk about as quintessential autumn. It is overcast with periods of rain. The ridge is engulfed in a heavy mist. The rain is so thick she can hear it as it drips off the giant maple leaves. When it clears up, Cate heads out with Fredrick to further explore her new neighbourhood.

Near the top of the lane, Cate sees a man raking up leaves. He waves and calls Fredrick over for a pet.

"Are you new around here?" he asks, as he squints into the sun that has just peeked out from the clouds, lifting his hand to his brow.

"I suppose so. I'm staying temporarily at my daughter's house, the rental at the bottom of the lane," Cate replies.

"Well, welcome to Cobble Hill," he says, holding out his hand. "I'm Reg. Me and the wife, we're the first homeowners here. Almost forty years ago now."

"Hi, Reg, I'm Cate. Perhaps you met my daughter, Celeste, and her husband, Grayson?"

"You know what, now that you mention it, I think they had a yard sale a few weeks back," Reg says. He scratches his stubbly chin. "Is it the house with the bright yellow jeep out front?"

"Yeah, that's the one."

"I remember your daughter alright," Reg says with a leery grin. "She's quite the beauty. I can always remember a pretty face."

Cate is unimpressed with Reg's ramble. It goes from bad to worse.

"You know, in the good old days, when I first moved here, I had a view from my house of the bay, but that was before the Indians stopped allowing the cutting back of the trees. They've fished all the fish out of the ocean, you know. And they won't let us fish anymore neither, except for certain kinds."

Cate is surprised to hear Reg express such clear disdain for the Indigenous people, but she doesn't say anything. She has no wish to create conflict.

"I best get back to Fredrick's walk," Cate says, as an excuse to move on.

A little further on up the road, Cate sees another older man out walking with his dog off-leash. She sighs, not up for another draining conversation.

"Hello there, I'm Hank and this is my dog, Sparky," Hank says as he approaches.

Hank has a friendly demeanour, and somehow his white-grey hair and beard make Cate think of leprechauns. Sparky comes running over to inspect Fredrick, who lowers his tail and puts down his head.

"Don't worry about him, he just likes to act tough," says Hank.

"Hi, Hank, I'm Cate and this is Fredrick," says Cate. "We just moved in at the bottom of the road."

"The house with the yellow jeep?" asks Hank.

"Yeah, that's the one," Cate says.

"Well, welcome to the neighbourhood," Hank says. "I was just about to take Sparky to Bright Angel Park. Would you like to come along? It's not far from here, and if you haven't been there yet, you're missing out on something special."

"No, I haven't heard of it, and I suppose we don't have anything else to do, right Fredrick?" Cate says on an impulse.

"I'm just over on the next court," Hank says.

Cate follows Hank up the hill. A green Toyota hatchback is parked in the driveway. Hank gets out his keys and whistles for Sparky. Cate gets in the passenger side and lifts Fredrick on her lap. For some reason she can't explain, Cate trusts him.

Fifteen minutes later, Hank turns off the highway onto a rubbly road and parks in a gravel lot. They all file out of the car, and the dogs start in sniffing. Cate can see right away why Hank loves Bright Angel so much. The ancient trees stretch forever up into the sky, creating a ceiling of green foliage, with just enough space in between the branches for the sun's rays to sneak through and the ground to become a carpet of moss.

They walk along the river that runs through the park, the gurgling, clear water a pleasant backdrop of tranquility. The dogs are in heaven, scampering down the pathways and investigating the lush, dank scents. Cate is happy she chose to come along and decides she will bring Fredrick back often.

Cate settles into her new neighbourhood and quickly becomes good friends with Hank and his wife, Dorothy.

When Halloween rolls around, the couple invite Cate and Fredrick to a block party at their house. Shortly after dark, Cate hitches Fredrick to his leash, grabs a bottle of red wine, and walks up to join the group who are already huddled in the dark around the fire, drinking hot rum and handing out candy to the children who come along trick-or-treating. One of the neighbours, who appears to have a had a few too many beers, gives Cate a hard time.

"How come you've got that poor dog tied up on a leash?" Bob asks.

"He's a city dog," Cate says. "He'll just get into trouble."

"Well, you're in the country now," Bob says. "Go on, let him be free."

Cate caves in to the pressure and lets Fredrick off his leash, against her better judgment. When she calls for him shortly after, he is gone. Cate grabs the flashlight she brought along and starts to search for him, but he isn't anywhere in sight. Cate starts to panic. Several of her neighbours join her in the search. Cate ventures closer to the main road, her heart beating faster as she thinks about Fredrick getting hit by a car. Just as her imagination is getting carried away, Bob returns with Fredrick in his burly arms.

"No need for alarm," Bob says as he walks up, his ball hat askew. "I was ringing doorbells down the street and found him curled up on Ned and Izzy's couch, all warm and cozy. Ned was just about to head out to look for his owner."

"I told you he would only get into trouble," Cate says.

Cate is relieved, but she's had enough drama for one night. With Fredrick safely on his leash, she heads home.

A few days later, Cate accepts an invitation from Celeste's good friend Megan, who has taken it upon herself to introduce Cate to some more people in the community.

"Do you want to come with me and my husband to a hockey fundraiser at a local bar?" Megan asks.

"Sure, that sounds fun," Cate says.

Cate meets Megan and her husband, Charles, at the bar. She remembers Megan from when she visited Celeste and Grayson in the summer and recognizes her massive mane of blonde waves as soon as she walks in. Megan waves from the table, and Cate joins them.

"It's so good to see you again," says Cate, giving Megan a quick hug hello before sliding onto the bench beside her. "It was kind of you to think of me."

"It's no problem," says Megan. "It's good to see you again too. And I'd do anything for Celeste's mom. By the way, have you had any luck with your job search?"

"Ugh, don't even mention it," says Cate. "As it turns out, I have to update my certification to teach in BC. It's looking like it's going to be quite the go-around."

"Sorry to hear that," says Megan. "But for tonight, let's just kick back and have a good time."

Cate takes Megan's advice to heart and gets a bit tipsy. She flirts with one of the single dads, a friendly and outgoing guy originally from Scotland named Finn, who has a good singing voice and entertains the crowd at the karaoke station. After he finishes a set, Finn walks over to Cate and Megan's table.

"Would you like to go for drinks sometime, just the two of us?" Finn asks.

"Moving in on the new girl in town already?" Megan asks, a mischievous look in her big blue eyes.

"What the heck," says Cate, feeling bold.

Cate gives Finn her phone number, and he promises to be in touch.

Lying in bed that night, Cate thinks about Finn. She reflects on how messed up her relationships with men have been.

Her first loves were Clarence and Murray, all between the ages of six and ten, purely innocent with romantic dreams of kissing and stealing furtive glances. In grade five, the girls and boys were already dating, but she wasn't ready for that. And when the most popular and handsome boy in the class ditched his girlfriend and invited Cate to the gully to make out, she couldn't do it. His ego was bruised, and when she returned to school the next day he made fun of her in front of everyone and called her frigid.

In grade seven she made out with a boy in her class in his friend's clubhouse over the school lunch hour, but she wasn't really into it and it was soon over. In grade nine she had a crush on a boy and she went to the school dance, loaded on straight up alcohol stolen from her parents' sparse liquor cabinet, gulped hastily from a plastic margarine container. They necked up in the bleachers and he gave her a hickey, and all of a sudden he was popular and she was named the school slut.

She met Danny when she was fourteen, working as a waitress, her first job the summer after grade nine, and he was eighteen. Cate thought she was in love and cried hysterically when her family moved to Calgary after her father was diagnosed with severe rheumatoid arthritis.

In grade ten, she dated Joe from the cinemas, but she broke up with him in the spring, never going past first base.

It was just before summer holidays, not long after she'd turned fifteen, that Cate was raped. It was a set-up by a girl who was jealous of her. Carly tried to set her up with a friend of her boyfriend's, but when Cate saw him from the window of the truck, all tall and awkward looking with a huge afro, she said thanks, but no thanks. A few weeks later, Carly invited Cate to a party at her farm. Cate had two beers, and then there was a tequila station set up where the boy she'd rejected was pouring shots. Carly pressured her to try one, so she took one gulp and within minutes almost fell right into the bonfire. Carly dragged Cate into an old tool shed. The boy from the schoolyard came in, and soon he was on top of her, pulling off her jeans. Cate was like a rag doll. Tears poured down her cheeks, but she didn't have the strength to push him off and he ignored her pleas to stop.

When he was done, Carly came in from where she'd been waiting just outside the door and the two of them dragged Cate across the gravel and loaded her into a car and drove her home. Cate stumbled inside, her parents already asleep.

Cate never did know the full details. She always wondered if they'd drugged her with something in that single shot. She had tried to tell her parents, but somehow it was like they couldn't hear what she was saying, it was too much. Nothing happened. No charges were laid. Cate repressed the traumatic memories but not enough to stop her from trying to live up to what she had been called, a slut. Funny thing though, because she was the furthest thing from a slut. Cate was a romantic, innocent, trusting, naïve teenage girl, who didn't know how to spot a snake charmer when she saw one.

The summer after, Cate worked at a restaurant in Calgary where she hooked up with a guy for a one-night stand. It was just sex. Cate's ego took it as proof of her maturity. That fling didn't last long, and there were a few others before she met Celeste's father, Billy, at the beginning of grade eleven. They met at a bar. He was twenty years old, working in construction, driving a hot car. Cate was fifteen. They'd been dating just over a year when Cate got pregnant with Celeste on December 26, 1982.

She and Billy had driven up to his grandpa's house for the holidays. She was using a diaphragm, but when Billy snuck into her single bed in the room next to his in the middle of the night, having had a bad dream and needing consoling, the diaphragm remained tucked away in her overnight bag. The next morning, she realized what she'd done, but she talked herself out of thinking she might be pregnant because she'd only finished her period four days before, and after all, it was only the one time.

After two missed periods, Cate went to the doctor for a pregnancy test. She called from the pay phone at the cinema where she worked, and the nurse receptionist congratulated her that her test was positive. Cate had just turned seventeen.

Cate stayed with Billy through the pregnancy, hoping it would work out. But the cards were stacked against them, and when she found out Billy was cheating on her and had been all throughout their courtship, she decided to let him go.

Not long after, she gave her naïve, abused, ashamed, and vulnerable heart to John. They were neighbours. He was best friends with her brother. His mom and dad played bridge with her mom and dad. Everyone approved. And Cate was definitely attracted to him.

When Celeste was born, John came over bearing gifts. When he went to Europe for the summer, he sent her postcards asking how Celeste was doing, was she walking yet, was she talking yet? Cate's insecurities about being a single, teenage mother and his charm worked to create a vision. She wrote out two pages of what she wanted in a man, and when she was done, John's name appeared in her mind in golden handwriting and Cate thought it was surely the work of God.

Cate's history with men concluded with the twenty-six years spent in a relationship with a man who was abusive, controlling, and sexually dysfunctional. But it turned out she was more resilient than even she knew. She not only survived, she kept her inner light burning, ever so softly.

Now, Cate is ready to move forward. She's older and wiser, more at peace with herself, and more confident. She tells anyone who will listen that she'll never be stupid enough to marry again, but still, she yearns to meet someone kind and loving, who will be good to her.

Chapter 2

*I*T'S EARLY NOVEMBER AND A brisk wind has Cate head-down, coat pulled up around her neck. She is running a few errands in Duncan, and as she exits the bank on Station Street, she almost bumps right into Finn.

"Excuse me," she mumbles, before she recognizes him. "Oh, Finn, hi, how are you doing?"

"Hi, Cate, it's great to see you," Finn says, rubbing his bare hands together. "Sorry I can't stay and talk, but as it is, I'm in a bit of a hurry."

Cate is attracted by his Scottish accent and notices that in the bright sunlight his cobalt blue eyes glimmer even more than usual. She hadn't realized he was so short the other night at the bar. He's not much taller than her, she decides, and with her heels, she'd likely be taller.

"No worries," Cate assures him, "I'm on my way to yoga anyway. But maybe I'll see you around sometime?"

"Yeah, sure, it would be great to get together," Finn agrees. "I'll message you, soon." He leans in for an air-kiss on her cheek, and then he dashes off across the street. Cate watches him covertly behind her sunglasses. She notices how nice his bum looks in his tight jeans.

Later that evening Cate is tucked into bed early, all cozy in her pajamas and reading a book when she gets a text from Finn. "I'm just finishing up at work. Do you fancy popping by the restaurant for a drink?"

Cate surprises herself and texts back, "Yes." She throws on some clothes and drives down the dark country roads of Shawnigan Lake, her heart beating in anticipation.

When she walks into the dimly lit restaurant, Finn greets her at the door and leads her to a booth by the bar. He grabs a bottle of wine and pours them both a glass, then slides onto the red leather seat beside her. They talk and it doesn't take long before Cate's nervousness melts away. Finn kisses her softly, and she likes it. Cate is aroused but says she has to go and kisses him goodnight.

The next night Finn texts again. "Want to get together?"

"Sure, why don't you come over here?" she replies.

Cate gives him her address, and fifteen minutes later the doorbell rings. Fredrick goes crazy, barking like a maniac, but Finn just laughs when Fredrick jumps up, and gives him a good pat.

"Fredrick, get down," Cate says in her best stern voice. "Come on in, take a seat," Cate says as she points to the living room couch.

She has lit candles all along the fireplace mantle, and the atmosphere is romantic. She opens a bottle of wine that is ready on the coffee table and pours them both a tall glass.

"You know what attracts me most about you?" Finn asks, after an hour of light conversation. He drains the last sip and sets his empty glass down.

"No, I don't," Cate admits. "Why don't you tell me?"

"It's your eyes," he says, while gazing intently at her, as if to confirm his observation. "They are sultry as hell, but it's more than that. When I look into your eyes, they seem to hold all the wonder of the universe inside them."

Apparently this is a stellar pickup line. Cate gets up from her seat on the chair across from Finn and sits down on his lap, then takes off her shirt and bra. They end up in her room.

A few days later Cate is at her desk, working on an assignment from her course to write a letter to her present-day self from her eighty-year-old self, with the task of trying to imagine what might occur in her life over the next thirty-five years.

Dear Present-Day Cate:

First of all, I must inform you of the likely shocking news that you are still alive. I know you've always thought that because of the diabetes gig and your lack of success in achieving good results, you would likely die young from complications. You didn't. The naysayers were wrong. Perhaps even more shocking is the discovery that you are completely healed from diabetes, no longer needing insulin or medications of any sort. So, try not to be so hard on yourself. You're doing your best, and it is enough.

I'm so happy to tell you that you became a published writer and in fact went on to become an accomplished, internationally bestselling author, with a long list of award-winning novels to your credit. The made-for-television version on Netflix was extremely intriguing and the producers did an excellent job in their portrayal of your series.

Perhaps your greatest accomplishment, though, was the epic opening of your Wellness Centre. You see, your dreams come true, my dear. There are even more incredible surprises in store for you in the years ahead, along with some spirit-testing challenges, but never doubt you are on the right path. You have everything you need and more. I encourage you to embrace your life with enthusiasm and not to worry so much. All is well.

Love, Your Future Self

Finn and Cate are only seeing one another a few weeks when a red flag appears. Cate expresses that she wants to have intimacy that isn't only sex, like going to the movies and for long walks, but it doesn't happen. Finn seems to always have other plans or commitments that keep him from following through. Cate feels like the last item on Finn's list of priorities.

In the meantime, she's officially addicted to Bikram yoga and the Cowichan Valley. She's completely enamoured with her new life. She loves that she's living smack dab in the abundance of nature: the farmer's field with cows grazing in it, the forest, and the ocean. She's charmed by the idiosyncratic oddities of the community, of Old Farm

Market and Fisherman's Wharf and the pub, where everyone already knows her name. She explores teaching opportunities while going through the necessary procedures to become certified to teach in BC. She writes every day, working on her book and her writing course. Despite her dissatisfaction with Finn, her life feels full.

A week goes by and Cate doesn't hear a word from Finn. She's sitting on the couch eating potato chips and watching Food Network when he texts.

"Want to hook up at the pub?" Finn asks.

"It's closed on Mondays." Cate replies. "I can come over to your place."

"No," Finn writes. "It's a mess and my kids are home."

"Do you want to come here?"

"Too tired for the drive. Another day?"

Cate puts down her phone. She feels frustrated, disappointed, and unimpressed. Having a messy house is a problem for Cate, who is nothing if not a meticulous housekeeper. Her love language is quality time, but Finn is barely making any time for her. She doesn't want a relationship of stolen moments that are only about sex. She wants more. She longs to feel special.

Cate finds herself feeling lonely, the house on Longwood so quiet and still. She chooses to let go sulking about it and be grateful that her solitary life gives her the freedom to do whatever she wants. She gets out *The Artist's Way* and reads her next assignment, which is to write her present-day self from her eight-year-old self.

Dear Present-Day Cate:

I'm writing to remind you of how happy you were when you were me. Your light shone brightly in the lives of everyone you met. What that boy did to you when you were four didn't touch your soul; it happened to your body. God was holding your spirit, loving you tenderly throughout it all. Your soul is a treasure worth protecting. I am the acceptance you are searching for; it is inside of you. You need to let go of looking in the world for answers and discover what you already know inside. You don't have to accept the stories you've made up about yourself. Reclaim your self-confidence from me, who loves myself unconditionally. Remember, your eating disorders didn't start until after the farm. You still need to process that so you can let it go. Learn from me, the girl without diabetes or thyroid disease, who loves and accepts herself exactly as she is. There is no victim here. My wish for you is to love yourself now as much as you did when you were me. You need to forgive yourself. It wasn't your fault. It never is.
Love, Your Past Self

Cate drives from Cobble Hill to catch the ferry from Duke Point to Tsawwassen to meet up with Taylor, who is making the road trip from Calgary to Vancouver with some of his friends. She has Fredrick with her and has been relegated to the pet compartment, which is sparse, cold, and dreary. The uninviting space can't dampen her spirits, though, she is so excited to see her son. She passes the two-and-a-half-hour ferry ride reading Eckhart Tolle's *New Earth* and writing in her journal. Fredrick, curled up in her lap, keeps her warm.

She disembarks in the unfamiliar terminal, and all the hallways look the same. The signage is unclear and she is hopelessly lost. The crowds of people and her navigational challenges have her feeling anxious. Her heart races and beads of sweat break out at the base of her spine as she detours down yet another hallway, unable to locate the exit. She has an irrational worry that she'll never find Taylor. Then she hears a familiar, deep voice calling out to her, and her anxiety quickly melts away. She runs over to greet him. Taylor gives her a huge bear hug, easily lifting her off the ground, despite his lean and lanky build. He smiles, his blue-grey eyes turning up at the corner just like her brother Michael's.

"Hi, Momma, and you too, Freddy, ole boy," Taylor says as Fredrick paws his shin in excitement. He crouches down to pat Fredrick on the head and ruffle the fur under his neck.

Cate and Taylor talk non-stop all through the busy parking lot, making their way to where Taylor has parked his car. His friends, who made the trip out from Calgary with him, are waiting.

"Hi, Cate!" greets Todd as he vacates the front seat for her. "It's good to see you again."

"Thanks, Todd, you too," Cate says, climbing in. Turning around she says hi to Calum and Neil. Before long they are laughing together, telling old stories about when they were boys in junior high school.

Taylor navigates the car smoothly through the hectic traffic of downtown Vancouver, then finds a parking spot not far from Stanley Park. Everyone gets out and Cate hitches Fredrick to his leash.

"Can I walk him, Momma?" Taylor asks, reaching out his long arm. "I miss taking him for walks."

"Of course," Cate agrees easily, handing the leash over.

They've just started out on the pathway when the rain

sets in. They get drenched as they run back to the shelter of the car. Taylor uses Google Maps to find the way to a Vietnamese restaurant that has good reviews on Tripadvisor. They leave Fredrick to dry off on an old blanket, the window left open a crack, and go inside to enjoy a hot meal.

Too soon it's time for Cate to catch the last ferry back to the island.

"Well, it was short but sweet," Cate says as she gets out of the car. She holds back her tears, not wanting to embarrass her son in front of his buddies.

"Yeah, Momma, it was perfect," Taylor agrees. "Thank you for making such a huge effort to come all this way to see me. And putting up with these guys," he jokes, in an attempt to lighten the mood.

The three boys all wave goodbye, and Cate carries on with Fredrick, through the terminal, and onto the ferry.

When Cate gets up the next day, the sun is high and the leaves wax brilliant through her living room windowpane. She performs a guided self-hypnosis. She sits cross-legged on the cushion in her sacred space. She closes her eyes and breathes. She chooses a Goddess card from the deck. It is Isis: past lives. She lets that settle in, then counts backwards from ten. She pictures herself skipping down a cobbled path. She envisions herself as a fairy nymph–like creature, full of innocence and playfulness. In her mind's eye, Cate can see the stones of the path are in the middle of a glassy lake. She continues to count backwards as she enters a meditative state. She feels as though all of time, since the very beginning, is passing through her awareness in a flash of light. She loses all sense of present reality. Her breathing alters. Her heart pounds. Her throat stretches and tightens.

She tilts her head back. She hisses like a snake and releases breath from her mouth. She cries. A joyfulness washes over her, and then she is thrown back into time and back into her body. She picks up her journal, and her pen scrawls across the page as though directed by a force not her own. What she draws resembles a map of some sort, but even she can't comprehend what, if anything, it means. In the moment it seems irrelevant, because all she is present to is the freedom she feels, if only for a few precious, fleeting moments.

The first snowfall of the season transforms the island, a blanket of white that covers the lush green grass. Schools close and children build snowmen. Cate is inclined to just sit on a cushion in front of the big bay window and watch the snowflakes fall gracefully earthward, as she sips from a steaming cup of hot coffee. The ocean is visible through a gap in the trees where the fallen leaves have created a slight opening. Cate gets up off her cushion, called by the irresistible pull of the ocean. She is drawn to connect with the ancient trees, to celebrate their glory and Mother Earth herself. She moves into tree pose. She plants her left foot and roots into the ground. She pushes her right foot into her thigh. She lifts her arms to the sky and imagines they are branches, reaching for the sun. She bends her arms and brings her hands together in prayer. *Om shanti.*

Cate pulls open the living room drapes the next morning to cloudy skies. All signs of snow have disappeared, and the rain has returned. She takes Fredrick with her on an artist's date into Victoria. The Malahat is slick with rain. She grips the wheel tightly and lowers her speed, turning down the music to focus on the road. They make it without incident, and just as they drive past the sign announcing they are in Greater Victoria, the rain stops and the sun appears.

Cate parks in a parkade on Yates and hitches Fredrick onto his leash. They walk along the leaf-strewn streets, taking in the crisp smell of fall. Fredrick pounces puppy-like, trying to catch the dancing leaves. Cate spots Munro's, an independent bookstore, and thinks how nice it would be to browse through books, but there's Fredrick to consider. She happens to notice a street person by the bus shelter, his belongings in a backpack, sitting on an old worn blanket, and approaches him. She ignores the stories in her head, conceived from ignorance and fear, that whisper to her not to trust a homeless man.

"Um, excuse me?" Cate begins, with hesitance.

"What can I do for you?" he answers, a broad smile lighting up his face.

"Well, uh, I was just wondering, would you mind keeping an eye on my dog while I go into the bookstore for a bit?" she asks.

"Sure, why not?" he replies, already stroking Fredrick's scruffy neck.

Cate thanks him, offering to pay him a little something for his services, and he grins again before agreeing. She passes him a crisp ten dollar bill, gives Fredrick a pat with instructions to be a good dog, and goes inside.

The store is warm and cozy. Cate immediately goes into her happy place, surrounded by the sight and smell of new books, of ink and paper and ideas and words and creativity. She lets her hands drift across rows of book covers. She chooses a beautifully designed journal and a book, *In the Realm of Hungry Ghosts,* by Gabor Maté. When she walks back outside, Fredrick is all cuddled up with the man who was his temporary charge. They both look content. Cate sheds a single tear as she lets go the fear she'd been holding, that he might be mentally ill or a crack addict, or that he might steal Fredrick and attempt to sell him for money. She feels ashamed, for all she sees before her is a man like any other, who happens to be down on his luck.

Back home, Cate is happy for her little adventure. She feels lighter. She takes her new book and reads on the couch, drifting in and out of sleep. After her rest she feels inspired and heads into the office where her journal lies waiting.

> *Gritty eyes. The size of my thighs. The lies and the guys; my most excellent disguise. I cannot deny that as each day passes by, I wonder how I'll survive. The what, where, and when, like an old mother hen. I don't know how it will all unfold yet, but I have no regrets. I get wet, thinking about sex. I'm vexed. And yet. My heart is whispering to me that there is so much more beckoning at the door of the Healing Room. The Healing House. The Healing. Accept the gifts you are being given, give up the ego-driven. Skip-to-my-loo-my-darling. A kiss tossed to the curb, worse than money.*

Cate fills the tub and climbs in. She starts to weep; a river of tears runs down her cheeks and drip off her breasts into the bathwater. In her head she hears Alanis Morissette singing, "this cross I bear that you gave to me." She curses John and rises from the tub. She stands naked in front of the mirror and wonders if she can learn to love herself. She finds some cocoa-butter lotion in the cupboard under the sink and massages it with healing-intentioned hands, into her skin. She opens like a flower, swaying side to side in the flow of a rush of energy channelled through her breath.

Rejuvenated, Cate gets dressed with the intention of making progress with her book, but when she gets settled in the big leather chair in the office, her mind draws a blank. She can't concentrate. Irritated, she gets up from the desk and grabs a pillow from the couch, then starts boxing with it. She forces her fists deep, a technique she learned in therapy. Jab. Jab. She feels the anger rising. She yells, in a grizzled, pained voice, but stops, self-conscious. In the silence, her anger shifts to sadness. She lets go a deep, wounded cry. She sits down on her meditation pillow and reaches for an amethyst stone. She closes her eyes and sees a purple light. She focuses on the light. She breathes in, deeply. Her tears disappear. She returns to the office and her book in progress.

The last word written on the page is *destination*. Inspired, Cate writes about her volunteer experience in Africa with Dana. She describes Cape Town, the city of contrasts. She remembers how devastated they both felt when they toured the seemingly endless rows of shanty-town dwellings. How the tour of Robben Island, led by an ex-prisoner who was the same age as Dana when he was imprisoned for speaking out against apartheid, had them outraged with the pain and injustice. She writes about lighter things, like her imaginary adventures with her nephew Sam. She writes about Thailand with Taylor and how their relationship evolved as they navigated the trials of travelling in a strange country together. Cate continues her exploration, recounting counselling sessions with Arlene and Lynn. She recalls one session in particular where Lynn used EMDR, a trauma therapy, to help Cate confront her childhood abuser, how she saw him as a cartoon wolf. She sees herself push him into a space capsule, tucking his tail in before closing the lid and blasting him into outer-space.

She writes about searching, to arrive somewhere. In an epiphany of awareness, she realizes there is no destination. There never is. She remembers the letter, from her eight-year-old self. What she is searching for is inside her. She has everything she needs. It's been inside her since the moment of her birth. She writes and writes, the epiphanies flowing, deep into the darkness of the night. She finishes her book, or so she thinks. It's three in the morning, but she pours herself a glass of wine and toasts herself and her accomplishment. She feels incredibly lonely, yet somehow, it feels okay.

Chapter 3

*I*T'S DECEMBER 15 AND CATE is on an Air Canada flight from Victoria to Maui where she is meeting up with her family for the holidays. She has a window seat, beside a boy of perhaps nine or ten, whose parents are sitting across the aisle. After takeoff, Cate pulls her ever-present journal and a pen out of her carry-on bag, then folds out the tray and settles in to write.

> *Feeling a whirlwind of emotions as I fly ever closer to Maui. I'm beyond excited to see Celeste. Praying she is doing better than when I last saw her in August. I miss Taylor already, too. I've never had a tropical Christmas before, and hanging out with my family in Maui has me super-stoked. But then there's John. I'm nervous to see him. Terrified, actually. When I left him, we'd been planning this holiday, and when I tried to disinvite him, he lost it. It makes me shiver as I*

remember: the furious look in his steel-grey eyes as he swiped his huge forearm across the desk with a vengeance that had papers and pens and files flying all over the office. The venom in his voice as he accused me of trying to steal our children from him. The old drama.

Cate pauses and takes a deep breath, the emotion of her words on paper triggering her heart to beat faster. The boy beside her looks up from his video game.

"You alright, ma'am?" he asks.

"Oh, yes, I'm fine, thanks for asking," Cate replies.

"That's good," he says. "By the way, do you know what those clouds out there are made of?" he asks, gazing across her to look out at the massive mounds of white fluff.

"Clouds are large collections of very small drops of water," Cate replies as she tucks her journal in the back-of-the-seat pouch.

"But, how come they look like cotton candy?" he persists.

"Well, I can't say I know the answer to that one. What do you think?" Cate challenges him. He's stumped for a bit and sits in silence.

"I guess I'll Google that one when we land," he decides.

It carries on like this, but Cate doesn't mind. She gets out her phone and shows him photos of Fredrick and the seals by the wharf. The boy is a stranger but feels more like a friend. It touches Cate to make this unexpected connection even though she has a knack for creating space for people to open up with her.

It's been a few years since Cate has been to her brother Michael's house in Maui, but as soon as she arrives at the airport, the thickness of the humid air fills her lungs and her memory. The sun dazzles in the sky, brilliant and welcoming. Cate is waiting at the carousel for her luggage when she looks up and sees Taylor. His smile is huge and contagious. He bends down to give Cate a big hug.

"Hi, Momma, welcome to Maui!"

"Oh, Taylor, it's so good to see you! You've grown another inch I think," Cate exaggerates.

"Momma, it's only been a month since I saw you, and besides, I haven't grown since grade ten," Taylor laughs.

The two of them fall into their familiar pattern, one talking over the other, trying to get all the stories in at once. They walk hand-in-hand to the pick-up zone where Celeste is waiting with the car, and Taylor tosses Cate's bag into the trunk.

"Who gets the front seat with me?" laughs Celeste, as she gets out of the car to give Cate a quick hug.

"Well, I suppose it should be me as the elder," Cate says. "But considering your brother is a foot taller than me, I'll take the back seat."

Celeste is already sun-browned, having arrived in Maui with Grayson two and a half months earlier. Her long, dark hair, fine like Cate's but thicker, is steaked with golden highlights. Her dark brown eyes, framed by thick, long lashes, seem less clouded over in pain to Cate; she appears healthier and happier. The energy in the car is charged with enthusiasm.

"Do you feel as good as you look?" Cate asks Celeste.

"I'm not totally recovered yet, Mom," Celeste says, "but I have come a long way. What about you? You look incredibly relaxed from when I saw you last."

"Yes, well, living in your house is such a gift. I love my life on the island."

"I bet living on your own, out of the shadow of Dad's perpetual gloom, has a lot to do with it," Taylor says.

"Speaking of your dad, how are you managing living with him?" Cate asks, her fair eyebrows drawn into a frown.

"It's all good, don't worry, Momma," Taylor says. "I manage to avoid him most of the time, seeing as how I work the evening shift at the pizza joint, and he's always been a little softer on me."

The three of them talk non-stop all the way to Michael and Ashley's home in Wailea. Celeste manoeuvres the car into the garage, and Grayson comes out to greet them. At six foot one, his head seems to almost touch the door frame, at least from Cate's perspective. He looks just as tanned and relaxed as his wife. He's grown a beard-goatee-type thing, and his blonde hair is long, almost touching his shoulders, swept back and streaked by the sun.

They walk into the house where John is watching television. He looks up briefly to say hello, then returns his attention to the TV. It is all rather awkward. Cate wheels her luggage over and then carries it up the stairway to her room at the end of the hall where she is bunking with her mom in one of the guest rooms. Her mom is lying on the bed reading a book when Cate walks in.

"Oh, I didn't hear you come in!" Donna exclaims. She sets her reading glasses on the nightstand and gets up as quickly as her ageing body will allow. She throws her arms around Cate for a hug. "It's so good to see you! How is life on the island treating you?"

"It's wonderful, Mom," Cate says. "Trying to get my Alberta teacher's license accredited in BC has been a total pain in the ass, but other than that, my life is good. What about you? Is your hip holding up?"

"I just knew you moving out there was a good decision," Donna says. She tucks the tendril of curly grey hair, that is forever escaping its clip, behind her ear. "My hip is great; thanks for asking. That operation has been a godsend."

They catch up more on one another's lives while Cate rummages in the closet for hangers, unpacking her things and settling in. When she is finished, the two of them join the others in the media room, and the six of them decide to go out for pizza.

When they arrive at the restaurant, Cate makes sure to sit as far away from John as possible, at the far end on the other side of the table. She manages to avoid conversation with him, and the meal proceeds without incident.

It's getting late when they return. Celeste, Donna, and John all say goodnight and head straight off to bed. The night owls, Grayson and Taylor, convince Cate to join them for an all-night poker game.

"I'll be the dealer," Cate says, reaching for the deck of cards. Grayson grabs two cold beers from the fridge, one for him and one for Taylor, Cate already sipping her customary glass of red wine.

"Well, we put in a good effort," Grayson says, stifling a yawn just past midnight, "but I guess it's a failed mission. I can't keep my eyes open."

They all agree. Taylor and Grayson tidy up the poker chips while Cate rinses out their glasses, and they call it a night.

Cate is the first one up. She puts on a pot of coffee and takes her journal poolside to write.

> *I see him now with the clarity only distance and detachment can create. How is it that I couldn't see his dark side growing, his good side diminishing? Love is blind, they say, and apparently that is true.*

I can't change the past, but at least, at last, I am free to be me. Watching him as he stalks about in a cloud of gloom, I worry about Taylor, still living with him in that taupe house on the hill. Taylor has such a good heart, feels sorry for his dad. Like I used to. I don't want my experience of John to alter Taylor's relationship with his dad, but there is a voice in my head urging me to be more forthright with him. Sometimes I think I should tell all of my children, but it doesn't feel right to burden them. I tell that voice, which is likely only fear, to be quiet. I hold my tongue and pray, giving my worry to God.

Celeste and Taylor wake up and come out by the pool to join her. Cate tucks away her musings and joins them in conversation. They wish to head into town for a walk around the shops, and Celeste wants to treat them to a cup of artisan coffee and then walk down to the beach after. Donna walks in and overhears the conversation.

"Oh, can I join you?" Donna asks.

"Of course," Celeste assures her.

"Let me just check the weather," Donna says as she turns on the television. She adjusts her reading glasses, pushing them over the bump on the bridge of her distinctive aquiline nose that both Cate and Celeste inherited. "Oh my, it's already 22 degrees, too hot for me to walk that far."

"What about you, Grayson, do you want to grab a coffee with us?" Cate asks.

"Ah, thanks for asking, but no thanks," Grayson says. "I need some alone time to get work done that is starting to pile up."

Cate is relieved when John says no too. He was out golfing in the hot sun without a hat or sunscreen the day before, and now the top of his head, which is balding, is sunburned and he feels heat-stroked. Celeste tries to cheer her father up, encouraging him to come along to distract himself, but he just whines and complains.

Cate, Taylor, and Celeste throw their swimsuits and towels into a cloth bag and walk down to the shops of Wailea. Celeste takes Cate and Taylor to the coffee house that serves up delicious macadamia nut lattes. They aren't gone long when Celeste receives a distressed text from John.

"Sorry guys, I have to go," Celeste says, getting up from the table. "Dad wants to go to the clinic after all, and since I didn't list him as a driver on the rental, I'll have to take him."

"Seriously?" Cate moans, rolling her eyes. "We just got here."

"He really should have thought of that before we left," Taylor agrees.

"I know, but it will just be worse if I ignore him," Celeste says. She tucks in her chair. "Hopefully it won't take long. See you later."

Taylor and Cate walk down to the beach and stretch out on their towels in the hot sand.

"I hope it's not too weird for you, with things so strained between your dad and me," Cate says.

"To be honest, it does feel a little strange," Taylor admits. "But I appreciate you putting yourself in this situation so that I get to spend Christmas with both you and Dad. I know he can be a bit of a pain in the ass, but he's my dad and I love him."

"I know," says Cate. "It's all good."

She reaches out and pats Taylor's hand. They sit in comfortable silence, each lost in their own thoughts.

After an hour or so Cate receives a text from Celeste, "I'm on my way with Dad and Gran. You 2 still there?"

"Yes. We're just down from the shops," Cate texts back.

A few minutes later, Taylor spots Celeste and waves her over. John is beside her, wearing an old golf shirt and a ball cap on his sunburnt head. He is loaded down with mats, food, a water cooler, and snorkelling equipment. Donna is trailing behind them.

"How did it go at the clinic?" asks Taylor.

"I was told to drink lots of fluids and stay out of the sun," John says. "I'm feeling a little better."

Cate isn't impressed that John chose to come down to the beach after being advised to stay out of the sun. She notices his dark stubble. He looks unshaven and un-showered, his typical holiday mode, but she stays quiet.

Once everyone has settled in with their gear, Celeste and Cate walk to the edge of the ocean by the rocks to practice yoga.

"Can I join you?" Donna asks, walking over, wobbling a bit in her orthopedic sandals.

"Sure, Gran," Celeste agrees. "But the poses we'll be doing will likely be too difficult for you."

"Oh, don't worry about me," Donna assures her. "If anything is too hard I'll just figure out a different way to do it or plop these old bones of mine down in the sand."

The three begin their practice standing with their feet planted in the wet sand, facing the ocean. Donna is the same height as Celeste, and although Cate is several inches shorter, she has her hair in a bun atop her head, creating an illusion of perfect symmetry.

Celeste moves her slim, fit, dancer's body in flow with Cate's. Donna does her best, but she's bitten off a bit more than she can chew. Even sitting in the sand is difficult for her, but she so wants to be a part of it. Celeste slows it down and cuts it a little short.

"I think we've all had enough," Celeste says. "Do you two want to go in for a dip?"

The three generations of women galivant in the ocean, laughing like children while the waves wash away the tiny grains of sand that have become encrusted on their bodies.

A bit later, Grayson shows up. He has prepared blender drinks for everyone to enjoy. They sit in a circle on the sand and toast one another.

"To this kick-ass beach!" says Grayson.

"And the bad-ass ocean!" Celeste adds.

"To gratitude!" chimes in Cate. They clunk their plastic glasses, and then Taylor takes it up a notch.

"To the generosity of Uncle Michael and Aunty Ashley, for sharing their pimp space with us!" Taylor says.

Cate counts her blessings and wonders if her time in Maui by the ocean with her family is part of her healing journey, despite the toxic energy that emanates from John.

Everyone is starving when they get home. Donna is feeling sore from the yoga and excuses herself to go lie down. Celeste and Cate depart for Whole Foods to stock up on groceries. They go a bit crazy, loading up on alcohol, super jazzed that booze is sold at grocery stores in the US, and embracing the fun energy. Two hours, three hundred dollars, and two carts later, they are ready to call it a day.

When they get back, everyone pitches in to put the groceries away and they assemble a picnic-style meal.

On the beach the next morning, Celeste, Grayson, and Cate do a meditation practice together. They hold hands, close their eyes, and sit in silence, exchanging energy. When they feel grounded, they open up and share their feelings.

"John's negative energy is really challenging me," Cate begins. "Since I left, I've become more sensitive."

"I know," Celeste says. "I've tried to ignore him, but that doesn't seem to be working."

"It's been all I can do to not lose my temper," admits Grayson, "especially when he stalks around and criticizes everybody. I just can't tolerate it when he's verbally abusive to anyone, but especially my wife." Grayson reaches over and takes Celeste by the hand. "I don't know how you have so much patience with him."

"I'm trying to be patient with him because I know he's got a serious mental illness, but I'm fucking sick and tired of his passive-aggressive bullshit," Celeste vents.

"I know, but what can we do?" asks Cate.

"I think we all have to hold him accountable," says Grayson. "Sick or not, we can't let him get away with his outbursts."

"That's a good idea but easier said than done, trust me," says Cate. "I'm going to try and avoid him as much as I possibly can."

"Also easier said than done," says Grayson.

"I'm sorry we agreed to this family holiday," Celeste says in quiet voice. "I've made so much progress with my health these past few months, and his abusive energy is wearing me down."

Cate is furious, but there isn't much more to be said. They all agree that venting has helped, at least a little.

Later that afternoon, Cate decides she needs some alone time and chooses to go down to the beach on her own.

She finds a quiet spot and lays out her towel. She hydrates herself with ice-cold lemon water and munches on a snack of pineapple and almonds. She's feeling peaceful and relaxed when John shows up with his speakers blaring reggae music. She remembers her earlier conversation with Grayson and Celeste, and instead of reacting she just picks up her things and moves.

After dinner that night, everybody crams into the Charger on a mission to find a Christmas tree.

They aren't out and about long when Taylor spots a fresh-cut Christmas tree church-lot sale. There are aisles and aisles of trees to choose from, and they end up with a seven-foot Douglas fir that they can barely tie safely to the roof of the car. Working together, they manage to get it back to the house all in one piece. John and Grayson set it up in a bucket in the corner of the media room. Cate can hardly wait to tell Ashley, who had thought it would be impossible to find a real tree in Maui.

Cate crawls into bed. Her mother is asleep, snoring softly. Cate feels grateful. Sharing a room at their age, like high school kids, has been a great opportunity for them to bond.

A version of the Alanis Morissette song, "Thank You," plays in her head. *Thank you, Maui, thank you, Thailand, thank you, technology, thank you, Michael and Ashley, thank you, me, thank you, bank account that still has some money.*

Cate wakes up feeling sad and oppressed. She's tired
of pretending and tiptoeing around on eggshells because
of John. She wonders what on earth she was thinking,
planning to share the holidays with him. She's living in fear
again, of his judgment and negativity. It hurts her newly
healing heart to be back in his space, so soon after finally
finding freedom.

Cate encourages herself to laugh in the face of his
heaviness and surround herself in an invisible shield of
strength and courage. She's grateful that she is not with
him anymore and that she never will be, ever again.

Soon it is the day that Michael, Ashley, and Sam are arriving
from Calgary, and their house guests are all nervous and
excited.

Celeste and Grayson offer to clean the house spic and
span while Cate and Donna shop for fabric leis for the
evening celebration, wine for Michael, earrings for Ashley,
and a game for Sam. They aren't back at the house long when
they hear the car pull into the garage, and everyone except
John races to the back door to greet them.

"Aunty Ashley!" beams Celeste. "Welcome to your home!"

"Thanks, Celeste," Ashley laughs, setting down her huge
purse on the counter to give Celeste a hug. "You look
absolutely amazing—Maui must be treating you well."

Celeste and Ashley are the same height and of similar
build, with long, dark-auburn hair. Everyone who meets
them thinks they are blood relatives, not aunt and niece
through marriage.

Michael rolls their luggage into the back entrance.
He looks worn from travel: blue-grey eyes heavy-lidded,

his thin face drawn. Then he smiles and his eyes turn up at the corners, just like Taylor's.

"It's so good to see you," Michael says, first to Celeste, then Cate. Cate reaches up to tussle her brother's thick, wiry hair with affection, and Michael gives Taylor a knuckle pound.

"Hi, Mom, how is Maui treating you?" Michael asks Donna.

"Oh, you know I just love it here," Donna says. "I'm just tickled you included me."

"The first thing I want to do is jump in our swimming pool," Sam says, already beginning to peel his shirt off his slim, chalk-white torso. "Can I go up and change into my swimsuit, Mom?"

"I think that's a great idea after that long flight," says Ashley. "But make sure you put on sunscreen, there's a bottle under the bathroom vanity, I think."

Everyone heads off in different directions to change into their swim gear and meet out at the pool. Sam reappears slathered in 80 SPF, streaks of oily white cream in blotches. Grayson gets the blender going for cocktails, and Donna puts a tray of munchies together. Celeste and Cate play treasure hunt games with Sam, who has tied a kerchief around his head, his thick blonde hair sticking up in rooster tails. Taylor and Sam play stunt Olympics in the pool. Their legs stick up in the air, Taylor's long legs twice the length of Sam's, as they dive to the bottom to perform handstands.

When it's time for dinner, everyone chips in to prepare an easy, casual meal. Even John joins Michael at the barbeque.

When the dishes are tidied away, Sam gets out Uno and plays a few rounds with Taylor and Cate before switching it out for an intense game of Risk, with Michael and John joining in. The game goes way past Sam's bedtime, and Ashley has to break up the party.

After Ashley gets Sam tucked in, she comes back downstairs and requests a family conference to set the ground rules. She puts the kettle on for a cup of tea. Everyone grabs a drink refill and they gather outside on the patio.

"First, I want to say thank you for being thoughtful about keeping our home clean," Ashley begins. She pushes her glasses up over her small, critical eyes, soft-lined at the corners, and coughs into her sleeve. "It was great to see everyone pitching in to make dinner and cleaning up after."

"Sounds like there's a 'but,' coming," John interrupts, folding his arms across his barrel chest.

"Yes, John, there are a few things that are bothering me," Ashley says, the soft lines around her eyes tightening. "And I feel it's important to address them right away."

Ashley continues with the itemized list she has jotted down on a piece of lined paper. John sighs and rolls his eyes. When Ashley goes over the house rules, like washing sand off with the hose out front and drying off completely before entering the house, John is quick to say it wasn't him who clogged the shower drain. When Ashley asks for support in getting Sam, who is only eight years old, to bed by nine o'clock, Celeste and Donna agree, and Cate apologizes for extending the Risk game with her competitiveness. John takes a huge glug from his beer and let's go a giant belch. Grayson appears distracted, checking his phone every few minutes. Michael and Taylor are both quiet, saying little but paying close attention. It all ends up feeling a little sticky for everyone, but at least they know what the expectations are.

Cate doesn't sleep well, her earlier resolve to be a fierce Warrior Goddess somehow forgotten.

After a few days, the motley crew manages to get into a groove of sorts, and by the time Christmas Day rolls around, everyone is in relatively good spirits. Sam and Cate spend an entire day getting groceries and supplies, then baking a selection of delectable treats, including Sam's favourite, sugar cookies.

On Christmas Eve they decorate the tree together and eat baked goods while listening to Christmas tunes. Cate has brought a special ornament for each of them to hang on the tree.

"Thank you so much, Aunty," Sam says when he unwraps his Snoopy Santa. "You remembered how much I like Snoopy." He hangs the ornament with ceremony on the tree and then gives Cate one of his signature nose kisses.

Christmas Day starts with stockings and presents, followed by a delicious brunch that they all prepare together. After the dishes are all washed and put away, Cate reads her book and writes in her journal, relaxing by the pool. Celeste and Cate work together to bake up coconut cream vegan pies for dessert while listening to eighties top hits.

"Do you want to join me for some yoga at the beach?" Celeste asks Cate when the dinner preparations are done.

"I'd love that," Cate says.

When their practice is complete, Cate and Celeste sit facing one another in the sand and connect knee to knee. They hold hands and commune silently with one another. Tears form in their eyes.

"I'm so grateful you had the courage to embark on your healing journey," Cate says to Celeste. She pauses to push a tendril of Celeste's hair behind her ear, then places her hand on her heart. "I'm thrilled you asked me to sublet your place too. It's turned out to be an incredible part of my own healing."

When they finish their meditation, they discover that the rest of the family has come down to the beach to join them. Grayson totes a jug of alcoholic yumminess, the exact contents of which even he is unsure.

"Will you bury me in the sand, Aunty?" Sam asks, just before the sun sets.

Cate scoops handfuls of sand and packs it around his body, tucking his gangly legs and arms in tight. Cate imagines he is like a puppy waiting to grow into his paws, and that he will be tall like Michael.

Taylor and Grayson ride their boards in the waves.

There is a peacefulness in the air as they all walk back to the house to finish preparing dinner. Even John appears content, the dragon asleep in his cave.

As they get ready to sit down for Christmas dinner, Skype rings. It is Dana, reaching out from Thailand to wish them all season's greetings. She is all smiles, her dimples in full form.

"Hey, family!" Dana yells out from halfway around the world. "Merry Christmas!"

Everyone takes a turn sharing stories and asking her about her adventures abroad. They all sing "We Wish You a Merry Christmas" before saying teary-eyed goodbyes. No one minds that the turkey ends up being over-done, the stuffing dried out, and the salad mushy, for they are all full up with love.

After clearing the food and dishes away, they cozy up in the media room to watch their classic Christmas movie, *Home Alone*.

Celeste falls asleep halfway through the movie.
She's watched it a hundred times or more anyway. When
the credits come on, Cate turns off the TV. She whispers
goodnight to Taylor, the only one still up, and then decides
to sleep out under the Maui sky. As she drifts off she feels
as though God is tucking her in under a blanket of stars.

It's Boxing Day and Ashley announces she has a surprise.
Everyone is dying of curiosity, wondering what
she has up her sleeve.

"You need to dress up, smart-casual, and be ready to
leave at five o'clock sharp," Ashley says. "That means no
flip-flops, Sam."

Just before five, everyone gathers on the driveway. Cate
thinks Ashley looks stunning in a crème linen pantsuit and
a pair of beige, pointy-toed, high heels with matching clutch.
She wonders about her own choice of a short, above-the-
knee, cotton, striped dress with black patent, open-toed
pumps, but it's too late to change so she bundles into the
car with everyone else. Michael stops in the valet parking
of the Wailea Fairmont.

"We're here," Ashley says, a controlled grin on her face.

As they walk through the upscale lobby and out onto the
immaculate grounds, the excited chatter builds. Cate figures
they must be attending a luau, but she is wrong. They walk
up a grassy hill to the top, and Cate discovers a private table
reserved just for them, overlooking the ocean. The white
table linens are pressed crisp, and the silverware and crystal
gleam in the late afternoon sun. Ashely has arranged private
service complete with a special menu that suits everyone's
dietary needs. Two servers lead everyone to their seats.

Cate is disappointed to discover she has been seated between Taylor and John, but she hopes for the best.

When the sun begins to set, a native fire-lighter appears, dressed in traditional attire, and lights the torches surrounding the table. Champagne flows and soon the appetizers arrive. Cate is feeling totally happy and spoiled.

"You sure look hot in that sexy dress, Cate," John blurts out of nowhere.

It's like a pin bursting a balloon. Cate wishes she were anywhere but there. She is at a loss for words, and everyone else seems rendered speechless too, except John who continues to babble in a drunken diatribe.

When some strangers approach, ignoring the sign, Private Gathering, John makes it even more awkward by engaging in conversation with them. They are about to take a selfie when John calls out, "Hey, I can take your photo for you!" He almost falls over when he gets up to take their picture.

"Is she your daughter?" one of the men in the group asks John, pointing to Cate.

It's all very uncomfortable. But then the servers start bringing out the main courses and the intruders say goodbye and John is too busy devouring his meal to talk.

As the food is being cleared away, Celeste and Grayson start dancing to the music. Everyone walks down the hill to the beach, throwing off their shoes to walk in the soft sand barefooted. Celeste performs ballet at the edge of the tide that is kissing the shore.

When it's time to go, the mood is merry as everyone carries their shorn shoes back up the incline, across the grass, and through the hotel lobby to return home. Another day in paradise. If only they hadn't invited the snake.

The next few days are filled with more family time and exploring. In the early hours of the last day of the year 2011, Cate completes *The Artist's Way* writing course.

> *My creativity heals myself and others. My writing is an expression of my creativity. I am grateful for the insights I have achieved. I am proud of myself, for following through with my commitment. I am full of enthusiasm for the future, excited to discover what lies ahead and what will unfold.*

Cate quietly gets dressed and then tiptoes from the room, so as to not to wake up Donna. She is heading out on a road trip to Hana, with just Celeste, Grayson, and Taylor. She's excited for the adventure and relieved for the reprieve from John, if only for a day.

In Paia they make a quick pit stop for breakfast. They savour hot coffee and chocolate croissants before going into Manna Foods to buy a selection of salads and cheeses for a picnic lunch. Then they are back on the road.

The road to Hana is breathtaking but hazardous. The road is so narrow that in many parts it can't accommodate two vehicles. With the sharp turns and sudden bends, a car can be approaching from the opposite direction, and there isn't even a shoulder to pull onto. Cate proceeds with caution and hopes they don't end up with a scraped-up car, or worse. The road snakes through the rainforest where thousands of trees, hanging vines, and tropical plants grow in an explosion of colour. They listen to the classical station on the radio, the rhythm of the music seeming to move with the undulations of the road.

After a few hours they stop at a turnout and climb the waterfall. Grayson spots a sign for a tree museum and spontaneously starts singing, "They took all the trees and put them in a tree museum, then charged the people a dollar and a half just to see 'em." But this tree museum is free, and the four of them dance amongst the orange trees, fragrant with fruit and glossy-leaved. They sing and laugh all the way to Hana, arriving just after noon.

They are sitting on the beach, enjoying their lunch, when it starts to sprinkle.

"Remember how the spitting rain turned into a monsoon on our honeymoon?" Celeste asks Grayson.

"Do I?" laughs Grayson. "I was the one who carried you through the deluge and back to our hotel."

"No problem," Cate declares. "I am the Wish Magician, and I say to these clouds, be gone!"

They all laugh, but then miraculously the clouds disappear. They walk to the Seven Sacred Pools and edge their way down the craggy cliffs over the rough black rock. The water is ice-cold, but they go in anyway and the boys find a cave to explore while Celeste and Cate recline on the rocks, inhale the warm air, and absorb the sun's rays. After a while Celeste joins the boys and Cate watches as her children swim in the dark water with delight and abandon, feeling joyful and blessed to be alive.

Too soon, it's time to make the drive back. Cate wants to be through the narrow section before dark. They are slightly delirious, perhaps from too much sun, with Celeste telling hilarious stories. They laugh so hard their jaws ache, and then they get sleepy, drifting into total silence. Hearts are brimming. Cups are running over.

By the time they reach Paia, it is almost six and everyone is starving so they stop for pizza.

Their final destination on their big day out is the movie theatre in Kihei where *Mission Impossible* is showing. They are all completely exhausted as they load into the car and

Cate drives them back to Michael and Ashley's, laughing all the way, like sleigh-riders.

"What's that sound? That's the sound of a tool box falling down the stairs," quips Celeste, followed by other, what she thinks to be hysterical, quotes from *Home Alone*. Blissful laughter fills the air.

Three weeks have gone by, and Cate's time in Maui is over. She's heading back home to winter on Vancouver Island. She will remember this gift, always. But she's ready to be back on her own. She is definitely done spending time with John. She's looking forward to seeing Finn again, wondering what direction that will take. She anticipates with excitement the adventures and memories that will be made in the new year that lies ahead, confident that she has been building a solid foundation to dream upon.

Chapter 4

BACK ON VANCOUVER ISLAND, CATE is excited to be reunited with Fredrick, ready to get back into her routine. She sends a text to Finn.

"Driving up the Malahat now. There in 10 minutes."

She pulls onto Finn's gravel driveway and leaps from the car, throwing the keys into her handbag. As she climbs the wooden stairwell she can hear a ruckus inside Finn's apartment. Her knock on the door goes unanswered, so she tries the knob and discovers it is unlocked. She crosses the threshold to arrive into total chaos. The apartment is a mess, as Cate is discovering is par for the course.

"Finn? It's Cate," she calls out to no answer. She steps over a pile of dirty laundry before she turns into the kitchen where she sees Finn on his phone. He waves to her but doesn't interrupt his call. Fredrick comes scampering over, his tail wagging like crazy, and she bends down to pet him while he licks her hand. Cate starts to pick up Fredrick's

belongings, which are scattered all over the place.
His water dish and food bowl, crusty with remnants, are
on the kitchen floor. She gathers everything up and puts
it into Fredrick's Rubbermaid storage container and waits
a few more minutes, but Finn is still on the phone. The
television blares. Finn's teenage kids yell at one another.
It is all she can do not to cry.

"Text me later," she yells over the din. "I'm going to take
Fredrick home."

Finn barely seems to register, and Cate departs without
a reply.

On the drive home, Cate is lost in thought. She
knows that Finn is not her love. She reminds herself she
isn't looking for love, but that doesn't mean she doesn't
want something more. She considers the many red flags,
the biggest of which is her discontent. She doesn't feel
appreciated. She tells herself not to be judgmental, that these
little things don't matter, but they do. Cate is beginning
to understand that acceptance isn't about settling, it's about
choosing. She wants something Finn can't give her, and
she knows it isn't fair to either one of them to keep dragging
it on.

When Cate gets home she cuddles up with Fredrick
on the couch. She cries softly into his thick fur, grieving
her loss. When she is done, she feels inspired to write and
gets out her journal.

> *Angels dancing on my shoulders. Fairies skipping
> lightly over the Earth, leaving not a trace. Seashells
> still covering my wounds. I'm yearning for something
> deeper. A knowing in my heart, rooted in my Spirit.
> I know the dance. The Teacher was here and danced
> and called us to love. If you have ears, listen, he said.*

The purpose of our existence is love and only love.
Part of loving myself is not accepting less than I desire.
Part of loving myself is listening to my heart.

The next day, Cate receives a call from Celeste's friend, Megan, the cupid who introduced her to Finn.

"Hi, Cate, welcome back to winter on the island," Megan says.

"Thanks. It feels even colder after three weeks in the sunshine, but I'm glad to be back," says Cate.

"So, how was Maui with the ex?" Megan pries.

"Ugh, don't even go there," Cate moans with exaggeration. "But spending time with the rest of my family was wonderful."

"That's good to hear," says Megan. "How is Celeste doing?"

"She's so much better; you'd hardly recognize her," Cate says. "Her decision to go on an extended leave from work and travel around the world with Grayson was definitely a good one."

"It was total drama here," Megan says. "I'm relieved the holidays are over. But speaking of over, how are things with you and Finn?"

"What are you, a psychic?" Cate asks. "To be honest, I haven't cut it off with him yet, but I need to."

"Yeah, well, I saw that coming," Megan says. "But don't worry, I have another single, attractive man to introduce you to."

"You can't be serious; I haven't even broken up with Finn yet!" Cate says.

"You don't have to date him, just show him around
a bit," Megan persists. "His name is Ethan and he lives in
Saudi Arabia, but he is here visiting his daughter, who used
to be one of my clients. Come on, Cate, he doesn't know
a single soul."

"Oh, what the hell, why not?" Cate says.

Megan gives Cate Ethan's contact information, and they
hang up with plans to get together later in the week.

The next day, Cate gets the unfortunate news that it will take
at least another eight weeks before her teacher certification
in BC is approved. She's frustrated that the process is taking
so long and worried that she will spend all of her savings for
the future if something doesn't change. Cate attempts to be
patient and trust that something will come along eventually.
She doesn't want to return to Calgary; the very word sounds
like gravel in her ears. She consoles herself that she still has
time, that she doesn't have to make any big decisions, yet.

Ethan sends Cate an email, inviting her for lunch with him
and his daughter. Cate is intrigued and a little surprised
that he has suggested including his daughter but says yes.

When she walks into the restaurant, Cate realizes she
has absolutely no idea what Ethan looks like. She glances
about the room, and then an attractive bald man of medium
build, with strikingly intense blue eyes, stands up and waves
tentatively. He's very fair-skinned, clearly not Saudi Arabian,
as Cate had anticipated. She wonders where he is from.

"Hi, Cate?" Ethan says, moving around the table and
taking a step closer.

"Yes, that's me," Cate says, shaking his hand. A small shock of electricity bolts through her hand and up her arm, but Cate keeps her composure, turning to face his daughter, who remains seated.

Chloe is striking and exotic looking, with her olive skin and curly raven hair that falls down past her shoulders. She has unusual, dark blue eyes that look almost black, her pupils are so huge. Cate wonders if Chloe's mother might be of mixed race.

"Hello," Chloe says, so quietly Cate can barely hear her.

Cate isn't sure whether it's proper to sit in the vacant chair beside Chloe or Ethan, but chooses the one beside Chloe. When she pulls out her chair, Cate notices that Chloe is dressed in an oversized coat, that she is far tinier than she thought from the first impression.

The waitress brings them menus and they order. Ethan answers Cate's questions about life in Saudi Arabia and tells her he is originally from Winnipeg. Chloe gives Cate a bit of the drill.

"Papa, I think we need to go," Chloe says, glancing at her phone. "My appointment is in five minutes."

"I'm sorry," Ethan says. "Where did the time go?"

When Chloe stands, Cate notices they are about the same height.

"Please, let me get this," Ethan says, offering to pay for the bill.

"Thank you, that is so generous of you," Cate says. "You'll have to let me treat you next time."

On the drive home, Cate feels excited. She hopes there will be a next time. Her mind drifts.

Ethan is nothing like I expected. Not that I expected anything. It was a little awkward with Chloe there. But then there was that unmistakable shock of electricity when I shook his hand. It's too soon to tell if anything will come of this, but I'm intrigued.

The days come and go. It's the second week of February when Cate and Ethan meet up again, this time at a small, cozy little Noodle House in Duncan.

Ethan has already arrived when Cate walks in. She sees him sitting at a table for two by the window. He looks up as she walks over, a genuine smile on his face.

"Cate, it's so good to see you again," he says as he stands up. He goes around the table and pulls out her chair.

"Yes, it's good to see you too," Cate says. "I was glad when you reached out to suggest we meet for lunch, just the two of us," Cate says.

Cate sits down and soon they fall into an easy flow of conversation that is the perfect balance of intensity and calm, what Cate likes to call a Goldilocks state. They share a half litre of red wine and order tasty noodle bowls that are fresh and full of crisp, tender vegetables. As they talk Cate finds herself feeling more and more attracted to him. She appreciates his polite manner and warm smile, not to mention his fit body, biceps bulging under the short sleeves of his snug, navy-blue T-shirt. In Cate's eyes, Ethan is the epitome of acceptance and non-judgment, like her brother and her son. She is particularly impressed by his love, commitment, and support of Chloe, whom she finds out over the course of their conversation is not his biological daughter. Cate senses that Ethan is equally enthralled with her, but she isn't ready to share her burgeoning feelings yet.

They talk for hours, long after their meal and drinks are cleared away and Cate has paid the bill. Finally, she looks around, as if waking from a dream.

"What time is it anyway?" Cate asks. "We seem to be the only people here."

"It's four o'clock," Ethan says, looking at his watch.

"I can hardly believe it," Cate says. "Where did the time go? I'm sorry, but I need to get home and feed my dog, Fredrick, I'm afraid." She reaches for her purse and rises from the table. "Thank you so much, I've really enjoyed the afternoon."

"Me too," Ethan says. "Perhaps we can do this again, sometime soon?"

Ethan walks Cate out to her car, parked just outside on the street, and hugs her somewhat awkwardly before she gets in and drives away with a smile on her face that says more than any words could possibly express.

Soon comes sooner than Cate anticipates. Megan sends Cate a text the next day, "Want to come over to my place for poker night?"

"Sure, sounds fun," Cate replies.

"Should I include Ethan on the guest list?" Megan texts back.

"Yes, please!"

Cate arrives at Megan's home to discover several of the other people that were invited dropped out last minute, so it's a small, intimate group, perfect for nurturing connection. Drinks are poured and the cards are shuffled. It's a jovial group and even Megan's kids join in for a few rounds.

They play cards until after midnight, laughing and telling stories between hands. When Cate gets up to leave, Ethan decides to go too. They stand outside by Cate's parked car, neither one of them wanting the night to end. Their bodies seem to gravitate toward one another like two magnets. Within minutes, they are kissing. Their lips fit together like two pieces of a puzzle. They stop for air.

"Do you want to come over to my place?" Ethan asks.

"I'd love to," Cate says, catching her breath. "But it's late and I think I best be going home."

Cate feels guilty that she hasn't broken it off with Finn and a little alarmed at how quickly she is falling for this man. Ethan looks disappointed, but he agrees, it is late. He leans in for one final kiss goodnight.

A few days later, Cate's mom flies out from Calgary for a week-long visit.

The first night of her stay, Cate and Donna end up in deep conversation, staying up until three in the morning to share myriad revelations, discoveries, and emotions. The experience is almost ethereal, a transcendence from the ordinary to the divine. For the first time in their lives, both women are able to set aside their egos and really be present to one another.

"I'm sorry I haven't been the mother you felt you needed," Donna says with true conviction. "I did my best, but apparently my best was the shits."

Cate pauses and looks her mother in the eye.

"I'm sorry I've made you feel that way," Cate says. "But you're right, I used to think I needed something that you weren't able to give me. I need you to know, Mom, that story is from the past."

Donna cries, softly, as she takes in that piece of truth.

"You always encouraged me and told me I could do anything I set my mind to."

"Thank you for saying that," Donna replies. "I suppose I have come a long way, compared to my mother's skills in developing my self-esteem. Remember the story of when I was getting ready for the prom and my mom said, 'You can't make a silk purse from a pig's ear'?"

Donna's injection of humour lightens the moment. She takes Cate's hand in hers.

"I'm so grateful to be here. I think we are both healing some deep pains from the past."

As their conversation continues to unfold, Cate and Donna realize that they've never been able to see one another clearly because their vision was blocked by their own pain and neediness. With love and commitment, they unravel their stories and get to the heart of the matter. They feel their connectedness, that they are one, part of the same source. Cate feels Donna's brittle bones, and Donna feels Cate's dried-up pancreas. They behold one another's pain, and instead of backing away from it, they embrace it.

Cate decides she wants to introduce Donna to Ethan and texts him to ask if he'd like to meet up with them for dinner. He agrees, and they decide to meet at a family diner–style restaurant on the wharf that is famous for its deep-fried fish and chips.

The waitress directs them to a cozy booth and they place their orders. Within minutes the three of them are totally engaged in conversation.

"Brr, is anyone else feeling a bit chilly or is it just me?" Donna asks, giving a little shudder of her shoulders for emphasis.

"If you'll excuse me a moment," Ethan says, getting up from his chair.

Donna looks over at Cate with a quizzical expression, both ladies' curiosity piqued. When Ethan returns minutes later he has a sweater, which he places gently on Donna's bare shoulders.

"Is that better?" he asks.

Donna hardly knows what to say, and it isn't easy to render her speechless.

"Did I not mention to you, Mom? Ethan has earned the nickname Mr. Charming Pants more than once already," Cate says with a giggle.

Ethan blushes, ever so slightly, and soon the three of them are back in the thick of conversation, talking about politics and religion, prejudice and poverty, and everything under the sun.

After dinner Donna takes it upon herself to invite Ethan over for an after-dinner drink. There is clearly more than one cupid afoot. Ethan agrees without hesitation and meets up with them at Cate's.

Not long after the wine is poured, Donna starts to yawn rather over-dramatically.

"Wow, I didn't realize how tired I am. I really must get myself off to bed," Donna says. "Goodnight you two, and Ethan, it has been an absolute pleasure."

Donna has barely left the room when Ethan moves closer to Cate and they start kissing. Cate can feel that she's falling for him, that she wants him, but it's still not the right time. She pulls away, reluctantly.

"I think you should go," Cate says. "It's too soon."

Ethan looks disappointed for a moment, but he quickly switches gears.

"I hope we can do this again," Ethan says at the door. He takes Cate by the hand. "Because I agree with your mom, it was an absolute pleasure."

The next day, Ethan sends Cate a text, "Meet me at the pub for a drink?" Cate feels torn. She doesn't want to abandon her mom again, but Donna encourages her to go. Cate can hardly apply her lipstick with a steady hand, she is so full of excitement.

Cate walks in and spots Ethan already settled in a cozy booth. She leans in to kiss him before she sits down. They order wine and water and settle in.

"So, tell me more about your marriage," Cate asks, catching Ethan by surprise with her forthrightness, wasting no time getting right down to it.

"Well, what do you want to know?" Ethan asks.

"I'm just curious, how you met her, how you knew you were in love, why it ended…" Cate trails off, wondering if she is prying too much.

Ethan tells her about how he met his wife and about how he first discovered that she suffered from alcoholism. Cate listens intently and then it's his turn to ask her about her life. Cate shares the outline of her own dysfunctional marriage, how she endured similar challenges, being married to a man who was mentally ill with severe depression. They relate to their different but shared experiences of marital discord. Their bond deepens. Cate decides to take it up a notch.

"I'm curious, Ethan. What character traits matter most to you?" she asks.

Ethan sits in quiet contemplation for a few minutes before replying.

"I think being open and honest are probably the most important things to develop trust in a relationship," Ethan says. "But I also value behaving with integrity and character."

"Are you serious?" Cate says, her eyes widening. "Open and honest are the first two words I chose to describe myself when I put together an authenticity outline just a few months ago."

Suddenly Cate is certain that meeting Ethan is not a coincidence at all.

"It's kind of miraculous, us meeting up," Cate says. "You coming to Vancouver Island from Saudi Arabia to support Chloe. Me coming to Vancouver Island to support Celeste and start over. Megan being best friends with Celeste. Megan having counselled Chloe in the past and somehow deciding she should introduce us, all cupid-style. I feel like, perhaps, it's destiny."

"It does kind of feel like that, doesn't it?" Ethan agrees.

"Can I interrupt our conversation to kiss you?" Cate asks.

"Yes, please do," Ethan encourages her.

Cate leans over across the table to kiss him, fully, deeply, on the mouth.

"I really have only one question left," Cate says somewhat brazenly, pulling away from their embrace, "but you can't answer it in the pub."

"Shall we go to my place for a nightcap then?" Ethan replies.

It is Cate's turn to say, "Yes, please!"

Within minutes the bill is paid and they are in their respective cars on the way to Ethan's beach house condo.

They go inside and Cate looks around the sparsely furnished room while Ethan pours them both a glass of wine. They sit down beside one another on the grey suede couch, but they have only taken one sip when Ethan takes Cate by the hand and leads her to his bedroom. They begin to get undressed.

"I forgot to mention, I'm a bit of a cyborg," Cate admits self-consciously as she unhooks her insulin pump.

Ethan doesn't skip a beat, only smiles and says, "More like the Six Million Dollar Woman to me."

Their intimacy is nervous and exploratory, gentle and beautiful. Afterwards they lay in bed and talk. Ethan places Cate's hand on his heart and they both know, without saying it yet, that they are falling in love.

On the drive home Cate spots two deer by the side of the road. She remembers the three deer she saw in her front yard when she moved in and wonders what a deer totem means. She looks out at the inky black sky and imagines the Universe winking at her. Something is unfolding.

Giddy with emotion, Cate tries to sneak into the house, all raccoon-eyed and bushy-haired from lovemaking, but eagle-ears Donna hears her.

"Hello? Is that you, Cate?" Donna hollers from her room. "Come say goodnight."

Cate stands in the doorway to Donna's room, not sure which one of them is more uncomfortable.

"Yes, of course it's me—who else would be waltzing in at this hour?" Cate replies.

"Well, there's no need to get testy," Donna laughs as she takes in Cate's dishevelled appearance. "Judging by the lateness of the hour and those star-crossed eyes of yours, I'm guessing you had a wonderful time."

"You're right, Mom, I did have a wonderful time, but it's late," Cate says. "I promise to give you the juicy details in the morning." Cate comes around the side of the bed and kisses her mother on the forehead. "Goodnight."

Cate wakes up early. She is full of energy and excitement after her encounter the night before. Donna is still asleep, so Cate quietly brews a pot of coffee and gets out her journal.

> *I feel like a true love virgin. I've only just discovered now how it feels to be touched without demand. How it feels to be given to without expectation. I felt free to be me. He called me the Million Dollar Woman and it wasn't a line. He meant it. I could feel it. I can't believe I'm calling this love, it seems too new, too soon. But that is how it feels. For now, I will hold this awareness inside my heart, my secret. Until I'm sure he feels the same.*

A week goes by faster than either Cate or Donna can believe and soon it's time for Cate to drop her mother off at the airport.

Both women are lost in thought, reflecting on their time together. Cate parks at the departures drop-off area and helps Donna with her luggage, then stops to give her one last hug goodbye. Donna wipes a tear from her eye and then brightens up when Cate reminds her she will be in Calgary in just a few weeks, for her birthday. Cate drives back home in silence, full of gratitude for the gift of her mother.

The house is so quiet with Donna gone. Cate sends a text to Ethan, "Do you want to come over and make a meal together?"

Ethan agrees and picks Cate up in the Charger. He drives them down to the wharf where they buy some fresh halibut, then to the liquor store for wine. They pick up fresh vegetables at the market, along with some dark chocolate.

In Cate's kitchen, they set everything out on the counter and Ethan turns on the stereo. Adele belts it out as they chop and stir and sway together as they prepare the meal.

"Sure, she's got it all," croons Ethan a bit off-key. He winks and pulls Cate closer. "And yes, that is really what I want."

Between tasks and during tasks, they kiss and laugh, telling stories. Cate gets out the tablecloth and lights candles, but neither one of them has much of an appetite, they're so engrossed in one another.

After dinner Ethan gets up to take his plate into the kitchen, but Cate takes him by the arm.

"We can leave the dishes for later," she tells him, totally out of character. She leads him to her room.

A few hours later they emerge barefoot and half naked to finish cleaning up. It is late when they finish putting everything away.

"Would it be alright if I stayed over?" Ethan asks.

"I was hoping you would," Cate replies without hesitation.

It is their first sleepover. They are both a little nervous, but Cate is especially uncertain. She doesn't know how to tell Ethan that Fredrick sleeps at the end of the bed. She knows he's not crazy about dogs, even though he's never said as much. Cate sets Fredrick up on his doggy bed in the office, which has Fredrick clearly confused. Ethan falls asleep while Cate lies there, restless. She can feel the charge of his energy. She notices the soft, blue glow of his aura. It is a blue so pure and bright, yet somehow soft and Cate feels almost mesmerized. Then Fredrick is scratching at the door so she sneaks him in on her side of the bed, laughing at the silliness of it all but taking it in stride. Everything feels perfectly natural and comfortable for her, and soon she is sound asleep too.

Later she feels a caress on her shoulder. Ethan is awake, wanting her. They make love again, this time slowly, with less urgency. Cate lays her head on Ethan's chest and buries her face in to inhale the intoxicating scent of his skin. They fall asleep just as the sun is starting to peek in from under the blinds.

They get up late, which is unusual for both of them, and Cate puts on a big pot of coffee. They make breakfast together, whipping up some scrambled egg wraps. They share a lazy morning until it is time to part ways to run errands and get exercise.

One of Cate's errands is a pit stop at the Country Grocer. As she places a couple of local tomatoes in her basket she hears the announcement. "The store will be closing in five minutes. Please proceed to the checkout."

Cate hastens her way to the till.

"I'm so sorry to keep you late, leaving it right to the wire, but I've been too busy falling in love to get my chores done," Cate apologizes.

The cashier smiles and laughs and swoons right along with her.

When they next arrange to get together, Ethan arrives at Cate's for dinner bearing flowers and wine. Cate is so dizzy in love, she spills her dinner on the floor and drops her utensils, but Ethan doesn't seem to notice or mind as they talk non-stop about anything and everything. They forget all about the chocolate defrosting on the counter and abandon the dishes again, they are so full of desire for one another. They make love and cuddle for a while before Ethan gets up and begins to get dressed.

"I was hoping you'd stay over again," Cate says, with a look of disappointment.

"I'm sorry, but Chloe is staying at the guest house with me now and I told her I would be home," Ethan says.

"Can't you just call her and say you changed your mind?" Cate asks.

"I like to follow through on my promises," Ethan says. "But let's plan another sleepover soon." He leans over and kisses Cate, finishes dressing, and lets himself out.

Stickiness from the past has Cate feeling rejected. After Ethan leaves she curls up on his side of the bed and breathes in his scent. She sleeps restlessly.

In the morning Ethan calls. Cate gives him the brush-off. She pouts and sulks as she putters about the house, ignoring his persistent attempts to reach out. Cate tries to distract herself, sticking to her routines. She gets out her journal.

> *Why am I so damn triggered? I'm in such a funk over nothing. I see my dysfunction staring me in the face. It's a disgrace. I can't seem to find a trace of the woman who replaced the old me, the one who was with John.*
>
> *In my marriage, we both used withholding as a manipulation technique. If he made a sexual advance that I didn't return or respond to, he rolled over and ignored me, giving me the cold shoulder. No sex, no connection, no affection. Then I sulked and skulked*

*for days, ignoring him completely. Sometimes it would
take weeks to repair. More often we just stayed stuck
in the muck.*

Cate closes her journal and picks up her phone. Ethan
hasn't given up on her. He continues to send texts.

"I feel sick to my stomach. Please, can I come over?"
he writes.

Cate continues to ignore him, but something shifts.
She busies herself with household chores.

"Please, Cate, don't shut me out," Ethan persists. "I want
so much to resolve this. I want us to be back the way we
were. I want to make you happy."

Cate reads Ethan's words and knows she needs to stop
being so damn stubborn. She recognizes the old habit
pattern, from a different relationship.

"Okay," she replies, finally ready to let go.

Cate hears a knock on the door less than ten minutes
later.

"Can we walk?" she asks Ethan quietly when she opens
the door.

Ethan agrees and Cate throws on her jacket and rubber
boots. It is a chilly, early spring morning. The gravel
crunches beneath their feet.

"Cate, will you please tell me what I've done to hurt
you?" Ethan asks.

"You don't know?" she replies.

"No, I honestly don't."

Cate pauses. This is so foreign for her. She isn't used
to being asked to share her feelings openly.

"I, well…" Cate tries to express herself, but her throat
constricts. She chokes and stumbles on the words, but Ethan
encourages her to take her time. He takes her hand and

places it on his heart. Cate swallows and stops where she is standing. She looks deep into Ethan's eyes and sees his soul, pure and strong. Then, somehow, she finds the words she wants to express her pain and hurt, still with her after all the work she has done since leaving John. She opens her vulnerable heart to him and he receives it with love. He remains calm and accepts everything she has to say. She cries and shakes and has to stop often and take a deep breath. Ethan just listens without interruption. Cate is blown away. It hits her hard, how much she has to learn, how little she knows about being in a healthy relationship with a man. But she knows she wants it, that she's willing to do the work. She lets everything go and leans in. They stand there in silence on the road for a long time and then, holding hands, they return to Cate's house. All is well again, at least for now.

Cate reaches out to Finn again, asking him if they can please get together. He tells her he is sorry but he just doesn't have time. She had wanted to break it off with him in person, but as it is, she writes him a long message. Her phone rings, seconds after she hits send.

"Hi, Cate? I just read your text and I'm a little shocked that you want to break up," Finn says.

"I'm sorry, Finn. I've been trying to tell you for weeks now, but you keep blowing me off," Cate tells him. "The truth is, I've met someone else."

There is an awkward silence.

"Who is he?" Finn asks. Cate can almost feel the heat in his words. "Have you fucked him yet?" he asks.

Cate is hurt and shocked by Finn's over-the-top reaction.

"I'm not going to dignify that with a response," Cate says. "What I do or don't do is my business."

Finn hangs up before Cate can say anything else, leaving her more than a little rattled, but at least it's over.

The next day, Cate wakes up with a crazy-assed cold. Her throat is sandpaper sore and her face feels on fire.

"Can I come over?" Ethan texts.

"I'm sick," Cate texts back.

"It's perfect then, I've caught a nasty cold too. Let's be in misery together?"

It seems a good point, so Cate agrees. She throws her wrinkled, sweaty pajamas into the laundry basket and has a quick shower, then applies a coat of mascara to her fever-runny eyes.

When Ethan arrives on her doorstep minutes later, instead of wine and flowers he is bearing Kleenex and lozenges. It is perfect. They order in Chinese food and snuggle up on the couch to watch movies, their sore throats making their laughter sound like two sea lions. This makes them laugh even harder, and Cate begs him to stop, but they've become slightly delirious. A tear runs down Cate's cheek. Ethan wipes it away tenderly and the mood shifts. Cate places his hand on her heart.

"There is absolutely nothing I want to change about you," Cate confides. "There are no red flags. None. Everything feels perfect."

"I feel the same," Ethan says. He mirrors Cate's action, placing his hand on her heart. "I've never felt this way before, but it feels incredible."

"I love how you not only handle my intensity, you seem to welcome it," Cate says. She presses her hand against his chest, then moves it up to his neck and pulls him in for a kiss. She tilts her head back. "I've never felt completely accepted, for exactly who I am, and I am grateful."

"I welcome your intensity, it's part of you. I love who you are and every expression of you," Ethan says.

"Pinch me, I'm dreaming," Cate laughs.

Ethan pinches Cate's arm playfully. She breaks out in a cough, but nothing can ruin the moment.

"I want to give you everything, to make you happy," Cate says.

"How perfect," Ethan says, "because you already do." He takes her hand in his. "It sounds like you're making a commitment."

"No way," Cate denies, laughing and giving his hand a squeeze. "It's only a pledge."

At the beginning of March, Ethan has to return to Saudi Arabia to take care of a few things and extend his compassionate leave as Chloe continues to struggle. She has moved into the beach house and is finishing her school year working from home.

Ethan's flight leaves ridiculously early in the morning, so on his last night Cate and Ethan decide to book a room at a quaint hotel in Sidney, near the airport.

They share a magical evening and then, when it's still dark outside and Cate is sleeping, Ethan departs without waking her.

Cate wakes up, disoriented. She reaches for Ethan, only to find an empty bed. She can still smell the lingering scent of their love-making. She sighs as she remembers, he is gone. Her heart aches. Reluctantly, she pulls herself out from under the covers. She sends him a text, then takes her journal to sit at the table by the window. She stares out at the ocean, deep in thought.

> *We've been together every day this past week, Ethan and I. We've shared amazing romantic dinners and beautiful wine, and I've never talked and kissed and cuddled so much in my life. Our love-making is divine. His attention and focus are as intense before and after as everything in between. I'm falling in love, but I have so many questions. I'm scared shitless, really. Will I be in a full-on committed relationship with Ethan? Will we stay here on Vancouver Island, or will we end up in Saudi Arabia? Will we build a dream home together, here or somewhere else entirely? Will we create our dream life? Will I be his wife? And what about Chloe?*
>
> *I said I would never marry again. But I admit, I would love to be married to him. Thrill for it. I'm swooning, over-the-mooning in love and I want to crow and shout from the rooftops. Adele is right, love is the one and only.*
>
> *I am going to put my faith completely in God, for God's wisdom is infinite and boundless. One thing I know for sure, I'm on the road to healing my heart. Ethan's love is the antidote, the medicine I've been craving.*

To distract herself during Ethan's absence, Cate takes on a thirty-day yoga challenge.

In her first class, Cate experiences a Bouja moment.
She moves into fixed firm pose. The instructor gives
a directive. "Create maximum pressure in your lower
abdomen." Cate attempts to do as she is told but can't feel
any sensation at all. A memory returns to her of a vision
she had during a yoga class a few years before.

> *Cate is standing in front of the mirror, in tree*
> *pose. She is looking at her reflection. The yoga*
> *instructor is talking about emotional containers when*
> *Cate suddenly sees the aura of her container in the*
> *mirror. It is inside her womb, and it is torn. Cate cries*
> *silent tears as she intuits that the tear is from the sexual*
> *abuse she endured when only a child. She sees the tear*
> *as a barrier toward creating healthy physical and*
> *emotional boundaries, and weeps.*

During her next yoga practice, when Cate enters into fixed
firm pose, she imagines her womb healing. She sees a golden
thread that is unravelling from a spool labelled "Love"
sewing the tear back together. Gratitude floods through her.
She embraces the healing energy as she connects with and
listens to her body. Joy overcomes her. In the mirror she sees
herself smiling. She winks back at her reflection.

Summer arrives and Cate has less than a week before she
has to let the Calgary school board know her intention for
the fall. She has been praying for a job offer so that she can
stay on Vancouver Island with Ethan, who has chosen to
leave his job in Riyadh to support Chloe. Ethan's decision
to take a leap of faith encourages Cate, but it's the eleventh

hour and she's almost out of options. She has sent applications to every school board, public and private, listed on the island. She checks her answering machine every day but hears nothing. Then, only one day before the deadline to give her notice of resignation, she receives an invitation for an interview from a private school in Victoria for children with learning disabilities.

The day of the interview Cate puts on her grey wool power suit with a white blouse. She styles her hair sleek with the straightening iron and applies a fresh, minimal look with makeup. She clips her pearl earrings on, slides into her black patent heels, and grabs her leather briefcase with her notes and questions. She leaves with time to spare to make the forty-five-minute drive into the city.

Cate walks into the reception area with confidence, but it is crammed full with other applicants. Cate takes a seat until the principal conducting the interviews calls her name.

"Welcome, Ms. Henderson," the principal says. "Please take a chair."

The principal asks Cate questions about her experiences teaching and her philosophy toward learning. Cate answers with open and honest professionalism, and when it is over an hour later, Cate is confident it went well. Still, the competition is fierce, and Cate just can't be sure.

The next day, Cate receives a callback and is offered the job. A huge weight lifts from her shoulders. She dances around the house, giddy with relief, then calls up everyone she loves to share her good news, starting with Ethan.

"I got it!" Cate says, her voice high. "It looks like we get to stay together after all."

"Congratulations!" Ethan says. "I'm so relieved."

"I know," Cate says. "I feel like we need to celebrate. How do you feel about me organizing a little get-together here this weekend?"

"That sounds perfect," Ethan says. "Who do you want to invite?"

"Let's keep it simple, just us and Chloe, Megan and Charles, Hank and Dorothy."

At the party Ethan pops a bottle of expensive champagne and everyone toasts to Cate's new job, her happiness and success. Cate imagines it is going to be just what she has been yearning for.

Chapter 5

*I*T IS STILL EARLY MORNING when Cate arrives at the beach condo. Ethan and Chloe are walking over to the Charger when she pulls into the lot and parks her car.

"Looks like you two are ready for an adventure," Cate says as she grabs her purse and locks the door.

"Hi, Cate, you're right on time," Ethan says. "We should make it to our appointment with time to spare."

"Perfect," says Cate, hopping into the front passenger seat. "Is this the two-bedroom that you found on Craigslist, Chloe?"

"Yeah, it is. I hope this place is a good fit," Chloe says as she buckles up her seatbelt in the back. "It's so close to my new school, I would be able to walk."

"That would certainly be handy," Ethan says.

"Yeah, and it looks like it's close to downtown too," Chloe says as she moves her finger to zoom in on the location in Google Maps.

"I suppose I need to start looking for a place too," Cate adds. "Now that I've got this new teaching gig. And of course, Celeste and Grayson arrive back in Canada in a couple of weeks and will want their house back."

The three of them settle in comfortably for the drive to the city. Chloe puts in her earbuds, and Cate and Ethan talk easily.

"We're close now, there's the sign for Goldstream," Cate says, pointing out the window. "I meant to go and watch the salmon spawning in the spring but never got around to it. Have you been?" she asks.

Chloe takes out her earbuds and joins in on the conversation.

"No, I haven't," Chloe says. "And I'm not interested either. I'll never be able to eat salmon again if I do."

A few kilometres later Ethan turns left onto McKenzie Avenue.

"We're only ten minutes away now and we're early," says Ethan. "Do you want to take a quick spin by your new school to show Cate?"

"Sure, why not?" Chloe says.

Ethan pulls through the gate and onto the winding drive. Cate is impressed with the school grounds, which remind of her of the private school in one of her favourite movies, *Scent of a Woman.*

"The brick buildings are beautiful," says Cate as Ethan navigates the road that curves by the headmaster's residence and the other buildings. "I hope it turns out to be everything you are hoping for, Chloe."

The rental property is five minutes away, and Ethan finds the address easily. He parks the car in the cul-de-sac of the cozy neighbourhood. The house is mid-century builder, iconic sixties style, stucco-clad with a hipped asphalt roof and front stairs leading to a screened single door.

Cate walks through the open front door to an in-process renovation, with workers and piles of wood everywhere. She manoeuvres around a bucket of paint after almost tripping over it. They have to pick over the mess to take a tour. This place is small, but Cate thinks it has potential. When Chloe discovers the second bedroom has a sunroom, she instantly claims the space.

"Papa, this place is perfect, don't you think?" Chloe asks as the three of them head back to the car.

"Yes, it is," Ethan agrees. "And I'm wondering, since Cate needs to find a new place to live too, what do you think of the three of us moving in together?"

"That's a great idea," Chloe replies without a moment's hesitation. "What do you think, Cate?"

"Um, well, gee, I don't know," Cate says, caught totally off guard.

"It's probably a terrible idea, at least according to the advice gurus," Ethan laughs, "but what do they know?"

Cate thinks to herself that it is likely too soon and it has the potential to jeopardize everything. But in the moment, it feels right and Cate chooses to follow her heart.

"Well, if you're sure," Cate says, turning around to look at Chloe. "I would love to. You know," she continues, "we're not the only ones with changes afoot. I was talking to Taylor the other day, and he was accepted at the University of Victoria. He moves out here in August. I can hardly wait for you two to meet him."

"That's awesome news," agree Ethan and Chloe. "And what about Dana, have you heard from her?"

"Dana is still content to traipse around the world," replies Cate with a sigh. "But hopefully she will return to Canada someday soon and you will get the chance to meet her too."

Later that afternoon, when Cate is back home and snuggled up with Fredrick on the couch, she gets out her journal.

> *Wow. So much has happened in such a short time. I'm reeling with the enormity of it all. It feels like a set of dominoes was knocked over when Chloe decided in the spring that she couldn't stay at her boarding school for her grade twelve year. Ethan tried so hard to convince her to stay, to push through the hard stuff. He thinks she will regret it, but she is so stubborn. As for me, I thought it was bordering on audacious for Chloe to choose switching to a day school, which of course required Ethan to make the tough decision to quit his job in Saudi Arabia, give up his income, and move here to support her. But who am I to say? In the end, I guess it's working out for me because now, here we are, the three of us, moving in together at the beginning of August.*
>
> *The house we looked at today was a perfect fit according to Chloe, but I have to say it isn't my style. It felt boxy and dark, but perhaps after the renovations are complete. I'm not sure, but I think the drive to my new school will be at least half an hour. It all happened so quickly. I'm super-jazzed. I'm so in love with Ethan, and I have a strong feeling that this is the real deal,*

*twin souls finally reunited at our age. What a kick-ass
life surprise. It tops everything I have dreamed about,
all the images on my vision board.*

*I'm thrilled that Taylor is moving to Victoria, that
we will be living in the same city after this year apart.
Relieved too that Taylor will finally get out from under
John's black cloud.*

Two weeks before Cate moves out and into her new digs
with Ethan and Chloe, Grayson and Celeste return from
their year abroad. Cate moves into the spare room. She tells
Celeste she'd like to plan a dinner party at the house to
introduce everyone.

On the evening of the party Cate is full of nerves.
She frets over every detail of the meal. She makes sure
the tablecloth is ironed and the table is set with the linens
and good silverware. She places a bouquet of bright yellow,
blue, and pink gerbera daisies with a few leaves of greenery
in a vase. She hums and haws over what to wear, eventually
choosing a simple outfit of a pair of jeans and a purple silk
blouse that brings out the green in her eyes. She is stirring
the alfredo sauce when the doorbell rings.

"I'll get it," yells out Grayson, who is in the living room,
having just selected an easy-listening Leonard Cohen album
for the turntable.

"Hello!" Grayson says, opening the door wide to greet
Ethan and Chloe. "Come on in."

Celeste appears from their bedroom, fastening an
earring, and gives Ethan and Chloe big hugs. Cate makes
formal introductions. In no time, everyone is comfortably
engaged, drinking wine and sharing stories around the
coffee table.

The dinner is delicious and the evening goes off without a hitch. It's after eleven when Ethan and Chloe depart amid more hugs and promises to get together again soon.

"So, what did you think?" Cate asks Celeste as soon as she closes the door behind them.

"I'm a little surprised," Celeste says. "Neither one of them is as I imagined."

"Oh?" says Cate, a tinge of concern in her voice.

"Yes, but don't worry, it's all good," Celeste adds. "It's clear you and Ethan are madly in love, and I'm really happy for you, Mom."

When Cate, Ethan, and Chloe move in together at the beginning of August, Cate quickly discovers that she and Ethan are perfectly suited to live with one another. She appreciates how Ethan keeps a clean space, always putting his dirty clothes in the basket right away and leaving a fresh, wiped down sink after he brushes his teeth.

"What do you think?" Ethan asks one day soon after the move when he can't find a casserole dish. "Do you want to clean out the kitchen cupboards and reorganize them?"

"I think it's a great idea—let's get right on it!" Cate says.

Cate is further impressed when she finds out that Ethan values routines and schedules as much as she does.

"I was wondering," Ethan asks one evening after supper, "would you mind if we made a commitment to work out at the gym on weekend mornings?"

"Sure," says Cate. "Let's sit down on Sunday evenings and make a rough outline of our upcoming week so that we're both on the same page."

"There she goes, Mrs. One-ups," Ethan laughs.

Living with Chloe doesn't flow quite as easily, but Cate still finds herself forming a deep attachment to her. She loves that Chloe goes crazy for Fredrick. She carries him around everywhere she goes and snuggles up with him on the couch or in her bed, her own personal therapy dog.

Chloe is a typical teenager, with little motivation for being tidy, but she helps out preparing meals, setting the table, and putting the dishes in the dishwasher. She expresses appreciation often, always sure to thank Cate when she does her laundry for her or makes a meal.

In their free time, the three of them get into philosophical conversations or watch movies on TV, squished together on the overstuffed, red couch. They take Fredrick for long walks. It isn't perfect, but it is real and, for Cate, it feels like they are becoming a family.

Ethan enrols in a multi-engine aircraft training course, with the intention of applying to the major airlines, but he has never had so much free time. He goes daily to the fitness studio that is a short bus ride away, where all three of them purchase memberships. Cate and Chloe join him on the weekends. Cate also finds a Bikram yoga studio on the drive home from work.

Before school starts, Cate spruces up the dark, tiny, cramped space she's been allocated as a classroom, on a very limited budget. There are two large cement pillars in the middle of the room, and the space feels more like a dungeon than a classroom. She shops at the teacher store on Douglas Street for supplies and decorates the bulletin boards and gets herself familiar with all the new computer programs she will need to use to grade students and write reports.

Taylor moves out on the September long weekend before classes begin. Cate is beyond excited for her son to meet Ethan and Chloe, but she has been so busy preparing her classroom she doesn't have the energy to host a family dinner.

"Why don't we pick up Taylor and treat him to pizza at Stromboli's?" Ethan asks.

"What a great idea," Cate says.

Taylor sends Cate a text once he is settled in, and the three of them pile into the Mazda to go pick him up at his new student residence. Cate puts Taylor on speakerphone, and he gives Ethan the directions to his building. When they pull into the campus parking lot Taylor is already waiting for them on a bench by the bus stop.

"It's so good to see you!" Cate says as she gets out of the car and gives him a huge hug.

"You too, Momma," Taylor says.

"How was the drive out?" Cate asks.

"It was all good. The scenery on the way through the Rocky Mountains never fails to impress me," Taylor replies.

"It's wonderful to finally meet you in person," says Ethan as he jumps out and opens the back door. Taylor and Ethan exchange man-hugs, and then Taylor scrunches into the back seat beside Chloe.

"I'm so grateful to have a new sister," Taylor says. "Now that we're living in the same city we'll have the opportunity to get to know one another better."

Over dinner Ethan, Chloe, and Taylor all fall into easy, relaxed conversation. Cate is over the moon with joy and gratitude that her crazy-blended family seems to be off to a good start.

School begins after the September long weekend, and Cate soon discovers how in over her head she is. Her students all have a variety of learning diagnoses and are working at different levels in every subject. She has to work sixty hours a week to keep up with the demands of individual student reports, marking, learning new computer programs, and constant student drama. Every day when she returns home with no energy for anything else, she questions her decision to accept the job, but the past is the past and she's determined to follow through with her commitment.

Winter hits the West Coast with a string of wet, gloomy days. Cate encourages herself to push through her exhaustion.

On a Friday in late November, Cate packs up her homework and rushes to make the five o'clock yoga class. She makes it just in time. She lays out her mat and takes a long sip of water, ignoring the buzz behind her ears. When the class shifts halfway through from the standing series to the floor, Cate feels a wave come over her and she passes out.

Cate wakes up in the emergency room of the hospital with no idea how she got there. She looks up at Ethan, who is sitting next to her bed, holding her hand.

"What happened? Where am I?" Cate asks, as she looks around.

"You're in the hospital. You've been unconscious for a while and they are running some tests," Ethan says.

Cate remembers feeling faint and checking her blood sugars, but they were 6.7, totally normal. She recalls wanting to cry out for help, but then everything goes blank.

"Sorry to be such a drama queen," Cate laughs and winces through a half smile. "Now you know just how much I'm willing to do for a little attention," she says, trying to convince Ethan and herself that there is nothing to worry about.

She is starting to feel almost back to herself when the doctor comes in.

"The good news is, your tests are all normal," the doctor informs Cate. "I believe you have suffered from what is referred to as a vaso-vagal attack, which is basically a sudden drop in heart rate and blood pressure that leads to fainting."

"Oh, well that is good news, I guess," Cate says. "I do have low blood pressure."

"You might be more susceptible then," the doctor says. "These events are often triggered by a stressful event though. Have you been under any stress recently?"

"Have I?" Cate laughs, and looks at Ethan. "My new job is incredibly stressful."

"Well, I suggest you go home and try and get some rest."

Cate wakes up the next morning aching all over with a high fever. She can't seem to shake it and ends up missing an entire week of work. *Seems my body had to pull out all the stops to get me to rest,* she admits to herself.

As Cate struggles with her health, Chloe does too.

"Papa, why didn't you make me stay at Shawnigan?" Chloe asks, expressing regret with her decision to change schools, just as Ethan had anticipated.

Cate sighs. She already knows how stubborn Chloe can be. No one makes her do anything, not even Ethan.

Cate is marking papers at the kitchen table and Chloe is watching an old episode of *Arrested Development* when Ethan interrupts them.

"Chloe, do you mind turning off the TV so we can talk?" Ethan asks.

"Um, yeah, okay, I guess," Chloe stumbles as she reaches for the remote and pulls Fredrick into her lap. "What's up?"

Cate looks up from her pile of marking to listen in.

"Well, I received an email today from your English teacher," Ethan says. "How come you didn't hand in your novel review?"

"What, are you like spying on me now?" Chloe says.

"Now, Chloe, that's a ridiculous response," Ethan says. "When your teachers email me that certainly isn't me spying on you."

Chloe starts to cry and wipes at her eyes.

"It's not my fault," she whimpers so quietly Cate can barely hear. "I haven't been able to focus at all. It's that stupid medication I'm on."

Cate isn't surprised. Several times when she's popped into Chloe's room to call her for supper or fetch Fredrick for his walk, she has found her staring vacantly at a blank computer screen.

Chloe sees a counsellor once a week. Her doctor keeps trying to find a better medication to help with anxiety and depression, but nothing seems to work. All of it feels heavy for Cate.

Cate barely has time to write in her journal anymore, but when she has a bit of energy she picks it up and scribbles a few lines.

What the fuck are you doing? You had a chance at total and complete freedom. To finally live your life for you. And here you are, back in the thick of family drama and responsibility, by your own damn choice. Love is so irrational. I'd always wanted a fourth child. Be careful what you wish for, they say. I do love Chloe, so much. It just feels too fucking hard. I need a break. I'm wearing down, breaking down, feeling like a failure.

When Cate is feeling better she decides to give herself a break and goes away for the weekend. She hauls Fredrick along to a bed and breakfast in Shawnigan Lake. She brings her never-ending pile of homework, planning, and marking, but she appreciates the reprieve from Chloe's sullenness. She revels being smack in the middle of nature, a healer almost as potent as love. The fresh air on walks while Fredrick romps blissfully through the forest recharges her, and she returns to Ethan and Chloe with renewed hope and energy.

At the beginning of December, Cate wakes up in the night with a burning hot sensation in her leftknee. It is bright red. It encompasses her entire kneecap.

"Are you awake?" she asks, poking Ethan lightly on the arm.

"I am now," he answers sleepily. "What is it?"

"My knee," Cate answers, turning on the bedside light and pulling back the sheet to show him.

"Wow, that's intense," Ethan says. He gets out his phone and they google webmd.com. There are a variety of explanations listed, including gout and infection. None sound life-threatening, so they try to get some sleep. With Cate's tossing and turning it isn't easy.

In the morning it is even worse and seems to be spreading. The pain is increasing. Cate calls work and explains the situation, but she has a parent-teacher interview scheduled that morning that is very important to her, so Ethan drives her to the school and waits in the car for her before taking her to a walk-in clinic.

The doctor on duty diagnoses an infection and writes Cate a prescription for some antibiotics with instructions to go to the hospital if it gets any worse. Ethan stops at the drugstore to pick up the medication and they go home, but within several hours Cate's knee has swollen to twice its usual size and they decide it is time to go to the hospital.

The hospital is understaffed and those on duty are overworked. It is chaos. They sit for hours in the crowded waiting room.

When the doctor finally examines Cate's knee he speculates it might be infected in the bone. He has to take a sample and it isn't easy to obtain. Cate is anxious and the pain makes it worse. She chews on her lip as they wait for the results.

"The bone is clear," the ER doctor shares the good news, "but there's an infection in your tissue." He scribbles a note on his clipboard. "You'll have to come in every day for the next ten days for antibiotic administered through an IV."

Cate is off work until after the Christmas break.

Chapter 6

CATE'S HEALTH CONTINUES to deteriorate rapidly. By the first week in January she is so weak she can hardly hold up her arm up to write on the whiteboard, and the simple act of composing reports on the computer sends shooting pain up her arms. Cate is exhausted all the time but determined to keep working.

When Ethan urges her to go part-time she agrees, but it isn't long before she realizes she's beaten, that even part-time is too much. Cate resigns from her job at the end of March with a heavy yet relieved heart.

Later that month Cate makes an appointment with her family physician. She lists all of her symptoms and challenges and waits while the doctor writes notes on a pad of paper.

"Well, Cate, based on what you've described, it sounds like you're developing another autoimmune disease, most likely lupus," she says, not pulling any punches.

Cate has heard of lupus before but she doesn't know very much about it.

"Lupus? Is there a cure? Are you sure?" Cate's voice trembles.

"No, there isn't a cure, Cate. I'm not one hundred percent sure this is lupus, but there are some tests I can conduct. I will refer you to a rheumatologist, but I must warn you there is a long waiting list to be seen by most specialists here in Victoria. If you are diagnosed with lupus, you are going to have to take a bunch of drugs for the rest of your life that are very hard on your body."

Cate lets that set in. She starts to cry, but the doctor has zero bedside manners and reminds her that her fifteen-minute time slot is up. Cate drives home in a daze. She bursts into tears as soon as she gets in the door and sees Ethan. He holds her, tries to console her, and encourages her not to jump to any conclusions before the tests come back.

The next day, Cate gets a call from the doctor's office informing her that her appointment with the rheumatologist is in four months, at the end of July.

Cate isn't impressed with the western medical system, which doesn't feel at all supportive. She decides to look into alternative options. She watches documentaries about Lyme disease and a movie titled *Doctored* about the failings of the modern western medical system.

In one of the documentaries it suggests that chiropractors have treatments that can be helpful in dealing with autoimmune diseases, so Cate makes an appointment with Dr. Weber, who has a clinic just a few blocks from their home. The X-rays show Cate's spine is off-kilter, so she goes for adjustments to realign.

A friend of a friend tells Cate about a doctor in Nanaimo who runs an integrative functional medicine clinic, so she and Ethan drive up for a comprehensive assessment. When the test results come back, there still aren't any definitive answers. Blood tests show high levels of metals, including mercury and lead, and the doctor recommends she start chelation treatment. It's no one's idea of fun, driving two hours to Nanaimo and back once a week, but Cate feels positive that at least she is doing something.

"How fortunate are we?" says Ethan on one of their drives. "We have all the time in the world, the drive is scenic, and the company is magnificent."

"Oh, hello, Mr. Silver Lining Pants," Cate says with a smile.

It's hard for her to argue with such compelling logic. She is grateful that through it all, she is with such an amazing man who really is as good as it gets.

As her emotional well-being receives much needed healing energy, Cate's physical pain seems to escalate. The pain in her joints, especially her knees, is constant. To make matters worse, digesting food becomes a game of tummy roulette. It's so unsettling and unpredictable. After enjoying a favourite meal, minutes later the food seems stuck in her intestines, growing spikes and spinning like a whipper snipper in her lower abdomen, causing her to double over. It's often accompanied by heartburn and nausea too.

At her next chelation treatment, Cate brings up her digestive issues with her nurse, Freida.

"Do you have any suggestions on how to deal with bloating, nausea, and sharp pains in the abdomen?" Cate asks.

"It could be related to a food allergy or sensitivity," Freida says. "We recommend our patients try the elimination diet for two months."

"Elimination diet? What's that?" Cate asks.

"You take wheat, dairy, chocolate, coffee, alcohol, and sugar out of your diet," Freida says.

"All the good stuff then," Cate laughs.

Cate is diligent in following the diet plan, but nothing obvious emerges, so she has allergy testing done through a laboratory in the States. The ten-page report reveals that she is allergic to wheat, corn, grapefruit, ginger, mold, grass, dust, cat dander, pollen—to name a few. She does her best to avoid her allergens, but no matter how she eats or how her blood sugars test, regardless of more sleep or less stress, Cate continues to suffer from frequent flare-ups in both her gut and knees. Sometimes, the joint pain is so intense she can barely walk Fredrick to the dog park and back.

At the beginning of April, Celeste texts Cate.

"Grayson and I are coming into the city. Want to meet us at Mole for lunch?"

"Would love to," Cate texts back.

Cate meets up with Celeste and Grayson at the restaurant and they grab a booth by the window. She starts to chatter away about her allergy testing when Celeste takes out her phone to share some of their photos from when they were in Greece. Cate scrolls through the images when, in amongst the travel selfies and scenic shots, she spies a photo of a pregnancy test wand showing positive.

"Um, excuse me," Cate pauses for half a second. "Is this what I think it is?" She holds out the phone with the photo, but before Celeste can answer Cate knows by the smug looks on both their faces.

"You're pregnant!" Cate blurts out.

"Yes, we are!" Celeste and Grayson crow in unison.

"Oh my God!" Cate jumps up and hugs them both. "I'm going to be a grandma! I'm so delighted! When are you due?"

"The third week of October," Celeste says.

Cate squishes in beside Celeste on the bench.

"Ooh, can I touch your tummy?" Not waiting for an answer, she presses the palm of her hand onto Celeste's still flat abdomen. "I can't believe there's a little person in there! Hello, Baby! You know, this is crazy, but I had a dream just the other night that you had twins—maybe there are two babies in there."

"Ugh, I hope not!" Celeste groans. "That would be double the work."

"True, true," glows Cate, "but Grayson is a twin, so I think the chances are more likely. Have you had an ultrasound yet?"

The three of them are so excited, when their server comes over to bring their food, she can't help but overhear. She congratulates Celeste and Grayson on becoming parents and Cate on becoming a grandparent. Cate is incredulous but thrilled that she is going to be a grandma.

When she gets home, Cate shares the good news with Ethan and Chloe. That night she dreams about the future. She wakes up, excited to record the events in her journal.

> *Grandma Cate. I can hardly wait. I hope I have my strength back by then. That I don't have lupus. If I do, I might be too weak and disabled to play with my grandchild.*

I had a dream last night that was so vivid. I was on a sandy beach with a boy of three or perhaps four. He was my grandson. He had long, wavy blonde hair to his shoulders, streaked from the sun. His skin was bronzed and healthy, glowing. We were making castles in the sand. He looked up at me, pushing a strand of hair out of his eyes, just like my dad used to do. His eyes shone brightly in the sun and the way he looked at me, I could feel the love between us. When I woke up, I could still feel the love in my heart.

Before long, it's June and the school year is ending. Chloe graduates from grade twelve.

On the day of her graduation dinner and dance, Chloe looks stunning in the classy black dress Ethan bought for her at Holt Renfrew. When she walks across the stage and accepts her certificate from the school principal, Chloe glows with pride. She exudes confidence. Cate hopes Chloe's ambition to get a Bachelors in Art at the University of Toronto will be a new beginning for her that brings her happiness and success.

When their one-year rental contract in Victoria is up, Ethan and Cate decide to go with Chloe to Toronto to help her get set up. Hank and Dorothy agree to look after Fredrick. Ethan finds an Airbnb apartment in Rosedale for the month of August, never imagining from the online photos that they were moving into such a prestigious neighbourhood.

Cate, Ethan, and Chloe have fun exploring the city and campus together and checking out attractions like the Toronto Zoo and Canada's Wonderland. Cate encourages

Chloe to enrol in a two-day English preparation course offered by the university, knowing she has anxiety around writing essays, but Chloe doesn't follow through. Cate is happy when Chloe tells them she registered with the mental health support services on campus.

Ethan and Cate take Chloe to Canadian Tire where they purchase the things that will make Chloe's room in residence more comfortable, like towels, a kettle, and a fan. They purchase office supplies and some back-to-school clothes. They take long walks and watch movies.

The day before Cate and Ethan are departing back to the island, Ethan makes a reservation at a restaurant in Yorkville that has become one of their favourites.

Ethan and Chloe have some paperwork to complete at the university while Cate gets in some last-minute personal shopping. Cate arrives early and sits outside the Bay Street subway station, people-watching. She reaches into her purse for her journal.

> *Streets crowded with people in the after-work rush hour. Business women and men dressed in high fashion mix with sweaty cyclists and swanky cars and loud taxis. The skyscrapers loom into the sky, creating a man-made canopy of steel and cement. Horns are honking. Controlled chaos. My time in Toronto is at an end. It's been fun, but I'm ready for some tranquility back on Vancouver Island, excited to begin the next chapter. I'm at peace that we've done everything we can to give Chloe the best start possible. Now it's all up to her.*

When Cate and Ethan get back on the island it is the beginning of September, the leaves have started to turn. Their friend Melissa just happens to be looking for someone to rent out her home in Mill Bay over the winter, and it seems the perfect fit.

Melissa's house is a two-storey on a quiet street just a few blocks from the ocean. It has windows all along the south-facing wall that make the living room and kitchen super bright. The kitchen is spacious, with white cupboards and a breakfast bar. It is rustic, warm, and cozy with a fireplace and dark-stained, wooden floors. There is even an extra bathroom and bedroom in the basement for guests.

It's just the two of them for the first time in their courtship, and Cate is giddy with the freedom and lightness.

Ethan passes his multi-engine exams with flying colours. He is ready to get back to work and stop spending his savings. But when he finds out the beginning pay scale for a new pilot is even lower than the beginning salary for a new teacher, he is discouraged. With Cate still unable to work because of her health, the couple decides to explore options more deeply.

Cate gets out the purple notebook she uses for making to-do lists and turns to a fresh page. She jots down the title, "Priorities." Together, they brainstorm a list of things to consider, like balance, exercise, pay, and time with family. Then they rate the work options Ethan is considering: pilot for Transport Canada, pilot instructor in Riyadh, commercial pilot for one of the airlines, or instructor pilot at the military base in Moose Jaw. They rate each one from one to four against the priorities they have identified and discuss how each possibility fits. It is soon crystal clear that the gig in Riyadh offers the most financial benefits, but the Transport Canada job, based out of Richmond, BC, would have them closest to family, so it is their first choice.

It's a very competitive situation. Many highly qualified applicants are in the running, and Ethan doesn't have any experience flying a multi-engine plane.

Cate can hardly wait. She knows the outcome will have a profound effect on her future.

Celeste's due date in October comes and goes and she shows no signs of going into labour. Everyone is on pins and needles. The midwife and doula are both confident that things are going along fine. Then one night when Cate is already fast asleep she gets a call close to midnight from Grayson.

"Hi, Cate?" Grayson says. His voice cracks.

"Grayson? Is everything okay?" Cate asks despite knowing by the late hour that something is wrong.

"Actually, no, there are complications," Grayson informs her. "Celeste's water broke and there was brownish-green gunk in the fluid, I think our midwife called it meconium? Anyway, she seems concerned so we're at the hospital now. Can you meet us there?"

"Of course," Cate assures him. Her grogginess disappears in a flash, replaced by worry and concern. She switches into action mode.

"Do you need me to bring anything?" Cate asks, grateful they live so close to one another.

"Yeah, that would be great, we left in a bit of a hurry," Grayson says.

Cate gets a pen and jots down the long list of items Grayson asks her to bring to the hospital. She gets dressed and throws her blood glucose supplies, insulin pens, and snacks in an overnight bag, then kisses Ethan.

"I'll text you from the hospital," Cate says.

Cate stops in at Celeste and Grayson's house and assembles as many items as she can find, including a bag for the baby with diapers and receiving blankets and sleepers.

When Cate arrives at the hospital, Celeste is deep in labour. She isn't going to be able to have a home birth after all.

Twelve hours go by. There is another complication. The doctor informs them he has to perform a caesarean section. Cate sends Ethan a text, "Celeste has to have a C-section. Will text later."

Cate is shown to a waiting area down the hall from the delivery room. She is exhausted after a night without much sleep. She drifts in and out. She has anxiety dreams of being chased and going blind and driving out of control down winding mountain roads. It takes longer than she imagines, but then, in the early afternoon of November 6, the nurse comes in and shares the good news. A baby boy has been delivered, healthy and perfect.

The nurse leads Cate to the operating room. She can see Celeste and Grayson peering down at a little bundle wrapped in a blue blanket, lying on Celeste's breast. Celeste looks up with tears in her eyes.

"Hi, Mom," she smiles. "Come and meet your beautiful grandson."

"Oh my, he's so perfect," Cate coos. At over nine pounds, he is a chubby boy with a skiff of light brown hair on his otherwise bald head. He reminds Cate a bit of Taylor when he was born. "Have you two chosen a name for him?"

"Yes, we decided as soon as we saw him," Celeste says. "We're going to name him Oliver."

Cate thinks Oliver seems the perfect match for her gorgeous grandson. Cate gives thanks for the joy and the miracle of birth, that her daughter and grandson are okay. She is grateful for the cycle of life, which has come full circle. When she gets home she jots down an entry in her journal before tucking into bed.

> *Little boy, conceived in love, welcome to the world. Little boy, your grandma loves you, more than you can ever know. I'm here to help you learn and grow, to share my grandma wisdom with you. I will always be here. I will support you in everything you do. You are perfect just as you are. You are a gift from God. There is only one you. I promise to love and cherish you, for always.*

Later in November Ethan receives the news that he didn't get the job with Transport Canada. Cate is disappointed but relieved they have a solid plan B.

Ethan reaches out to an old colleague who is still working in Riyadh, and within a few weeks the process is underway and it looks like they will be moving across the world, to the deserts of the Middle East.

Neither Cate nor Ethan knows what the timeline is going to be, so they choose to just enjoy each day. They create routines that work for them, one day flowing into the next, glued at the hip.

Every day starts with a pot of coffee and couch time. Cate writes in her journal while Ethan reads online news. Every so often one or the other looks up to share some tidbit or aha.

"This article I'm reading in *International Living Magazine* claims you can live in Panama for less than $1,500 a month," Ethan says. "Apparently it's tax-free there too."

Cate knows by this time that taxes are a sore spot for Ethan.

"I can't comment on the tax rules, but I seriously doubt you and I could live anywhere in the world for only $1,500 a month," Cate says.

"Why do you say that, Ms. Bubble Popper?" Ethan teases.

"I just think when people make such outrageous claims they are living a far more frugal lifestyle than either you or me is interested in, that's all."

After an hour or so Cate and Ethan go into their big, bright kitchen and chop and stir and prepare breakfast as a team, Cate singing and Ethan humming along. After breakfast, they take Fredrick for a walk along the ocean. Hand in hand, they discuss their plans for the day while Fredrick scampers along the water's edge. They look for sea lions and sometimes they even spot dolphins out on the horizon. The conversation flows and they never seem to run out of things to say.

After their walk, they change into gym gear and drive to the fitness studio up the hill. The studio is bright and airy, with floor-to-ceiling windows along two sides of the building. They work out for an hour and half, although if Cate is suffering, sometimes all she manages is a slow half-hour on the elliptical, the rest of the time passed reading a book. By the time they get back home they are ready for lunch, wondering where the morning got to.

On Saturdays, Ethan and Cate clean the house together, top to bottom. They pump up the volume on their iPad, their chores playlist giving energy to their tasks. Even something as mundane as cleaning is a point of mutual compatibility. They are both fastidious, paying attention to the details. Ethan gets naked and cleans the shower last. Cate drops her sponge to join him. One thing leads to another.

Following their mutual scrubbing, clean and satiated, they get dressed and head to the kitchen, switching from coffee to wine and adding some cheese to make it officially happy hour. They toast their love and share their ideas and feelings openly.

Some evenings, they bring themselves to invite family and friends into their idyllic world. Their regular visits with Celeste, Grayson, and Oliver are deeply fulfilling. New grandparents helping new parents adjust to the demands of a new baby. Cate is over the moon to be a part of it all, changing diapers and rocking Oliver to sleep. But Cate and Ethan don't need anyone else's company. Cate experiences a sense of belonging inside of their relationship and discovers truth to the adage, home is where the heart is.

For the Christmas holidays, Ethan books a condo in Whistler for one week. Ethan's parents, Aubrey and Roger, fly out from Winnipeg, and Chloe makes the trip from Toronto to join them.

Cate's never been to Whistler before and is blown away. The village ski resort is a postcard for winter on the West Coast, with the snow-covered mountains and Christmas decorations and lights adorning every tree, awning, and storefront.

On arrival at the condo, Cate steps into an inviting living room where two oversized, leather recliners and a chocolate corduroy chesterfield border a shag area rug. There is even a real wood-burning fireplace set into the brick of the feature wall.

Ethan introduces Cate to his parents for the first time. She's seen plenty of photos of them, and even though they are smiling in almost every one, Cate is struck immediately by the positive energy they both exude.

"How lovely to finally meet the sun in my son's life," says Aubrey, immediately after giving Cate a warm hug. She is petite, like Cate. She has a thick head of silver-white hair that she wears short, and her face is so much like Ethan's, with the same intense blue eyes and fair skin.

"That's so kind of you to say," says Cate, a blush rising to her cheeks.

"Ethan tells us the long list of your outstanding qualities every time we speak," says Roger. He is a big man, with a ring of powder-white hair around his otherwise bald head, and Cate can't help but think of the stereotypical "gruff teddy bear."

"It's wonderful for us to see our son so happy, after everything he's been through," Roger says, his expressive, bushy, black brows drawing up as he smiles.

"I'm thrilled that me being with Ethan makes you happy," says Cate. "He's the most magnificent man I've ever met."

"Now, now," Roger says. "We don't want Ethan's head to get too big for his hat."

"That would take an awful lot of compliments," says Cate with a laugh.

Everyone settles into the comfortable space of the condo and into a cheery routine. Chloe and Ethan ski while Cate, Aubrey, and Roger ride the up the world-renowned gondola. They meet up for lunch at the top of the mountain, taking in the spectacular views. They celebrate Aubrey's seventieth birthday at a five-star restaurant in the heart of town.

After four days of festivities and fun, everyone crams into the Mazda for the drive through the stunning scenery en route from Whistler to Horseshoe Bay, where they board the ferry to cross the ocean to the Duke Point terminal on the island.

They celebrate Christmas with Donna, who moved from Calgary into an apartment in Oak Bay just a few weeks earlier. Taylor, Celeste, Grayson, and baby Oliver all join them for Boxing Day dinner at Cate and Ethan's home in Mill Bay.

Everyone is sitting around the tree, opening gifts and engaging in lively conversation, when the room suddenly gets still. Celeste passes a small, square package to Cate, her brow furrowed. She reads the tag, "To Cate, Love Ethan."

Cate looks at the silver-wrapped parcel, which is clearly a jewelry box. She wonders how she is going to say yes. She opens the gift paper and lifts the lid to reveal a stunning set of silver hoop earrings.

"My heart almost stopped," Donna laughs out loud, breaking the tension.

"Perhaps a ring will be part of the near future," Aubrey says, expressing what everyone was imagining.

"Sorry," Ethan blushes. "I didn't mean to cause any drama."

Two days later Cate is in bed reading a book, waiting for Ethan to join her, when she hears some rustling in the walk-in closet. When Ethan climbs into bed beside her, he passes her a gift bag.

"What's all this?" Cate asks. "Didn't you spoil me enough for Christmas?"

"Just look inside," Ethan directs her, impatient with excitement.

Cate peers in and sees a silver Birks ring box. She takes it out and opens the lid to discover a perfect, single diamond on a slim, white gold band.

"Ethan, I love it!" Cate swoons as she takes it of the box. "It's perfect."

Ethan takes her hand, his own just a little shaky, and slides on the ring. He doesn't have to ask, but he does anyway.

"Cate Henderson, will you be my wife?"

Cate nods her head yes even as she answers him, her voice thick with emotion.

"Yes, yes, a million times, yes."

They make love and curl up beside one another, then begin to plan their wedding day.

Chapter 7

*E*ARLY IN THE MORNING, EVEN before the sun has risen in the sky, Cate awakens. It is the tenth day of January, the day of her wedding, and she is too excited to sleep.

"Today's the day," Cate whispers to Ethan as she moves over to spoon in behind him.

"Good morning, my Love," Ethan says, sleepily. "Is it that time already?"

Cate drapes her arm over Ethan and reaches for his hand under the covers.

"It's stupid-early," Cate says, looking at the alarm clock on the nightstand. "Not even five, but I'm too jazzed up to sleep any longer."

"I love it when you're jazzed," Ethan says. He rolls over to face her and places his hand on her heart. "And I happen to have a great idea of what to do with your jazzy energy."

An hour later, fully satiated, they patter out to the kitchen barefooted to begin the day as usual, with coffee and couch time, followed by breakfast and a dog walk along the ocean. There is a stillness and calm to the air that seems a reflection of how they are feeling. They breathe in the tranquility as they walk, hand in hand, back home. They are ready.

Ethan drives Cate to the hair studio and drops her off, then heads into Duncan to pick up the bouquets of red roses and white lilies they chose just a few days before. He drops the flowers off at the winery where the wedding will take place and then returns to pick up Cate. She emerges looking radiant, her ash-blonde hair styled in soft waves that frame her face.

When they get back home Donna is just pulling up in the driveway.

"Oh, what great timing," Donna says as she steps out from her car. "I wasn't sure when I drove up and your car wasn't here if I had the time right. You did say to come over around one, didn't you?"

"Yes, Mom, your timing is perfect," Cate assures her as Ethan fetches Donna's overnight bag from the trunk.

"I'll just put your bag in the guest room," Ethan offers while Cate unlocks the back door.

"Thanks, Ethan, and if you don't mind, could you set up the ironing board for me?" Donna asks. "My skirt needs a go-over. Oh, and have you two had a chance for some lunch? I'm quite hungry after that long drive."

At first, Cate allows her mother's neediness to irritate her, but she quickly switches gears. She chooses to feel love and understanding instead. She lets the heaviness of old stories that have been completed, but still show up once in a while, evaporate.

"I'm not going to have lunch today, I'm saving room for later," Cate says. "You two can sort yourselves out."

Cate disappears into her bedroom. She sits at her vanity and scrutinizes her face as she applies makeup to create a soft, natural look. She chooses a cool cherry shade of red lipstick, then slips into her barely beige, lace and raw silk, knee-length dress. She puts on the silver hoop earrings Ethan gave her for Christmas just as he enters the room. He stops in his tracks and looks at her with love and appreciation.

"Can I help you with that?" Ethan asks as he moves in closer to assist Cate in fastening the pearl and silver choker that is a gift from Donna around her neck. He presses up against her and kisses her where his hands have just grazed, then takes a step back.

"You look incredibly beautiful, as always."

Ethan disappears into the closet to dress in his midnight navy suit and comes out looking ever so handsome. The slim cut fits his body perfectly. His black, patent leather shoes are shined to a military-grade sheen, and all that's left to do is sort out his tie.

"Wow, don't you two clean up well!" Donna says, looking up as she stacks her plate in the dishwasher.

"Thanks, Mom, you look fabulous too." Cate admires her mother's choice of a deep purple, velvet skirt and soft, flowing, silver-grey blouse. "Are you ready to go?"

"Just about," Donna says. "I just have to give my teeth a quick brush and put on my lipstick."

Minutes later they are on the road. They arrive at the winery right on time. Their photographer, Susan, is parked in the lot, unpacking her gear for the photo shoot.

"Hi, Susan," says Ethan, as he steps from the car. "Do you need any help to set up?"

Susan thanks him for the offer but assures him she has it all under control. She adjusts the strap of her camera and picks up her tripod.

"It looks like it was good idea to take photos before the ceremony," Cate says, looking up at the clouds that have moved in thicker and darker.

"Yes, very lucky," Susan agrees. "By the way, those sexy, high-heeled shoes really show off your gorgeous legs. Do you mind if I take a couple close-ups, just for fun?"

"Thank you, and please, feel free to use whatever artistic license you desire," Cate says.

"Great, let's get this underway before the rain starts up," Susan says.

Ethan and Cate pose in a variety of locations throughout the property. When they are on the bridge beside the waterfall, droplets of rain begin to splash onto the ground. They open up the red and navy umbrellas they purchased, which add a splash of colour.

Susan finds an old wooden swing behind the restaurant that makes a quaint prop. As the rain falls heavier, they move inside the winery where the rows of wine bottles stacked on oak planks provide the setting for more sensational shots.

Susan takes the last few photos and then it's time to head inside for the ceremony, just as the rain gets heavy.

There is a fire crackling in the stone fireplace, cozy and inviting. The Justice of the Peace, Liz McPherson, is already set up at a podium. Donna has taken a seat with Megan, their only witnesses. Liz asks Ethan and Cate to approach the podium and begins.

"We are gathered here today to witness the legal joining of Cate and Ethan," Liz says. She gives a brief statement and then asks the couple to say the vows they have written for one another. Cate and Ethan hold hands and look into each other's eyes.

"I wasn't looking, but there you were," Cate begins. "You are my rock, our love my foundation. You inspire me to be my highest self and fulfil my highest purpose. Because of you, my heart knows true love."

Ethan squeezes Cate's hand gently, then says his vows.

"Meeting you has changed my life. I never knew I could be this happy, and it is all because of you." Ethan pauses to take a deep breath. His hand, holding the paper with his vows written on it, trembles ever so slightly. "You light up the room with your contagious optimism, and you share it with generosity. Your love fills my heart like nothing I have ever felt before. I want to spoil you and shower you with love every day for the rest of your life."

Cate smiles. She can hear her mother sniffling back tears. Then it is time to exchange their rings.

"With this ring, I commit to adore and cherish you, to do everything in my power to have you feeling thrilled, every day, for all of our lives," Cate says as she places the white gold band on Ethan's finger.

"With this ring, I commit to support you, to love you, to hold you up and celebrate you, every day, for all of eternity," Ethan says as he does the same.

"You are now man and wife," Liz announces.

Cate and Ethan have hired a personal chef to create a custom menu, and the celebrations begin with champagne and an artisan selection of amuse-bouches. The newlyweds gather with the intimate group of guests in the smaller of

the two dining rooms and everyone toasts their
congratulations. Susan and Liz join in on the storytelling
and laughter as if they are old friends. After an hour
of socializing, it's time for the guests to leave.

The staff have set up a table for two in the middle
of the large dining room, with candles and the flower
arrangements set on crisp, white table linens. The meal
is served in courses, over several hours. Cate is immersed
in the experience, the delicious tastes and textures of the
three-course menu and the engaging conversation, oblivious
to the rest of the world.

After several hours it is time to go home. They step
outside to pouring rain. They get soaked running the short
distance to the waiting taxi. They laugh as they shake the
drops from their umbrellas and tuck into the warm and dry
back seat of the car. Ethan gives the driver the address. Cate
tries to focus on the conversation, but she has more pressing
things on her mind than small talk with a stranger.

When they make love on their wedding night, it is like
all the other nights before, except somehow different. For
Cate, it feels as though each touch affirms their commitment
to one another. Ethan brings her to the heights of passion
over and over again. Their souls collide, in bliss that Cate
imagines to be like heaven. She has no words to convey the
intensity of how she feels, but she doesn't need to say a thing.

Life feels like a grand adventure for Cate. She and Ethan
are flying to Las Vegas for a brief honeymoon, having
decided to postpone their plans for a longer honeymoon
in Costa Rica or Panama until their lives are a little
less uncertain.

Cate has never been to Vegas before, but Ethan has been several times and he assures her it is all that it claims to be: a fast-paced, over-the-top, materialistic conglomeration of gambling, eating, drinking, shopping, entertaining, and partying.

Cate and Ethan are booked for four nights at the Bellagio, famous for its spectacular water fountain. They arrive in a taxi that takes them up the immaculate driveway and past the fountains that are in full display. Ethan pays the taxi driver. They walk into the lobby arm-in-arm, their feet practically gliding across the magnificent marble floors. Ornate chandeliers hang from the ceilings. There are marble columns and elaborate arches, and priceless pieces of art and mirrors on every wall. Everything embodies bling and opulence.

"Ethan, this really is over-the-top," Cate exclaims. "I feel like Cinderella with her prince." Her enthusiasm is contagious and Ethan agrees.

"It is beautiful. I wonder what our room will be like?" Ethan says.

After checking in at the front desk and getting their room keys, they take the elevator to the twenty-second floor. They open the door to their deluxe romance studio, which looks more like an apartment, it's so large. Cate is the first to spot a gorgeous bouquet of flowers and a bottle of champagne in a bucket of ice on the glass coffee table. There is an envelope addressed to them, and Cate opens it.

"Congratulations on your recent nuptials, Love Michael, Ashley, and Sam," Cate reads out loud. "How thoughtful of them; we'll have to send them a thank you soon."

They take a few moments to take in the breathtaking view of the city lights from the floor-to-ceiling windows. They check out the bathroom complete with a rainforest showerhead and soaking tub big enough for two. They are both smiling ear to ear, like cats and canaries as Donna would say. Cate grabs Ethan by the hand and twirls herself around before turning to kiss him firm and deep on the mouth.

"Come on, let's open this champagne and start the celebrations," Ethan suggests.

There is a loud pop as Ethan expertly releases the cork, and then he pours the bubbly yumminess into two flutes.

"To living the dream with the love of my life," Cate toasts.

"Ditto!" Ethan agrees. "All the way."

After they unpack their things and hang up their clothes neatly in the closets, Cate and Ethan head out to explore. They are starving after their travels and choose the steakhouse at the hotel for their first of many sumptuous, decadent meals. They splurge on imported Japanese Wagyu beef accompanied by frites with three different dipping sauces, along with the customary bottle of red wine.

In the gambling room Ethan spots a blackjack table with a low limit and two available seats.

"Can you please present your identification, miss?" the dealer asks as Cate slides onto a stool.

"Are you talking to me?" Cate asks, incredulous, her hand to her heart.

"Yes, I am," he insists.

Cate produces her photo identification and laughs with mock indignation.

They have a good run of beginner's luck and by the end of the evening they are up a few hundred dollars. It is past midnight, totally out of character for them, when they finally make their way back to their room. Cate soon discovers the real excitement is only about to begin.

The sun peeks in from under the blackout blinds. Cate stirs from a deep and satisfying slumber. She opens her eyes to see Ethan staring at her with his intense blue eyes.

"Pinch me, I must still be dreaming," Cate says.

Ethan laughs and pinches her softly on her arm. She playfully nibbles his bicep and soon they are beginning the day as they ended it only a few hours before.

Over the next four days, Cate and Ethan take pleasure in all the over-the-top experiences that Vegas has to offer. They buy tickets for two Cirque du Soleil performances. They eat and drink like kings and queens. They window-shop, but it seems they both have everything they desire. They play blackjack at various casinos along the strip. They try their luck at the slots a couple of times. Their wins and losses end up balancing out, and they even have a few extra American dollars in their pockets when all is said and done.

"I absolutely loved our time in Vegas, but I'm glad it's time to go home because I'm bone exhausted," Cate says.

"I know what you mean," Ethan agrees. "I don't think I can eat or drink another thing. I'm ready to get to the gym and back into our routine."

"I must admit, I love doing everything with you as my partner," Cate says, a smile on her lips. "And I love, love, love being your wife."

Back on the island, Cate and Ethan settle back into their routines. They call up Chloe for their weekly FaceTime chat.

"I can hardly wait to hear all the details of your honeymoon," Chloe says. "Did you like Vegas, Cate?"

"I loved it," Cate says, "but I need a holiday from my holiday to recover."

"We took some great photos and are just putting together an album we can send you when we're done," Ethan says.

"That would be great," Chloe says. "Does it feel different … being married?"

Cate and Ethan had shared with Chloe before they got married that they didn't think having a legal piece of paper would change anything. They just had to have the paperwork for Cate to be able to move to Riyadh.

"Well, to be honest," Cate says, "it does feel different. I'm glad we kind of got pushed into it. I love being your dad's wife."

"You know, I've been thinking about it, and I think I would really like it if we were a family legally too," Chloe confides. "How would you feel about adopting me?"

Both Cate and Ethan are a little surprised, but not totally. They had given Chloe a certificate declaring the three of them to be an infinity family, along with a yellow-gold band to symbolize their commitment to her when she moved to Toronto.

When they hang up, Cate and Ethan talk about it some more and agree to start the process right away. Ethan calls a friend for the contact information of a lawyer he knows in Toronto, Julianna. He reaches out to her to start in on the paperwork immediately.

Ethan receives the news that his application to the Pilot Instructor Academy in Riyadh has been accepted. There is a human resources induction involved, which leads to a trip to Manchester, England. On the day he is scheduled to depart, Cate drives him to the airport. They are on the road when Ethan's cellphone rings.

"Hello, Ethan speaking."

There is a long space of time while Ethan listens, his brow turning into a deep scowl. It is clear to Cate that something is wrong.

"Okay, thank you so much for letting me know," Ethan says. He hangs up and turns to Cate. "That was Hugh, calling to let us know that he found out from Reagan that Chloe is in a really deep depression."

Hugh is the father of one of Chloe's closest friends.

"Shit," Cate sighs. "I never got any sense she was struggling when we talked last week. And it really sucks that you're just about to leave the country."

"I know, I know." Ethan says, his voice heavy with concern. "Hugh said Reagan is worried that Chloe might be suicidal. What are we going to do, Cate?"

"I don't know," Cate admits. "All I know for sure is that she needs us. I have to go to Toronto, on the first flight possible."

In the brief time before Ethan's departure they sketch out a tentative plan. Cate braces herself mentally and digs out her figurative firefighter's hat. As soon as she gets back home she books her flight, arranges for Hank and Dorothy to look after Fredrick, and books accommodation at the Hyatt, a few blocks up from Chloe's university residence.

On the plane, Cate has a chance to think and process. She retrieves her journal from her carry-on bag.

> *God? It's me again. I know, it would seem I only reach out when I'm desperate, but isn't that human nature? Anyway, this time it's important. It isn't about me, it's about Chloe. You just brought her into my life,*

and I can't believe it was for nothing. I need her. Ethan needs her. The world needs her. So, God, if you're listening, please find a way into Chloe's heart. Send her a message of love and hope. I am open to being your vessel. I am willing to give it everything I've got. Please, give me the strength and courage I need to support her, to show up and be what she needs.

Cate is a bit overwhelmed with navigating the busy Toronto Pearson airport on her own but remembers the basic layout from their trip out in August. Outside the terminal she joins the cue for a taxi. The driver is friendly and helps Cate hoist her heavy suitcase into the trunk.

"To the Hyatt in Yorkville, please," Cate says, hopping into the back.

The driver talks to her about politics, his journey from Pakistan to Canada in the eighties, and the crazy construction as he drives her to the hotel. Cate is grateful f or the distraction and just listens and nods.

When the taxi driver pulls up into the drop-off area, it is clear to Cate that the hotel is posher than she had anticipated, but that's the least of her problems. She rolls her luggage through the revolving glass doorway into the ornate lobby and checks in at the desk. Once Cate has unpacked she sends Chloe a text.

"Hi, Chloe, it's Cate. I'm in Toronto."

"WTF?" Chloe replies.

"Reagan told Hugh you aren't doing well and he called Dad and me."

"Oh."

Cate suggests she can come pick her up, but Chloe says no, she'll come over to the hotel. She sends a text when she is in the lobby, where Cate meets up with her. She looks unkempt, so small and frail, a ball cap over unwashed hair. Her shoulders sag, as if she's carrying the weight of the world. Chloe falls against Cate. They stand there for several seconds before Chloe steps back and Cate suggests they go up to her room.

Over the next several days Cate does her best to support Chloe and invites her to move into the hotel with her for a brief reprieve from life in residence, where her roommate is just adding to her stress. They order in room service and watch movies and go down to the hotel spa to be pampered with massages.

When Ethan's business in Manchester is finished, he changes his return ticket from Victoria to Toronto. The three of them work together to find solutions. They meet with university administration and a private counsellor.

In the end, Chloe tells them that she doesn't have the mental wellness or strength to cope with the challenges of her classes, and she withdraws from university. It's the middle of March when Chloe makes her decision, and Cate and Ethan only have two more weeks until their lease with Melissa is up. Chloe comes back with them to Mill Bay for some island tranquility while they pack up their belongings and try to decide what to do next.

On the weekend, Cate invites Taylor and Donna up for a family dinner and game night. When they arrive, Cate and Ethan are busy prepping beet and rice burgers in the kitchen. Chloe runs to the door.

"Taylor! I've missed you," Chloe says with a hug, "and you too, Donna," she adds. "Come on in. Papa and Cate and are in the kitchen."

"Looks like the party has already started," Donna says, observing the two half-full wine glasses on the kitchen counter.

"You bet it has," Cate says with a smile. "Can I pour you two a glass?"

"Not for me, I'm afraid," says Taylor. "I'm the designated driver."

"I'll just have a wee sip," says Donna. "What can I do to help?"

Cate gives Donna the task of setting the table. Chloe and Taylor offer to take Fredrick for a walk before dinner.

After the meal they get out a deck of cards to play a few hands of gin rummy.

"I hope it's okay," says Taylor, "but I just wanted to say how sorry I am that you had to drop out of school Chloe."

"Thank you," Chloe says, "I really appreciate that. It's been really tough."

"Well, I'm of the belief that everything happens for a reason, but sometimes we don't know what the reason is right away."

Everyone concurs, Taylor's advice is wise. They continue to play a few hands until Donna suggests it is high time they get back to the city.

When Cate crawls into bed later that evening, Ethan is tucked in reading the financial news. She reaches into her nightstand drawer and gets out her journal.

> *My mother's heart is overflowing with joy. I'm so damn proud of my son. From the very beginning he has been nothing but accepting, welcoming Chloe into his life as his sister with open arms. Chloe doesn't let just*

anyone in, but she has shared with me how much she
loves Taylor, and when she lit up when he arrived today
it pretty much said it all.

In the morning Cate, Ethan, and Chloe sit down to discuss
a variety of options. Chloe wants to return to Toronto, so
Ethan and Cate decide to move to Toronto with her. They
agree to take it one month at time.

Ethan goes online and finds a two-bedroom apartment
where the three of them can stay for the month of April.

When they arrive in Toronto it is raining hard. They're
locked out of the apartment building, unable to get a hold
of the landlord. The three of them, one soggy dog, and their
massive collection of luggage, overflow the sidewalk.

The landlord arrives twenty minutes late. He escorts
them up the elevator to their apartment. Cate looks around
and feels completely overwhelmed. The second bedroom
turns out to be a fold-out futon in an office. There is
something that looks like chocolate ice cream smudged all
over the freezer compartment of the fridge. There is who
knows how old laundry in the washing machine, reeking
of mold and mildew. The floors are covered in stains and
dust and dirt.

"I can't stay here." Cate is emphatic.

Superman Ethan gets on the phone and sorts everything
out. He absolves them of their commitment and then books
them a room at the Fairmont, the one hotel he can find with
a vacancy that takes dogs. They load up their belongings and
hail a taxi van.

The three of them are beyond exhaustion. After
checking in, they find their way to the room. It is very
squishy. A compact space with two double beds and not

much else. Fredrick jumps at the door, needing to go for
a comfort break, and Cate and Ethan leave Chloe to take
him to find some grass. It is still raining lightly.

"I don't think we could have found a smaller space
if we'd tried," Ethan says as he attempts to convince Fredrick
to join him under the protection of an over-hanging awning.

"Well, I'm the one who called it quits on that apartment,"
Cate laments. "But it really was filthy."

"Fortunately, it's only temporary," Ethan says.

"Let's hope," Cate says, crossing her fingers.

It takes three days to find a new apartment. They secure a
lease for a two-bedroom on Blue Jays Way in a condo tower.
It has Ikea style bright orange and neon green furniture, but
it's clean, there is a grocery store a few blocks walk away, and
there is a dog park just around the corner, past a parking lot.
Chloe has her own room and bathroom and Cate and Ethan
have theirs. They stock up the fridge and cupboards and
unpack their things. Cate discovers on Google Maps that
there is a yoga studio a few blocks away.

After a few days, Cate creates an opportunity for some
time for herself. She makes herself a cup of rooibos tea and
retreats to the sanctuary of her and Ethan's room to write.

> *Bustling, noisy, dirty, windy Toronto pisses me off.*
> *I try to protect myself against the gusts of wind when*
> *I walk to the yoga studio, but it is futile. My bare ankles*
> *freeze.*
>
> *The arrogant, perfectionist yoga teacher pisses me*
> *off too.*
>
> *At my last class, I was in corpse pose, almost*
> *wishing it was a permanent state. Death sounded*
> *so tranquil. In stillness, I felt like I was drifting away.*

I realized it wasn't exhaustion as I fell into a low blood sugar on my mat. I could feel myself moving placidly toward unconsciousness. Then survival set in. I literally dragged my body across the room to my purse where I fumbled for sugar and my blood metre. The room full of yogis were oblivious to my distress. I walked back home, the wind biting at me like a swarm of angry bees.

I'm so fucking overwhelmed. I'm frustrated with Chloe's stubborn resistance to every suggestion Ethan and I make.

I think about running away. But then there's Ethan, the love of my life. And even though Chloe is driving me crazy, I love her too. I've been waiting my whole life for her. I know this is all part of my higher purpose. I remember my promise to God and encourage myself to forge on.

Ethan discovers a message in his inbox from his new employer. The Saudi government is instituting a new visa process and the bottom line is, his visa won't be ready for a least another month. Cate is jubilant. She isn't sure she could do this all alone.

Chapter 8

CATE AND ETHAN HAVE BEEN working with their lawyer, Julianna, on the adoption process, over the phone and through emails, for months. Now that they are in Toronto, Ethan reaches out to Julianna and she clears up her busy schedule to meet them in person.

Julianna's office is a short taxi ride from the hotel, in an immaculate glass and steel building on University Avenue. A security guard at the elevator asks Ethan and Cate for identification before he allows them entrance. When they step off the elevator, a professional looking, young receptionist greets them and then asks them to take a seat.

A few minutes later a petite Black woman dressed in a Chanel suit and elegant flats walks in. She is wearing large, round-framed, charcoal coloured glasses. Her hair has been straightened into a slick, classy looking, long bob. Cate guesses her to be in her late fifties, early sixties.

"Hello, I'm Julianna," she says, holding out her hand to Ethan and Cate in turn. "I'm so pleased to finally to meet you after all our email exchanges, although it's too bad it's under such unfortunate circumstances. How is Chloe doing?"

"She's stable at the moment," says Ethan. "Thanks for asking."

Cate adds "thoughtful" to the growing list of qualities she admires in Julianna as she leads them down a hall to a conference room.

The room is a purely functional space, with one circular table in the centre, four chairs tucked in around it, and a couple of pieces of art on the walls, no windows. There is a large stack of file folders piled up in the centre of the table.

Julianna invites them to take a seat, and the three of them get down to business, going through emails and legal documents, looking for precedents that will support their request that parental consent on behalf of Chloe's biological parents be waived. Julianna asks a ton of questions. Fortunately, Ethan is extremely organized and has kept an electronic file that documents everything.

Cate is impressed with Julianna's efficiency and professionalism but is even more struck by her wise, genuine, and warm manner.

Several days later Julianna calls to tell them the court date has been set for April 23.

On the day of the hearing, Chloe, Ethan, and Cate take a taxi to the provincial courthouse. They walk through the security where they are required to place their coins and handbags in trays to be inspected, then into the sparse, white lobby where they wait for Julianna and her protege, Alicia.

A few minutes later Ethan spies Julianna, toting a large case on wheels, which more than likely holds the contents of their case.

"Chloe, this is Julianna and Alicia," Ethan says.

"So nice to meet you, my dear," Julianna says, extending her hand to shake Chloe's pale and shaking one.

"Papa and Cate have had nothing but good things to say about you," says Chloe with a nervous smile.

They wait outside the courtroom in awkward silence until their case is called.

Cate is surprised at how non-regal and unimpressive the courtroom appears. It is nothing like the grandiose settings depicted on *Law and Order*. There are no windows for air flow, and it smells stale, like old vinyl and mothballs. The walls are painted a nondescript greenish grey. There are projectors and computers on a table in the middle of the room, with cords dangling and trailing across the floor to electrical outlets on the wall. Cate takes her seat beside Ethan and waits in silence for the proceedings to begin.

Moments later, the judge arrives and everyone stands. She begins by asking the court clerk to call the lawyer representing Chloe's biological mother and engages in a brief debate with him. It is soon clear that he is not answering her questions to her satisfaction, and it isn't long before she tells him his presence is no longer needed. Cate is surprised by this development. She looks over at Julianna, whose poker face gives away nothing.

At this point the judge announces her decision that their request to waive the need for parental consent on behalf of the biological parents is approved. She reads from a section in a huge volume of law that she feels proves it unnecessary, since Chloe is eighteen, an adult able to make her own choices. Then she turns her attention to Chloe.

"What are your wishes, young lady?" she asks.

"I want to be adopted by Ethan and Cate," Chloe replies without hesitation.

The judge appears to be satisfied.

"I hereby grant this adoption to be of legal standing," the judge declares.

Cate is surprised. She feels certain the judge must have made up her mind before setting foot in court. Julianna had prepared them for an uphill battle, but instead the judge came to a swift and sure conclusion. Even Julianna looks shocked. It takes a few moments to sink in before Cate lets go tears of joy and relief.

"Thank you so much, Julianna," Chloe says, getting up from her seat.

"It was our pleasure to work on this case," says Julianna with a smile. "You are a very special young woman, and these two are the real deal," she says, gesturing to Ethan and Cate. "I'm just so happy I was able to play a part in the three of you legally becoming a family, as you so clearly already are in your hearts. And I must say, I never imagined we'd have such a successful outcome today."

"We couldn't be more thrilled," says Ethan.

"And I'm confident our success was due in large part to your diligence," says Cate. "Thank you for working so hard to advocate for us."

Back in a taxi, Ethan asks the driver to make a pit stop at a liquor store where he purchases an obligatory bottle of champagne to celebrate.

When they get back to their apartment, Ethan makes impromptu dinner reservations at an upscale Italian restaurant nearby, then pops the cork. He pours them each a glass and then calls up Roger and Aubrey to share the wonderful news over FaceTime.

"Can you believe it?" Cate says, practically shouting into the screen. "We thought we were just going to appeal the need for parental consent, but the judge skipped right to it and granted the adoption!"

"That is quite the miracle," Roger agrees. "We're both so happy for all three of you."

"It really is a miracle," Ethan says. "Julianna told us our case has set a new precedent, that adoptions have always required consent of the biological parents, no matter how old the adoptee is. She even had one case where her client who wanted to be adopted was fifty-four."

"Wow, that's saying something," says Aubrey.

"Thank you, Grandma and Grandpa," says Chloe, a tear in her eye, "for always supporting me."

"I suppose this means you're legally our granddaughter now too?" Roger says with pride.

They talk a while longer and then Ethan, ever conscientious, says they need to go if they are going to make it to the restaurant in time for their reservation.

Over dinner Chloe shares with enthusiasm her goals and dreams, including her desire to go back to university in the fall. Cate is reluctant to support Chloe with her decision as she doesn't feel like she's made enough progress with her mental health challenges, but Chloe seems so confident that Cate can't resist agreeing. Ethan says that he will stand by whatever decisions Chloe makes, but he urges her to take it slow and not rush into anything. By the end of the meal they are all riding high on a wave of optimism for Chloe's bright future.

Back at the apartment Cate is emotionally exhausted and wound up all at the same time. She logs into her email account and sends a group message to Donna, Celeste, Dana, and Taylor to share the good news of the adoption, with promises to fill them in with all the juicy details when they talk next. When she clicks out the light, it is almost two in the morning, Ethan fast asleep beside her.

The very next day it all falls apart. Chloe wakes up with an upset stomach. Things spiral downward quickly from there. She goes to a walk-in clinic and has a total meltdown. She calls Ethan in hysterics, telling him that the doctor doesn't believe her, that the doctor yelled at her. Ethan tries to calm her down, but she hangs up on him.

Cate and Ethan are thrown back on the rollercoaster of Chloe's emotions. They try to distract each other, but they are both too consumed with worry. Cate recognizes, her heart heavy, that the adoption is not going to be the solution to Chloe's struggles that she had hoped.

When Chloe returns a few hours later, she goes straight to her room and closes the door, without a word to either one of them.

"Well, at least we know she's safe now," says Cate. "But I need some quiet time to process all of this. Do you mind if I spend some time alone in our room?"

"Of course, my love," Ethan says. "Take as much time as you need."

Cate sits down on the edge of the bed. Her heart beats, too loud, too fast. It feels like it has risen up into her throat.

She rolls out her yoga mat and sits cross-legged, her hands resting gently on her knees. She chooses a crystal to hold next to her heart and inhales deeply. She exhales, releasing the tension. She closes her eyes and attempts a quiet meditation, but she can't focus so she gets up and retrieves her journal from her night table.

> *I'm reeling from the impact of falling so hard, so far, so fast. It's almost unbelievable. For Chloe to go from celebrating and acting like she has the world by the tail, to crying in hysterics that she has a serious, mysterious illness that is likely life-threatening, in under twenty-four hours, seems almost impossible. I can't help but wonder if there is something more to her struggle with mental health than just anxiety and depression. Can I even use the word "just" in this context? I feel way, way out of my league. Praying for some insight because I have absolutely no idea what to do next.*

Cate and Ethan do their best to support Chloe, but she remains in an extremely low depression. She ups her counselling to twice a week, and Cate and Ethan attend a family session with her, but Chloe just doesn't seem able to follow through with the work.

At the end of April, their lease at Blue Jays is up. Time for more transitions. Ethan and Cate move Chloe into a temporary residence near the university, and they move with Fredrick to a new rental in a more family-centred area of Toronto where there is a huge park, tree-lined streets, and old brick houses renovated into suites.

Once they are all a little settled into their new spaces, Cate and Ethan invite Chloe over to spend the day with them. They take Fredrick for a walk to the park and stop at a small Chinese grocer to pick up a few fresh vegetables for dinner.

"I'm going to the three o'clock Bikram class at the yoga studio a few blocks over," says Cate. "Would you like to join me, Chloe?"

"No, thanks for asking," Chloe says. "I'll stay here with Fredrick."

Ethan decides he will go for a workout at the gym beside the yoga studio.

When the two of them return a few hours later, Chloe is snuggled up with Fredrick on the couch, watching television. She falls asleep while Ethan and Cate prepare a tofu vegetable bake. Chloe wakes up and joins them at the dinner table but picks at her food. She is even more quiet than usual.

"Are you okay?" Cate asks.

"I'm fine," Chloe answers.

Chloe's actions don't seem to support her statement, and Cate suspects she is far from fine. Chloe has so many walls around her heart.

Chloe gets up from the table and scrapes her half-eaten dinner into the compost, then loads her plate into the dishwasher. She thanks them for the meal, then says she is ready to go back to the residence. Ethan asks her to stay to have an important discussion with them. Chloe looks sullen but scoops up Fredrick and plunks down on the couch.

"We've done some research and have come up with a few treatment plans for you to consider," Ethan begins, taking a seat at the table beside Cate.

Cate produces a stack of notepads and printouts, and the two of them share outlines, timelines, graphs, and a table of options. They're just getting into it when Chloe starts to cry.

"This is all really unnecessary," Chloe says through her tears. "I'm doing so much better. I don't need any help."

"I know you're managing okay right now," Ethan concedes, "but you don't have the stress of school or work, plus we're here."

Chloe is silent. She picks at her skin and pulls at her hair.

"It's obvious you are still struggling," Cate says, breaking the silence. She gets up from her spot beside Ethan and sits next to Chloe. "Everyone needs some support sometimes. We just want to help you. We love you."

Cate tries to console Chloe with a hug, but she brushes her away. Fredrick jumps down; even he can feel the tension.

"I don't care what you want," Chloe says. "I don't want to go into treatment." Chloe cries so hard she can barely speak.

"Would you at least give one of these treatment centres a try?" Ethan asks. The more Chloe resists, the more impatient Ethan sounds.

"You don't need to yell," Chloe whimpers.

Ethan takes a deep breath. Cate knows it is all he can do not to yell. Then Chloe suddenly gets up off the couch, her head lowered and eyes downcast.

"If it will get you two to leave me alone, I'll go to one," Chloe says. "But don't expect a commitment."

She leaves without her customary hugs and doesn't even say goodbye.

The mental health treatment facility that Chloe has agreed to check out is an hour and a half bus ride away. Upon arrival they are greeted warmly by the director, a middle-aged woman with a sunny disposition. She gives them a tour of the facility, including the yoga room, art studio, and the kitchen, where they offer cooking classes.

After the tour, the director introduces them to the psychologist who would work with Chloe. Maggie is young and striking, with a slim figure and long, chestnut-brown hair. She takes them to her office and outlines the different treatment options available, which range from as little as one counselling session a week to a full-time day program. Chloe seems to be at ease with Maggie. When Chloe agrees to the assessment, Cate is surprised and hopeful.

The results of the assessment are ready just over a week later. Ethan gets a call from the clinic, and the three of them make the long journey back.

Cate is shocked when the director informs them that as parents of an adult child they have no privileges or rights to view the results. She advises that their role is to pay the fees and support Chloe. Cate and Ethan are shown to a waiting room and offered a cup of coffee while Chloe meets with Maggie.

Chloe emerges almost an hour later looking pensive and withdrawn, but she informs them she will agree to meet with Maggie for one-on-one counselling once a week.

Each of them retreats into their own world on the bus ride home. Cate takes her journal out of her bag and attempts to write while the bus lurches along.

I feel like I'm watching a tsunami rolling toward me and there is nothing I can do. Trapped, with no control over what's coming. I know I have to let go, that this is Chloe's journey. I was foolishly hoping she would agree to a full-time day program. I believe in my heart that she needs an intensive intervention and that she would benefit so much from the routines, medication options, and involvement of a fully qualified team of professionals. But this isn't my cupboard.

She is doing the minimal, probably just to get Ethan and me to back off and leave her alone, like she said. She told us she wants us to leave Toronto, so we are going back to the island, soon.

This isn't how I thought my role as her adoptive mother would be, but it is what it is and I must accept it.

Chloe gives them the brush-off, making excuses for not being available until it is time for Ethan and Cate to fly back to Vancouver Island. A few hours before they have to leave for the airport, Chloe shows up on their doorstep.

"I didn't want you guys to go with things like this," Chloe says, stepping into the entranceway. "I know you mean well, that you want the best for me, it's just hard."

"Thank you so much," Cate and Ethan say, almost in unison.

The three of them laugh awkwardly. They tell one another how much they love each other, and agree to continue with weekly FaceTime chats.

"You know, it's only a few weeks until our family celebration," Cate says. "Did you print off your plane ticket?"

Chloe assures them she has everything in order. Then it is time to for them to go.

Cate and Ethan move into a two-bedroom, basement suite up-island, in the lake community of Shawnigan, for the month of July.

Ethan gets word that there are still issues and delays with his work visa. He won't be starting work until after the five-week, Islamic religious holiday, Ramadan. Cate is relieved. For a while she wasn't certain if they'd have to cancel the plans they made for family celebrations of their marriage and Chloe's adoption. She is even more thrilled that although he hasn't started work, Ethan's officially on the payroll. With all the flying back and forth to Toronto and medical bills, it is a blessing.

A couple of nights later Cate and Ethan are chilling out, watching an episode of *House Hunters International*, one of their favourite television series. The featured couple are checking out three properties in Tamarindo, Costa Rica.

"Now that we have confirmation that I won't be starting work for another five weeks, what do you think of us going to Tamarindo for our second honeymoon?" Ethan asks during a commercial.

"You can't be serious?" Cate says, completely caught off guard by Ethan's uncharacteristic impetuousness.

"I'm totally serious," Ethan says. "We don't have a place to stay after our shindig in Winnipeg, so why not take advantage of this opportunity and enjoy some tropical tranquility, just the two of us?"

Cate has to agree, it sounds tempting. When the show is over they get out their laptop and start browsing. They book their flights and put down a deposit on a condo, and it feels amazing for Cate, a hard-core planner who has been living in stress, not knowing what lies ahead. Now she can focus on planning the family celebrations in Shawnigan and Winnipeg and prepare for their second honeymoon in Costa Rica.

Ethan and Cate are hosting their first family celebration with Cate's side of the family. They purchase balloons and streamers and order flowers to make it festive. They hire a local caterer to supply the food, including tables and chairs and all of the linens.

Chloe flies in from Toronto a few days before. Cate is nervous, waiting for Chloe at the airport, but when Chloe walks through the security she is all smiles. She greets them both with huge hugs, and it would seem that the drama of a few weeks ago is all but forgotten.

Dana flies in from Calgary the next day, where she has been living with her father since her return from Peru. Taylor picks her up from the airport and they drive up together. Dana will finally meet Ethan and Chloe for the first time. When they are ten minutes out, Dana sends Cate a text.

"Almost there, so excited to see you."

"Me too, see you soon," Cate replies.

Cate has knots in her stomach. She bites her lower lip. She has no idea how this introduction is going to unfold. Dana wasn't very accepting when Cate told her about Ethan's proposal. She said it was hard to get on board when she hadn't even met him, that it all happened so quickly. Which was true enough. And then when Cate shared the adoption news, Dana wasn't very supportive of that either. Cate hopes that no matter how Dana feels, there isn't drama. As she paces the driveway she spots Taylor's car approaching. She takes a deep breath.

"Maman!" Dana cries out, using the French term for mother, a habit she started during her early years in French immersion. She jumps out from the car and throws herself against Cate, almost knocking her over despite her willowy build. "It's been way, way too long."

"I know," Cate agrees, taking a step back to look at her daughter. "You look amazing, still tanned and glowing from your time in Peru."

Dana's thick mane of dark blonde hair is gathered in a messy knot on top of her head. Her large, hazel-green eyes, the same colour as Cate's, glow bright in the sun.

Taylor comes around to join them, and then the three of them are talking one on top of another, descending the stairs that lead to the apartment. Chloe and Ethan are sitting on lawn chairs under the shade of the spacious covered deck.

"Dana, it's so good to meet you," Ethan says as he gets up to greet her. "You're so much taller than I imagined."

"Yeah, well, it's hard to gauge height over FaceTime," Dana concedes. "I get it from my dad. It's good to meet you too, Ethan. It has been trippy to see Mom go bonkers for you."

Chloe and Dana exchange awkward hellos. Ethan offers drinks all around, and they settle in for a long chat. Taylor and Ethan's chill personalities seem to lighten the mood a little, and as the late afternoon sun dips toward the horizon everyone appears a little more comfortable. They order in pizza and play a few hands of cards, and then Taylor and Dana set up a two-person tent at the side of the house.

On the day of the party, it is one of those rare hot and sunny days on the island. The kids help to get everything set up in the morning. Ethan stocks up on wine and beer at the liquor store and fills up coolers with ice.

Just after noon, Donna is the first to arrive. Ethan is outside sweeping the walkway and greets her with a big hug.

"Cate is inside, still getting ready," Ethan says.

Donna sets her packages down on the kitchen table and calls out, "I'm here!"

"Come in, Mom," Cate yells back, "I'll be right out!"

Cate greets her mom and leads her by the arm back outside where Taylor, Chloe, and Dana are still blowing up the last of the balloons. Ethan offers to pour Donna a drink. Before they know it, Michael, Ashley, and Sam, who flew in from Calgary and are staying at the Fairmont in Victoria, pull up in a SUV. Celeste and Grayson are the last guests, Oliver hoisted on Celeste's hip. When he sees Cate he almost topples over as he reaches out for her.

"Come on over to Grandma, little love," Cate says as she scoops him up in her arms. Cate ogles her grandson while intermingling with her guests. Over the course of the afternoon there are bocce-ball tournaments on the lawn and long conversations over many cocktails. Cate hears Michael, his unique machine-gun rat-a-tat meets Santa Claus ho-ho laugh filling the air, and feels jovial. She goes into the kitchen to look for Oliver's soother and walks in on Celeste and Dana in the middle of a conversation.

"I don't know what to think about all this," Dana is saying. "Like, am I supposed to just be all happy that all of a sudden I have a new stepsister?"

"I know what you mean," Celeste says, nodding her head. "It's weird enough to see Mom in love with someone else, but to adopt his daughter?"

"Oh, you two are in here," says Cate, pretending like she didn't hear a thing. "Did you put Oliver's diaper bag in here, Celeste? He's starting to get a bit fussy, so I was going to give him his su-su and rock him a bit."

Celeste blushes and fetches Oliver's bag. Cate rejoins the party, but her jovial mood has been taken down a notch.

The caterers arrive and set the table with the china service and crystal wear. They have silver warming bins for all the hot food, and serving tables are overflowing with a huge variety of appetizers and mains, including the feature dish of barbequed wild Pacific salmon. Champagne is poured and everyone congratulates Cate, Ethan, and Chloe.

After a few glasses of wine, Cate is able to put the conversation she overheard out of her mind to focus on the positive energy of the rest of her guests. There are many tears, and emotions run high. When dinner is complete, the caterers pack everything up. Dana takes photographs with her new camera while guests chat in small groups, sharing family stories.

It is getting dark outside by the time everyone has left. Ethan and Cate pick up all the strewn glasses and bottles.

"Does anyone want to help me build a fire in the pit?" Dana asks just as Cate and Ethan are heading off to bed.

Taylor is the only one with any energy left, so the two of them get a fire going.

"Did you think Celeste looked stressed?" Cate asks Ethan as they crawl into bed.

"Yeah, a little, but that's to be expected with a six-month-old," Ethan says.

"You're right, I worry too much," Cate says with a sigh. "I did overhear a conversation between Celeste and Dana this afternoon. Apparently, they aren't adapting to this new blended family thing quite so easily as Taylor."

"That's not surprising, especially for Dana who has only just met us," Ethan says with a yawn. "But try not to worry, my love. These things take time."

"I suppose you're right," Cate concedes.

Cate drifts off to sleep, heavy with emotion.

Ethan and Cate leave Vancouver Island for Winnipeg on the last day of July. Chloe is joining them to celebrate all over again with Ethan's side of the family.

Roger meets them at the airport. He pulls up in the old Honda as soon as they step into the pickup area. He is full of smiles, as usual.

"Are you sure you have enough luggage?" Roger teases as he helps Ethan to heft everything into the trunk. They won't all fit, so he stacks a few on the back seat, and Chloe and Cate squish in beside them, barely able to get their seatbelts fastened. It's not far, and soon Roger is turning into the driveway.

Aubrey is at the front door, wiping her hands on a tea towel, waving hello. The boys roll the suitcases up to the front landing. Aubrey ushers everyone into her pristine kitchen where she has prepared a veritable feast of various cheeses with crackers, raw vegetables with a creamy dip, chips, mixed nuts, and a fruit plate. Wine is poured. They take their drinks and load up their plates before heading out to the patio by the pool to enjoy the hot, humid weather, typical of summer in Winnipeg.

After a few hours of eating and drinking and conversation, everyone pitches in to clean up. The mosquitos are out in full force so they head inside to play a few hands of cards at the kitchen table.

"What should we play?" asks Ethan, going into the hutch for a pack of cards.

"How about a few hands of Screw Your Neighbour?" suggests Cate.

Roger agrees and fetches a pad of paper from the side drawer to keep score, while Aubrey puts together a plate of cookies and fruit. Chloe starts to yawn midway through the sixth round, and they all agree, it is time they went to bed.

Cate crawls into the freshly laundered sheets and sighs with contentment before she drifts off, her mind a whirl.

When they wake up, Cate caresses Ethan's arm, then lets her hand drift further.

"Good morning, my love," Cate says, with an unmistakable look of desire in her eyes.

There is a lot to do before Ethan's brothers and their families arrive, but Ethan can't resist Cate's advances.

They emerge from their room looking rather ruffled and pleased with themselves. Lucky for them, they are the first up. Ethan puts on a big pot of coffee. They pour themselves a cup just as Aubrey comes in to join them. Aubrey whips up a light breakfast of toast, fruit, and yogurt, and soon Roger comes down, followed shortly by Chloe.

While they eat they discuss the plans for the day, when the caterers will arrive, where to set up the tables, and all the other little details. With all five of them working together, they get all of their tasks done early.

Everything unfolds without a hitch, much like it did in Shawnigan, only instead of bocce-ball tournaments, the swimming pool is the main attraction. Ethan's brothers and their wives and all the nieces and nephews join in on antics in the pool. The catered meal service is exceptional, and everyone has a great time. Soon it's time for farewells.

The few days in Winnipeg go by quickly. Chloe returns home to Toronto, and Ethan and Cate catch their flight to Costa Rica.

Tamarindo turns out to be a surfer's paradise, but neither Ethan nor Cate surf. Fortunately, Ethan has booked them an amazing condo.

They walk in through the main entrance to discover modern decor set in an open concept, high-ceiling space. Light pours in through the windows that line the entire far wall, including sliding doors off the kitchen that showcase a circular balcony looking over lush green tropical gardens. On the black marble kitchen counter there is a bottle of wine and a packet of coffee along with a welcome binder.

The fridge and pantry both need stocking up. They haven't rented a car, having read a review on Tripadvisor that said it was unnecessary, so they walk into town over dusty, gravel roads. It takes longer than advertised, and they are hot and sweaty when they arrive at the small local market. The selection isn't great, but they find enough things to throw together a picnic-style supper and mushroom omelettes for breakfast. Ethan picks out a bottle of cheap Argentinian wine and they walk back to the condo.

In the morning Cate feels rested and ready to embrace the adventure. The bright morning sun creeps high into the clear blue sky, with not a cloud in sight. Ethan makes a pot of coffee and brings two mugs out to the table on the balcony where Cate has already started writing in her journal.

> *It was a bit disappointing, looking out the window as we made our descent into Liberia and seeing only dust and dry, brown grass. I had imagined Costa Rica to be a lush jungle.*
>
> *The drive on a narrow road, which really only had room for one car with a crazy driver who clearly had no fear, was terrifying. But once we were at our building, everything shifted. It was beautiful and, after a quick tour, Ethan lifted me up and carried me to the bedroom and onto the king-size bed. Boom!*
>
> *It was more contrasts as we walked into town amid honking cars and stray dogs and surfers smoking pot in the bars along the main road. Lucky for me I'm with the love of my life, and I can be anywhere in the world with him and it feels like heaven. I hope I can put to rest my concerns for Chloe, Dana, and Celeste, and just relax into the flow of us.*

Ethan has already started sautéing the mushrooms, onions, and garlic when Cate closes her journal and goes into the cool kitchen to join him. They finish preparing their simple breakfast together and enjoy a satisfying meal. The tidy up is quick, and they throw on their workout gear, ready to find the local yoga and fitness studio that the owner of the condo mentioned.

It takes about twenty minutes to get there, door to door, but Cate is happy to walk barefoot in the sand. The studio is located off an oceanside restaurant and hotel. When they walk through the door, the lady at the desk greets them in Spanish, "Buenos dias."

Ethan explains they only speak English, and she switches over easily. She tells them it is fifteen dollars each for a drop-in and twenty dollars for the yoga classes, then takes them for a tour.

Floor-to-ceiling windows cover two sides of the yoga studio, showcasing the lush jungle Cate imagined. She is excited to practice yoga in this space and grabs a flyer with the class schedule before joining Ethan in the gym.

The walk back to their condo isn't as relaxing as the walk in. The beach is crowded with cheeky vendors selling everything from massages on the beach to snorkelling adventures to wooden whistles carved into the shape of birds. They shout out, "Senora, for you, very special price."

After showering and changing at the condo, Ethan and Cate return to the beach where they grab a light lunch at a local beach bar. They eat greasy fries and nachos and drink tangy margaritas, unusual choices for two wine drinkers who appreciate healthy, fresh food.

They've worn their swimsuits under their clothes and walk back to the busy strip of beach to bathe in the sun and frolic in the ocean. Ethan rents them two recliners and a table with an umbrella.

The pushy entrepreneurs encroach on their space. A wrinkled old geezer has the nerve to peek his head under Cate's canopy umbrella while she's reading her book. Cate summons her patience and instead of being rude, she suggests to Ethan that they go back to their condo where there is a quiet pool to relax by.

At the pool Ethan pours them sangrias from a plastic pitcher, having stopped to pick up more wine and fresh fruit on the way home. They stretch out on the recliners and talk about their lives and their dreams, dipping in and out of the cool water when it gets too hot.

"I don't want to be a bubble popper, but the next time we plan a tropical holiday, my vote is for Panama," Ethan says.

"I agree." Cate takes a sip of her sangria. "This pool is beautiful and I love the condo, but Tamarindo is just a little too small-town and touristy for me."

Ethan, with his fair, freckled skin, has plastered on the sunscreen, but after a few hours he's had enough sun for one day. They pack up their things and head inside to make dinner and make love before falling asleep, hand in hand.

For the ten days of their vacation in Tamarindo, they fall into an easy routine. Neither one of them has any interest in taking a tour or going zip-lining; they're here for some much needed rejuvenation. They check in over FaceTime with Chloe every few days. She fluctuates from high to low, as is her way, but somehow the miles between them and the mañana attitude of Costa Rica has allowed Cate to detach a bit from the drama. It is exactly what she needed after the stress of the last few months.

When it is time to leave, Cate feels more relaxed than she has in ages.

As the plane ascends into the cloudy sky, Cate stares out the window. She has no idea what lies ahead. She worries about Chloe and stresses about how long she has with Ethan before he gets the call to start work in Riyadh. She wonders if Dana is settling down, if Celeste is coming around. Then Ethan is ordering them wine and water and flipping through the in-flight movie menu, asking her which flick she wants to watch with him, and her concerns evaporate, if only for a few hours.

Chapter 9

CATE AND ETHAN STAY A few nights in a hotel by the airport while they look for a new place to live. They are only back in Canada one day when Ethan receives the news that his temporary visa has been approved and he is expected to begin work in Riyadh in a few weeks.

The couple chooses to rent a one-bedroom apartment in Victoria for the month of September. Lucky for her, Cate finds out that Melissa wants to rent out her home in Mill Bay over the winter again and is happy to lease on the first of October on a month-to-month basis.

The apartment is one of several units in an old house that has been converted. It's small but has a contemporary look that suits Cate. The location turns out to be phenomenal, only blocks from The Village, downtown, and the ocean.

Cate struggles to accept that Ethan will be leaving, despite the fact that she expected the news. She's stressed out, now that the time for his departure has come and no one seems to have any idea how long the temporary visa is valid for. Cate does her best to cram in all the love, experience, and connection she can into every moment, but the time goes by all too quickly.

When it's time to say goodbye, Cate feels the angel wing that is Ethan's being torn from her shoulder socket, where it was fastened so securely it had become a part of her.

At the airport, Cate kisses Ethan over and over until he can't delay his departure through the security gates any longer.

"I have to go now, my love," Ethan says.

"But I don't want you to," Cate says. She places her hand on his heart.

"I know," Ethan says. "But I'm sure you'll join me soon. Until then we'll talk, every day, twice a day, over FaceTime."

They kiss one last time and Ethan leaves. Cate stands there, immobile. She stares at the empty space where Ethan stood. She can see traces of his aura, like the last snowflakes drifting after a storm. Cate walks out to the parking lot, gets into her car, and drives.

Soon, reality sets in. Back at the apartment, Cate forces herself to carry on but wallows in her grief. She hates the uncertainty of not knowing how long they will be separated, but even a day feels too long. She throws herself on the bed where she and Ethan made love so many times. His scent lingers. She inhales deeply and cries softly into his pillow. Her tears soak the wrinkled cotton pillowcase that is his.

Time ticks by with exasperating slowness. Cate tries to keep herself busy, hanging out with Donna, Celeste, Oliver, and Taylor whenever possible, but they have their own lives. Cate feels like she is just drifting along, an oxygen bandit. Her bouts of painful digestion and lead-legged exhaustion become more frequent and intense, and her blood sugars are all over the place. No surprise; she is an emotional creature.

The move up-island, back into Melissa's house, helps to distract Cate, if only momentarily.

During her regular chelation treatment at the clinic in Nanaimo, Freida has some news to share.

"I've been pouring over your test results, trying to make a connection that makes sense, and I noticed that the test we did for Lyme disease showed as indeterminate," Freida says.

"Yes, I remember," Cate says. "I had been so certain it was Lyme's after watching that documentary."

"Yes, well, I think your symptoms support a Lyme diagnosis, especially the recurrent-remission cycle of your flare-ups. It's worth following up if you're interested, but I'm afraid we don't have the lab testing available here in Canada."

"I'm willing to try anything," Cate says.

Freida recommends a doctor in Seattle who specializes in treating chronic Lyme's, and Cate makes the necessary arrangements to go for a consultation.

The ferry ride to Seattle is noneventful. Cate takes a shuttle bus to the hotel she booked online. It's a no-frills, no-luxury Holiday Inn–type establishment. Cate doesn't even unpack. She finds her toiletries case and digs out her toothbrush to give her teeth a quick once-over before climbing between the thin sheets.

In the morning, Cate sets out on foot with her paper map that she picked up in the ferry terminal. There is a light wind and she pulls her scarf around her neck. She unfolds the map. It all looks so simple and straightforward. The clinic appears to be only a few blocks away. But Cate's lack of navigational skill has her walking in the wrong direction and in circles. She can't find the address, and her phone doesn't work because she didn't think to buy a plan for use in the United States. She has a slight breakdown. She stands immobile in the middle of the street as tears streak down her cheeks.

"Do you need some help?" a kind-hearted stranger asks.

"Um, actually, yes, I do," Cate answers, surprised. Cate smooths out the wrinkles in her map and points to the red dot that indicates the doctor's office. "I'm trying to find this address."

"That's just a few blocks north of here," the stranger tells her. "But you're welcome to use my phone to call the office," she says.

Cate dials the number for the clinic and explains her dilemma to the receptionist, who gives her foolproof directions.

Cate arrives to her appointment late, a sweaty, haggard mess. The receptionist asks her to take a seat while the doctor finishes with his current client. Cate flops down in a chair, exhausted from her ordeal. She flips through a stack of out-of-date magazines. Twenty minutes go by before her name is called.

The doctor asks Cate to take a seat while he looks through the thick file of lab results that Cate brought with her. He pushes his glasses back up onto the bridge of his nose and squints over at her.

"How long have you been having these flare-ups, as you describe them?" he asks.

"Since the end of 2012," Cate answers.

"Hmm," he says, looking back at a particular paper in her file. "It looks like you had testing done for Lyme's back in June of 2013 but tested indeterminate. Did you ever notice the tell-tale, red, bull's-eye rash?"

"No," Cate admits. "And I don't recall being bit by a tick. But I did have a cellulitis infection on my left knee in November of that year, after spending some time in the woods of Shawnigan Lake," Cate says.

The doctor continues to ask Cate questions. When he finishes, he tells Cate that Lyme's seems a likely explanation for her symptoms.

"I would recommend you try a course of antibiotics," he says. "If Lyme's spirochetes are present in your tissues, it will cause a severe reaction. Let's schedule a follow-up appointment when you finish this first course of medication." He hands her a prescription.

Cate thanks him and leaves the office feeling a bit numb. She makes her way back to the ferry terminal for the journey home.

Within hours after taking the first pill Cate becomes weak in the knees. Her legs are so heavy she can't walk. She has to crawl across the floor and up and down the stairs. The pain is almost unbearable. Cate lies in bed. She moans and tosses and curses God, who clearly is busy with more important world calamities.

Celeste calls. She offers to come over to help. When she sees how much Cate is suffering, Celeste makes a call to a doctor of a family friend who has an outstanding reputation in homeopathic and alternative medicine. Before she knows it, Cate is booking flights to Calgary to consult with Dr. Kensington.

Celeste supports Cate one hundred percent. She packs a bag for her and Oliver, and they take the flight with Cate to Calgary. Cate books a car at the airport, and Celeste installs Oliver's car seat. Celeste drives them to the hotel downtown where Cate has made a reservation.

It is -28°C with the wind chill. Cate feels grateful that there is an underground parkade at the hotel. They drop off their suitcases in their room and grab a bite of lunch at the hotel restaurant before climbing back into the car and out onto the snow-covered roads. Celeste drives with extreme caution and drops Cate off at the office door. She bundles Oliver up in layers of warm blankets and brings him in to wait while Cate has her exam.

Dr. Kensington is an older woman; Cate judges her to be at least sixty. She has sharp features: small, intelligent-looking eyes, a prominent nose, and strong cheekbones. After several hours of testing and interviews, Dr. Kensington concludes that Cate does have Lyme disease.

She supports Cate in her decision to go off the antibiotics and starts her on an intensive treatment program of vitamins and remedies from Belgium called UNDA numbered compounds that are formulated from plants. She prints off a menu plan that supports the immune system, which eliminates sugar, processed foods, and alcohol and focuses on a wide variety of vegetables and fruits.

"You will need to book follow-up appointments with me every four months to monitor the situation and adjust the protocol as necessary," Dr. Kensington says as Cate heads for the door with her cache of naturopathic remedies. "I know it's a big commitment, especially with your pending move, but it's essential for us to be diligent to achieve success."

"It does sounds like a lot, but I'm determined to make this work," Cate says.

Celeste drives them back to the hotel. Oliver falls asleep on the way, and Celeste carries him up to their room and tucks him into bed.

"Would you like a cup of tea, Mom?" Celeste asks, turning on the kettle on the bar and selecting a packet of English Breakfast for herself.

"I'd love one," Cate says, pulling off her boots and rubbing her feet. "Might help to warm us up a bit; damn, it's frikkin' cold out there."

"I know," Celeste agrees with a shiver. "We've been on the island so long, we've forgotten how brutal winter in Calgary can be. But speaking of brutal, how are you feeling about your visit with the doctor?"

"It was heavy ... to get the diagnosis," Cate says with a deep sigh, "but at least I know what I'm dealing with and I have a plan of action. You know how I thrive on plans."

Cate opens up with Celeste, but the weight of her emotions makes her tired. She abandons her half-finished cup of tea and crawls into bed beside Oliver.

When Cate wakes up, the room is quiet. She checks her phone and discovers she has been asleep for over two hours. There is a note from Celeste scribbled on the hotel stationary, "Oliver and I have gone for a stroll in the mall. Sleep well."

Cate is grateful for the peace and quiet. She gets out her journal.

> *My suspicions are now confirmed. I have Lyme's.*
> *It explains why I feel like shit. Feeling like shit makes*
> *being separated from my one and only even harder.*
> *We FaceTime and email, but it's not the same, and*
> *besides, the Internet in Riyadh is sketchy and unreliable.*
> *Ethan tells me soon we will be together, but soon*
> *isn't soon enough. I want to be held. I want the*
> *groundedness that his solidity provides. But apparently*
> *this is my demon to tangle. I'm so grateful I'm not*
> *all alone, that Celeste is here with me. I know she is*
> *worried about me, though, and with her, I feel I need*
> *to be strong. Perhaps that is a good thing.*

They head back to the island the next day, and Cate gets back into her routine.

Celeste brings Oliver for visits often. He is a delightful distraction for Cate, but when she tries to carry him for very long her hips ache, her knee gives out, and her arms throb. She loves to read to Oliver. He points to the illustrations and makes sounds that resemble words.

Cate's daily walks with Fredrick shift, depending on how she is feeling. Some days she can barely make it back up the hill as she drags her lead legs while Fredrick pulls on his leash. She feels like a lumbering gorilla as she trudges along, each step a giant undertaking.

Ethan's temporary visa expires and his employer has to send him home until the situation can be resolved.

At the beginning of December, Ethan flies from Riyadh back to Victoria.

The first two weeks of their reunion, Cate and Ethan barely leave the house. Cate suffers from a kick-ass flare-up, but Ethan's love and attention distract her from her pain. Then Chloe flies out from Toronto, and Roger and Aubrey fly in from Winnipeg to be with them over the Christmas break.

On Christmas Eve, the house is filled with joy as Taylor and Donna drive in from Victoria with plans to stay overnight, and Celeste, Grayson, and Oliver arrive for dinner. Drinks are poured and food is served and games are played, all punctuated with peals of laughter. Roger makes manhattans and Cate serves up her gluten-free, vegan baking.

"I have frikkin' amazing news to share," Taylor says as he reaches for a second cookie. "I received confirmation today from the university in Paris. My application for the exchange program was accepted."

"That is *frikkin'* amazing news," Cate says. She goes over and gives Taylor a big hug. "Although they would be crazy not to accept you."

Cate is in her happy place, her authentic space.

When Grayson takes his little family back home and Donna has tucked into bed, Taylor and Chloe decide to watch a movie. Cate and Ethan are too tired to join them, but before she goes to sleep Cate jots a quick note of gratitude in her journal.

> *I'm sorry, God, for all my tantrums these last few months. Having Ethan back and all my family gathered around me, I am reminded of how incredibly fortunate I am. Thank you.*

I'm still thick in the throes of Lyme's, but I'm ready to change my attitude. I've got this. My love is with me, and inside of his love, I'm ready to stop bemoaning my fate and accept my life with gratitude. Lyme's is my low, my love is my high. Just as the ocean ebbs and flows, just as my heart beats loud, then soft.

In the morning the gang all returns to open stockings and exchange gifts. Cate and Ethan prepare Christmas brunch together. They chop and grate to create a build-your-own breakfast burrito buffet with eggs, tofu, and all the fixings. Celeste brings over a dish of sweet potato fries smothered with guacamole, and Grayson pours mimosas.

After breakfast is cleared away, everyone heads down for a walk along the ocean. Cate pushes the stroller along, bringing up the rear. Oliver points with delight at Fredrick and the seagulls and the boats out on the horizon. Soon Cate's legs are too tired to continue.

"I just remembered, I need to get that turkey in the oven if we want to eat early," Cate announces. "You guys carry on and I'll see you back at the house later."

"I'll take Fredrick," Taylor offers as he backtracks from his position at the front of the posse.

Cate suspects no one is fooled by her attempts at bravado, but they go along with her anyway. Celeste takes over the stroller and Ethan walks back with Cate, taking her by the crook. She has to stop every few minutes to catch her breath.

Ethan gathers some newspaper and starts a fire in the fireplace, and the house is soon cozy and warm. Cate gets the turkey washed and dressed and into the oven, then sneaks off for a nap.

When dinner is ready everyone gathers around the table. Roger leads them in prayer.

"Thank you, Lord, for this food and for this family. Amen."

Grayson and Celeste pack up Oliver and his litany of baby things as soon as the meal is over. They want to get him home for his early bedtime. Donna and Taylor stay for a few hours, and the kids play a few rounds of Catan, the new board game Taylor received as a Christmas gift. It is close to ten when Taylor drives Donna back to Victoria.

Roger and Aubrey depart a few days later, and then Chloe returns to Toronto and it is just Cate and Ethan again.

Ethan's permanent work visa is issued at the end of January. He flies back to Riyadh, leaving Cate at Melissa's until her visa is approved. Cate has no idea how long it will take for her visa to be processed, but she hopes she and Ethan will be reunited soon.

Most days Cate finds somewhat bearable. She reminds herself of Dr. Weber's words of wisdom—we heal from the inside out—and tries to focus on finding her inner strength. It's hard for Cate to stay positive when she doesn't have her health and vitality, but she does her best. Donna's now-infamous saying, "Sometimes our best is the shits," comes into her head frequently.

When Valentine's Day comes around, Cate finds her resolve to be positive disappears, to be replaced with more dreary sullenness. She cuts out paper hearts from old magazines and pastes them onto a collage. She writes Ethan's name in different coloured marker and different sizes all over the page. She feels the heaviness with the deepest intensity yet. "Stupid Valentine's Day, stupid holiday," Cate mutters under her breath.

It's clear to Cate that Ms. Grouchy Pants needs to be given the boot. She encourages herself to follow her own advice. She sits down on the pillow in her sacred space and moves into a meditative state. She closes her eyes and takes several deep, cleansing breaths. She clutches her jade green crystal that is smooth and egg-shaped. When she opens her eyes, she feels grounded. She gets up off her pillow and gazes out the window. The picture is clear-sharp, bright green and blue, vivid and beautiful. She hears a plane fly overhead. Charlie, the neighbour's beagle, barks excitely. It is all so familiar and perfect. Cate knows that despite how much she wants to be with Ethan, as soon as she's gone she's going to miss this house of healing and time with her family.

Cate picks up Celeste and Oliver and they head into Victoria for the day. It is unusually warm and sunny, and they decide to go the petting zoo at Beacon Hill Park. Oliver chases the goats around their pen, pulling his hand away when the goats try to nibble on his fingers. Celeste shows him how to wash his hands thoroughly with soap and water, and Cate treats them all to an ice cream.

After lunch it's time for Oliver's afternoon nap, so Cate drives back up the Malahat and drops them off at their house. She kisses Oliver goodbye and embraces Celeste warmly.

"Thank you for a lovely day," Cate says. "It has lifted my spirits, spending time with you two."

"You need to get out more, Mom," Celeste berates her. "Staying cooped up inside and pining for Ethan isn't good for you."

"I know, I know," Cate concedes. "I never regret it when I can muster up the energy to get going. Do you want to come over for some Vietnamese takeout and a sleepover soon?"

"That sounds like a great idea," Celeste says, then waves goodbye as Cate puts the Mazda in gear and drives away.

Cate has some errands to run and drives into Duncan. A wave of melancholy comes over her as she thinks about her approaching departure and how that decision is going to have her missing out on watching Oliver as he grows up. When she stops in at London Drugs to pick up her prescriptions, Cate purchases a huge bag of potato chips.

When she gets back home, Cate plunks down in front of the television to watch old episodes of *CSI*. She munches on chips, along with some chocolate and cheese. She opens a bottle of wine and pours herself a drink, going all-out on a total binge, a classic case of what Cate calls, in her habit of mixing metaphors, "Her eyes screwing her stomach in the ears."

When she is done stuffing herself, Cate feels incredibly fat. She grabs her rolls hanging over her pants. Not a muffin top, she thinks to herself, but a whole cake. The ten pounds she's gained since becoming ill feel more like twenty. Cate wonders if she'll ever fit back into her clothes. She longs for what was, then insults herself for all the shit decisions she's made. She pines for the days when she felt sort of good about her body and she didn't have Lyme's.

Chloe flies out from Toronto to visit Cate for a week in March. They hang out together, doing run-of-the-mill, everyday stuff like walking Fredrick, reading novels, and watching episodes of *Mad Men*. They have many heart-to-heart conversations. They FaceTime with Ethan every day and wax philosophical about the problems in the world with corruption and greed and the destruction of the Earth.

"The world is such a mess, I think we should just move to Panama where life is simple," Ethan says, for the umpteenth time.

"You're incorrigible, Ethan," Cate says. "We haven't even been there, and I'm certain Panama doesn't hold the answers to all the world's problems."

"Okay, okay, then maybe we should buy our own island," Ethan continues. "Where a benevolent and wise king with integrity and character rules with the best interests of the people always at the forefront of every decision."

"Hmm, and would that wise king be named Ethan by any chance?" asks Chloe.

Ethan just laughs and continues to share his dreams of tranquility and abundance. Their laughter is good medicine for all three of them.

The week seems to disappear in no time. Cate drives Chloe to the airport and stays until it's time for her to go. Just before going through security, Chloe gives Cate a big hug. She has tears in her eyes.

"I don't want to go," Chloe says, wiping at a tear. "This past week has felt so safe and supportive."

"I'm so glad," Cate says. "Hold on to that. When times are tough, remember, you are always in my heart."

Cate returns to her quiet existence. She fills her days with errands, like getting her passport photos done and Fredrick's vaccinations up to date. Most of the time she is counting the minutes between FaceTime chats with Ethan or visits with her family. She reads several books and writes in her journal every day.

> *I wake up to the rat-a-tat-tat of a woodpecker trying unsuccessfully to discover a tasty breakfast inside a telephone pole. Can't blame him for mistaking it for a living tree.*
>
> *Still pining for Ethan. Ms. Moping Moper.*
>
> *I remember when I first moved to the island, when it was just me and Fredrick, before I ever met Ethan, and how deliriously happy I was. I have what Oprah calls an "Aha!" moment. I realize that with or without Ethan, with or without my health, with or without anything but the gift of my breath and my footsteps walking me through the incredible gift of my life, I can access joy. I feel God's love filling my cup and it is overflowing, spilling all over the floor.*

Chapter 10

*I*T IS THE END OF April, and Cate is packing up, preparing to move out of Melissa's house in a few days. Her visa clearance still hasn't been issued, but Melissa and her partner want to move in for the summer. Cate has decided she will stay in a hotel until her paperwork is ready. She is cleaning out the fridge when her phone rings.

"Have you been watching the news?" Celeste says, the words tumbling out in a heated flurry.

"Uh, no, I haven't I'm—" Cate begins. Celeste interrupts her.

"Mom, there has been an epic-sized earthquake in Nepal. In the area where Dana is trekking," Celeste says.

"What?" Cate says, unable to put the two events together. Then, "Oh my God, an earthquake? In Nepal?" Cate's heart almost stops. She tells herself to calm down. She listens to her intuition, which tells her Dana must be okay, that she would know if the unthinkable happened. But the red devil on her right shoulder questions and plants the seeds of fear.

"Mom, are you there?" Celeste interrupts, her voice almost a shriek.

"Yes, I'm here, I'm, I'm…" Cate's tongue is thick. She can't articulate.

"All I can do is imagine my sister trapped and hurt," Celeste says, her voice rising an octave. "We have to do something, Mom."

"What can we do?" Cate asks. She gives her head a shake and blinks back tears.

"You can start by contacting the Canadian Emergency Response. I'll call the Foreign Affairs hotline and register Dana as missing," says Celeste.

Cate agrees and promises Celeste she will phone her back as soon as she gets any information. She googles the number for Canadian Emergency Response. When she calls, the line is busy, and then when it finally rings she is put on hold. While she is waiting, Cate turns on the TV where news of the earthquake is being broadcast on every channel. The images are devastating.

The operator finally comes on the line. She takes Cate's contact information and Dana's name and age. She asks for Dana's passport number, but Cate doesn't have a clue. Cate hangs up, her hand trembling. She walks into her room in a daze and falls on her knees.

"Please, please, let her be alright," Cate begs. She attempts to pull herself together, but the tears won't let up. She tries to hush her fearful thoughts. Cate closes her eyes and visualizes Dana's beautiful smiling face. She's seen so little of her daughter the last few years, yet in her mind she can see her clearly.

The time between Cate first hearing of the earthquake and receiving a text from one of Dana's friends saying she is okay is one of the longest, most terrifying times of her life.

Just when she's feeling relief flood over her, Cate reads reports on the news and on social media of aftershocks and landslides in Lang Tang National Park, where Dana was last seen, where the stories spill out about no survivors. Cate's heart beats too fast. She feels on the edge of hysteria, like she is on an extreme eight-cups-of-coffee-later caffeine high.

Cate almost wears out a path in the wood flooring, pacing back and forth. She decides she needs to be with Celeste. She packs a bag and asks Hank and Dorothy if she can drop off Fredrick for a night, sharing with them the drama that she is engulfed in.

"Of course, bring him on over," Hank says without hesitation.

When Cate drops Fredrick off, Dorothy asks if she'd like to come in for a visit and a drink but Cate declines. She has an urgent need to be with Celeste.

Cate drives over to Celeste and Grayson's house. She knocks on the door, but when no one answers she lets herself in. As soon as she walks in it is like being hit by an invisible force field.

Celeste is at the kitchen table on her iPad and phone simultaneously, and her home looks and sounds like a call centre and a disaster zone all in one. When Celeste gets off the phone, she comes over and gives Cate a quick hug hello and then begins immediately with the drill, telling Cate everything she needs her to do. Cate tries to comply, but she sucks at technology, so she offers to look after Oliver instead, giving Celeste the freedom to focus completely on her rescue mission plans.

Three intense days go by with no news. Cate's mother's heart is certain that Dana is alive, but her skeptic's brain continues to play with the fear. Celeste's intensity adds to the drama, but Cate's overseas chats with Taylor, in Paris on exchange for a semester, and her talks with Ethan help her to stay calm.

Her phone rings when she is back at home, washing dishes. She drops a plate. She doesn't stop to dry her hands but answers. The connection is horrible, the line full of static.

"Maman? Is that you?" Dana asks.

"Yes, my love, it's me." Cate drops into a chair, relief flooding over her whole body. "Are you okay?"

"I'm safe, Maman," Dana tells her. "I don't have much time; there is a big group all waiting to use this one cellphone that works. I just needed to let you know I'm alive, I've survived," says Dana.

The call lasts barely a minute, but it is one of the best minutes ever.

Cate moves out of Melissa's house and into a suite in the Oswego Hotel in Victoria. Celeste arranges interviews with several news agencies. She is determined to have Dana rescued. Photos of Dana appear on local Canadian television stations. A firefighter from Burnaby, BC, sees Dana's face and recognizes her as a friend of his daughter. He organizes a group of twenty volunteers and gets permission from the Canadian government to fly into Kathmandu. He works with the captain of the Nepalese army, and they coordinate a rescue by helicopter that takes Dana and her travelling companions to safety. The Canadian government organizes a flight on a C-17 back to Canada.

Cate's visa still hasn't been issued, and she is grateful for this strange synchronicity of events that has her still in Canada instead of in Riyadh, able to be reunited with her daughter.

On the day of Dana's arrival at the Victoria airport, Celeste leaves Oliver with Grayson and drives in from Cobble Hill to pick up Cate at the hotel to drive to the airport together.

Cate and Celeste make their way to the arrivals area and wait at the door. Celeste is the first to spot Dana in the crowd. She looks exhausted yet somehow radiant, a scarf draped over her thick hair frames her face.

The three women hold on to one another in a silent embrace. Cate is flooded with myriad emotions; relief, gratitude, tenderness, love, disbelief, and joy. Tears stream down her cheeks. After what seems a long time, they move apart. They all start talking at once, over top of one another. So many questions.

"It doesn't feel real, already," Dana shares. "One minute I was drinking tea and reading my book, the next my friend Manish was pulling me to safety as the hostel we were staying in crumbled to the ground."

Dana talks all the way to the car. She is grateful to find the picnic basket Celeste packed for her, full of her favourites: vegan brownies, energy balls, fresh fruit, and even a traveller's mug of green tea. On the drive back to the Oswego Hotel, Dana falls asleep.

The next two weeks Dana stays with Cate and Fredrick at the hotel. Dana deals with culture shock, survivor guilt, and post-traumatic stress. Cate does her best to hold and behold her daughter, to love and support her.

Then Cate receives the email that she has been waiting months for. Her visa authorization has been approved, and she expects the final documentation she needs for entry into Saudi Arabia to be issued imminently.

Cate decides to fly to Toronto and wait for her documentation there so she can say goodbye to Chloe. She is grateful she was gifted the time with Dana, but she is ready.

On Cate's last night, Celeste invites Cate, Dana, and Donna to drive up to her house up-island, having agreed that Dana can move into the spare room until she figures out what to do next. They order in Indian food and play with Oliver. They say their goodbyes.

Cate knows in her heart they are all going to be okay. When it is Oliver's bedtime, Cate tucks him in. As he is falling asleep she says goodbye to him, but there is no way to explain to a one-and-a-half-year-old where she is going. Cate tells him how much she loves him. She tells him Grandma will always come back.

When it's time for Cate and Donna to drive back to the city, there are more tears as they hug Dana and Celeste goodbye.

"I hope you find healing, here with your sister," Cate says to Dana. She takes her finger and points it to Dana's chest, a ritual Cate and Dana have practiced since watching the movie *E.T.* "I'll be right here."

Her last night in the hotel, Cate sleeps fitfully. Details of her upcoming pilgrimage play over and over in her head. Her alarm is set for four a.m., but she gets up at three, unable to sleep anymore.

Donna picks her up to drive her to the airport. It is pitch-black, only a sliver moon in the sky. Cate shivers and can see her breath in puffs as she speaks.

"Thank you so much, Mom, for insisting on taking me," Cate says.

"You know you'd do the same for me," Donna says, holding onto Fredrick's leash while Cate hoists her two huge suitcases, a carry-on, a computer bag masquerading as a purse, and Fredrick's canvas crate into the trunk.

"Yes, I suppose you're right," says Cate, "but I still appreciate you."

On the drive to the airport, Cate checks her phone. She has a new email from Ethan in her inbox. Ethan, the man who once upon a time before Cate didn't like dogs, has written an email to Fredrick. Cate's heart melts as she reads it out loud, and her mom swoons along too.

Dear Fredrick,

I imagine you are feeling a little anxious with all the changes you can't possibly understand. This will be the longest time you've had to endure being in your travel bag, but don't worry, because you've flown from Victoria to Toronto before and you rocked that. I will be at the airport to greet you and Mom, and I will be sure to bring some treats with me. After I give you a good petting and a scratch under your chin, you can have a comfort break, and then it's only a short drive until you arrive at your new home. You won't find the lush forests and oceanside you're used to on Vancouver Island, but I will take you to all the good grassy areas to explore, including the dog park where maybe you will make a new friend.

In your new apartment there is a cozy comforter for you to curl up on at the foot of our bed, and I bet you'll love scratching and dragging your nose through our carpets,

*although they are a little threadbare. I'm sure you'll adjust
to your new home quickly, and after a while you will forget all
about the discomforts of your travels. You've got this, Fredrick!*

Love, Dad

Cate's flight to Toronto goes smoothly. Fredrick settles
down in his bag by her feet and doesn't bark at all. When
she unzips the compartment to let Fredrick stick his head
out for some air at the terminal in Toronto, a little boy
who was on the plane turns to his mother.

"Mommy! There was a dog on our plane the whole
time!" he says.

"Would you like to give him a pat?" Cate asks with
a smile.

The boy is clearly delighted. He asks his mom if it is
okay, and when she says yes, he crouches down and pats
Fredrick on his head.

Cate is staying at the Hyatt, which has become sort of a
home away from home for her in Toronto, while she waits
for all the paperwork to be completed. As it is, there is
another delay.

After four nights in the hotel, Julianna, who has
become a dear friend since the adoption, insists that Cate
and Fredrick come and stay in her guest suite rather than
extend at the hotel. Cate is grateful for the invitation and
happily accepts.

Cate, Chloe, and Julianna hang out as much as possible,
between Chloe and Julianna's work schedules. They take city
hikes around the cemetery and walk up and down the steep
stairwell at Casa Loma.

It is Thursday, May 22, when Cate's envelope with her final paperwork arrives from DHL, just in time for the flight she already booked that departs that evening. Cate is thrilled and grateful. She sends Ethan a text with her flight information, and they have a short conversation over FaceTime. She sends texts to Julianna and Chloe.

"Wonderful news," texts back Julianna. "Shall we invite Chloe over for a casual farewell lunch at my place?"

"That sounds perfect," Cate texts back. "I'll reach out to Chloe and pick up a few things from Whole Foods."

Cate walks the few blocks to the store and chooses some fresh ingredients to make a salad with some baked salmon and stops at the liquor store for a bottle of champagne. When Julianna gets home, Cate already has the table set and everything ready.

Julianna is fetching three champagne flutes from her sideboard when the concierge rings that Chloe has arrived.

"I hope you're prepared for the intense heat of the desert," Julianna says, taking a sip of her champagne.

"How does one prepare for something like that?" Cate laughs.

"You've got to promise to send me a photo of you in an abaya," says Chloe, laughing along with her. "But don't worry, I'm sure you'll be fine once you get used to it."

Chloe shares stories from her childhood, when she lived in Riyadh years before, and Julianna contributes her fair share from when she was in Saudi Arabia visiting her niece and her family. The conversation shifts to the challenges of learning about a different culture.

"Take it from me," says Julianna. "I know from my experience as a visible minority growing up in small-town Nova Scotia, some people are going to judge you by the colour of your skin and your blonde hair and make assumptions that most likely aren't true."

"I never thought about that," says Cate. "But you're right. I'm sure I'll find that difficult, but I'm going to take it as a learning opportunity, to develop my empathy."

"It will likely have you rethinking your ideas on feminism too," adds Chloe. "It's like stepping back in time, compared to how far things have come toward equality of the sexes here."

Cate takes comfort in their storytelling and appreciates the extra time in Toronto to connect with both of them on a deeper level.

On the flight to Frankfurt, Cate is wedged in the middle seat between two large-ish men with Fredrick at her feet. She has her diabetic supplies stacked on her lap, feeling more like a sardine than a human being. When the food service commences, Cate finds out they didn't order her a special gluten-free meal as requested. She skips dinner, opting for an energy bar from her stash of snacks. She dials back her insulin dose, but not enough. She starts to drift off. She mistakes her loopy feelings for anxiety, fatigue, or the air pressure in the plane, but then she is going low and she knows it, but she's too low to stop it. She goes unconscious.

The man on Cate's right saves the day when he recognizes something is wrong. He calls a flight attendant, and she finds a nurse on board who puts cubes of sugar in Cate's mouth. Within minutes Cate comes out of it, confused and disoriented but conscious, to everyone's relief. Cate finds out later that the man's deceased wife had diabetes and he suspected Cate might be in a hypoglycemic state.

After her ordeal, Cate receives royal treatment from the flight attendants. They bring her food from business class and check in on her every hour. Then, before Cate knows it, they're landing in the Frankfurt airport without any further drama.

Cate has only been in this airport once before, years ago. True to form, she gets lost trying to find her gate. She's so nervous that someone will challenge her about Fredrick that she can't focus or relax. Since she can't take Fredrick into a restaurant, she buys a bag of potato chips and a bottled water at a kiosk, finally finds her gate, and settles down in a chair with Fredrick at her feet. He is relieved to be free from his crate.

A trio of children spot Fredrick and come over to pet and adore him.

"Are you going to Saudi Arabia?" one of them asks.

"Yes, in fact, I am," Cate says.

"We are too!" the little girl exclaims. "Our grandpa lives there. Did you know he has three wives?"

It goes on like this. Fredrick seems tired out from their attention, and Cate is too. She packs up her things and takes Fredrick into the handicapped washroom. She encourages him to use the doggy training pad, but he's been so well-trained to do his business outside, he stubbornly refuses.

Cate chooses a seat in a quieter area and lifts Fredrick onto her lap for cuddles. He climbs up to rest his little muzzle on her shoulder and snuggles up, so out of character. It's clear to Cate that he is stressed out too.

On the flight from Frankfurt to Riyadh, Cate is on the aisle. It is less cramped. Her seat-mate is a young Saudi man. They mostly ignore one another, watching movies on their miniature screens, with the odd polite exchange. During the meal service Cate is surprised when he orders a beer. She had thought that it was against the Islamic religion to consume alcohol, but then she thinks about all the Catholics she knows who use birth control and recognizes it is likely the first of a huge list of stereotypes she has about the Middle East culture and the Islamic religion. She finds herself looking forward to dismantling everything she thinks she knows.

Six and a half hours later, Cate and Fredrick arrive in the Kingdom of Saudi Arabia. Like a deer in the headlights, Cate disembarks from the plane. She walks along the gleaming, marble-tiled corridor, past a massive marble fountain, and down the escalator to a long cue of people waiting to clear customs. She is modestly dressed, all in black. She doesn't yet own an abaya and feels nervous when the Saudi officer dressed in a traditional white thobe and ghutra directs her to the lineup for persons newly entering the country. There is a women only line, which is short and moves quickly.

Cate presses her diabetic-calloused fingers on the fingerprint scan several times before she is successful. She starts to ramble about Fredrick's passport. Then she looks up, and amongst a sea of faces she sees Ethan just outside the window in the baggage area. He's smiling and looks more handsome than ought to be legal. Cate forgets all her worries and smiles back, ear to ear. The man behind the counter stamps her passport and Fredrick's paperwork.

"Welcome to Saudi Arabia," he says.

Cate walks through the doors, into Ethan's arms. He holds her and kisses her on the cheek, ever so briefly, in respect to Saudi customs. Cate feels his angel wing slide swiftly back into place and imagines golden threads attaching it back to her shoulder, where it belongs. Her heaviness evaporates.

Ethan leads her out of the air-conditioned airport terminal. Cate is enveloped by a sheet of heat like she's never experienced before.

As it turns out, Fredrick managed to hold his bladder for the entire twenty-plus hours of their journey. He earns a new nickname, Mister Iron Bladder. He takes a comfort break on the rocks beside where Ethan has parked his vehicle. Cate lifts him up and climbs into the black Honda Pilot with Fredrick on her lap. In no time they are at the security gate of the compound where they will be living.

The compound is surrounded by high cement walls topped with curling, electric barbed wire. Security officers with guns and walkie-talkies ask for their identification. Once they are through the checks, it is a short five-minute drive to their apartment.

Cate lets Fredrick out to sniff the desert air. She stops Ethan, who is unloading her luggage from the trunk, and places his arm around her waist. She kisses him, long and deep, then lets out a huge breath of relief.

Chapter 11

*E*THAN TAKES CATE'S LUGGAGE INTO the building and up the stairs to their apartment, then returns to show Fredrick his new neighbourhood. Fredrick sniffs the foreign scents with curiosity and wags his tail, nose close to the ground, then pulls on his leash, ready to go.

At the apartment, Fredrick seems unsure about the slippery tile steps and barks in protest, but Cate encourages him, producing a treat from her purse. Fredrick heads to the living room to investigate while Cate looks around the cramped space.

"Do you want something to eat? Or maybe a shower?" Ethan asks.

"What I need is you," Cate replies, "but I think after my long trip I need to take a shower first."

"I was hoping you would say that," says Ethan. He moves in to kiss her. "I need you too."

Ethan shows Cate to one of the two bathrooms where he has laid out a fresh towel and a face cloth. The shower is anything but deluxe, yet for Cate it feels like the best ever.

After she dries off, Cate wraps the towel around her and patters barefoot over the grey tiles to the bedroom where Ethan waits. The towel doesn't stay on very long. It has been four months since they've been together.

Cate delights in rediscovering the freckles on Ethan's shoulders and the scent of his Old Spice body wash, among other things. She tries to take it slow, but she can't resist; she wants all of him, next to all of her.

After, Cate tries to engage in conversation, as is their custom, but exhaustion overcomes her.

"I'm sorry, my love," Cate says as she nods off mid-sentence, "but I can't keep my eyes open."

"It's all good," Ethan assures her. "Sleep well." He pulls the sheet up over her shoulders and they fall, intertwined, into deep, blissful sleep.

When Cate wakes up she's disoriented.

"Where am I?" she asks out loud, rubbing her eyes. But then she feels Ethan's body beside her and remembers. She smiles.

"Good morning, Mister," Cate says, turning over to face him.

"Welcome to your new life in Saudi Arabia," Ethan says.

Fredrick barks, as if he wants to be a part of the conversation. Cate laughs and picks him up to join in on the cuddle-fest, giving his tummy a good rub while she and Ethan talk about the day ahead of them. Cate is grateful it's Saturday.

Fredrick barks again, impatient to get outside. Cate slips on some clean shorts and a blouse from her luggage, slides into her flip-flops, and grabs his leash, still coiled up at the front door.

"I'll put on some coffee while you take Fredrick," Ethan says, throwing on his robe.

Cate takes Fredrick down to find the little piece of grass that Ethan had shown him when they arrived in the dark of night. Even at this early hour the air is hot and stifling. Cate notices that all the buildings look exactly the same: a light beige, as if they've been carved from the desert sand. The grounds appear to be meticulous. Around the corner she spies a swimming pool set in amongst palm trees and thick, green shrubs. Cate hears the cheerful chirping of birds. The sky is hazy with dust.

Fredrick isn't inclined to explore in the heat. He pants and his tongue almost touches the ground, so they return to the comfort of the air-conditioned apartment.

"Back already?" Ethan says as they walk through the door.

"It's frikkin' oppressive out there," Cate moans. "It's going to take some time for both of us to adjust."

Ethan laughs and pours Cate a cup of coffee while she rummages around for Fredrick's kibbles and pours a scoop into his dish, along with some fresh water.

Cate is thrilled; it is their first couch time in ages. She shares in detail all of her travel ordeals. Ethan is concerned to hear that her blood sugars dropped so low.

"Why didn't you text me in Frankfurt and let me know how you were doing?" Ethan says.

"I'm sorry," says Cate, "but I was so anxious, I couldn't figure out how to get onto the airport Wi-Fi."

"Well, I suppose the important thing is that you're okay now," says Ethan.

"I think it's time for breakfast," Cate says, distracted by her grumbly stomach.

"How do you feel about me prepping us up some wrapless wraps?" asks Ethan.

"That sounds divine, thank you," Cate says.

Cate explores the apartment in the light of day. The decor is dated and lacks visual appeal, with oversize furniture out of place in the tiny space. The furniture and heavy drapes are a deep, dark purple. The tables are a light, orangey-toned particle wood, solid and heavy. The kitchen is more like a large closet. There is no dishwasher, and the washer in the kitchen is some kind of crazy-fangled, washer-dryer combo that Cate knows will become her nemesis quickly. She doesn't complain though. The accommodations are free, and more importantly, she's reunited with her beloved.

After breakfast Cate starts to unpack. When Ethan returns from his shower, she abandons her task.

They spend most of the day finding their way back into their flow. Later in the day, Ethan suggests they walk up to the compound market with Fredrick to pick up a few fresh groceries.

"Do I need to wear my abaya?" Cate asks.

"Absolutely not," says Ethan. "What you have on is perfect. The compound is our own little oasis where we can live just as we would back home. I can't believe I didn't tell you that."

"You very well may have," says Cate, "but the learning curve has been steep. It's hard to keep all the rules and regulations straight, especially with jet lag brain."

The limited selection of produce and few aisles of dry goods at the tiny grocer has Cate homesick for the abundance of her neighbourhood Thrifty's store back home.

When they get back from their walk, jet lag hits Cate in a wave. She crawls into bed for a short nap but ends up conked out for two hours.

Ethan has already started seasoning some chicken breasts for the barbeque when Cate emerges all groggy-eyed and disoriented.

"Hello there, sleepyhead," Ethan says with a smile. "Do you feel better after your rest?"

"Um, I suppose you can say that," Cate concedes, "if by better you mean not as though someone has drugged me."

"Don't worry, my love," Ethan says, "it is all normal. Your body will adjust soon enough."

Ethan has to work on Sunday, the work week in Saudi Arabia being from Sunday to Thursday.

Cate has never seen him in his pilot suit before, and when he walks out of their bedroom adjusting his Velcro name tag, all Cate can think is, *Top Gun eat your heart out.* There's no time for love-making, though. Cate pushes aside her desire, content with a kiss goodbye at the door.

After Ethan leaves, the stillness descends upon Cate. She decides to take Fredrick with her to go explore the compound a little more, up to the collection of shops and the main outdoor pool. She strolls past the International School and the recreational centre. It is very quiet, with few people about.

It isn't long before Cate decides it is too hot to explore any further and she takes Fredrick home.

Cate grapples with the remote controls for the television. She scrolls through the channels, but there is nothing that interests her. Most of the shows are in Arabic or reruns from the 1990s.

Cate rolls out her mat on the dusty grey living room carpet and attempts to practice some yoga postures, but she can't get into her flow. She reads for a bit, but finds her eyes heavy. She flakes out on the couch for several hours. When she wakes up she gets out her journal.

> *I remember hearing what I thought to be a fable about it being so hot somewhere you could fry an egg on the sidewalk. Clearly it wasn't a fable. It was referencing Saudi Arabia. Fredrick lifts his little paws as if the sidewalks are a skillet. Ethan tried to prepare me, but how do you convey to someone from Canada, where it rarely gets above thirty, the intensity of this heat? When I go outside I feel like I'm entering an oven. I think about the fairy tale of Hansel and Gretel.*
>
> *I'm a bit delirious. A little overwhelmed. What have I gotten myself into?*

Ethan returns from work while she is writing. She sets down her pen and closes her book, then jumps up from the couch. Fredrick is excited too. It's a race to the door to greet him. Fredrick wins, but Cate receives a kiss before Ethan stoops down to pet him.

One of the first tasks that needs Cate's attention is her application for an Iqama, the national identification card. Ethan is on the late shift so he makes time before work to drive her to the administration building in the parking lot through the first set of security gates on the compound.

Cate puts on her abaya, a second-hand gift from the wife of one of Ethan's colleagues. The abaya is a black, floor-length garment that is loose-fitting with sleeves that fall below the wrist. It is required by law to be worn by all women in the kingdom. For Cate, it feels like a tent with a hole for her head. She feels like an imposter, but she resigns herself to her fate, for it is the custom and she has heard that the religious police have no tolerance for deviations from the law.

Everything proceeds without incident, and within half an hour, Cate's Iqama application is complete.

"We have time to meet Quinn at the coffee shop," says Ethan as they hop back into the truck. "Would you like that?"

"Sure, why not? I like Quinn," Cate says.

Cate met Quinn in Victoria when Ethan was home for Christmas. He is a little younger than Ethan, quick to smile and make a joke, always a mischievous look in his eye.

Quinn is already seated with some other Canadians at a table in Costa Coffee when they arrive. They make introductions and place their usual order: a mocha for Ethan and a soy latte for Cate.

The atmosphere is genial, with stories of life on the compound, the crazy drivers in the city, where they're from in Canada, and what brought them to Riyadh.

"My first day at work was a real eye-opener," says Quinn. "After teaching military cadets at the base in Moose Jaw, it was quite an adjustment."

"The ten-hour days with two debriefings and two flights are long enough," says Ethan. "But when you add in ground school and the daily met-brief, it can be darn right gruelling."

"You've been here before, so you have one up on us," says Quinn. "You have to promise to share your tricks."

"I don't know what tricks I have, but I'm happy to share my experience," Ethan says, getting up from his chair. "For now, I best get going if I'm going to get into work on time."

Ethan and Cate say their goodbyes and Ethan drives them back to the apartment. He grabs his packed lunch and heads off, leaving Cate to figure out what to do with the rest of her day.

Cate feels uninspired by her options. She sifts through emails, scrolls through Facebook, reads her book, and writes in her journal. She takes a long nap with Fredrick curled up by her feet.

The next day Cate has to complete another step in the application process for her Iqama. Ethan books a car and driver to take her to a hospital in the city to undergo a medical exam.

This is Cate's first time outside the compound since she arrived in the dark of night. In the light of day, she sees the desert stretching out in all directions, piled high with garbage, plastic grocery bags, and plastic water bottles caught in the wire fences that line the road. She notices a ton of construction projects, some on the go, some abandoned. There is Arabic graffiti on the sand-coloured walls. Camels of different sizes and shades of brown and black amble along the side of the road. Tent-type lodgings, remnants of a Bedouin society, dot the landscape. Pop-up road entertainment offers everything from horse rides to ATVs to blow-up slides. People hawk their wares from the back of their vans or trucks: Spiderman figurines, balloons, watermelon, Turkish rugs—a strange assortment of offerings in Cate's opinion. Dusty, hazy skies encompass it all.

Upon arrival at the medical facility, Cate enters a packed waiting room that is mostly all young men. She feels nervous and very aware of her gender. After a few minutes Cate hears, "Madame Heen-der-sin?"

"Yes, that's me," she says, as the Filipino nurse with her chart smiles, takes her samples, discreetly packaged in brown paper bags, and shows her down a corridor.

The nurse directs her to the female "water closet" and asks Cate to provide an additional urine sample. The water closet (or WC) as the Saudis refer to the washroom, consists of a squat-style hole in the floor, a shower head, and no toilet paper. Cate is perplexed, but does as she is told, relieved Ethan suggested she bring tissue and hand sanitizer.

Cate leaves the plastic cup with her specimen on the counter, then is shown to a seat where the nurse draws several vials of blood. Cate is asked to sit in another waiting area until a female nurse, face covered, shows her to a cubicle where she is told to change out of her abaya, blouse, and bra for a chest X-ray.

A half hour later everything is done. Cate sends a text to the driver and he picks her up at the entrance before driving her back to the compound.

Cate hasn't had time to adjust to her new life in the Middle East when the time comes to sort out Ramadan travel plans. Before Ethan goes to work, he suggests they take Fredrick for a walk up to the compound travel agency to look at flight itineraries, but when they see a huge lineup, they decide to wait for another day.

The next item on Cate's to-do list is to find someone to look after Fredrick while they are away. It is a five-week holiday, so Cate anticipates she will have to split Fredrick's care amongst several families. She scans through the compound community Facebook page, but doesn't have any luck.

"I've scoped out a possibility for Fredrick," Ethan says over dinner. "I read on the work WhatsApp that there is lady named Lena who has a dog sitting business; I'll get her number."

A colleague at work provides Ethan with Lena's phone number and when Cate calls her, Lena invites them over to her villa to introduce her to Fredrick and discuss arrangements the next day.

As soon as Lena opens the door, Fredrick jumps up on her in excitement. She is dressed in a long floral sundress, and her grey hair is clipped into a loose bun at the nape of her neck.

"Fredrick, get down," Cate admonishes him.

Lena laughs. "Hello to you too," she says with a thick British accent. Her smile is broad and authentic. She gives Fredrick a scratch on the head. "Don't you worry, Mum," she says to Cate, "I'm practically a professional dog whisperer."

Lena proceeds to demonstrate her competence by calling Fredrick into the kitchen and producing a dog treat that requires a shake of his paw to receive. Cate knows with absolute certainty that Lena is going to be the perfect holiday mom and all they have to do is work out the details.

On Saturday morning Don and Peyton, a couple from Australia that Ethan already knows quite well, invite them over for coffee. Don greets Cate warmly at the door. His large rugby-player shoulders fill the door frame and his smile is almost as huge. He gives Cate a big bear hug, like they are already good friends.

"So, this is the beauty that has our Ethan so smitten," Don says. "It's a pleasure to finally meet you, come on in."

Cate walks into their renovated villa. It is obvious that they have serious style. Don leads them to the kitchen where Peyton is putting some muffins onto a plate. She looks up with a smile and comes over to welcome them.

"Nice to meet you, Cate," Peyton says as she places her hand on Cate's shoulder. "Ethan has told us so much about you."

Cate is struck by Peyton's natural beauty and great sense of style. She has her dark hair pulled back loosely with a clip, a few strands delicately framing her heart-shaped face. She's wearing minimal makeup, a white, loose-fitting blouse, and torn denim jeans.

"Can I interest you two in a cappuccino?" Don asks. "We have filtered water, and Peyton roasts our coffee beans, imported from Australia."

"How can I resist?" Cate says. "That sounds divine."

Don whips up cappuccinos for all four of them and they talk about important things like life balance, mindfulness, and making conscious choices. Don tells some funny stories about life in Riyadh. Cate feels relaxed in their company and grateful for the opportunity to meet such down-to-earth people. She hopes they will become good friends.

On Sunday, after Ethan goes to work, Cate feels restless again. She decides it is high time to check out the neighbourhood pool. As she puts on her bathing suit she feels a bit self-conscious that it doesn't quite hold everything in the way it used to, but then she laughs at herself because who is there to impress anyway? She grabs the book a stranger on the plane gave her, a bottle of water, and a towel, and slips into her flip-flops for the two-minute walk.

There is no one else at the pool so Cate chooses the least dusty looking lounger to lay her towel out on. She stretches out and closes her eyes under her shades to bask in the hot sun. It isn't long before the metal clasp on her bathing suit top burns into her chest. She gets up to take a dip, the pavement like a floor of fire as she dashes the short distance to the pool. Even the water in the pool isn't cool, but at least it is somewhat tepid.

Cate feels refreshed when she gets out and lays back on the recliner. She opens her book and reads some more. Her eyes drift closed. She wakes up startled and checks her phone. She was only asleep short while.

Cate lives for weekends. Every Friday and Saturday morning she and Ethan make love first thing. Cate decides it is the most glorious way to begin the day.

Ethan usually goes to the gym after breakfast, but today they are going back to the travel agency to book their flights. Ethan suggests they try the location in the Shaheen building, just a block outside the compound where they went for her Iqama. Cate puts on her abaya and Ethan drives.

Just outside the security booth, Cate spots a sign that says, "Security level: substantial." She has a mini panic attack.

"That sign has said substantial every day since I've been here, it never changes," Ethan laughs.

"You could've at least warned me." Cate punches him playfully on the shoulder.

Later that afternoon, Ethan takes Cate for her first trip to Lulu's, one of the big supermarkets in the city. Cate isn't sure what to expect and is delighted when it turns out to be a treasure trove of choices. She can hardly believe her good fortune.

"Why on earth have you waited so long to bring me here?" Cate asks. "This place is frikkin' amazing!"

"You've only been here two weeks," Ethan says, "and besides, I've never been here, so I didn't know what we were missing out on."

"I've been so worried that the grocery stores would only stock unknown, foreign brands and exotic fruits and vegetables I don't recognize. I never imagined I would find all these great gluten-free products!"

"I'm thrilled you're so happy," Ethan says. "Perhaps we should make this a weekly tradition?"

Cate agrees. She dances across the tile floors as she finds things like Illy coffee, organic strawberries, extra-firm tofu, and brown rice spaghetti to toss into their cart. She is in her happy space when Ethan tells her they need to hurry up and make their way to the cashier if they're going to get through before the mandatory closing for prayer. The cart is already full to bursting, so they hustle to the till just in time.

After all the groceries are put away, Cate is starting to get dinner organized when she hears the now familiar FaceTime ring.

"Hi, Chloe," Cate says, placing some lettuce in the sink. "You're ringing a bit early."

"Yeah, I know, but I really need to talk," says Chloe. "Is it okay if we FaceTime now?"

Cate says of course and Ethan pulls up a chair to join them. Chloe shares her stress about the pressures at work. She's concerned that she isn't ready to go back to university, but she hates working in the service industry.

"Have you considered taking a few courses at Ryerson, or a smaller college?" Ethan asks.

"That's a good idea," says Cate. "It could be less stressful, while giving you the challenge you are craving."

"I can't afford to not work full time," Chloe says.

"We could help out with expenses," Ethan says.

"It's not just money, it's my social anxiety," Chloe says.

Cate and Ethan do their best to support and encourage her, but Chloe rejects all their suggestions. It is an uphill, familiar battle that doesn't end well.

Cate creates a routine of sorts. She walks Fredrick twice a day along the now regular routes through the neighbourhoods or around the perimeter. She reads, writes in her journal, and practices yoga as best she can with her inflamed joints that seem to have gotten worse with the heat. She goes to the pool and up to the market. She cleans the apartment, unable to keep up with the never-ending need to dust away the accumulation of sand. She prepares nutritional meals for her and Ethan that mostly follow the guidelines that Dr. Kensington gave her. She follows her treatment regimen. She and Ethan FaceTime regularly with family back home. Somehow each day feels full, if not necessarily all that satisfying.

Cate walks the dusty path up to the medical clinic for her first appointment with Dr. Patel. Cate thinks he is likely close to her age, another Brit. He appears to listen attentively while she shares her history and lists her diabetic and thyroid medications, careful not to mention anything about Lyme's or the homeopathic and naturopathic remedies she is taking. Dr. Patel enters the data into his computer. He prints off a prescription.

"You can have this filled in any pharmacy in the city and then submit your receipts to us for reimbursement," says Dr. Patel as he hands her a slip of paper. "All of your supplies will be completely covered by the company insurance."

"Thank you," says Cate, getting up to leave. She walks back home through the thick heat.

On the next trip into the city, Ethan takes Cate to the Saab bank, where he already has an account, to get her own Visa and debit cards. Cate is quiet.

"Are you okay?" Ethan asks. "I'm all ears if you need to get something off your chest."

"You're so perceptive," Cate says. "Thank you for asking. There is something I'd like to talk with you about, but I'm not quite ready."

"Okay, well, when and if you are, I'm here."

They drive the rest of the way in comfortable, easy silence. The traffic is as mad as ever, but today, Ethan is able to ignore it and stay calm.

At the bank the Saudi manager, dressed in the traditional thobe and ghutra, greets Ethan with a warm handshake. He says a curt hello to Cate, then proceeds to ignore her, his full attention on Ethan. He seems puzzled as to why on earth Ethan would want to provide Cate with her own account.

"You can just give her a card in your name, sir," he sort-of jokes, holding up his hand to cover his mouth, as if in doing so Cate can't hear the exchange. "And I'm certain you will want to stipulate her spending limit."

"Thank you, but my wish is for my wife to have her independence," Ethan says, then adds with diplomacy, "That's how things are done in Canada."

When they get back home Cate is ready to share her emotions.

"Ethan, can we have that talk now?" asks Cate as she flops down onto the couch with Fredrick on her lap.

"Of course," says Ethan. "It sounds serious, though. Should I pour us a drink?"

"Yes, please. A cool glass of iced tea would be divine."

Ethan pours them a drink and they sit together on the couch.

"I've been questioning our decision to move to Riyadh," Cate begins. "I don't think I realized how different it would be, and I'm not sure I can adjust to this life. The exchange we just had with the bank manager kind of says it all."

Ethan listens patiently while Cate vents all of her frustrations. When she is done, he honours her feelings but encourages her to give it a little more time. Cate agrees it is too soon to know, then goes on to express her doubts about the protocol she's on to treat Lyme's.

"I can't help but wonder if I will ever feel energetic again," Cate says with a heavy sigh.

"It sounds like you are feeling a little impatient with the process, my love," Ethan says, taking her hand in his. "I want to remind you that you make good decisions. You gave the move here so much careful consideration. And I remember you telling me that the antibiotic treatment didn't feel like a good choice for you."

"You're right," Cate says, feeling lighter already. "You are a wise man."

Ethan gathers Cate in his arms. She presses herself against him, aroused, and he distracts her from her troubles.

Cate and Ethan get invited to a squadron party, hosted by Don and Peyton. Cate is excited to see them again, to meet some more new people, and for the opportunity to wear something other than a bathing suit, yoga gear, or an abaya. She dresses up in a colourful silk wrap dress and puts on a little makeup, embracing her femininity.

Don welcomes them at the door and ushers them into the backyard. It is set up beautifully with white, twinkly lights draped along the pergola, a long, cloth-covered table, vases of flowers, and votives of electric candles. They have placed fans discreetly throughout the garden to keep it as comfortable as possible in the heat of the Saudi Arabian summer.

Cate and Ethan mingle with the diversity of guests. There are people gathered from all over the world, including South Africa, Germany, Australia, and the UK. Laughter rings through the air as everyone consumes a few sangrias and various other home-brewed alcoholic beverages. The buffet, featuring a variety of Indian curries, chutneys, poppadums, and naan bread, is delicious.

After several hours, Cate starts to yawn and Ethan suggests it is time to go. They thank Don and Peyton for their hospitality and walk back home in the starlit night. Cate takes Fredrick out for a quick break and when she returns the lights have been dimmed and candles lit.

"I hope you aren't too tired," Ethan says with a smile.

When Cate gets up the next day, the house is quiet. Ethan has already gone to work. She had made an impassioned pledge before she arrived that she would get up with him every day, but she hadn't realized how difficult it would be when Ethan is on the early shift and has to set his alarm for 4:00 a.m.

Cate takes care of Fredrick and makes herself a cup of tea, then gets out her journal.

> *Feeling present to my blessings, to the possibility of good friends, good food, and conversations. Feeling grateful for the little things, like the companionship of my sweet Fredrick, toes painted red, swimming pools, and sunshine every day.*
>
> *We had a fabulous FaceTime with Taylor the other day. He has a break before his exams and is going to take a few weeks to travel through Europe. We decided to go big and meet up with him in Greece over Ramadan. I'm so excited. Greece is one of the travel destinations on my vision board.*
>
> *Today is no different than any other, yet somehow my joy feels so abundant, my cup is full and running over. All my worries I shared with Ethan, about moving here and my treatment, feel almost ludicrous today. My emotions can be so up and down, yet the simple act of sharing them with someone I trust, with Ethan, makes all the difference. I am an emotional creature. I am a sensitive woman. It is okay. I can accept my contradictions. I accept who I am. All is well in my world.*

Ethan and Cate decide it is time to tackle the unpleasant task of appliance shopping in the city. Cate throws on her abaya, which still irritates her, and climbs into the truck.

The traffic is horrendous. Cate glances into the other vehicles crowded around them and sees drivers on their cellphones.

"Clowns to the left of us, jokers to the right, here we are, back in the madness again," she sings in her country twang, and Ethan laughs it all off along with her.

They arrive at the Extra store without incident, all in one piece. There isn't a great selection and they don't recognize many of the brand names, but they find a Samsung washer and dryer that will fit the space in the shower stall in the second bathroom if they stack them one on top of the other. Ethan knows of a carpenter on the compound he can hire to build an appropriate housing unit.

While they are there they decide to go all out and purchase a dishwasher, water cooler, and a microwave. At the cashier, Ethan fills out all the delivery information and pays the bill with his Visa.

"I'm so excited to have a proper washer and dryer that won't shrink my clothing, and a dishwasher instead of handwashing every dish!" Cate says on the drive home.

"Yes, I think we will find the money and effort well worth it," Ethan agrees.

When they get home neither one of them feels like cooking so they walk over to the compound restaurant for dinner. The menu isn't very exciting, but they serve a decent curry for a reasonable price.

As they are sitting down, Quinn walks in.

"Hey, fancy running into you two," Quinn says. "Mind if I join you?"

They get into a deep discussion on mental illness and stigma and stereotypes. Quinn shares his news that he and his girlfriend, Sophia, got engaged, and Cate and Ethan congratulate him. Cate wonders if Quinn will become a good friend too.

The appliance delivery man calls a few days later when Ethan is at work. He only speaks Arabic and Cate only speaks English. After much confusion, he hangs up on her. When Ethan gets home, Cate relates her frustration, but he assures her he will sort it out. Ethan calls the Extra store. He speaks slowly into the phone and is told it will be delivered the next day.

Ethan finds out he has to fill out paperwork at the visitor centre for a delivery truck to be allowed on the compound. The mission fails a second time.

It takes several calls to the manager at the store but eventually, two weeks later, the appliances arrive. Cate can hardly wait for them to be installed.

As the delivery is unloaded it soon becomes apparent that the washing machine is missing. Something that would be so simple in Canada is as complicated as it gets. Ethan attempts a stilted conversation with the delivery man, but it's clearly going nowhere so he calls the manager, again. The manager assures him it is no problem, the missing washing machine is on order and will be delivered next week, *Inshallah*.

"What the heck does 'Inshallah' mean?" asks Cate, who has been listening in on the conversation.

"It translates roughly to 'God willing,'" laughs Ethan. "Unfortunately, it's the blanket excuse whenever things go wrong, and as you're beginning to find out, that happens often."

Early in the morning a few days later while Ethan is at work, Dana rings up on FaceTime.

"I feel like I need more support from you, Maman," Dana says.

"I'm not sure what else I can do from here," Cate says. "I was hoping the counselling Ethan and I are financing would help you get your feet back on the ground."

"It is helping, and I'm grateful for that," says Dana, "I just wish you were here."

They lose the connection and Cate calls back.

"Sorry about that," says Cate. "What horrible timing with the stupid Internet here. You were just saying you wished I was there."

"Never mind, it doesn't matter," Dana says, clearly frustrated.

"I have a hard time when you close up when I don't understand or agree with you," says Cate. "I can't read your mind and I honestly don't know what you want from me."

"I get tired of always having to spell everything out to you," Dana says. "You're my mother, you should know me better, you should know what I need."

Cate is thinking about how to respond when Dana says a stiff goodbye and hangs up.

Unsettled about her stilted conversation with Dana, Cate makes the impulsive decision to go out and about on her own on the shopping bus to Ikea.

As women are not allowed to drive, the compound administrators organize two buses every day to take bored housewives to various shopping malls throughout the city.

The buses leave from the shopping centre parking lot at eight forty-five so Cate leaves the apartment early. She is the first one to arrive, but more women slowly trickle in and soon there are twelve women ready to go. Cate doesn't know anyone, but she doesn't mind some quiet time. She sits at the back of the bus, listening to a playlist on her iPad. She looks out at the littered landscape through the dusty window.

At Ikea, Cate is delighted to discover it is much the same as Ikea stores back home. She finds a plethora of items to spruce up the apartment and fills her cart with pillowcases, photo frames, candles, and dishes. As she heads to the cashier, she wonders how she'll ever carry everything back to the apartment from the bus stop but decides she can figure that out later. She feels very progressive using her new Saab Visa card with her name on it, even though Ethan receives a notification each time she uses it.

Cate waits outside for the bus, sitting on a cement pillar with her bags of parcels piled around her feet. A Saudi woman who is dressed in complete niqab starts to yell at her in Arabic. Cate has no idea what she is saying, but by her emphatic gestures she thinks the woman is objecting to her lack of head scarf. It doesn't feel good to be yelled at, but Cate's not about to let some stranger with different customs intimidate her. She stares back with defiance, leaving the scarf she had brought along tucked in her purse. Then another woman comes along, perhaps a niece or daughter, and drags the distraught woman away, still cursing loudly.

There is a potluck barbeque party the next day at the central pool, an early celebration of Canada Day, hosted by the Canadian Community of Riyadh. Cate has never been to the pool and is impressed with how attractive the space is. The pool is very large, shaped like a kidney bean, with lounge chairs and tables with umbrellas scattered about.

Ethan introduces Cate to some of the guys he works with and their wives. They see a few people they already know, like Quinn and the couples she met at the coffee shop.

After the meal there is a slideshow of Canadian scenes and landmarks projected onto a big screen accompanied by a playlist featuring Canadian musical artists. They have a good time. Cate feels happy to connect with other people. She meets a woman from Nova Scotia named Joan who looks of Indigenous ancestry, and Joan tells her she is a member of the Mi'kmaw Nation. Joan exudes a positive, Earth-mother energy. She has sparkly mahogany eyes and brown-black, bone-straight hair pulled back in a low ponytail. Cate discovers over the course of conversation that Joan is a yoga teacher and will be offering classes after Ramadan.

The next few days are consumed with preparations for the Ramadan holiday. Cate fetches her suitcase from the storage room; it feels like she only just unpacked. She makes a huge batch of chicken, carrots, and rice for Fredrick and washes all his toys and dog-bed. She sorts out her diabetic supplies and Lyme's remedies. She is full of anticipation, excited to be reunited with her family, ready for connection and adventure, starting with meeting up with Taylor in Athens.

Chapter 12

*I*SHMAEL ARRIVES RIGHT ON TIME. He is the driver that Peyton recommended, and as soon as Cate meets him she understands why Peyton thinks so highly of him. Ishmael is very friendly and polite. He helps Ethan to carry the heavy suitcases down the stairs and out to the truck. He also has excellent English, and on the drive to the airport Ethan and Cate talk about their family in Canada and Ishmael talks about his family in India.

It isn't long before Ishmael is pulling into the chaotic drop-off area at the international departures terminal. He helps unload the luggage and shakes Ethan's hand.

"I will text you when we get back," Ethan says. "Thank you so much."

"It is good, sir," Ishmael says with a smile. "I will be here, no problem."

There is a huge lineup at the check-in counter. Throngs of people mill about, cutting in and out of line, trolleys stacked high with cardboard boxes and luggage wrapped in clear tape. Cate is grateful for the air conditioning that blasts cool air, her polyester abaya stuck to her skin from the few minutes outside.

Once they have their boarding passes, Cate and Ethan make their way to security. There is a boarding pass verification station where they are separated when a Saudi official directs Cate to the women only search area, curtained off from the scrutiny of male eyes. The Saudi women who check the carry-on baggage seem uninterested in detecting any inappropriate items, more engaged on their phones than watching their screen. Cate is on the other side before Ethan is even halfway though the men's line. She stands by the notice board and waits.

They have over an hour until the posted boarding time. Ethan finds a semi-quiet spot for them to sit. Cate goes off in search of the WC, but when she discovers the floor covered in an inch of water she changes her mind. It is one of many cultural differences Cate hasn't adapted to. She decides to wait until she boards the plane, "cameling it" as she's taken to say.

She returns to her seat where Ethan is reading one of his financial newsletters and rests her head on his shoulder. She falls asleep.

"They're announcing it's time to board," Ethan says, touching her shoulder.

"Has it been an hour already?" Cate asks, squinting as she opens her eyes.

It is a six-hour flight to Milan. By the time Cate gets herself sorted out and buckled in, it is past midnight. She falls asleep almost immediately after takeoff.

Cate wakes up feeling rested and chipper only to find out Ethan couldn't sneak in even a wink. They watch a rather lame movie together until it is time for the meal service. The coffee is watery thin and the omelette with canned mushrooms is bland. When cleanup is complete the captain makes the announcement for the cabin crew to prepare for landing just as Cate has nodded off again. She opens her eyes half-mast as the air pressure makes her eardrums ache. She retrieves a stick of gum from her purse and offers one to Ethan.

Cate is surprised to find the terminal in Milan deserted. It feels kind of eerie.

Ethan looks for their connecting flight on the departures screen, but it doesn't show yet. Since they don't know where the gate is located, they wander around in a bit of a daze until Ethan spots a small café that is open for business. They grab a seat at a table for two and Ethan brings them delicious Italian cappuccinos. They connect to the Wi-Fi and log in on their phones, then write a few emails and read a few articles. An hour later their flight is listed on the departures screen. Their gate is in another terminal so they have to go through passport control.

Terminal A is a whole new world, nothing like the deserted B. There is a plethora of shops and restaurants and hordes of people. Cate decides to do a little shopping and get into holiday mood.

"It's past noon somewhere in the world," Cate says as she takes Ethan by the crook and leads him to a seat at a bar. They order two glasses of Amarone, and with the first sip

Cate is in heaven, her first real wine in weeks. Ethan decides the lacklustre breakfast they had was insufficient and orders a savoury cheese plate to share. Cate is in her happy place.

"This is definitely the way to pass time in an airport," she says to Ethan, clinking his glass in good cheer.

Several hours later it is time to board their flight to Athens. As soon as Cate steps onto the plane she can see why they got such a good deal on Aegean Airlines. There are no entertainment systems to help pass the time, and meal service turns out to be a fast-food style meal of pasta. Cate can't eat pasta, but in this case, she isn't the least disappointed. Even Ethan chooses to set his portion aside.

"Lucky for us we chose that delicious cheese plate," Cate says as Ethan reseals the aluminum container of congealed pasta.

"You can say that again," says Ethan. "And, lucky for us, this flight is only two and a half hours."

As they approach the city of Athens, Cate looks out the window. Athens is nothing like she imagined. The dusty, hazy sky reminds her of Riyadh, not the brilliant blue of the postcards and travel brochures. Later she will find out the Greece of her imagination is to be found in the pristine islands, not in the city.

They disembark and collect their luggage only to discover there is a fee for a luggage trolley and they have no euros. Ethan goes to the currency counter and exchanges American dollars for a few euros at a ridiculous exchange rate. He loads their six pieces of luggage onto two trolleys and they each push one out to the taxi lineup, where they

soon realize their luggage will never fit into a typical taxi.
Ethan hails a limo, which is far more expensive, but it is one
of the costs of living abroad.

The limo drives through thick traffic, the city sprawls
in all directions. Athens is a strange mix of ancient and
modern architecture. Cate periodically nods off. It takes
more than an hour, but then the taxi pulls into the drop-off
zone of their hotel.

Cate steps onto the curb just as Taylor strolls up to greet
her. He looks handsome, tall and tanned with a full-on
Grizzly Adams–type beard.

"Momma!" Taylor exclaims as he scoops Cate up in his
customary huge hug, lifting her right off the ground.

"Taylor, it's so good to see you!" Cate says.

Taylor greets Ethan with a handshake that pulls into
a one-armed man-hug, and they all start talking over one
another, full of stories that they want to share.

"Are you sure you brought enough luggage?" Taylor
teases as the taxi driver helps Ethan to unload it all onto
the sidewalk.

"Make fun of us if you must," Cate says, "but not
everyone can manage with just a backpack."

Taylor reaches for a suitcase just as a porter materializes
with a trolley. He tells Ethan he will take care of everything,
and Ethan passes him a five-euro tip.

They check in at the desk and the attendant informs
them that the room they booked is on the executive floor.
She outlines the privileges of the club room, including access
to the Panorama Lounge.

Cate is happy. The hotel is well-appointed and clean.

"I think we should drop off our luggage in our room
and head up immediately to the lounge," Cate suggests.

Ethan and Taylor agree and soon they are outside in the brilliant blue sky of a rooftop lounge and pool area. The views of the city are incredible.

"Look, there's the Acropolis!" says Taylor, pointing to the infamous tourist attraction in the distance.

"I'm so excited to see it," says Cate. "And to explore the rest of Athens. But for now, I want to hear all about you."

The three of them sit down at a table under an awning and order drinks, wine for Ethan and Cate and a cold beer for Taylor.

"I'm super-stoked that my classes are almost over," says Taylor. "Uni in Paris has been an amazing experience, but I'm ready to get back to the island."

"What about your relationship with Becky?" asks Cate.

"It's the real deal, that's for sure," confides Taylor, a blush on his cheeks, "but we both have another year left of school, and with her in the UK and me in Canada, we'll have to figure out how to do the long-distance thing."

Cate tells Taylor about her adventures getting to Riyadh and the challenges of the foreign culture.

"What's your job like at the pilot academy?" Taylor asks Ethan. "Is it challenging?"

"I love my work," Ethan says. "But, yes, it can be very challenging. The cadets I train how to fly often have poor English, and with the culture differences thrown in, I'm often off to a slow start before I begin." Ethan laughs. "Some of the higher ups even defend the cadets when they lie or cheat. It's bizarre, but rewarding still."

After a few hours they agree they've had enough sun and it's time to switch gears. They go back to the room to shower up and change, and then they decide a meal is in order. Ethan suggests they keep it simple and have dinner at the hotel's main restaurant. The food and wine do not disappoint.

"Shall we explore our neighbourhood and walk off some of this meal?" asks Cate.

The boys agree and they head outside into the humid, heavy, pollution-filled air. The hotel is located in a quaint community where white-washed stucco buildings with clay tiled rooftops in shades of burnt orange and dusty yellow dot the landscape. They walk along the cobbled streets in deep discussion for a good hour or so before returning to the hotel.

When Ethan and Cate wake up just after dawn, Taylor is still sound asleep so they get dressed as quietly as they can and sneak out of the room. They go to the executive lounge where there is hot coffee. They find two comfortable chairs and settle in. Ethan reads financial articles on his phone and Cate gets out her journal.

> *Pinch me, I'm dreaming. How is it that this is my life? It all feels unreal, globe-trotting from Saudi Arabia to Athens, Greece, staying in a luxury hotel with my husband and my son. I'm over the moon with gratitude for my good fortune. I'm so excited to explore this ancient city, to share this experience with both of them. My relationship with Taylor is so important to me, but it isn't easy to maintain connection living halfway around the world. It's wonderful that he agrees to FaceTime often, but there's nothing like the live experience.*
>
> *When we were all talking at the pool bar it made my heart burst with joy to witness Ethan and Taylor so relaxed and open with one another. Two of my favourite men. I feel like the luckiest woman alive.*

An hour or so later, Taylor walks in, having found the note they scribbled in the dark, and joins them for coffee.

"Happy belated Mother's Day," Taylor says, handing Cate a card.

"Oh, my goodness, how thoughtful," Cate says. "I wasn't expecting anything."

Inside the card is a folded piece of paper. Taylor has written her a poem. Cate reads it quietly to herself.

"Do you mind if I read a few lines of this out loud?" she asks.

Taylor gives his permission and Cate begins.

> *Is there a greater gift than what you give to me?*
> *Perhaps the things I value most you taught me how to see.*
> *And like the webs that, invisible, connect us all,*
> *my heart to you is bound across all seas.*
> *The universe itself, indeed, is small.*
> *I love you like the sunshine loves the trees.*

"Thank you so much." Cate's voice catches in her throat and she tears up. "This is the best gift ever."

Cate tucks her card into her purse and the three of them make their way to the breakfast buffet. They fill up their plates and sit down to talk about their plans for the day and decide to begin with their top-rated attraction, the Acropolis.

The Acropolis is a short taxi ride away. The driver drops them off on a street close to the entrance, already crowded with tourists. They walk to the ticket booth where Cate is surprised to discover that as a student at the university in Paris, Taylor's admission is free. She feels grateful for the little things.

It is a challenge for "Ms. Lyme Legs" to ascend the steep steps, but Cate manages with tons of water breaks and pit stops to make it to the top. It is well worth her effort, as she beholds the breathtaking scenery and exquisite details of the preserved remains of the ancient civilization of Greece. The stones on the ground prove to be quite slippery, polished to a sheen with so many tourists traversing them day after day. Cate walks carefully, grasping Ethan by the crook on one side and Taylor on the other. Soon the sun is directly overhead and the heat beckons for them to be on their way.

Taylor is designated as their unofficial tour guide. He takes them to the Plaka where they view the temple of Zeus. It begins to rain slightly, so they seek cover in a side-street restaurant, deciding it's time to eat anyway.

"Did you hear about Serena Williams winning the French Open?" Ethan asks Taylor.

"I did, it was all over the French media, but I have to admit, I don't really follow tennis," says Taylor. "I remember Mom telling me you are quite a skilled tennis player yourself."

"I don't know about skilled," Ethan says with a blush, "but I do enjoy the game. I'm thrilled for Serena."

Cate knows next to nothing about tennis, or any sport for that matter. She changes the subject.

"It looks like the rain has stopped," says Cate as she looks out the window to the street. "Are you two ready?"

The three of them window-shop and watch the changing of the guard in front of the parliament buildings. They take in the tribute in honour of the tomb of the unknown soldier.

By late afternoon Cate is ready for a rest and a change of pace. They grab a taxi back to the hotel and change into their swim gear to take advantage of the rooftop pool. Cate and Taylor get deep into their novels and Ethan reads the financial news. They order wine and beer and everyone concurs, life is good.

After a few hours, hunger sets in. They depart the poolside haven and go back to their room to shower and change, then catch a taxi to the restaurant that the hotel concierge recommended. As it turns out the road is blocked by police because of a demonstration.

"It's a sign of the civil unrest here," says Ethan. "Greece is in a huge financial crisis and the future doesn't look very stable at the moment."

"It's true," pipes in the taxi driver. "There is a political demonstration just about every day. But don't worry, I can take you to a popular restaurant down by the harbour."

It is nine o'clock when they finally arrive at Zorba's. They are starving. Cate is impressed when the waiter leads them to a table situated right next to the water, so close she can dip her toe in if she desires. As it is, the water is murky, with a skiff of oil running along the surface. Cate chooses to keep her toes safely tucked inside her shoes.

The waiter suggests they share the whole sea bass, served tableside, and it is delicious. Over dinner the three of them get a little tipsy and the talk turns to matters of the heart.

"I'm dying to hear more about Becky," says Cate. "How exactly did you meet?"

"Well, I think I told you already that she is on the same exchange program as me, that she studies at Cambridge?" asks Taylor.

"Yes, you did," says Cate, "but did you meet in class, or at a bar or a party? And when did you know you were in love?"

"Whoa, one question at a time, Momma!" laughs Taylor. "We met at a party. I can't say I remember when I knew I was in love though. It just seemed to happen when I wasn't looking."

"How funny," Cate chuckles and caresses Ethan's arm. "That's exactly how I felt when I fell in love with Ethan. Totally unexpected."

When the waiter returns to clear away their plates he offers to bring dessert menus.

"I'm too full for dessert," says Cate, "but I'd love a shot of ouzo."

The waiter pooh-poohs her choice of ouzo, which he claims is overrated. He informs her he will bring them all something else to try. They have no idea what liquor they partake in, but it is light and slightly herbal and they agree it suits their palates.

They all wake up at almost the same time the next morning. Over breakfast, Taylor googles attractions and suggests they go to the Banaki Museum. They spend a few hours looking at art and artifacts and then walk over to the chic, upscale district of Kolonaki. They look in the elaborate window displays of designer shops and then find a restaurant to have lunch.

"I vote for another afternoon lying about by the rooftop pool," says Taylor when the meal is done. Cate and Ethan agree and they catch a taxi back to the hotel.

"Are you any closer to deciding what career you want to pursue once you have your degree?" asks Cate, taking a sip from her margarita.

"This semester in Paris has taken my French to another level. I'm pretty sure now that I do want to pursue a career in education, teaching languages and humanities at the secondary level," Taylor says.

Cate and Ethan agree Taylor will make an excellent teacher. Cate has always supported her children to make their own choices, but she feels a little thrilled that her son wishes to follow in his mother's footsteps.

On their last day in Athens, Cate feels mixed emotions. The reunion with her son was far too brief. Yet, ahead of her lie new adventures and connection with more of her loved ones, including her precious grandson. When it is time to say goodbye, Cate holds him for a while in a silent embrace.

"Send me a text when you arrive in Paros," Cate says. "I love you, so much, too much, very much."

Taylor smiles. He and Cate used to say this phrase all the time, a phrase they picked up when they volunteered together in Thailand. He gives his mom another huge bear hug and then departs for the ferry bound for the legendary Greek Island of Paros. Cate wipes a tear from her eye and watches until her son disappears into the crowd.

Chapter 13

*A*T THE CALGARY International Airport, Cate and Ethan rent a car and Ethan drives to Michael's house. It is late when they pull into the driveway, but the front light is on. Ethan is unloading their luggage from the trunk when Michael appears at the door.

"Hey, buddy, could you use a hand?" Michael calls out, slipping on a pair of shoes.

"Hi, Michael, thanks, that would be great," says Ethan.

"It's so good to see you, Broski," says Cate as she limps up the stairs to give her brother a big hug.

"You go on in, let me get this," Michael says. He takes her heavy carry-on from her. "It's good to see you too, Sis."

The boys bring everything into the foyer.

"Sam is in bed but he wanted me to give you one of these," Michael says. He leans in to kiss Cate on the nose. "Ashley is tucked in too, reading her book. Can I get you guys anything?"

"I think we're good, thanks" says Cate. "If not, we know our way around."

"We're both way past ready for bed," says Ethan.

"Alright then, I guess I'll see you in the morning," Michael says. He gives Cate another big hug.

Ethan moves their things into the guest room. Cate plops down on the bed, ready to just crawl in, but she's too grungy from travel not to shower. After a quick rinse-off and brush of her teeth, she kisses Ethan, then falls like a zombie into travel-weary sleep.

Cate is wakened by the sound of construction vehicles outside the window. She checks her phone. It is not quite five in the morning, and five hours of sleep is not enough. She tosses and turns. Her restlessness awakens Ethan and he makes a move. Soon Cate is delighted to be awake.

They throw on some clothes and head out to the kitchen. They snoop through the cupboards and pantry until they find coffee beans and a grinder. Ethan fills the drip coffee maker with filtered water and adds the ground beans. There is no creamer to be found, so they have to settle with some soymilk Cate discovers on the fridge door.

While they wait for the coffee to brew, Cate gets out her journal.

> *I already miss my son and the energy of Athens. True, it was a dirty, crazy, chaotic city, but we had so much fun. Walking up the ancient ruins of the Acropolis was incredible. What an experience. I thinks perhaps I pushed myself too much, to keep up with Ethan and Taylor. After the long flight and the jet lag that had us both up at five, I'm feeling rough. My legs*

are heavy and my arms feel like two anvils are tied to my wrists, but it's all good because I'm here in Calgary with my brother and Sam, and soon I'll be reunited with Dana too. I will try and carve out some time to meditate, but with only a few days to cram in connection, it might be a challenge.

I haven't had word yet from Taylor. I hope he is okay. Last night I dreamt of him lying in an alley, robbed of his passport and money. I sent him a text this morning, but no reply. Do you ever stop worrying about your kids, I wonder?

Just then Sam comes up the stairs, dressed in Snoopy pajamas and wearing a fedora with a feather.

"Hello desert-dwellers," Sam says. "I didn't think you would be up."

Cate puts her journal down and gets up off the couch to give Sam a hug.

"Yes, well, we did get in rather late, but you know Ethan and me, we're early birds. I suppose you are ready for some breakfast," Cate says. "What do you usually have?"

"My dad always makes my breakfast for me," says Sam.

"I see you found everything to make coffee," says Michael, appearing as if on cue. "Did you two sleep okay?"

"We had a great sleep," says Cate. "Although not quite enough of it, no fault of the bed."

"That's the good thing about being on holiday, you can always catch a nap later if you need it," says Michael as he pours himself a cup of coffee. He gets out a packet of bacon and starts to fry up a few slices for Sam.

Sam tells Cate and Ethan about his school musical performance in between mouthfuls, and Michael disappears to get ready. Ashley strides into the room in a flurry of rushed energy. She hardly acknowledges her guests as she assembles a lunch, grabs an energy bar, and pours herself a coffee in a to-go mug. Soon all three are heading out the door, with plans to connect over dinner that evening.

Cate and Ethan have a quiet morning. They talk over breakfast and get themselves sorted. A little after ten o'clock Dana calls, excited to see them.

"Can I come to Uncle Michael's and pick you up in my new used car?" Dana asks.

"That would be awesome," Cate agrees, equally excited to be reunited. She hasn't seen her since the early days when Dana got back after the earthquake.

Moments later Dana honks her arrival. Cate and Ethan lock up the house and Cate slips the spare key Michael gave them into her purse.

As Cate walks down the driveway to the curb, Dana jumps out of the car and runs around the side. She grabs Cate by the arm and twirls her around, then presses Cate's head against her chest.

"Maman! It's SO good to see you!" Dana whoops.

"It's so good to see you too," says Cate, her heart full.

"What do you think of my new wheels?" Dana asks, sweeping her arm in the direction of her rusted out, old Dodge hatchback.

"It's wonderful that you were able to save up for your own car," says Cate. "Congratulations."

Ethan hops into the back seat and Cate takes her place in the front, beside Dana.

"There's this sick new restaurant in Marda Loop that only sources local. I'd like to take you guys there for an early lunch," says Dana as she drives.

"That sounds lovely," says Ethan, "but you must let us treat you."

Dana laughs and calls him Mr. Moneybags and agrees he can foot the bill.

At the restaurant they find a cozy booth and place their orders. Dana rummages around in her bag and produces a belated Mother's Day card for Cate and a Father's Day card for Ethan. Both cards are handmade, featuring Dana's original artwork and poetry.

> *"Dear Ethan, thank you for being so wonderful to my mother, and me, and our whole mix-mashed family. You inspire me in your dedication, follow-through, generosity, and attitude toward life. Thank you for being a part of my life. Love Dana."*

"Thank you, Dana," says Ethan. "This is so thoughtful of you."

"Yes," agrees Cate. "And your artwork is nothing short of amazing."

When lunch is over, Dana announces she has a few errands to run but she will see them again later for dinner. She drops them off at Michael's.

Cate suggests to Ethan they unpack their things, and she takes a nap. When she wakes up Ethan is in the shower and she decides to join him.

After getting dressed, Cate and Ethan head over to Dr. Kensington's office for Cate's appointment. Dr. Kensington tut-tuts as she conducts a variety of tests.

"Unfortunately, your body isn't responding as well I'd hoped," Dr. Kensington says. She tests Cate's levels again, just to be sure. "Are you following your regimen strictly, as I suggested?"

"I'm following the dosage regimen exactly when we're at home," says Cate. "It's harder when we're travelling and skipping time zones. As for the diet, I'm strict about it on

the weekdays, but then I cheat a bit on the weekend.
I thought you said sticking to it eighty percent of the time
was reasonable, considering this is a long-term plan."

"You're right, I did say that," says Dr. Kensington.
"It sounds like you're doing a great job. I'm going to change
a few of your doses and introduce two new remedies, and
we'll see if that makes a difference next time."

Sixteen hundred dollars and two and a half hours later,
Cate departs with Ethan toting a huge box of pills and
potions to last the next four months.

When they get back, the house is busy. Michael is
unpacking groceries and Ashley is preparing dinner. Sam
is studying at the kitchen island getting ready for end of
the year exams. Ashley puts out some snacks and Michael
pours the wine.

"So, how are you adjusting to life in Saudi Arabia?"
asks Ashley.

"It hasn't been easy," says Cate. "I won't deny that.
But I'm with Ethan, and I know it will be all good."

"Have you ridden on a camel yet?" asks Sam.

"No, and I don't intend to," laughs Cate. "But when
you're done your homework I'll show you a few photos
of camels. It's quite hilarious, actually, to see them riding
around in the back of trucks when we're out and about
in the city."

"Sweet," says Sam. "Can I do the rest of my homework
later, Mom?"

Ashley checks his work.

"Okay, I'll agree to a compromise," Ashley says. "If you
finish two more problems you can be done for the day."

When Sam finishes his math homework he sits down
on the couch with Cate to look at her photos of Riyadh.
Dana arrives just as they are about to sit down to dinner.

Michael barbeques the chicken, and Ashley asks them to take a seat at the patio table that she has set with matching placemats, napkins, and summer dishes. The meal is delicious.

After dinner Sam organizes a bocce-ball tournament on their massive back lawn. Ashley shows the video of Sam's voice recital, and Cate shows them photos of Riyadh. Dana tells stories about the earthquake, about the villagers and how generous they were to her. Cate feels content, reconnecting with her family under the black, star-studded sky. The Cheshire-cat moon winks with a crooked smile.

The next morning when everyone has departed for the day, Ethan heads down to the exercise room to have a run on Ashley's treadmill and Cate sits down at the table to write in her journal.

> *I finally heard back from Taylor. Of course, he is fine, just forgot to check in with me. He said that Paros was spectacular and, if I'm ever to go back to Greece, I must check it out.*
>
> *Reconnecting with Dana has been a whirlwind. She is in one of her up spaces, radiating enthusiasm. She confided to me that things have been tense with John. I wish she could create some healthier boundaries with him. It's not my cupboard, but I know how toxic his energy can be, and when he is in a deep depression he is at his worst.*
>
> *Dana said she appreciates Ethan's solidity. My heart is overjoyed that she loves him and he loves her. It's not the same; he isn't her dad, but it's something. I know it isn't always like this in blended families, and I know it hasn't been easy for her to adjust.*

She is feeling the urge to travel again. I wish she would settle down and make some roots, but who am I to say? Dana has her own life journey and I support her, even when my mother's mind worries.

Cate and Ethan meet up with Dana at Community Foods the next morning. They select salads and wraps for a picnic lunch. Dana suggests they take their goodies to Princess Island Park. It is a beautiful day, the air bright, pure, Canadian. Dana spots an old-fashioned wooden picnic table to sit and eat.

"I won't play it down, it's been fucking hard to readjust," Dana says. "I still have flashbacks, and sometimes work at the coffee shop feels so unsatisfying. But, I'm glad I moved back to Calgary. My new roommates are awesome."

"If you need extra support, just let us know," says Cate.

"Well, I have started a fundraiser on Facebook," Dana tells them. "I hope to raise seven thousand dollars for the villagers who gave me food, water, and shelter after the earthquake."

"We'll be sure to make a donation," says Ethan. "I'm really proud of you for giving back like that."

Dana entertains them, playing on her ukulele and singing a few songs she wrote. She returns her instrument to her backpack.

"I'd really like some one-on-one time with my mom," says Dana.

"No problem," says Ethan. "I'll walk over to the strip mall to browse the shops and leave you two to chat."

Cate and Dana walk hand in hand, then take a seat on the ground under a huge poplar tree. Cate happens to have her Goddess Guidance Oracle Cards in her bag and they decide to choose their summer solstice spiral spreads together. For the synthesis, Dana chooses Maat, the Goddess of fairness and justice.

"I wonder if this means there will be a peaceful resolution with Dad?" Dana wonders aloud.

"I hope so," says Cate.

"Who did you draw, Maman?" Dana asks.

"I picked Dana, high priestess," says Cate. "How cool is that? The Goddess with your namesake." Cate reads the message out loud. "You have Divine knowledge that can help others through your spiritual teaching." Cate puts down her card and takes Dana's hands in hers. "I have a strong feeling that the goddesses are encouraging us to work together. Maybe we can start a regular weekly dialogue."

"Thank you, Maman, for making some time for just me," says Dana.

"I know that is something that feels important to you," says Cate. "And I want to remind you how amazing you are. You have so many talents. I'm confident a bright future lies ahead of you."

"I hope you're right," Dana says. "I've been painting a new series and teaching yoga on the side. It would be amazing if I could earn a living just doing my art."

"Then that is my wish for you too," replies Cate. "Now, I think it's time we went and found Ethan."

Cate and Dana pack up their cards and brush off the grass that clings to their pants, then walk over to the mall. Cate sends Ethan a text and he meets them outside the main doors. It is time for them to go back to Michael's to get dinner ready.

Ethan makes a pit stop at Safeway and he and Cate purchase the items they need for chicken and vegetable skewers and a Greek salad. They choose a bright and cheery bouquet of gerbera daisies for Ashley and pick out a few bottles of wine at the liquor store and then they are on their way.

The simple act of preparing a meal together has Ethan and Cate in their flow. Soon, Ashley gets home from work and Michael returns with Sam after picking him up from his voice lesson. It is a full house and the conversation is animated. Over dinner they discuss politics and the NDP in Alberta, ethnicity, religion, human rights, and government conspiracy theories. After dinner they get into a heated game of Risk, but as it approaches eleven o'clock, Cate yawns.

"This has been so wonderful," Cate says, getting up from her chair, "but my eyes won't stay open a minute longer."

Everyone agrees and the troop disperses to their bedrooms.

"Sleep well desert-dwellers," says Sam.

Their last day in Calgary is a Saturday. Michael and Ashley don't have to work and Sam is off school. Ashley invites Dana to join them for brunch at noon for one final hurrah. Dana reaches out to see if Cate wants to join her yoga class in the park that morning and Cate agrees.

Cate parks the car in a lot closest to the gate, grabs the yoga mat she borrowed from Ashley and her bag from the back seat, and walks toward the river. She sees Dana standing in the centre of a clearing with four other yogis gathered around her.

"Namaste," Dana says.

Cate rolls out her mat and takes a seat.

"We'll just wait a few more moments to see if any more will be joining us," says Dana to the group. "While we wait, I invite you to close your eyes and visualize a scene that brings you joy."

Cate closes her eyes and imagines herself with Ethan on the cliff edge by the ocean near Melissa's house in Mill Bay. She pictures Fredrick scampering in the sand along the shore.

Another young man joins the group and then Dana begins the class, leading them in a Vinyasa flow. Cate has to modify every posture, she is so sore and tight. At one point, when Cate is in Child's Pose, Dana comes over and gently readjusts her. She places her hand on her mother's lower back.

"I invite your body to manifest total, radiant health," she whispers in Cate's ear.

Dana ends with Savasana, which she accompanies with a Sanskrit song. When the song is finished and all is quiet, Cate sits up and smiles at her daughter. She feels lighter. Cate helps Dana to pack up her things after all the other yogis have thanked Dana for the practice and departed.

"I have a final parting gift for you before you go," says Dana, reaching into her large burlap bag. "This is a meditational healing CD I made just for you."

Cate is overwhelmed with her daughter's generosity. She holds her in a deep, silent embrace.

"Thank you, Dana, for everything. I feel so blessed to be your mother, for our deep spiritual connection and forever love."

"I'll see you back at Uncle Michael's," Dana says. She gives Cate a kiss on the cheek. "I have a few things I need to do first."

Cate stops at the farmers' market. She fishes out the list Ashley gave her from her purse and fills her cart with fresh fruit, organic eggs, and fresh-baked, artisanal bread.

Once the groceries are unloaded and put away, Cate heads into the guest room to freshen up and change. Ethan has already packed up his suitcase and is ready to go.

"How was yoga in the park?" Ethan asks.

"To be honest, my yoga practice was a challenge," Cate says, "but my connection with Dana was phenomenal." She retrieves the meditation CD from her bag and shows it to Ethan. "She gifted me with this."

"It's so good to see her in such a great space," Ethan says. "And don't worry about yoga, I know you're going to be recovered and back doing your Bouja moves in no time."

Ethan kisses Cate, firm but soft, then heads into the kitchen to help out.

Dana arrives just in time, a flurry of energy as she floats into the room dressed like Pippi Longstocking, with striped red and white leggings, her long hair woven in two braids.

"I made some energy balls that don't have any sugar or flour," says Dana. She places a pottery bowl, also one of her creations, on the table and takes a seat beside Sam.

"Well, that's all of us," says Michael. "I'd like to offer a blessing for this food and my gratitude for my sis and her wonderful husband, for coming all the way from Saudi Arabia to join us."

Everyone toasts to family, clinking an odd assortment of water glasses and coffee mugs. The usual chaos of enthusiastic conversation ensues.

When the meal is over and the dishes are put away, Sam and Dana perform a duet, Dana strumming along on her ukulele. Too soon it is time for Cate and Ethan to depart for the airport. There are hugs and tears and well-wishes on the front step. Cate waves goodbye as Ethan backs out of the driveway.

"I'm going to miss that crew," Cate says with a sigh.

"Yes, it was wonderful," Ethan agrees, "but there is more connection to be made just around the corner, when we arrive in Victoria a few hours from now."

Cate presses her hand to Ethan's heart. She notices her phone light up and picks it up.

"Hi, Mom, it's me," says Celeste, "I have a little boy who can't wait until you get here."

"No problem, put him on," says Cate.

"I so esited, Gwamma! Are you sweeping over at my house? Are you bwinging pwesents?"

"Oh, my goodness," laughs Cate. "Yes, little love, Grandma and Grandpa are on our way with presents and we are definitely going to have sleepovers too."

"I wuv you, Gwamma."

"I love you, Oliver, to the moon and back."

Chapter 14

*V*ICTORIA STILL FEELS LIKE HOME to Cate. As she descends the stairwell from the plane to the tarmac, she breathes in the seaweed scent of the ocean. The early afternoon sun peeks from behind clumps of white clouds. Her heart expands.

At the Avis car rental counter, Cate is jazzed to find out they have a Dodge Charger available. Sweet nostalgia sweeps over her as she recalls the many trips she and Ethan made in the Charger he rented in the early days, when they were falling in love.

On the way to Donna's apartment in Oak Bay they stop in at Origins Bakery, the liquor store, and Thrifty's for a few groceries. Celeste, Grayson, and Oliver are making the drive down from Cobble Hill to be a part of their welcome home shindig. Cate can hardly wait to be reunited with her family.

Cate buzzes the intercom at her mom's building, her arms heavy with paper bag purchases.

"Come on up," Donna's voice crackles with static.

When Ethan and Cate get off the elevator on Donna's floor she is waiting for them, all aglow with excitement.

"I'm so happy you're here," Donna exclaims, then pecks Cate on the cheek. "How was your visit in Calgary?"

"It was great, Mom," Cate says. "Dana was in a very positive space and Michael was same-old, agreeable Michael." Cate sets her packages down on the kitchen island. "It was great to see Sam so confident and comfortable with himself, now that he's entered into the awkward years."

"Yes, Sam is a character," Donna says. "He reminds me of Dana in many ways. Free spirits who follow the beat of their own drums."

"Hmm, I wonder who they get that from?" Cate teases.

Donna helps to unload the purchases, and then the buzzer for the front door sounds. Donna opens the door to her apartment just as Oliver gets off the elevator. He runs down the hall and jumps into Cate's arms.

"Gwamma!" Oliver squeals, his face lit up like the sun.

It is a flurry of confusion as everyone talks at once. Donna, Ethan, and Cate assemble plates of nibbles: cheese and crackers, raw vegetables, and hummus. Grayson has brought a bottle of wine; he opens it and proceeds to offer everyone a glass. Oliver wants a special drink too, but Celeste is one step ahead of him. She takes a bottle of organic grape juice out of his bag and pours it in a wine glass.

"Be extra careful with a big-boy glass," Celeste says.

Oliver smiles ear to ear as he clinks his glass and says "cheers" several times to everyone. He eats all the cheese on the plate Celeste has prepared for him and not much else.

"Gwamma, will you pway twains with me?" Oliver asks, a few minutes into the meal.

Cate is about to say yes when Celeste interrupts her.

"You need to eat everything on your plate before you can play with Grandma," Celeste says.

"But, Mommy, I so esited to pway with Gwamma," Oliver says with a pout, his big blue eyes, so like Grayson's, blink back tears.

"I know," Celeste says, gentle yet firm. "You need to eat or you'll wake up in the middle of the night starving," Celeste says. "I'll make you a deal that if you eat all your veggies you can play trains."

It is a casual evening. The adults take turns entertaining Oliver while engaged in telling stories and catching up, and Donna refills the plates and bowls.

"Does anyone want some dessert?" Donna asks. "I just remembered, Cate and Ethan brought over some yummy looking, gluten-free, vegan cookies and cupcakes from Origins."

"Yes, peas!" sings out Oliver, always the one with the sweet tooth. He drops the puzzle piece in his hand and runs to the kitchen.

"Okay, Mister," says Celeste, "but you can only choose one. Then it's time for your bath."

After dessert, Cate offers to give Oliver his bath. After she dries him off she pulls his pajama top over his head and he laughs when she tickles him. Cate cuddles him up. She buries her nose into his neck, where the fresh scent of baby shampoo and talcum powder lingers. She reads him three stories and sings him a song, cuddled up on Donna's bed. Oliver yawns and Cate traces her finger along his cheek, like she used to do when Celeste was a little girl.

"Goodnight, sleep tight, little one."

Cate tucks Oliver into his portable bed in Donna's room. She leaves the door open a crack, and the adults engage in more chit-chat. It isn't long before they succumb to their own weary eyes.

"We'd love to stay longer," Celeste says, as she gets up and packs Oliver's toys into his bag, "but morning comes early with our little one and we've got a long drive ahead of us."

Grayson plucks Oliver from his cozy nest and carries him out to their car.

"Oliver will be over the moon when I tell him in the morning that you two are coming up to stay with us for a few nights," Celeste says as she hugs Cate goodbye.

In the morning Cate wakes up feeling the most rested and refreshed she's felt since she left Riyadh. Ethan kisses her good morning, then throws on a T-shirt and a pair of jeans and goes into the kitchen to make coffee. While it is brewing, Cate gets out her journal.

> *Home sweet home. I can't get over how much Oliver has grown since I moved away. I'm blown away. Was it only a few months ago? Oliver knows all his farm animal sounds and sings the alphabet song. He reminds me of Celeste at his age, so engaged and social and interested in learning. My heart melted when his face lit up when he saw me, when he ran into my arms and embraced me like I'd never been gone at all. I was worried he might forget me, he is still so young. But he remembers.*

Donna comes out from her room in her pajamas.

"Good morning you two," she says. She stretches her arms up over her head with a yawn. "Have you been up long?"

"No, not long at all," Ethan assures her. "There is a fresh pot of coffee on though."

"You two are so awesome, how you just make yourselves at home. It's easy-breezy having you as house guests."

Donna fills her own mug and joins Ethan and Cate for coffee. Cate sets down her journal and the three of them chat about life in Saudi Arabia.

"Is it really true that it is illegal for women to drive?" Donna asks.

"I know, it seems archaic in this day and age," agrees Cate. "But yes, unfortunately it is true. I'm actually excited to drive our rental car."

"What time are you two heading up-island?" Donna says.

"I have an eye appointment this morning," Cate says.

"And we have a few other errands too," says Ethan. "We'll grab a bite to eat in Victoria and plan to get to Celeste and Grayson's after Oliver's nap."

Donna peppers them with more questions, but soon Ethan's tummy grumbles. He offers to make egg sandwiches and Donna happily accepts.

After breakfast Donna disappears into her room to get ready and Cate has a shower. Ethan takes his turn. When he returns, his naked body entices Cate. She locks the door.

Cate appreciates the opportunity for some time, just her and Ethan, something they've had little of since they left Riyadh more than a week ago.

After Cate's eye appointment they go for a lunch date at the oyster bar, just like the old days. They walk over to Outlooks, Ethan's favourite store, and he tries on some clothes and models them for Cate. He buys a few short-sleeved, button-down shirts. They make a pit stop for some drugstore items they can't buy in Saudi Arabia and then Cate gets behind the wheel.

"I don't think I'll ever tire of this drive," Cate says as she merges onto the Malahat.

"I agree," says Ethan. "I can't seem to get enough of these incredible views."

"Especially after the miles of beige landscape of Riyadh," says Cate.

Two hours later they arrive at Grayson and Celeste's cozy, cottage-style bungalow in Cobble Hill. As Cate pulls onto the drive, Oliver appears at the front door.

"Gwamma!" Oliver yells out. He pushes on his bright green crocs that are on the shoe mat and runs out to the car to greet them.

"Mummy said we're having four sleepovers! I so esited!"

Cate laughs and ruffles his hair, which has grown into a thick mass of soft blonde curls. Ethan unloads the car and puts their luggage in the spare room while Oliver and Cate snuggle up on the couch.

"Can we peas go to Bwight Angel Park?" Oliver asks.

"That's a great idea," says Celeste. "Does that suit you two?"

"Absolutely," says Cate. "You know how much I love it there."

"I'm going to take the opportunity to get some work done," says Grayson. "But you guys have a great time."

"Okay then, you go and use the bathroom, Oliver, and I'll pack up a few snacks," Celeste says as she heads into the kitchen.

"Can Gwamma and Gwampa come with us in our car?" Oliver asks.

"Yes, of course," says Celeste with a smile.

When everyone is ready, Oliver grabs Cate by the arm and pulls her along.

At Bright Angel the adults traipse around after Oliver. Cate catches him when he flies off the end of the slide, and Ethan pushes him on the swing. Oliver throws rocks and sticks into the river. Ethan tries to teach Oliver how to make smooth pebbles skip across the choppy surface of the water but he is too young, his coordination not developed enough to master the move.

They walk up the hill into the forest and Oliver discovers an old bone and withered feather. He spies an ancient tree with a massive trunk.

"Can we hud this twee?" he asks. "I just wuv dis twee."

"Absolutely," says Celeste. "Hugging trees is very good luck."

Oliver hugs the tree and insists everyone else do the same. The adults tire out long before Oliver runs out of steam.

"It's time for us to go home and get dinner started," Celeste tells Oliver.

"Can we have pasta, peas?" Oliver asks on the drive home. "Did you know I just wuv pasta, Gwamma?" he asks, turning his head to look at Cate.

They sing songs and tell jokes and count construction vehicles all the way home.

When they walk in, Grayson has already started making dinner. Oliver has a hoot helping out, right in the thick of things. He counts the cutlery and sets forks and knives at each table setting. He stirs pasta sauce and asks for a taste. Then he gets out his puzzles and sits on the kitchen floor.

"Tan we go for a walk and see the hawses?" Oliver asks after dinner.

It is a beautiful night and everyone agrees it is a great idea. Cate and Oliver make up silly stories, using their vivid imaginations, and Celeste makes different voices to create hilarious dialogue between the two horses on an acreage just down from their house. Too soon it is time to take Oliver home to bed, but he doesn't complain as Celeste assures him Grandma can read him his bedtime stories and tuck him in.

Oliver wakes up early and traipses into the guest room to wake up Cate and Ethan.

"Is it morning already?" Cate asks, rubbing her eyes.

"Silly Gwamma," Oliver says, jumping up on the bed to give her a big kiss. "Tan't you see the sun is up?"

Cate and Oliver play with his wooden train set while Ethan makes a pot of coffee, letting Celeste and Grayson sleep in for a change.

"Gwampa, will you make warm chocolate cashew milk for me, peas?" asks Oliver as Ethan takes a carton of coffee cream from the fridge. Ethan makes Oliver his special drink and brings over two large mugs of coffee for him and Cate.

Once Celeste and Grayson are up and ready for the day, Oliver suggests they drive to the Cowichan Bay harbourfront and count the boats and look for sea lions. They all load into the car, even Grayson.

As soon as he is out of the car, Oliver takes Cate by the hand. They walk over to the promenade that runs alongside the ocean. The tide is low and there are so many interesting things to explore. Oliver is fascinated with the tiny yellow, brown, and black crabs that crawl through the sand, creating the illusion that the ground is moving. Eagle-eyes Ethan spots a few sea lions out playing amongst the waves and a turkey vulture soaring overhead.

Oliver plonks down in the pebbly sand to gaze dreamily at the clouds in the powder-blue sky.

"I spy a tiger cloud," says Ethan.

"Where?" asks Oliver. "I tan't see it."

Ethan takes Oliver's chubby hand in his and points to the tiger cloud in the distance.

When it is time for lunch, Oliver asks Celeste if they can go into Duncan to his favourite Vietnamese restaurant. Everyone loads back into the car and in fifteen minutes they are pulling onto the street.

When his avocado and yam roll and tempura vegetables are delivered to the table, Oliver digs right in with gusto.

"Nummy!" Oliver exclaims after every bite.

The public library is just a few blocks away and Cate suggests they hang out there for a bit. They take Oliver to the children's area, and the adults talk while Oliver explores the fort and looks at books on the shelves.

"No, no, no, no, no," Oliver says to a little girl who tries to take a book from him.

Cate can't help but giggle, he looks so damn cute, wagging his finger and saying no in a sing-song voice.

"Oliver, remember what Mummy said about sharing?" Celeste intervenes.

"But, I had it first," Oliver pouts. Celeste gives him a stern look, hands on her hips, and he gives the book to the little girl, then runs into Cate's lap for a snuggle. Cate reads from a stack of books he has collected and soon the sharing incident seems all but forgotten. Oliver rubs his eyes and

Celeste declares it is time to go. Oliver cries a little but cheers up when Celeste tells him he can choose five new books to sign out.

"Sank you, Mummy," Oliver says as he clutches his cloth bag with his new books in it.

The next day, Celeste asks if Cate and Ethan will look after Oliver while she and Grayson go out on a much overdo date. They are more than happy to comply.

Cate and Oliver are working on a puzzle in the living room when Celete comes in wearing a red dress and heels.

"Mummy and Daddy are going out for a little while now," says Celeste as she puts on her lipstick in the hall mirror. "Be good for Grandma and Grandpa."

"I will," Oliver says, engrossed in his task.

"What, I don't even get a hug when Grandma's here?" says Celeste, pretending to cry.

Oliver jumps up and runs to the door.

"You look bootiful, Mummy," Oliver says. He gives her a kiss on the mouth, her red lipstick now smeared a little on both of them. "I wuv you."

Grayson walks in, handsome in jeans and a loose, untucked shirt. He hugs Oliver and tells him to be a good boy, and then the two of them are out the door.

Cate fixes Oliver a snack-lunch with a selection of his favourite foods and they sit out in the backyard at his picnic table. They read through a huge stack of books. Oliver makes the noises of all the transportation vehicles with exaggerated enthusiasm. Cate gets out his crayons and they draw pictures. They blow bubbles. Ethan teaches Oliver the

Pipa song his mom sang to him when he was little, while Cate plays the ukulele with an amateur hand and Oliver cries, "Again!" over and over.

Cate has so much fun she completely loses track of the time and soon Celeste and Grayson are back.

The next morning it is more of the same: Cate and Ethan engaged in activities with Oliver. It is their last day up-island and final sleepover.

"What should we do now?" Cate asks Oliver when they finish tidying up the toys.

"We did all my favowite sings," says Oliver. "Escept a hike up Cobble Hill. Want to go?"

"Are you sure?" asks Celeste, who is in the kitchen doing dishes. "Last time you said it was too hard and you could barely make it back down."

"Maybe we could just go up halfway?" Ethan suggests.

"Or we could go over to the ocean by where Grandma and Grandpa used to live and play at the park over there," Cate says.

"I pick what Gwamma wants," Oliver says and he runs to the foyer to put on his shoes.

Celeste plans a special dinner and they stop in at the store on the way home. Cate and Ethan dash into the liquor store beside the grocer for a special bottle of wine.

"Tan we light tandles?" asks Oliver as Celeste fetches her good linen tablecloth out of the hutch.

"That's a lovely idea, Oliver," Celeste says. "See if you can find some in the top drawer of the pantry."

Oliver opens every drawer and finds at least a dozen different candles. He sets them on the table in a zig-zag pattern and claps his hands.

When the dishes are cleared away, Celeste surprises Oliver with a cake hidden in the garage.

"A tate!" Oliver squeals in delight. "But it isn't even my birthday!"

"I know it's not anyone's birthday today," admits Celeste, "but since we won't get to see each other on our real birthdays, I thought today we could have a pretend one."

Oliver claps his hands as Celeste lights the candles on the cake and lets him try to blow them out. He devours his piece of cake in no time.

"Do you mind if I steal you away for a bit, Mom?" asks Celeste when dessert is done.

Cate is surprised and a little nervous by this unanticipated request. She senses a sticky feeling in the air, but she agrees. They go outside and walk around the block. The air is fresh, a beautiful calm night, but Cate's senses are heightened.

"Mom, I'm feeling really disappointed and sad," Celeste begins. "I told you back when you made the decision to move to Riyadh that I didn't want you to go, that I need you to be here to support me. To help me raise Oliver. I so wanted you to be a bigger part of his life, especially once I saw the deep bond you two created."

"I know," says Cate. "I grappled with the decision to go for those same reasons. But Ethan didn't get the job at Transport Canada, and this opportunity seemed like the best choice for us, for our future and our retirement."

"But what about family?" Celeste persists. "You always say your family is the most important thing to you, but this choice doesn't reflect that at all."

"I'm sorry you feel that way," says Cate. "I didn't think I had to choose between the two. I thought that with our three holidays a year and FaceTime connection, we could make it work."

Celeste tells her it isn't working for her. They both cry tears of grief, their hearts in deep pain. Celeste feels abandoned, but Cate doesn't know how to fix it. They vent their feelings, but nothing is resolved. They walk back in silence, a wall of pain between them.

They walk into the house, both trying to act like everything is okay, but they aren't fooling anyone.

"What's wong, Gwamma?" Oliver asks, fresh from his bath.

"Grandma's just sad because she's leaving in the morning," says Cate. Then Oliver starts to cry.

"No, don't go, Gwamma," he says through his tears. "Stay with me."

Cate's heart almost breaks in half. The guilt, grief, and family drama sit heavy. She wipes away Oliver's tears and tucks him into bed. She tells him she will be back again before he knows it and that they can talk on FaceTime every week, even though Celeste has told her she finds the FaceTime chats too difficult, that Oliver is too young to understand.

Before she goes to sleep, Cate tells Ethan about her exchange with Celeste.

"I must say, I'm surprised," Ethan says. A frown furrows his brow. "I mean, I know Celeste was upset when we left, that is to be expected, but to be mad at you, well, I just don't get it."

"I know, I think her anger hurts me the most," says Cate. "I can understand her being sad, but these heavy feelings are difficult for me to process. I think I'm going to take a few minutes to write in my journal."

> *I feel like a bowling ball landed on my chest. It hurts so much. I'm doing my best, but apparently my best isn't good enough. Worse than the shits. It is unacceptable, at least for Celeste.*
>
> *I never promised her I would be here to help raise Oliver. I would love that too. We all have to make tough decisions sometimes. This feels so foreign for me. Celeste has always been so supportive. I have valued the closeness of our relationship ever since she was born, back when it was just me and her against the world. And now, it feels like it is all falling apart.*

In the morning there are uncomfortable, awkward hugs goodbye. Oliver stands on the front porch and cries as Cate backs out of the driveway and Celeste looks stricken.

Cate shares more of her feelings with Ethan on the drive back to her mom's in Victoria, but her heart is still heavy when they arrive. As soon as she walks in the door to her mom's apartment, Donna knows something is wrong.

"Do you want to tell me what happened?" asks Donna.

"I'm sorry, Mom," says Cate, "but if you don't mind, I'd rather not talk about it right now."

Donna agrees, reluctantly. Cate does her best to stay present and enjoy her time with her mom. Donna's boyfriend, Jim, drives in from Sooke and they play a few rounds of bridge and snack on munchies for most of the afternoon. Donna is curious about their upcoming vacation in Panama, and Jim wants to know more about Saudi Arabia.

"Wow, can you believe how the time has flown?" asks Ethan, looking at his watch. "We'd better finish up this hand and get ready if we're going to make it on time for our dinner reservation."

After a quick tidy up, Cate and Ethan change for dinner. Ethan chooses light grey trousers with a navy button-down dress shirt, and Cate puts on her black and white polka-dot dress and black patent high heels.

"I didn't know we were going to gussy up," Jim says, looking down at his denim jeans and flannel shirt as Cate and Ethan emerge from their room.

"We aren't all getting dressed to the nines," says Donna, walking in to join them, wearing leggings and a tunic with bright coral Birkenstocks. "That's just Cate and Ethan's style."

The two couples walk in the calm, early evening breeze that is drifting in off the ocean waves. It is only a few blocks to the marina restaurant. They are shown to a table with an incredible view of the harbour. They take a few selfies on Ethan's phone and the waiter appears to take their order. Ethan chooses the Malbec Cate raved about the last time they were there.

The fresh seafood caught that day is transformed into heavenly dishes by the chef, and the four of them talk easily over a leisurely meal. Before long the moon is up and it is time for Jim to drive back to his place in Sooke.

"We best get ready for bed," Ethan says once they are back home. "Our flight out tomorrow morning leaves at six thirty."

Cate gives her mom a big hug goodnight before tucking into bed beside Ethan.

In the wee hours of the morning Cate and Ethan try to sneak out without bothering Donna, but she isn't about to let them leave without a final, teary goodbye.

"It was far too short a visit," Donna says as she hugs Cate in close.

"I know, Mom," says Cate. "But we'll be back soon enough at hajj, and in the meantime, we'll keep up with our weekly FaceTime chats."

"I love you, dearest daughter and son-in-love," Donna says as they wheel their luggage into the hall. "Have a safe journey, and give my love to Chloe."

Chapter 15

*T*HE TORONTO AIRPORT BUSTLES WITH
tourists who have arrived in throngs for the
Pan-American Games. The lineups for customs and
security are long and tedious, but eventually Ethan
and Cate collect their luggage and head outside the
terminal where the air is so humid, it's like breathing
the heavy, wet mist of a steam room.

Ethan flags a limo to take them to their Airbnb
on King Street. The owner of the loft meets them outside
the building. She gives them a thorough tour of her well-
appointed and tidy space. The sun pours in through floor-
to-ceiling windows on the south side, filling the space with
natural light. Cate knows that Chloe will love the sunshine,
not to mention the exposed brick walls and wood flooring.
She hopes the three of them will adjust to a routine that feels
nourishing and supportive. After the tour the owner has
them sign the necessary documents.

"Be sure to reach out if you need anything at all," she says as she departs.

Once they unpack their bags, Cate and Ethan walk to the grocery store they passed on the taxi ride over, just a few blocks away. They purchase the basics to assemble some easy breakfasts and snacks, coffee, creamer, and bottled water, but somehow end up with six bags to cart back. Mister Charming Pants grabs the four heaviest, leaving the two lightest for Cate.

When the groceries are put away, Cate feels too tired to make dinner and suggests Ethan reach out to Chloe to meet them for dinner at Terroni's, a restaurant on Queen Street that is a five-minute walk from them.

Cate and Ethan are shown to a table and are looking at menus when Chloe arrives.

"It's so good to see you!" they say, almost in unison. They get up to give Chloe hugs and Ethan pulls out a chair for her to join them. Chloe looks thin and pale.

"How have you been since we talked last week?" Ethan asks.

"Actually, I'm totally stressed about work," Chloe says without preamble. "I had a few panic attacks last week. Like, I was so embarrassed. But there is too much pressure with this hostess job. It triggers social anxiety for me. I don't know if I can do this."

"Slow down, take a deep breath," Ethan says in a soothing voice.

Chloe takes a moment to calm herself with a few breaths and then she continues.

"I'm sorry, but I've been feeling anxious and depressed for a few weeks. I'm really struggling. I'm sorry I didn't tell you before."

"It's okay, at least you're reaching out now," Cate says. She does her best not to react, she but wasn't prepared at all for this. Chloe seemed to be doing so well the last few times they spoke.

"Did you attend the free mental health group support meeting that I forwarded you?" asks Ethan.

"No," Chloe admits. "I haven't been in the space."

There is an awkward silence as they eat their meals. Cate finds herself unsure of what to say, feeling that old sense of walking on eggshells.

"We love you so much," says Cate. At least that much is true.

"And we'll support you," Ethan says. "You'll get through this, just as you've gotten through before, so don't give up."

Just then a clearer comes by to take their plates, oblivious that he is interrupting a serious conversation. Cate notices that Chloe's meal is only half finished.

"Has your waiter come by to offer you an after-dinner drink, dessert, or coffee?" the young man asks.

"Um, no actually," says Ethan.

"I will make sure he is fired immediately," he jokes.

"I would like a shot of Chambord," Chloe says as she laughs out loud at the waiter's cheeky comment. "I tried some at the hotel the other night and it's so good."

"Really?" says Cate. "I thought you decided alcohol wasn't a good choice for you."

"Yeah, well, I'm trying to lighten up, to not be so black and white about things," Chloe says.

Cate and Ethan decide to join her in an after-dinner drink. They order a cheese plate to share but Chloe abstains, having flip-flopped back to a vegan diet.

When they are out on the street, ready to part ways, Chloe bursts into tears.

"You just got here and I'm already anxious about you leaving for Panama next week," Chloe says. "I wish you could stay here. I miss not having the security of a home, of my parents."

"I know, it isn't enough time," Ethan says.

"But we promise to still FaceTime every week," adds Cate. "And we can plan more if you want."

Chloe sniffles and wipes at her eyes with the back of her sleeve.

"Let's just take it one day at a time and try to be present to the time we have together right now," says Ethan.

When they get back to the loft, Ethan doesn't have any energy left after the heaviness of the evening's conversation. Cate nestles her face into Ethan's chest and has a little cry before she kisses him goodnight. Ethan appears to fall asleep almost immediately, but Cate is unable to. She quietly gets out her journal and writes in the dim light of her bedside lamp.

> *I know Ethan and I are doing our best, but somehow it doesn't feel like enough. I've prayed and prayed for God to give me the strength and wisdom I need to support Chloe, but it feels like nothing ever sticks. Chloe keeps going around in circles. She will seem to make progress and exude enthusiasm one week, then take two steps backward and express hopelessness the next. Hell, sometimes in the course of one conversation. It breaks my heart that she continues to suffer from panic attacks. I had no idea. She keeps so much from us. I should have known*

*something was up when she asked if we could audio
only last time we chatted on FaceTime.*

*I don't have the answers and this isn't my
cupboard, but damn it's hard to be stuck on a sinking
ship when you can see the lifeboat bobbing up and
down in the distance.*

After breakfast the next day Ethan gets a text from Chloe.

"Can we take the ferry over to Toronto Island today?"

"Sounds great. Meet us here in an hour?"

Chloe arrives right on time. She looks much brighter
than she did the night before. Cate wonders if the time
with her and Ethan, unloading her feelings, helped. She
hopes so.

It is a bit of an ordeal of bus transfers and walking
blocks to get to the ferry terminal. Cate suffers from
inflammation and pain in her knees. She does her best
to keep up with the formidable Chloe, who walks as if her
life depends on the speed at which she travels.

They purchase tickets and bottled waters from a kiosk
and then join the long queue to wait for the ferry. It takes
almost an hour, but once they are on board Chloe leads
them to the railing to take in the spectacular views of the
city. Ethan takes the opportunity to snap a few selfies of
the three of them. The strong wind blows Chloe's and Cate's
hair into their eyes. Chloe, who never wears sunglasses,
squints into the bright sun.

Once they have disembarked from the ferry, Chloe
leads them on a tour of the island and they talk more about
her challenges.

"Another thing that makes my work so hard is my
manager," Chloe says. "I really don't like her. She doesn't

allow time for me to have a snack, even though we're supposed to get a break every four hours."

"That doesn't sound at all fair," Ethan says. "Perhaps you should have a conversation with her about it?"

Instead of addressing Ethan's suggestion, Chloe changes the subject.

"I tried an anti-anxiety medication last month," Chloe says.

"What?" says Cate. "I thought you were completely against medication. That's great news! How come you never mentioned anything to us?"

"Because I didn't want you and Dad to get all invested," says Chloe. "As it is, I went off it after a couple of weeks. I liked that it gave me more energy, but I felt like I was on speed."

Cate suspects Chloe only felt how people who don't have mental illness feel. She knows how impatient her daughter can be, and two weeks doesn't sound like enough time. She decides not to say anything.

"What does Maggie think of your choice?" asks Ethan. "I imagine it was her who suggested you try it?"

"No, it wasn't her. It was a psychiatrist Dr. Finlay recommended. I didn't like him either."

There doesn't seem like much more to say.

"I don't know about anybody else, but I'm ready for some lunch," Ethan says.

"We can always count on your dad's internal hunger clock," says Cate.

Chloe laughs along. They drop the heavy talk and walk over to a retro café where they eat their lunch in relative silence. When they are finished they walk along the beach. Soon it is time to catch the last ferry back to the city.

Cate and Ethan return to their rental and Chloe goes back to her apartment with plans to meet back up for dinner with Julianna in a few hours.

After a shower and a change of clothes Cate feels refreshed. Ethan calls them a taxi and they arrive at the posh restaurant in Yorkville where Julianna made dinner reservations. They wait outside the door until they see Julianna approaching. She looks sophisticated and glamourous, as usual. Heads turn in greeting; the manager kisses her bronzed cheek—Julianna seems to know everyone.

The server shows them to a prime table on the rooftop patio, surrounded by rich hipsters. They are just beginning to catch up when Chloe arrives. She is wearing her favourite leopard-spotted summer dress and she looks even better than she did that morning.

"My dear, don't you look stunning!" says Julianna, getting up from her seat to give Chloe a hug. "It has been too long since we got together."

"I know," Chloe says.

An evening of joyful companionship ensues. They order small plates to share and pair glasses of different champagne and wine selections with each dish.

"Have I mentioned to you the international women's conference I go to each year?" asks Julianna.

"Yes, I believe you did tell us it is being held in Chicago next month," says Cate. "It sounds very interesting."

"Excellent memory, my dear," says Julianna. "As it turns out, the Halifax Regional Women's Committee is also organizing an event for African Heritage Month in February that I want to attend too."

"Sounds like you're going to be busy travelling for the next few months," says Cate.

"Yes, but I almost wasn't going anywhere. I had such an ordeal with the airline, trying to use my e-upgrades to change from economy to business. It was such a run-around."

"Airlines can be such a pain," Cate says.

They end up in a heated conversation about the woes of modern-day travel and the lack of incentives from the airline membership plans, then onto deeper discussions on world issues. Julianna's animated stories have all four of them laughing, then crying, then laughing again. Julianna manages, it seems without effort, to distract Chloe from her difficulties.

"Well, folks, I hate to be the one to break up the party," announces Julianna, "but I think we must ask for the bill as I have an early conference call with a client tomorrow morning. I never imagined when I got into family law that I'd work such long hours."

"It's almost midnight as it is," Ethan says, looking at his watch. "As for the bill, this is our treat."

"You two are too generous," says Julianna. "Thank you so much. It was a wonderful evening."

Chloe has to work a lunch shift at the hotel the next day, so Cate and Ethan decide to head over to the gym. Ethan rocks a solid workout and Cate manages to stretch her tight muscles. When they get back and shower off, they take the opportunity for some intimate reconnection.

When she's done work, Chloe sends a text to Ethan.

"Can I come over?"

"Of course, see you soon."

Chloe arrives in a state of anxiety, the exact opposite of the night before. She looks like a racoon, her eyes black with smudged mascara.

"I can't do this anymore," Chloe says as she throws herself onto the couch. "I need more help."

"Can I make you a cup of tea?" asks Cate.

"Yes, please, a green tea or herbal if you have it," Chloe says, then continues to unload. "Maggie has been pushing me to start a new program. She wants you guys to come in a for a family meeting. I've been blowing her off, but I think I'm ready to give it a try, if you're willing."

"Of course, Chloe," Ethan says. "You know we're ready to do anything we can to help you and support you to be healthy."

Chloe sends Maggie a text and within hours Maggie replies, inviting them all for a family session at her clinic the next day. Chloe stays for supper and they play a few games of Catan.

"Is it okay if I sleep over?" asks Chloe, stretching out with a big yawn. "I don't feel like going back to my apartment."

"Sure, that's a great idea," says Cate. "There is a blow-up mattress and extra bedding in the hall closet."

The three of them have a lazy morning. Ethan makes a pot of coffee and reads the financial news while Cate journals and Chloe watches an old *Gilmore Girls* rerun on television. They have a late brunch of egg sandwiches and fruit and take turns sharing the single bathroom to get ready.

They have to catch a streetcar and transfer to the subway, then walk a few blocks to Maggie's clinic. It is located in a converted, old brick house just a few blocks from the subway station.

"Please take a seat," the receptionist says when they enter the waiting room.

Cate begins to leaf through a *Healthy Living* magazine when the receptionist calls over Ethan and passes him a stack of paperwork they both need to read and sign. Fifteen minutes go by.

"Maggie is ready to see you now," the receptionist says.

Chloe leads them to Maggie's office on the third floor.

"Hello, Cate and Ethan, I'm so glad you agreed to come," says Maggie as she shakes both their hands with a light grip. "I'm also really pleased that Chloe has decided to take this big step. Please, take a seat."

"Thank you," says Ethan as he sits down. "Chloe has said so many good things about how helpful it has been to work with you."

"Yes," agrees Cate. "And we're so proud of her for having the courage to try this program too."

"Well, speaking of the program, I'd like to begin with a short summary of DBT, which stands for dialectical behaviour therapy," says Maggie. "It's a cognitive-behavioural approach to wellness that focuses on developing skills and uses mindfulness to explore interpersonal relationships, distress tolerance, and emotional regulation. I have asked Chloe to commit to a treatment program that involves weekly group therapy as well as weekly sessions with me, for seven months." She pauses to flatten her skirt and push her glasses back up onto the bridge of her nose. "I must also insist you commit to join the parent support group, as it is an important part of the process," Maggie continues. "I know you live in Saudi Arabia, but you can join in on your first session this week and continue to be involved through Skype conferences."

It is a lot to take in, but Cate is thrilled.

"I'm absolutely willing to commit," says Ethan without hesitation. "Does this feel good for you, Cate?"

"Yes," says Cate, "I'm ready too."

The family meeting is held in a large open space in the basement of the clinic. There are fold-out chairs arranged in a circle. Cate and Ethan are the first to arrive. Maggie greets them at the door.

"I'm so thrilled to see you, come on in," says Maggie, shaking their hands. "I think it's going to make a huge difference for Chloe. Would you like a cup of coffee?"

Neither Cate nor Ethan is interested in drinking thin coffee from a Styrofoam cup. They take a seat and talk quietly together while the rest of the parents trickle in. Then it is time for the session to begin.

"Can everyone please introduce themselves and share a little of their story?" asks the group leader. "And if you're comfortable, I'd like it if you could tell us your goals for your loved one who is in treatment at the clinic."

Cate listens while other parents share their stories. One woman says her goal is for her son to stay on his medication. A father says his only hope is that his daughter doesn't try to take her life again. It is a sobering experience. When it is her turn, Cate's had time to reflect and knows what her goals are for Chloe.

"I want my daughter to learn healthy coping strategies to manage depression and anxiety, and body image and eating disorder challenges," says Cate. "I'm hopeful for a day in the future when she can pursue her dreams for an education and a life that feels fulfilling for her."

When the family meeting ends, there is a heavy emotional cloud over Ethan and Cate. Ethan opens up with Cate on the bus ride home.

"That meeting reminded me of an AA family support meeting I went to when my first wife was in rehab," Ethan says. "I feel like I should be feeling hopeful and uplifted, but I don't. I feel the huge weight of Chloe's challenges, and after listening to the other parents, it feels like there is one hell of a long road ahead of us."

"It was difficult," agrees Cate, "but at least Chloe is trying something. Maybe she's hit rock bottom and has the motivation she needs."

"I hope you're right," Ethan says with a sigh.

They hold hands in silence for the rest of the journey home.

Neither one of them has the energy for intimacy, but they are too wound up to sleep. Ethan cozies up with a blanket on the couch to watch the news, and Cate crawls into bed with her journal.

> *Back on the rollercoaster. I was dismayed to hear all in one sitting that Chloe tried and gave up on medication so quickly. I still feel strongly that she just hasn't found the right one, or the right dose or stayed with it long enough to give it a fair trial. I told her it wasn't any different than having diabetes, how my body doesn't make insulin so I have to inject it, but she insisted it isn't the same thing, that she should be able to do this on her own. That's one of the many things that sucks about having mental illness. The illness itself is self-sabotaging.*

*The very next day, she told us about this new
DBT program and that she wanted us to be involved.
That was the most surprising development yet. It felt
amazing to be included, but then Maggie told us that
the clinic considers parent involvement mandatory.
Still, she signed a contract for seven months. If she
sticks with it, that will be the longest she has stuck
with anything. I'm hopeful. I'm praying.*

Over the rest of their stay in Toronto, Cate and Ethan s
pend as much time with Chloe and Julianna as they can.
They take Chloe to Chapters to buy her some new books,
including a DBT workbook Cate finds in the psychology
section. They take long walks in High Park and Queen's Park
and encourage Chloe to join them for physical exercise
at the gym. They make healthy meals in the apartment and
play Catan.

On the last day before their departure, Cate and Ethan
meet up with Julianna and Chloe at the Art Gallery of
Ontario. Julianna and Chloe are both art buffs and they go
off together to explore the exhibits in depth. Later they meet
up at the gallery café for cappuccinos and dessert.

"I have to work tonight, and since you two are leaving
for Panama early tomorrow morning, I guess this is the last
time I'll see you," says Chloe.

"Yes, but don't worry, my dear," says Julianna, patting
Chloe's hand. "You and I are going to be much better about
getting together more often, isn't that right?"

"Yes, I would like that," says Chloe.

"We are both so grateful that you two have each other," says Cate. "Who would have imagined back in the days of preparing for the adoption that we'd become such good friends?"

"More like family," Ethan says. "And thanks to technology, we are always only a click away."

They say goodbye to Julianna, who heads to her car in the parkade down the street. Chloe walks with Cate and Ethan to the bus stop. They are heading off in different directions, so Chloe gives them big hugs goodbye.

"Thank you so much for your incredible support," says Chloe. "It means everything."

"It's all good," says Ethan.

"And I know you're going to rock this whole DBT gig," says Cate.

When they get back to the apartment, Cate and Ethan pack up their bags and climb into bed early. They have their alarms set for 4:00 a.m., ready for an 8:30 departure. Cate is ready to let go of the heaviness and relax into the flow and ease of vacation in Panama, just the two of them.

Chapter 16

ON THEIR AIR CANADA ROUGE flight from Toronto to Panama City, Cate and Ethan order wine and water and select the cheese plate and some chips from the on-board café, the only two gluten-free options available, then choose a documentary to view together on their iPad.

"That's how the guys with the big brains do things," Ethan says to Cate when the feature is over.

"This is how the guys with big hearts do things," replies Cate, pressing her hand to his chest.

"I'm so lucky you see me that way," Ethan says with a smile as he places his hand over Cate's.

The five-hour flight goes by quickly and soon they are over the city. They look out the window on Cate's side to see the sun's bright rays reflect off the ocean waves below. Farther on, skyscrapers nestled amongst a forest of dark green foliage come into view, seeming to reach out to greet them. Cate feels drawn to Panama's beauty before they've landed.

"I'm so excited," Cate says to Ethan as they disembark from the plane and walk across the hot, humid passageway into the tiny little airport. They breeze through customs and collect their baggage without incident.

Outside the arrivals area, they are unsure as to where to meet their driver. Then Cate spots a man holding up a sign with Ethan's name on it.

"Welcome to Panama. I'm Jack from Panama Transportation Services," Jack says, holding out his hand.

Jack helps them with their luggage and leads them to his car.

"If you don't mind me asking," says Cate, "where is your accent from?"

"I'm from the UK originally. I'm building a house near Coronado where you're staying. I just love it there."

Jack loads their things into his SUV and soon they are on the road. He takes them on the scenic route that confirms Cate's impression from the plane; it is a beautiful, modern, and clean city.

"This might sound strange," Cate says as they drive along the road that winds along the ocean, "but Panama City kind of reminds me of Miami."

"Funny you should say that," replies Jack. "It's often referred to as Mini-Miami."

Jack drives confidently over the Bridge of the Americas and shares with them other interesting facts about Panama.

"Panama is a great place to live for many reasons," Jack says. "There are good health care options, the infrastructure is decent, and you can get a private education for your kids for really cheap. The Panamanian people are so friendly and chill. One of the things I love is that the temperature hovers between 23°C and 33°C all year. After all the dark, drizzly cold weather in the UK, it's quite a lovely shift."

"That does sound nice," says Cate. "We're tired of the cold weather in Canada, and in Saudi Arabia it's too hot. The weather here sounds perfect."

Jack's description sounds wonderful, and Cate can't help but wonder if they haven't just stumbled upon their future retirement destination.

The drive through green hills, lush jungles, and valleys, past small towns and roadside fondas feels like a postcard for peacefulness to Cate. An hour and a half later, Jack arrives at the gate to Coronado. The sign reads, "*Coronado es vida!*" Jack informs the security guard he is taking them to Vista Bay, and he ushers them through.

They drive past Picasso's, a popular restaurant they read about online. There is a lively crowd. A little further on, Jack points to the right.

"There's Luna Rosa," Jack says, "You'll definitely want to check out the amazing Italian food there."

They pass a super-mini market on the corner and then they are at the security gate for the condominium building.

"We're guests of Ms. Barringer," Ethan informs from the back seat.

The security guard looks at his clipboard and seems satisfied.

"Ms. Barringer has been held up in the city on business, but she said her son will assist you," he says.

Jack pulls into the underground parkade and drops them off at the front entrance by the elevators. He shakes their hands with vigour and tells them to have a great time just as Ms. Barringer's son walks up.

"Hi there, I'm Ross," he says. "My mom says sorry she couldn't be here, she's caught up in traffic in the city."

Ross looks to Cate to be fifteen or so. He shows them to the elevator. Cate detects an unpleasant smell, of deodorizer trying to mask something else. She wonders if this is going to be another Airbnb dud but holds her tongue as Ross selects the twelfth floor.

Down the hall and to the right is their room. Ross opens the door to let Cate and Ethan in. He shows them where the information binder and welcome basket are on the kitchen table.

"Mom said to call her cell number if you need anything, it's in the binder," Ross says, then passes them a set of keys and disappears.

It is a bit stuffy, but bright with turquoise painted walls. It isn't a four-star, as advertised, but it's spacious and comfortable, not a dud after all. It doesn't smell, like in the elevator, but Cate opens up the sliding doors for some fresh air and steps out onto the balcony.

"Come check out the unusual sand," Cate calls out to Ethan as she leans over the rail.

"Yeah, I read somewhere that the black sand is volcanic ash," Ethan says as he steps out onto the balcony to join her. "I've never seen anything like it, but it's interesting, don't you think?

"Yes," Cate says, "and best of all, there are no vendors or panhandlers in sight, like there were in Tamarindo."

Cate and Ethan unpack their suitcases and look through the welcome binder, then decide to walk up the main road to Picasso's. It's as lively as it was when they drove by. They choose a table for two. The restaurant is outdoors, surrounded by villas and tropical trees. Cate can smell the ocean.

When the waitress brings them menus Cate orders a vegetarian green curry while Ethan chooses a pizza. After dinner they pay the bill and the waitress thanks them for their generous tip.

"There is live music tomorrow, I'm sure you'll want to come back to enjoy it," the waitress says.

Back at their condo they shower off the day and close the curtains of the master bedroom, which has a panoramic view. They pull back the cotton sheets on the king-size bed to fully reconnect before they fall asleep, hand in hand.

Cate wakes up to the sound of a parrot squawking, "Hola!" She can hear the ocean waves beat against the shore. The sun filters through the gauzy curtains. It takes her a few minutes to remember where she is, she's been in so many beds. She sighs with gratitude and reaches for Ethan's hand.

"Good morning, my love," Ethan says, already awake.

Ethan throws on a pair of shorts and goes into the kitchen to make coffee. Luckily Ms. Barringer left them a bag of local Duran, some powdered creamer, and a bottle of water, which is all they have in the fridge for now. They sit out on the balcony to enjoy the view. Cate gets out her journal.

> *Life is precious. I am precious. All is well in my world. Somehow along the way, inside all of the drama with my health, the earthquake, Chloe's challenges, and the big move, I lost my awareness of these truths.*
>
> *That is the past. The point of power is always in the present moment. I can choose to live in faith, to quiet the stories in my head. I can choose to love and approve of myself. I can choose to listen to and honour my body.*

My body speaks to me; she is tired, she needs to rest,
but I don't listen until I'm in a health crisis. I take
my body for granted. This body has nurtured three
beautiful beings inside her womb. This body has done
its best to work with insulin injections and medications
to manage diabetes and thyroid disease. This body
has survived the abuse of John, back when nothing
was ever enough. This body is working as hard as
it can to battle a Lyme invasion, the micro-spirochetes
driving into my cartilage like a corkscrew, but I still
criticize it, just like he used to do. I choose, right now,
to change. That isn't my story anymore. I choose to
surround myself with support, seen and unseen.

Cate puts down her journal. She feels a little lighter.

"If I'm hungry you must be famished," Cate says
to Ethan. "What do you say we take a walk over to that
super-mini on the corner and see what we can find?"

Ethan agrees and they walk over to the market. They
find bread for Ethan and some peanut butter, but the eggs
are stored on the shelf instead of in the refrigerator section
and Cate is skeptical, so they head to the cashier with their
scant basket.

"This market is clearly not going to do," Ethan says
as he unloads two bottles of water onto the counter. "I think
I better give one of the car rental companies listed in our
binder a call so we can drive into town."

As soon as they get back Ethan calls and arranges to
have a car dropped off later in the afternoon. Cate is grateful
she has some granola bars in her carry-on to tide her over.

Cate and Ethan leave their apartment to investigate the facilities in the building. They discover the rooftop pool and the gym, which have amazing views of the ocean and countryside. They decide to strip down to their swimsuits and lay out on two recliners by the pool to catch their first rays of tropical sun. The sweet sound of silence is broken when Ethan's phone buzzes.

"How is Panama?" texts Chloe.

"It's wonderful. And you?"

"Okay, I guess. Can we FaceTime?"

"We're at the pool, but we'll head inside and call you back in 15."

"That was Chloe," Ethan shares with Cate.

"I figured," says Cate. They pack up their things and head back to their condo to give Chloe a ring.

"I had my first group DBT meeting," Chloe says. "It was even harder than I expected. There's one girl in the group I kinda like, but the rest of them are all weird and make me feel uncomfortable."

"Congratulations," says Ethan, choosing to ignore her negative observations. "The first group was probably the hardest and it will be all downhill from now."

"We're so proud of you," says Cate. "Keep up the good work and check in with us as often as you want."

Chloe fills them in a bit more and after they hang up they're ready for some lunch. Cate suggests they take a quick shower and walk over to Luna Rosa, the restaurant that Jack recommended.

When they approach the restaurant, Ethan notices a sign out front, "*Abierto todos los días.*"

"My Spanish is limited," Ethan says, "but I think it means open every day."

"I guess we'll find out soon enough," Cate says. "Maybe we should consider some Spanish lessons down the road."

Just then a friendly looking woman, perhaps in her late fifties, opens the door and greets them.

"*Bienvenido a Luna Rosa*," she says with a smile, then leads them to a table for two by the window.

"This place is so beautiful," Cate says as she takes her seat. "I feel like I've been transported to Italy, and I've never even been there."

Wooden tables stained to a warm sheen are arranged in a cozy setting. There are mustard-yellow stucco walls and a circular ceiling with large beams. On the walls there are framed works of Italian artists and a huge map of Tuscany. Cans of Illy coffee line the back wall, bottles of wine are displayed in front. It smells like fresh tomatoes and basil, and Cate is in heaven.

When the waiter asks to take their order, Ethan requests two glasses of red wine. They order house salads and finish off with cups of frothy, creamy cappuccino.

"This could be one of the best cappuccinos I've ever tasted," raves Cate as she takes another sip. "I can hardly believe our good fortune, to be in a condo that's a stone's throw from this fabulous place."

Seth from the car rental company shows up with their vehicle several hours later than he agreed. Ethan fills in the paperwork. Seth mentions he has a friend in real estate who would be happy to show them some properties.

"Thanks for the offer, but this is our first time in Panama, we're just here for a vacation," says Ethan. Seth passes him a business card anyway.

As soon as Seth leaves, Cate and Ethan hop in the car, which turns out to be a bit of a clunker, and Ethan drives up to the town centre. They find a wine and deli store where Cate is pleasantly surprised by the variety and selection of wine, as well as gluten-free bean chips, manchego cheese, and chorizo.

Across the parking lot is an organic grocery store. Cate loads up their cart with fresh fruit, a whole pineapple, selling for only two dollars, and a bunch of bananas for even less. She discovers local lettuce, tomatoes, and cucumber, as well as organic, refrigerated eggs, butter, and coffee cream. Cate is almost dancing as they make their way to the cashier.

Their final pit stop is at the Movil store where Ethan purchases a SIM card for his phone at a crazy low price.

After a light dinner, Cate and Ethan tidy up together.

"I just remembered, our server told us there is a live band at Picasso's tonight," Ethan says as he washes the last plate.

Cate dries it and stacks it back in the cupboard.

"It sounds like fun to me. Do you want to go?" Cate asks.

Ethan doesn't typically get excited about amateur music, and he isn't one to dance, but he agrees. Cate spruces up a bit, putting on a white sundress with black and white wedge sandals and the silver hoop earrings Ethan gave her. Ethan irons a periwinkle blue linen shirt and wears it with his new white dress shorts and weave shoes.

Picasso's is packed, but they find a seat at the bar. They embrace the energy of the tropics and order two margaritas. They have a great time. The musicians are a talented group with enthusiasm to spare. They consume a few more drinks than is their normal. Cate tries to engage in conversation, almost yelling above the din, when there is a shift in the energy between them. They know it is time to go home.

They make love for the third time that day. Cate falls asleep thinking *I'm really, really liking it here.*

The next day Ethan heads up to the gym for a workout after breakfast, but Cate's Lyme's legs aren't up for it. Likely the margaritas, she thinks. Still, she doesn't regret it, they had such a wonderful time. She decides to take a dip in the pool on the main level, a stone's throw from the beach. The water is clear and cool. Cate swims from end to end with long, slow strokes. The feel of her body moving through water is therapeutic, supported, and peaceful. Cate focuses on her breath, the inhale and exhale.

After about twenty laps Cate is too tired to swim any longer. She rolls her towel out on a lounger and sunbathes. She is present to the energy of Panama, which to her feels even more tranquil than Vancouver Island.

In the afternoon Cate and Ethan head out in their squeaky-braked rental for a bit of an explore of the area. They drive up the main road and then make a turn by the international school. There doesn't seem to be much in the way of lots or houses for sale so they head back to the main road and turn left toward the golf course. There is a crazy mix of mansions and tear-downs, empty lots grown over with weeds and grass, and small, brightly coloured, Panamanian-style homes. Cate sees a house with pale yellow stucco and white and blue accents that catches her eye. She loves the rusty-orange clay roof tiles.

As they drive farther away from the main road it becomes more and more challenging, with massive potholes and crumbling asphalt, rocky gravel, and dead ends. Ethan is unable to proceed any farther, the car's belly scraping the ground.

"Well, living in this part of Coronado is definitely not going to be an option," says Cate.

"Who said anything about living here?" asks Ethan, a coy look in his eye.

Cate laughs at her blunder and tries to back-pedal, but it's all in fun.

Back at the condo Ethan and Cate put together some crackers and cheese and open a bottle of wine for happy hour. The sun is a little lower in the sky but it is still a beautiful day.

"Do you want to head down to the beach?" Cate asks after their snack.

"Sure, why not?" says Ethan.

They change into their swimsuits. Cate throws a candle and a lighter in her tote bag, along with her Goddess cards. They take the elevator to the lower level, with access to the beach just off the pool. They walk hand in hand along the black sand, like a sheet of midnight sky pulled down to the earth, the only two people on the entire beach. The sand is fine and soft under Cate's feet. The Pacific Ocean stretches out unobstructed in every direction. They spread their towels out adjacent to a craggy rock where the ocean waves beat. Ethan closes his eyes and Cate lights her candle. She sits in silent meditation and soon her breath and the ocean tide are in synchronicity. Cate gets out her journal.

*The tide is high, like the swell of my emotions.
Waves crash against the rocks with an intensity that
matches my passion. As the ocean ebbs and flows in
perfect rhythm, I think of my lover, how our bodies
move together in a similar perfect flow. So far, our time
together here in Panama has felt Divine, like a shrine
to love. I am overwhelmed with gratitude.*

The next day Ethan and Cate head off for an adventure to
Elle Valle. The road is winding, scenic, narrow. There are bus
shelters and fruit stands, ceramic shops, fondas, super-minis,
and simple Panamanian residences here and there amongst
the trees. Cate points out the views from both sides of the
road, of the lush green jungle and rolling red hills and
sweeping valleys.

Soon they are pulling onto a gravel road and Ethan spots
the sign for Casa de Lourdes. The building is surrounded by
green hills and dark forest, with a small meadow in front,
full of blue-petalled flowers in full bloom. The stone and
structure hint that the building is quite old, but it is well-
maintained. For Cate, it feels like a castle in a fairy tale.

"Who would have imagined such a place way up here,
in the jungle, in the middle of nowhere?" says Cate as she
walks along the cobbled path that lines the garden.

"It does feel rather spectacular," Ethan agrees.

Inside it is even more impressive. The foyer showcases
a grand piano with professional wedding photographs in
antique frames arranged on top. Wide arches line the wall
with French doors that lead out to the patio-style restaurant.
There is shallow pool with clear water and dark blue tiles,
the tables forming a semicircle around it. A hill rises up
from the pool, reaching with the trees to the sky.

The handsomely attired server shows Cate and Ethan to a table. They order a glass of Malbec and share an appetizer of melted cheese over roasted peppers and baby pickled onions.

"This reminds me of the salty, gooey fried cheese we had in Greece," says Cate.

"Ah, Greece," sighs Ethan. "Doesn't it feel like a lifetime ago?"

"It's true, so much has happened." Cate reaches out to place her hand on Ethan's. "It's been amazing, this Ramadan adventure. I loved all the connection with family, but this time with you here in Panama feels healing."

Cate devours the grilled scallops, while Ethan dives into the barbequed pork chops. They take some fun photos of one another. Ethan clowns around. He models his catwalk on the steps by the pool. They imagine Lourdes to be the perfect location for the wellness centre they dream of opening some day in the future.

After their long, leisurely dining experience, Ethan drives to the village of Elle Valle where there is an open-air market featuring artisan crafts and fresh fruits and vegetables. They walk amongst the stalls with rows of painted wooden frogs and woven Panama hats. Cate picks out some lettuce and fixings to make a salad and then it's time to make the drive back down the winding hill.

Cate wakes up to thunderstorms. Somehow even the storm feels welcoming to her.

"Since we can't enjoy the pool or the beach, what do you think about reaching out to that realtor Seth recommended?" Ethan asks.

"I think that's a great idea," says Cate. "I know it's crazy, we've only been here a few days, but somehow I can imagine us retiring here one day."

José picks them up an hour later under the awning just outside the front gates of their building. Cate sprints to the car, trying not to get soaked in the deluge.

"Wow, it's really coming down hard!" Cate says as she slides into the back seat. "Thanks for coming on such short notice, José, it's good to meet you."

Cate reaches across the seat and shakes hands. Ethan introduces himself and then José pulls out onto the road.

"The first place I'm going to show you is a modern condominium complex that is oceanside, just like the one you're in, only better," he says.

The show home is spectacular. It features open concept living and high-end interior design. There are several swimming pools and a golf course. Unfortunately, it has a big price tag too. Ethan tells José they would prefer a single-family home with their own yard, so he takes them to Azura. It isn't on the beach but in the countryside only five minutes from the Coronado town centre.

As soon as José drives through the gates, Cate falls in love with the beautifully landscaped community pool area. She skips across to the show home, which is pale yellow stucco. Inside, Cate discovers high ceilings and a huge, well-appointed kitchen with wood cupboards and granite counters. It is open concept too, with the living room adjacent to the kitchen, and patio doors leading out to a small backyard complete with a swimming pool. The workmanship is impeccable.

The builder comes in the front door and greets them warmly. They ask him a few questions and it is clear he knows his business. He gives them a few brochures to take with them and they return to the car, then José drops them back off at their condo.

After lunch they sit out on the balcony to crunch numbers. As they consider the situation, it becomes apparent that trying to run an investment property in Panama while living in Saudi Arabia would be more hassle than income.

The clouds begin to lift so they change into their swimsuits and head down to the beach.

Cate ventures into the ocean, but she's uncomfortable, not able to see what creatures and plants lurk under the murky water. She feels something slippery between her toes and lets out a little shriek.

"Are you okay?" Ethan says.

"Sorry," Cate says, "but something just slid through my toes."

"It was likely only some seaweed," Ethan laughs, then takes her gently by the hand and leads her out past the swell. The incoming tide rushes toward them and knocks Cate over, filling her nostrils with salty water.

"I'm ready to return to the safety of our towels," says Cate as she recovers her balance.

The next day Cate and Ethan pack up their things, ready to leave Coronado for the city. Jack picks them up right on time.

Ethan has made a reservation at the iconic American Trade Hotel in Casco Viejo. The old part of town is under reconstruction, with myriad one-ways and narrow roads.

Jack ends up going in circles, but Ethan saves the day, using the Waze App that Seth recommended, to direct Jack to the hotel.

"Thank you so much for picking us up," says Ethan, passing Jack his payment and a generous tip. "We really appreciated your positive spin and all the great advice."

"It was a pleasure to meet both of you," says Jack, shaking Ethan's hand. "I hope I'll see you back again sometime soon."

Cate walks through the entrance of the white stucco building into the air-conditioned lobby and onto a gleaming blue, black, and white mosaic tiled floor. The ceilings are crazy high and the decor is vintage classic. The friendly staff welcome them and the concierge at the desk checks them in. They take the old-fashioned elevator to their room.

They take a quick scan of their new digs while waiting for their luggage. It reminds Cate of the Fairmont in Banff, where high-end, ornate furnishings are crammed into a tiny space. There is a small, quaint balcony overlooking the park, elegantly framed by linen drapes.

When the porter arrives, Ethan tips him and thanks him in Spanish, "Gracias." They are both starving, so they put off unpacking to go down to the restaurant on the main floor.

The restaurant is bright and open, with beautiful chandelier lighting and huge plants in decorative pots throughout. The waitress greets them with a smile and leads them to a table near the window. They each order a glass of Malbec.

"This place is so amazing, I'm feeling like Cinderella again," says Cate. "Thank you so much for spoiling me like this, my love."

"It brings me so much joy to spoil you," says Ethan. "You deserve it, my dear."

Full and satisfied, Ethan and Cate head outside into the hot humidity and hail a taxi. They are going to the Balboa District to meet with the owner of a local forestry company that Ethan has been reading up on with the idea of perhaps investing.

By the end of an hour's conversation, both Cate and Ethan are on board, ready to commit to a sizable investment. They leave with the promise to be in touch soon.

They walk hand in hand along the boulevard, both of them aglow with excitement for their first investment together. The sun shines, the ocean glimmers, the pathway is luscious green, and Cate's heart skips to its happy beat.

Soon Cate's feet and legs are too tired to continue, so they take a taxi back to their hotel.

Cate takes a nap while Ethan googles restaurants nearby. He chooses a French restaurant in the old quarter that gets great reviews on Tripadvisor and is only a few blocks away. When Cate wakes, they freshen up and walk over.

The restaurant is located inside a converted museum. There isn't a single other guest and Cate feels certain it's not a good sign. An ancient looking man shuffles his way to show them to a table. The seats are uncomfortable and the worn red tablecloth has seen better days. Their meals lack imagination. Cate is disappointed but takes solace in Ethan's company.

After their lacklustre meal they walk along the water's edge under a moonlit sky back to their hotel. They fall blissfully asleep in a lover's embrace.

Cate and Ethan's day starts early. They grab a taxi and Ethan struggles to make himself understood in his rudimentary Spanish. Laughing, he finally gives up and uses Google

Translate to ask the driver to take them to the Panama Canal, to the Miraflores locks. The taxi driver takes them over the causeway and drops them off in the parking lot.

Once inside, they purchase tickets for the complete package, which includes a brief historical movie, museum tour, and viewing of the canal.

"The engineering and imagination for this project are mind-boggling," Cate says.

"I know," agrees Ethan, "I heard it was spectacular, but I never guessed it would be this impressive."

They press up to the railing to view the incoming ship, squished in by the crowd. The massive cargo ship soon comes into view. It inches along at a snail's pace and Ethan snaps a ton of photos.

"I'm so glad we chose to make this tour a priority," says Ethan, "but I'm starving."

"Me too," says Cate. "Let's head back to Casco Viejo for some lunch."

A few blocks away from the hotel they find VegeMoon. They hope this restaurant will fare better than the last.

There are old tiled floors, window boxes full of fresh flowers, and chandeliers designed from wine glasses. There is a different china teacup at each place setting.

Their waitress speaks little English and teases them for their lack of Spanish. They both order the pad Thai. The chef has created a novel interpretation featuring traditional rice noodles drenched in a peanut-based sauce that is so flavourful Cate decides she could drink it by the spoonful.

After lunch Cate and Ethan head out to explore the lively barrio. They walk through the bustling open market. Latino music blares. The energy is fun. They stop by the sea to take selfies, then it starts to pour rain and they dash for cover under the awning of a nearby building.

Twenty minutes later the torrential downpour comes to a sudden halt and they resume their stroll. On an impulse they purchase matching Panama hats. They pass the smelly fish market, the artisan shops and boutiques. They end the day at a rooftop bar where they eat a light meal and savour rich, complex red wine, while soaking in the views of the cityscape across the bay.

Before catching a taxi to the airport, they check out and indulge in one final romantic lunch in the hotel restaurant. There is a harpist playing modern covers in the lobby. They hold hands and savour the meal and one another until it is time to bid farewell to Panama.

On the drive to the airport, a limousine passes them accompanied by several policemen in a motorcade who have semi-automatic rifles strapped to their shoulders.

"What the heck is all that about?" wonders Cate out loud.

"There must be an important diplomat," explains the taxi driver.

At the airport Ethan gets their luggage checked through all the way to Riyadh and they breeze through security, then on to the Copa lounge to await boarding. They order a glass of wine and reminisce. Panama has been everything Cate was dreaming of, and more. With the reality of returning home, Cate's worries about Chloe resurface. She gets out her journal.

Hasta luego, Panama. I just met you, but you already feel like a dear friend. A safe place. A vibrant, happy space. I miss your tranquil energy already. I will carry this feeling of freedom inside of my heart.

When I get back to Riyadh, I resolve to focus on my own life and recommit to my letting go journey with my girls. My adult girls. It isn't appropriate for me to be so invested and attached to their choices. I will continue to support them and love them unconditionally.

I commit to love and support myself unconditionally too. And that means taking better care of myself, not eating so much rich food, drinking so much wine, and not getting enough sleep. It's been a crazy, beautiful, over-the-top five weeks, but I'm ready to go home and settle back into a healthy routine with my beloved.

Chapter 17

*B*ACK IN RIYADH IT IS quiet, peaceful, hot-as-an-oven in August, even at midnight. As promised, Ishmael pulls up to the terminal in the truck. He helps Ethan to hoist their luggage into the trunk.

The drive to the compound is quiet. Cate feels the melancholy that endings bring but looks forward to a return to flow and routine with Ethan.

In the morning Ethan and Cate drive over to pick up Fredrick from Lena's and then Ethan has to head into work. It is the first goodbye in ever so long. Cate holds him tight at the door and kisses him.

"I miss you already," Cate says.

"I know, we've been glued at the hip for five weeks and it feels strange, but I will be back soon enough," Ethan says.

"Mr. Realistic," Cate sighs. "But you're right, Ms. Slow-to-Transition just needs some time. I love you."

She kisses him again, then waves from the doorway until Ethan backs the truck out of the driveway and pulls out onto the road.

Alone, with only Fredrick for company, Cate feels heavy. She unpacks and throws a load of wash into her new machine. She is out walking Fredrick when the intercom at the corner suddenly blares.

"This is an announcement. There will be a test of the lockdown at nine hundred hours. There will be an alarm."

Fredrick freaks out and pulls on his leash to go home. Cate has a brief vision of a terrorist with a machine gun, but it vanishes as soon as it appears. Cate follows Fredrick's tug back home, where she folds clothes and cleans the cramped apartment.

She is on her hands and knees, scrubbing the tub, when she has a memory of Oliver scooping bubbles. She misses her grandson. Her phone buzzes, startling her from her reverie. She dries her hands and looks at the screen. It is Dana.

"Hi, Maman, can you talk for a bit?" asks Dana.

"Yeah sure, I'd love that," Cate answers. She abandons her task and flops onto the couch. "What's up?"

"I'm feeling kind of fed up with this city, with the stupid weather here," Dana begins. "I feel the urge to travel, and in fact I signed up to study yoga and Ayurveda at an ashram in India. The program starts in January."

"Wow, that's big news," says Cate. "I hope it will be a positive experience."

"Yeah, I'm jazzed. Now I just need to save up enough money."

Not more than an hour later, Cate is just getting back at her chores when her phone lights up again. It is Chloe. They exchange a few texts, but Cate feels drained, even within the sterile confines of text messages. It is just more of the same complaints without action. Cate attempts to practice the positive encouragement the parent group preaches. She writes phrases like, "I trust you'll come up with a solution," but it doesn't feel authentic.

Cate's frustration has her mind in a spin. Her heart beats too fast. She attempts a meditation but can't focus. She gets out her journal.

> *In the realm of my consciousness where I decide,*
> *I choose to manage my feelings around Dana's and*
> *Chloe's decisions with the tool of detachment.*

Cate stops to look at her vision board, a visual tribute of gratitude for everything and everyone she loves. She stares at the photo in the centre, of her and Ethan on their wedding day. She closes her eyes. The voices of fear and guilt continue to chatter inside her head.

"Hush," Cate says out loud. "I am safe. I am protected. My loved ones are safe and protected too." She picks up her journal and begins where she left off.

> *I feel worried about Dana's decision to uproot*
> *herself again. Something about this ashram feels fearful*
> *for me, but I can't put my finger on it. I can't tell if it's*
> *intuition or unfounded. I feel concerned about Chloe,*
> *exhausted by her ups and downs. I feel disappointed*
> *that Celeste rarely reaches out or answers my calls.*
> *This letting go gig is fucking hard.*

*I pray for a sign, for the wisdom of my intuition,
but all I hear is silence. Then, from out of nowhere,
I remember the letter from my eight-year-old self. From
the little girl who knew how precious she was. I can
see her in my mind, the embodiment of carefree joy.*

Cate smiles, gets up from her mat, and dances.

Cate participates in Joan's Thursday morning gentle hatha
yoga class every week. Joan's voice invokes peacefulness for
her, and the yoga practice feels supportive of her health goals.

One morning when class is over, Joan invites Cate
to walk up to Costa for coffee.

"One of the British gals on the compound is offering
belly dance classes," says Joan as she gives her green tea
a stir. "It sounds kind of fun. Would you like to try it
with me?"

"Belly dance?" says Cate. "Who would have thought,
here in Islamic centre of the world?" Cate pauses before
she answers. "What the heck? I'd love to."

Joan finds out that classes are being held in the mezzanine
of the sports complex and sends a text to Cate, "Meet you
out front at 6:45."

In the ten minutes it takes for Cate to walk from
her apartment to the complex she is drenched in sweat.
She takes a long sip of her water, which is already warm,
and plunks down on the cement steps to wait. Soon
Joan approaches.

"I love your outfit," Joan says as Cate stands up and
brushes the dust from the bottom of her bamboo capris.

"Thank you," says Cate. "I only wish I had an authentic belly dance costume, complete with a coin belt and bells."

"Now that would be a sight here in Saudi Arabia," Joan laughs.

The two women head inside and up the stairs. Cate has to stop every few steps to rest. They open the door to reveal a space that is bright and sunny. There are green foam mats on the floor. Cate thinks it would be a suitable enough space, if it weren't for the volleyball game going on in the court just below.

The instructor sets up her portable stereo and starts her CD. Shakira sets the tone while the instructor leads them in a hip rotation. Cate discovers her body responds to the movements as if they are a part of some long forgotten instinct, like she was born to move this way.

A few days go by, more of the same. Cate receives a text from Bonnie, one of the other new Canadians she has met at several get-togethers.

"I'm organizing a shopping trip, want to come along?"

"Sure, when and where?"

The next day Bonnie's driver pulls into Cate's driveway at nine o'clock and honks the horn.

"Hi," Cate says to Bonnie as she climbs into the back seat. Bonnie is pushing the dress code, wearing a coral-coloured abaya that looks more like a Japanese kimono. There is another woman Cate doesn't know in the seat beside her. She looks to be close to Celeste's age.

She is petite, with blue-black hair that hangs like skeins of silk to her shoulders. Cate guesses her to be of Japanese-Canadian heritage.

"This is Quinn's wife, Sophia," Bonnie says by way of introduction.

"I heard you two tied the knot over Ramadan and that you arrived last week," says Cate. "It's wonderful to meet you."

Along the way, Bonnie and Cate regale Sophia with stories of life in Riyadh. The traffic on Khurais Road is horrendous. All of a sudden, out of the corner of her eye, Cate sees a small white hatchback flying across four lanes of traffic directly toward them.

"Oh my God, watch out!" Cate yells to the driver.

It is too late. A semi-truck in the lane beside them clips the hatchback and sends it spinning out of control toward them, in what feels like slow motion. It crunches into the front passenger side. Bonnie's car goes from one hundred kilometres an hour to a standstill. The three women are dumbstruck for a few moments.

"What the fuck?" says Bonnie. She looks even more pale than usual, and her thin eyebrows are pulled into a deep scowl.

The driver mumbles an apology. Impatient passersby yell at them to move. The driver attempts to start the car, which has stalled, but it won't turn over.

"Is anybody hurt?" Bonnie asks.

"I'm fine," says Cate. "Just a little shook up."

"Me too," says Sophia. "Everything happened so fast, it doesn't quite feel real."

Cate thinks Sophia is more shook up than she admits; her chocolate milk–coloured eyes have lost the brightness they exuded moments before, and Sophia is drumming her tiny knuckles in a rhythm on her lap, a sure sign of anxiety.

It's 44°C outside and the car won't start. It's unbearable in minutes with no air-conditioning. Bonnie sends a text to her husband.

"I hope he's not in the air with a cadet," Bonnie says as they wait and the temperature in the car climbs.

Fortunately, Gabe is doing paperwork at his desk and texts back that he is on his way. The driver tries to sort things out with the policeman who has arrived at the scene. Soon Gabe drives up behind them. It takes a few hours to complete the paperwork and arrange for a tow truck, but in the meantime, the ladies have gotten out of the squashed vehicle and piled into Gabe's company car, the air conditioner on full blast.

When they arrive back to the compound, Bonnie insists on a selfie with Cate and Sophia in front of her scrunched truck, which has been towed to the compound auto shop. It was a harrowing experience, but they all are feeling lighter, mostly back to normal.

"Well, no one can say we didn't have an exciting adventure for Sophia's first day out," Bonnie says with a laugh.

A few days later Bonnie sends another text to Cate, "What do you think of an outing to the infamous souks?"

Cate is a little surprised that Bonnie is recovered and ready to face the insanity of traffic in Riyadh again but decides, what the heck, what else does she have to do with her time? Cate arranges for Ethan to carpool and books Ishmael to drive.

Joan and Sophia are keen to join in on the outing too. Ishmael picks up everyone at their villas and they head into the city centre. The skyscrapers glint in the bright Saudi sun despite the haze of dust.

As they enter the souks it is like they are transported to an entirely new world. Rows upon rows of old-fashioned stalls are sandwiched together amidst a squalor of people pressed up tight to one another. Ishmael drops them off at the main entrance and they file out of the car into the heat, then make their way to an office supply store. They all head off in different directions to explore the vast two-level, which feels to Cate like a Saudi version of a dollar store, a crazy mishmash of merchandise that doesn't seem to belong together, organized without an apparent system— not quite right, as Cate has become accustomed to saying.

On the way to the gold souk they have to pass by Chop Chop Square, where legends and rumours tell of cruel and inhumane punishment of criminals, from hangings to beheadings.

"This place gives me the creeps," says Joan. She shudders her round shoulders.

"It's hard to believe they still do that sort of thing," says Sophia. "I imagine it's a strong deterrent, though."

Cate gives a shiver. They all pick up their pace. Soon they are through the open-air square and in the gold souk. There must be over one hundred stalls. The same selection of gold jewelry seems to be for sale at each vendor. Cate wonders how anyone can make a living with the fierce competition. Bonnie finds the proprietor at stall 27 that was recommended to her and orders a gold necklace of her name in Arabic.

After a few hours in the chaos and heat everyone is ready to go home.

As part of their membership in the Canadian community of Riyadh, Ethan receives an invitation to attend the Red and White Ball.

"What do you think?" Ethan asks Cate one evening on their nightly stroll with Fredrick. "Does it sound like something you would like to do?"

"It does sound intriguing; I've never been to a ball before," admits Cate. "But I don't have a gown."

"I'm sure you can find one," Ethan says. "If you want to go, don't let that stop you."

"Well, it does sound like fun," says Cate with a smile. "Let's say yes."

"The invitation says we can invite two guests," Ethan says. "What do you think about asking Don and Peyton?"

"That's a fabulous idea," Cate says. "I'm already excited!"

Cate finds the perfect dress at Debenhams, a true-red, floor-length, organza gown that is gathered at the waist and compliments her curvy figure. It only needs a slight adjustment and the tailor on the compound is happy to make the alterations.

On the day of the big event Cate gets her hair styled at the salon on the compound. She dresses in her gown and fastens on the silver earrings she wore on her wedding day, then slips on gold, sling-back, high heels.

"You look absolutely beautiful," says Ethan. "Looks like I've got some work to do to catch up."

Ethan hops in the shower and dresses in his tuxedo, which fits his trim figure like a glove.

"Looks like someone caught up and passed me," Cate says with an attempt at a whistle.

When it's time to leave for the Diplomatic Quarter, Ishmael picks them up and then stops to pick up Don and Peyton at their villa. Don and Peyton climb into the truck, looking sophisticated and stylish as usual. The four of them get into a deep discussion on the way to the Canadian Embassy.

"I think human suffering is inevitable," says Don, "but we have a choice, through our actions and values, to transform suffering into sacrifice."

"That's an interesting point of view," Cate says. "I have a similar belief, that life's challenges are the sandpaper that smooth out our rough edges, to reveal the masterpiece God created us to become."

"It's all part of living our highest purpose," adds Ethan, "which is to love."

At the Diplomatic Quarter there is a group of army personnel dressed in fatigues with automatic rifles, who check their identification and then lift the gate for them to pass. Ishmael drops the two couples off at the entrance where there is a long line that stretches down the sidewalk.

"You can text me when you're ready to go home," Ishmael says. "I'll be waiting in the parking lot."

The lineup moves quickly and soon they are at the door where there is a security station.

"Please show your identification," says the guard.

They are ushered into a dimly lit corridor that to Cate feels like a prison cell. Another guard rifles through Cate's clutch, and a metal detector wand is waved across her body.

Minutes later they step across the threshold into a spectacular garden. Tall desert palms create a cool canopy over green-grassed lawns speckled with a variety of local flowers: pink and white Madagascar periwinkle, white oleander, and fuchsia desert catalpa. Festive, white, twinkly lights create a soft glow, draped in amongst the trees.

"Wow!" says Cate, her jaw dropping. "This place is absolutely gorgeous!"

A server in tails approaches and passes them each a flute of champagne.

"Is this the real deal?" Cate asks. She smiles and her eyes twinkle.

"This is it, Cinderella," Ethan says.

"Cinderella?" laughs Peyton. "I suppose it's fitting."

Ethan takes Cate by the elbow and leads her down the steps. Everywhere is a sea of red, white, and black gowns and tuxedos. Circular tables are covered in white and gold tablecloths, the chairs draped in linen covers. Buffet tables line the walls on each side of the garden.

"Please, everyone, take your seats," the MC says into the microphone. "We will open the buffet shortly. Over dinner there will be a slide show tribute to fallen Canadian war heroes and their families, the charity tonight's profits will support."

The buffet opens and Cate fills her plate with a delicious-looking assortment, then heads back to the table with Ethan.

When the slide show begins, everyone is silent. Cate feels tears form in the corners of her eyes and looks around; there isn't a dry eye in the house.

The servers have barely taken away the plates when the music begins. Cate is thrilled for the opportunity to dance. Ethan and Don decline, choosing to mingle with the other guests, but Peyton joins Cate and a group of women on the dance floor.

When the second set is finished, Cate and Peyton rejoin their husbands.

"Cinderella needs to kick off her slippers," Cate says to Ethan with a groan. "I think I might have overdone it."

"Shall I text Ishmael?" Ethan asks.

"Yes please, my prince," says Cate with a grin.

Cate wakes up the next day with a headache. Her feet ache too. She glances over. Ethan's spot is empty. She throws on her robe and hobbles out to the living room. Ethan is sitting on the couch beside Fredrick, a mug of coffee in hand.

"Good morning, how are you feeling today, my love?" Ethan asks.

"Like I've walked across the burning hot desert barefooted, uphill, there and back," Cate says with a laugh. "How about you?"

"My feet are all good, but I can't deny I popped a couple of Tylenols and glugged back a few glasses of water when I got up."

"I guess I better take Fredrick out," Cate says with a sigh.

"It's all taken care of, my love," says Ethan. "Why don't you grab a coffee and your journal and come join me?"

> *This Lyme disease is such a tease. Lying low, like a tiger ready to pounce. I was feeling so good the last few days, but of course I outdid myself last night and now I'm paying the price. My lead legs and bowling ball knees have burning feet to keep them company today. Even my arms feel tight, like two sticks of plywood dangling from my stiff shoulders. Oh well, the past is the past, what's done is done, but perhaps I will remember to calm it down a notch next time.*
>
> *The Red and White Ball really was a once-in-a-lifetime experience. I've never felt so much like a*

*princess in a fairy tale as I did last night, and I've
had some over-the-top thrills since I married Ethan.
I always enjoy connection with Don and Peyton. They
inspire me and remind me of the things that matter.*

*I'll get back into my healthy regime today and
hopefully, soon, I'll be back on track.*

"I'm dying to check out the Princess Nourah Women's
University," Bonnie says in a text a few days later. "Will
you come with me?"

"Sure, I can work on my blog while you chip away
at your dissertation," Cate replies.

Cate arranges for Ishmael to drive them. There is a
security gate, but Ishmael says something in Arabic and
points to Cate and Bonnie in the back seat and is waved
through.

The university campus is a transformation from the
desert sand and rubble, the noise and pollution of Riyadh.
Cate gawks out her window in wonder as they pass buildings
of intricate architecture set on lush green lawns. Palm trees
line the meridians and everything is pristine.

"Look, there's a monorail overhead," Bonnie says,
pointing to the right.

"I'm so glad I agreed to come," says Cate. "This place
is breathtaking."

Ishmael drops them off at the entrance to the library.
Cate feels safe, in a way she's never felt out and about in
the city. Bonnie leads them past the security. She signs them
in, flashing her Queen's University identification card.

"I can't resist pulling out my ID," admits Bonnie.
"It reminds me of my life back home."

They take an escalator to the next floor. There are ornate fountains and artifacts displayed in glass cases.

"It looks more like a museum than a library," Cate whispers.

Around the corner, Bonnie spots a Starbucks, bustling with young women. They are dressed casually, some with open abayas that reveal denim jeans and plaid shirts, no different than female students in Canada.

"This is so trippy," Cate whispers to Bonnie.

"I know, right?" Bonnie answers.

They find a table and set up their laptops and get started on their writing. Cate finds it difficult to concentrate with the noisy chatter and the uncomfortable seats, but somehow several hours fly by.

"Oh damn," says Bonnie, as she glances at her phone. "Look at the time, we're late to meet Ishmael."

Bonnie sends Ishmael a text that they are on their way, and they hustle to pack up their things.

Over the next few weeks, Cate and Ethan continue to flow in their routines. FaceTime chats are the usual mix of ups and downs with Chloe and Dana and steady calm with Taylor. Celeste rarely agrees to chats, but she does send updates now and again in emails or on Messenger.

Cate commits to her mindfulness practice. She reflects and observes in her journal.

> *I am reading Pema Chödrön's* When Things Fall Apart. *Ironic that it is a gift from Celeste. Pema contends that letting go of all limiting ideas is part of the path. She writes that when you feel fear you should feel lucky, as it is an opportunity to grow. I have a hard time with that. But if she is right, I must have achieved elephant-sized growth these past few months.*

I've been diligent with my health regime. I am rediscovering who I am, here in the desert, far away from the stress and demands of my girls, learning to trust my intuition. I listen to my body's messages. I love my body. I haven't indulged in a drop of alcohol since the ball, and I've been eating super nutritional meals, but I've taken it up a notch, showering myself daily with the same empathy and compassion I so easily give to others.

I feel present every day to the gift of Ethan's love, but I am also realizing that Ethan's love isn't the source of my healing. My love for myself is. He doesn't complete me, he complements me. I have to do my own work.

Bonnie organizes another off-compound adventure, this time to the Ishbilia coffee morning. She sends texts to Cate, Joan, and Sophia and they all meet up at the market to catch the company provided bus.

"Mind if I sit with you?" Cate asks Joan.

"Please do," Joan says. "This is exciting, I've never been to a coffee morning before."

"Me either," Cate confides. "I'm sure if it weren't for Bonnie I wouldn't have even known about it," Cate laughs.

Half an hour later, the bus pulls up to the gate of the compound. The security officer directs all the ladies to give him their Iqamas and take off their abayas to be left on the bus. Cate is surprised. She feels a little uncomfortable handing over her ID to a stranger, and it feels odd to be out and about in her normal attire.

"I hope that guy is legit," laughs Sophia, echoing Cate's fear. "Imagine if our Iqamas were stolen."

"Don't even go there," says Bonnie. "I've been to several coffee mornings here before, this is all normal."

Cate relaxes a bit and joins her friends as they make their way to the market square. It turns out to be a bustling centre of stalls with a wide variety of merchandise on offer, including jewelry, artifacts, clothing, and even Halloween and Christmas decorations.

"I'm in the market for a new abaya," says Cate. "The one I have was gifted to me when I arrived and it doesn't fit me properly."

"Oh, there's a super-talented seamstress who designs funky, well-made abayas just a few rows down from here," says Bonnie, always the one with the good info.

Cate follows Bonnie through the cramped rows of stalls. There is quite a large selection of abayas on display.

"What is your size?" asks a woman whom Cate presumes is the seamstress Bonnie had mentioned.

"I'm not sure, I'm not familiar with these sizes," says Cate as she looks at the tag on the neck of one of the abayas.

The woman looks Cate over and suggests a 52. After a few minutes Cate finds a black abaya with a red zippered front closure, red and white patterned trim, and pockets with the same trim as the hem. She slips it on.

"Wow, for an abaya, you're really rocking it," says Bonnie.

Joan, who is a few stalls over eyeing some Bedouin pieces of art, looks up.

"That does look great on you," Joan says. "A perfect fit."

"I love the pockets," Cate says, pushing her hands down into the them for emphasis. "How much?"

"This one is very special," says the seamstress. "Usually, I charge 500 riyals, but for you today, I give the good price, only 450."

Cate is happy to pay a good price and is delighted with her purchase. She joins her friends in perusing the other stalls and merchandise.

"Is anyone else ready for a coffee?" asks Sophia after an hour or so.

Everyone agrees they've had enough for one day and they walk over to the coffee shop. Cate plops her package on the floor and offers to treat her friends. She takes their orders and stands in the line.

"This is so lovely, spending time with you ladies," says Joan when Cate returns.

"We are a bit of an unusual group, when you consider the thirty-year age gap," says Cate, "and we seem to represent Canada's multicultural diversity too."

"I love the connection we're creating," says Bonnie. "It feels special."

"I was wondering," says Joan. "Would any of you be interested in creating a tribe? We could get together, maybe every week, to connect in meaningful sisterhood?"

"I'm intrigued," says Sophia.

The four ladies all agree it sounds like a great idea and hash out the details, sharing their thoughts on what a tribe of sisterhood might look like, until it is time to pack up and head back to the bus and home to the compound.

December arrives, Christmas just around the corner. It feels a little strange in Saudi Arabia, but Cate attends the compound events with Ethan. They meet up with Joan and Gareth, when the metal Christmas tree in town square is lit up and Santa comes to town on a tricycle. They go to the Christmas Bazaar, set up in the Al-Shaheen parking lot.

A few days before Christmas, Ethan comes home from work with the news that the academy has granted an extra day off work.

"Since we have a three-day weekend," says Ethan, "what do you think of driving to Bahrain to celebrate a romantic Christmas, just the two of us?"

"I think that sounds wonderful!" agrees Cate. "I'll see if Lena is available to look after Fredrick."

Lena agrees to take Fredrick for the Christmas holiday. Ethan and Cate google accommodations and find a good deal at the Meridian Hotel. When Ethan gets home from work, they pack their bags and load up the truck, drop off Fredrick, and are on their way.

Cate and Ethan head east on a three-lane highway. Ethan barrels along at the posted speed of 120 kilometres an hour. Cate looks out the window at the desert, dotted with black Bedouin tents and herds of camels.

"Have we passed the city limits yet?" Cate asks.

"I'm not sure," Ethan answers. "The city limits are nebulous."

"Nebulous?" replies Cate. "Hello, Mister Vocabulary," she laughs.

The sandy landscape transforms from beige to burnt orange, with tufts of pale green tumbleweeds here and there. They pass car carcasses, a solitary caterpillar tractor, and an abandoned Ferris wheel. Cate smells the salty air before she spots the steel-blue waters of the Persian Gulf.

"We're almost there now," says Ethan as he merges onto the bridge that crosses the water and connects to the tiny island of Bahrain.

There are five toll and customs booths to pass through. At the last stop there is a cheeky agent.

"Do you have any other wives?" the officer asks as he looks through Cate and Ethan's documents.

"Ah, no, I don't, just one," Ethan says.

"One with a pretty face is enough," the officer continues. "Me, I have three wives. I sleep well on Monday, Tuesday, and Wednesday." He laughs and waves them on.

They get a little lost with the unclear signage, but soon Ethan finds the hotel.

Inside the Meridian, it is festive. There is a twenty-foot Christmas tree in the lobby. The concierge welcomes them and offers them an upgrade to a club room for a small fee.

"I don't know if I'm more exhausted or hungry," Cate says.

"I can make you a reservation at the hotel restaurant," the concierge says, "and your luggage will be waiting for you in your room when you are finished."

Cate and Ethan thank her and make their way to the restaurant. After their meal they return to their room where their luggage is stowed by the door, as promised.

"I'm too tired to unpack tonight," says Cate. "Do you mind if we wait until the morning?"

Ethan agrees. They find their toiletry cases and give their teeth a quick brush, then crawl into bed. Cate reaches out to hold Ethan's hand, but finds something else instead. One thing leads to another. Apparently, they aren't that tired after all.

The next day, Cate and Ethan have reservations for the hotel's infamous Christmas brunch buffet. Cate puts on her favourite navy dress with her sexy wedding heels, and Ethan chooses his suit trousers and long-sleeve navy and white pinstriped shirt, minus the tie. They make a handsome couple as they exit the elevator.

There is a massive display in the lobby of tables laden with truffles, puddings, cakes, pies, and a chocolate fountain.

Cate makes a mental note to save room for dessert. The host, who has an elf hat perched merrily on his head, smiles and greets them with a "Merry Christmas," then leads them to their table.

"This is incredible," says Cate as she looks around at the huge buffet. There is a duet performing Christmas carols in the centre of the room.

"Would Madam like a glass of champagne to begin?" the host asks as he pulls out Cate's chair for her.

"We'd love a glass," Cate and Ethan answer at the same time.

Their server returns moments later with two glasses of champagne.

"To gratitude," says Cate, "for all this abundance."

"To enjoying it with the love of my life," counters Mr. One-ups.

The buffet is enormous, with all the traditional fixings as well as not-so-traditional fare like sushi and seafood. Santa Claus arrives, a comical sight with black hair sticking out from under his untidy white wig, but no one seems to mind. Cate and Ethan wine and dine and enjoy one another's conversation for three hours.

"That was over the top," says Cate, giving her tummy a rub.

"It was perfect," says Ethan. "But I think some rest and rejuvenation in our room is in order."

The next day, Cate receives a text from Joan, who is also in Bahrain for Christmas with her husband, Gareth.

"Would you two lovebirds like to meet up for a tour of the El Fateh Grand Mosque?"

Ethan thinks a tour of a mosque sounds interesting, so they make plans to meet in the parking lot later that morning.

It is Cate's first time setting foot in a mosque. She's a little nervous. She pulls her scarf closer around her face and adjusts her abaya.

At the entrance there is a large reception area where they are greeted by an imam.

"Welcome to our holy place of worship," the imam says with a smile. "I will be conducting your tour today, and please, feel free to ask any questions."

The imam leads them through the stunning structure, designed in an intricate configuration of shapes.

"The walls are covered in a local tile that keeps the building cool during our hot summers," the imam tells them. He shows them to a spiral staircase that leads to the viewing gallery. The stained glass windows are handsomely ornate.

"How does it work to fast at Ramadan if you're diabetic?" asks Cate.

"It is simple," replies the imam. "If you need to eat for your health, you eat. With Islam, it is easy, you just set your mind to it. You need only remember; there is only one God. And also, to engage in your five daily prayers."

It doesn't sound easy at all to Cate, but she keeps her thoughts to herself. Soon the call to prayer begins. They thank the imam for his time and head back to their cars.

On Christmas morning Cate produces stockings, which she had hidden in her suitcase.

"It's just like you to be so thoughtful," says Ethan. He reaches into his stocking to discover a Lindt sea-salt chocolate bar, some hand lotion, and a pair of socks.

Cate's phone lights up.

"Merry Christmas!" Celeste texts. "Do you want to FaceTime?"

Cate is thrilled and calls right back on the laptop. Oliver's sweetness tugs at her heart, but even though she misses him like crazy, misses all of her family, all she can feel is pure joy and bliss.

Cate and Ethan drive back to their compound later that day. They pick up Fredrick from Lena's. When Ethan brings in their luggage, he notices there is a letter in the mailbox.

"It's from the accommodation manager," Ethan announces. He opens the envelope and reads the letter, then lets out a cheer. "We've been assigned a villa and can collect the keys in five days!"

"This is the best Christmas gift of all!" exclaims Cate. "I can hardly wait!" She takes Ethan by the hand and twirls herself around, then kisses him full on the mouth.

Before she climbs into bed, Cate writes her last journal entry of the year.

> *A new year is about to begin, full of possibilities. We are moving out of our tiny, cramped apartment and into a three-bedroom villa with an office and a huge kitchen.*
>
> *My heart calls me to love myself and to nurture my love and partnership with Ethan. I feel ready to accept the relationships with all my children as they are, without judgment. I choose to cherish whatever*

opportunities I have to connect with Oliver and not worry about whether it's enough.

My friendships with Joan, Bonnie, and Sophia are blossoming into something beautiful I've never had before. I'm creating strong spiritual and emotional connections with women. I didn't realize until I had it what I was missing. I'm so excited to begin our tribe.

My heart calls me, to let go of the ties that bind and the fear that controls. To find my courage and strengthen my faith. To manifest my dreams into reality. I release all limiting ideas, beliefs, emotions, and patterns that create unwellness for me. I embrace, again, the healing.

Chapter 18

ON MOVE-IN DAY, CATE WAKES up early, ready to get at it.

"Are you awake?" Cate asks as she strokes Ethan's shoulder.

"I am, but I was hoping to get back to sleep," Ethan says with a sigh. "It was only four thirty when I last checked my phone."

"I know, it's crazy to get up so early on your day off," admits Cate. "But there is so much to do, my mind is racing. I'll go put on some coffee and take Fredrick out."

Cate checks her weather app. It is twelve degrees with an expected high of nineteen. She throws on a pair of old jeans and a wraparound blouse, the closest she has to scrubs.

When Cate gets back from her walk, Ethan is in the shower. He walks out, clad in a towel. Cate is enticed, but she is too distracted to follow through. *Perhaps later, when the move-in is complete,* she thinks to herself.

The men Ethan hired show up at nine, ready to work. Cate and Ethan have already boxed up several containers and loaded them into the truck.

At their new villa, Cate washes out kitchen cupboards while Ethan unloads boxes. Two of the workers paint the living room in the cool white Cate and Ethan purchased at Jotun just days before. Another team of men assemble the second-hand pergola they scooped for a good price on the compound Facebook page.

"Thank you for working so hard to get this kitchen shipshape," Ethan says, peeking his head around the corner.

"Ditto to you, for doing everything that needs elbow grease," Cate says. She gets up off her knees and wipes her hands on a towel, then gives Ethan a kiss.

They work hard all day but they aren't finished by the time the workers are ready to go. Ethan negotiates for them to return for a few hours the next day to paint the spare room bright yellow, the colour Cate chose to convert the second spare room into a yoga studio.

By late afternoon Saturday the bulk of their tasks is complete. Cate feels as though their new space is already becoming a home and she is thrilled.

The next weekend during their FaceTime chat with Chloe, she surprises them.

"I'd like to come to Riyadh to visit for a few weeks," Chloe says. "What do you think?"

"Uh, well, that's a great idea," stumbles Cate. "I'm a bit surprised, though, after you said at Christmas you couldn't get that much time off work."

"I know," says Chloe, "but I ended up regretting that decision. I wish I could learn to take yours and Dad's advice, but I never do."

"I don't know about never," says Ethan. "But if you think you can get time off, we would love to have you come. There is a ton of paperwork to be completed for a visit visa, so if you're serious, you better get started in on it right away."

"Can you send me the link for the website that lists all the documents I need?" asks Chloe.

"Absolutely," agrees Ethan. "And Cate and I will look into flights."

Chloe receives her visit visa in the mail just one day before her flight, in the eleventh hour.

Cate and Ethan can barely contain their excitement on the way to the airport to pick up Chloe. Cate chatters non-stop about all the things she wants them to get up to, and Ethan smiles ear to ear.

Chloe emerges from the sea of passengers who stream out of the arrivals area. She looks like a little bird, fallen from its nest. Cate's protectiveness is triggered. She picks up her pace.

"Hey, you made it!" Cate says.

"It's so good to see you two," Chloe says, visibly exhausted.

"Here, let me take that," Ethan says as he lifts the huge black travel bag off Chloe's thin shoulders. They exchange three-way hugs and then Chloe starts in with stories of her seventeen-hour flight, direct from Toronto.

"I managed to sleep most of the way," Chloe concedes, "but I don't think I've ever been so thirsty in my life. They're very frugal with their water service on Saudia."

"I know from our experience flying with them," Cate agrees.

"But you only have to ask and they are happy to bring you a bottle, even if they aren't offering service," Ethan says.

Out in the parkade, Ethan tosses Chloe's bag in the back of the truck and they are on their way to the compound.

"It feels like time has stood still," Chloe says as she looks out the window. "It hasn't changed a bit since I was here. When was that, Papa?"

"Hmm, let me think," Ethan says. He squints his eyes and looks to the heavens for insight. "That must have been back in 2010."

"I'm sure you'll find things have actually changed quite a bit," says Cate. "It's become more progressive just in the time I've been here."

At the villa Chloe goes crazy when she sees Fredrick. She picks him up and snuggles him, then hauls him in her arms up to the guest room.

Cate and Ethan finish preparations for dinner. Cate has a salad ready in the fridge and a salmon fillet dressed and ready for the oven. Ethan sets the table, just when Chloe steps into the kitchen.

"This is so thoughtful of you," says Chloe, "but I'm honestly too tired to eat. I just came down to say goodnight."

"Okay, Sweetie," says Cate, setting down the salad tongs to give Chloe a hug. "I hope you sleep well."

"Here's a bottle of water," Ethan says, kissing Chloe on top of her head. "You need to rehydrate."

Ethan has to work the early shift the next morning. Cate gets up with him, but Chloe stays in bed. It is almost noon when she makes an appearance.

"Good morning, sleepyhead," Cate says when Chloe appears. She is wearing flannel pajama bottoms and a wrinkled white T-shirt. "Or should I say good afternoon?"

"I know, I can hardly believe I slept so long. The jet lag really wiped me out," says Chloe. "But now I'm starved."

"There are leftovers from last night in the fridge," Cate says, as she folds up the last of a load of laundry.

"I'm not eating fish anymore," says Chloe. "I feel like my body can't digest animal protein, it makes me feel bloated."

"Oh, sorry, I thought you loved salmon. Would you like the salad, then?" asks Cate. "Or some toast?"

Chloe fills a plate with the salad and plunks down in front of the television.

By the time Ethan returns from work Cate is already stressed out by Chloe, who loafed around on the couch all day, reading or watching old movies. Cate couldn't even convince her to join her and Fredrick for a walk.

"I brought flowers for my two favourite girls," Ethan says when he comes in the door.

"That is so sweet," says Cate. She gives Ethan a kiss and takes the flowers to put them in a vase of fresh water.

"Thank you, Papa," says Chloe. But she doesn't bother to get up off the couch, where she is fully reclined, still in her pajamas and her nose in a book.

Chloe gets over jet lag after a few days and has a little more energy.

Cate and Chloe develop a routine of sorts while Ethan is at work. They take Fredrick for a walk after breakfast, read for a while, and then go to the gym before lunch.

In the afternoon Cate works on a new blog and completes household chores while Chloe reads some more. When the sun is at its warmest, midday, they sit outside under the pergola and play crib or get into deep discussions.

"I don't feel like you love me like a true mother," Chloe blurts out one afternoon.

Cate doesn't know how to respond, she is stunned into momentary silence. Her heart constricts.

"I don't know what you mean," Cate says. "I'm sure I love you differently than I love my biological kids. After all, I didn't meet you until you were seventeen. But I love you wholly and completely, with all of my heart."

"I guess I just imagined it would be different," says Chloe. "It's nobody's fault."

The next morning, Cate decides to ditch going to the gym with Chloe and stay home. She gets out her journal.

> *Wow. I feel so hurt. I can hardly believe Chloe said she feels like I don't love her like a true mother. That really stings. I love her so much. I've given her so much. All of me.*
>
> *Celeste and Dana have expressed similar feelings to me in the past. They've claimed I don't love them like a mother should. They have this notion that when you become a mother you turn into some kind of super-human, with no needs of your own. No faults. But what do they know of mothering? Mothers are just people, like everyone else, with the same challenges. I have sacrificed so much of my own needs in my desire to be a good mother and I'm tired of "should."*
>
> *All three of my girls expect so much. Often, it would seem, what I have to give isn't enough for them.*

On Thursday evening after dinner, Chloe gets out their favourite board game, Catan. It is the weekend, and Ethan doesn't have to get up so early.

After the first game, which Chloe wins by a landslide, Cate gets up to put together a bowl of nuts and chocolate chips to munch on and refills everyone's water.

"What do you think about going on an adventure to the Edge of the World tomorrow?" Ethan asks. "Gareth and Joan are going, and they invited us to come along."

"Haven't we been there already?" Chloe asks.

"Yes, we did go once," says Ethan. "But that was a long time ago and Cate has never been."

"That does sound fun," Cate pipes in as she sets the bowl down in the middle of the table. "We can pack a picnic lunch, and Fredrick will love the chance to explore in the desert sand."

In the morning Cate makes egg salad sandwiches and cuts up raw vegetables. She selects some apples and takes a loaf of her own homemade, gluten-free banana bread from the freezer, then loads up the cooler with napkins and paper plates and several bottles of water. Chloe strolls into the kitchen in her pajamas at eight thirty.

"We told Gareth we'd meet them at their villa at nine," Cate says. "Are you going to be ready in time?"

"Yeah, don't worry," Chloe says with a sigh. "It will only take me a minute to change and I'll just have some spinach before we go."

"Okay, we'll be pulling out at eight fifty-five sharp," Cate says. She has to bite her tongue. She rounds up a blanket for them to sit on during their picnic and throws Fredrick's things into the truck.

Ethan follows Gareth and Joan past wadis, small towns, and date farms, but mostly there is only desert stretching as far as you can see in all directions.

At a pile of old worn out and discarded tires, Gareth turns off the highway and into the desert. The truck shakes like a washing machine crammed too full with clothes. They encounter a herd of camels and Ethan stops the truck to take a few photos with the good camera.

"Are we almost there yet?" Chloe grumbles from the back seat.

"Almost," Ethan sighs.

They drive a bit farther and soon they round a bend. The spectacular sight of the massive sand columns looms before them.

"Wow," says Cate. "I never imagined anything so epic!"

"It is impressive," Ethan agrees.

Everyone files out of the truck. Fredrick scampers ahead, his nose to the ground. Cate is fearful to walk to the edge and nervous about Fredrick too. She hooks him back on his leash and plonks herself down beside Joan on a large boulder with a good view, while Ethan and Gareth venture on to investigate the tallest of the two towers. Chloe hangs back.

"Chloe seems very pensive," says Joan. "Is she always so quiet?"

"No, not always," says Cate. "But she is a huge introvert at the best of times. I think something is bothering her, but she hasn't confided in me."

"I still remember, and not all that fondly, when my girls were teenagers," says Joan. "And they're in their late thirties."

Cate takes comfort in the support of her friend. Soon Chloe, glued to her phone, returns. She sits down beside Cate and gives Fredrick a pat.

"Is it time for lunch yet?" Chloe asks. "I'm starving."

"We'll find a good spot once the boys get back," Joan says.

Gareth chooses a slightly shady spot under a rather forlorn excuse for a tree, and they unload their food hampers onto the blanket. Chloe picks at her food. Her sandwich and banana bread remain uneaten. She crunches on some vegetables and an apple and remains withdrawn throughout the lunch conversation.

On the drive home Chloe falls asleep and Cate and Ethan talk quietly.

"I'm worried about Chloe," admits Cate. "Since her DBT program wrapped up she hasn't been going for counselling and I feel like she's in a backslide."

"I agree," sighs Ethan. "It's clear she still struggles with food. I think we should have a conversation with her before she goes. Maybe she will consider more intensive treatment."

The next day when the three of them are out with Fredrick, Ethan broaches the subject.

"It's been so wonderful having you here with us," Ethan begins. "But living under the same roof, Cate and I have noticed you are seriously restricting your food."

"I'm not restricting," Chloe says. "Are you two freaking out just because I don't eat chocolate every day like you?"

"No, that's not it," Ethan says.

"And I wouldn't say we're freaking out," says Cate. "We're concerned. We want to support you to be healthier. We'd like to offer you the opportunity to go for intensive residential treatment, if you're ready."

"I can't believe you're even suggesting that," says Chloe. "You said yourselves, I made so much progress with DBT." She stops in her tracks and tears burst forth in a flood.

"I know," says Ethan trying to gather her in a hug, but Chloe pushes away. Ethan's hands fall by his sides. "And we stand by that, but I don't think you've had success with your eating challenges."

"That's so hurtful," whimpers Chloe. "I'm proud of my commitment to eating healthy. And there's no way I'll eat the hospital food they serve in those programs."

Chloe spirals into an emotional meltdown. She asks Cate for the keys and walks at a fast pace ahead of them.

When Cate and Ethan get back to the villa Chloe is in her room with the door closed.

"That didn't go well," Cate says with a sigh.

"No, she's clearly not in a frame of mind to accept help," Ethan agrees.

Cate and Ethan process their feelings together, but Cate has a huge knot in her chest, constricting her breathing and threatening to tighten further.

"I'm going to my yoga room to meditate," says Cate. She gives Ethan a kiss. "I'll be back down shortly and we'll make lunch together.

The yoga room is Cate's sacred space. She has a colourful hand-painted chest draped in silk scarves under the window. Her vision board leans against the wall, in the centre of the chest, surrounded by crystals and candles. Cate takes a seat. From the tray next to her cushion, she chooses a smooth turquoise stone to hold in her hand, then closes her eyes.

After ten minutes of deep breathing Cate feels more relaxed. She gets out her journal and moves to the chair in the corner to write.

*It is so fucking hard to live with someone who is
mentally unwell. I try to be supportive, but Chloe feels
offended and judged. It doesn't feel right not to say
anything, when it's clear she has a serious eating
disorder. Her obsession over her food choices and
her belief that everything, except spinach and sweet
potatoes, is unhealthy and fattening is so frustrating.
It's like she is unable to think rationally about food.
She denies herself nourishment and is constantly
hungry and fatigued. She said her hair is falling out,
and I can see it has thinned. That has to be related,
but she says its hormones. Being open and honest with
her hasn't helped. Instead, things are worse. I hope
we can move past this and enjoy this next week of her
visit. This whole situation really sucks.*

Cate comes downstairs to find Chloe has joined Ethan
in the living room.

"Anyone up for a game of Catan after lunch?" Cate asks.

"No thanks," says Chloe. "I want to read my book."

Over lunch everyone acts as though nothing has
happened, but the silence is almost as painful as the tears.

Over the rest of the week it continues much the same.
Chloe comes around a little, but there are no more deep
discussions or lively games. On the weekend Ethan drives
them to the Diplomatic Quarter for a change of pace, but
Fredrick seems the only one who enjoys the walk around
the park.

It is with mixed feelings that Cate says goodbye to her
daughter. At the airport she holds her in a deep embrace.

"Send us a text when you get home," Ethan says. He gives Chloe a big hug and kisses the top of her head. "And remember to ask for extra water this time."

"I will," Chloe says. "I love you."

Cate and Ethan watch until Chloe disappears from their sight behind the other side of the glass partition. On the walk back to the car, Cate feels a lump in her throat, but already she feels lighter. It has been so heavy, carrying the weight of Chloe's illness on her shoulders 24/7.

A week goes by and Cate feels a little lighter every day. She challenges herself with yoga and belly dance and creates a deep connection with her new friends.

Cate is working in the office, organizing some files, when she takes a break to log into her email. There is a message in her inbox from Chloe's boyfriend, Rick. In the subject line there are two words: "Chloe, emergency." Cate's heart starts to beat faster as she imagines the worst. She clicks it open.

"Hi, Cate, I didn't know how to call you over there. Sorry to reach out over email. I just got a call from our friend, Connor. He took Chloe to St. Joseph's Hospital. She is in emerg right now and I'm on my way. I have Connor's number for you. He said if you want to call, he's good with that. I can't tell you much more, other than Connor said that Chloe called him in a frantic mood, mumbling something about taking pills. I'm praying for her."

The words stare at Cate like daggers. The news hasn't fully sunk in before another message pops up, this time from Connor.

"Emergency. Chloe. Urgent. Ethan and Cate, my name is Connor. I'm a friend of Chloe's, from the hotel. She called me tonight in a state of emergency. She said she took a number of pills and drank a bottle of wine. She was quite incoherent, but I called an ambulance and went to her place. She is currently in St. Joseph's Hospital in Toronto. Her life does NOT appear to be in danger."

Cate stares at the screen in disbelief. She feels frozen in shock. Was it only a week ago she held her? She shakes her head. The only thing she knows is that she has to get a hold of Ethan. She tries to call him on his cellphone, but there is no answer. She sends him a text, "Call me." She tries not to panic. She attempts to call Connor but can't remember the country code for Canada. Her brain feels fried. She can't think what to do next, so she calls Lena.

"Hi, Lena?" Cate says with a trembling voice. "There is a family emergency. I, we, have to fly to Canada. Can you look after Fredrick? I don't know for how long."

"Yes, of course," Lena says without hesitation. "Is everything going to be okay?"

The tears Cate had been holding back are suddenly released in a flood. She cries into the phone. "I don't know."

Cate hangs up and sits in a daze, staring at the floor. She hears Ethan pull into the driveway and glances out the office window. His face is chalk white, his shoulders slump forward.

Ethan walks in the door and Cate throws herself against him. He holds her in silence for a few minutes, then pulls away.

"Why don't you start at the beginning?"

Cate takes Ethan by the hand and leads him to the office. She points to the message.

"It's easiest if you read it yourself," Cate says softly.

Ethan reads the message out loud. He lets out a noise Cate has never heard before, like a wounded animal.

"We need to fly to Toronto, immediately," he says.

"I know."

Cate makes a pot of coffee. Ethan calls Connor, but he doesn't have any more information. He and Rick are still in the hospital emergency waiting room.

They sit down with a pad of paper to sort out a plan. Ethan puts in a call to work to request compassionate leave and calls to book on the next flight out. Ethan is told the flight is sold out, but when he explains the situation, they manage the booking. They pack. They email their families. They reach out to Julianna, but she is in Halifax for the African Heritage Month conference. They call the hospital to get an update, but the staff say they can't. Confidentiality. It all goes by as if in a dream. Cate can't focus. She drifts around the villa like a ghost until it is time to go.

The trip to Toronto is gruelling. Their flight departs Riyadh at one in the morning to arrive in Frankfurt six hours later. They wait seven hours for the connection to Toronto. Nine more hours in flight. By the time they're in a taxi on their way to the Hyatt in Toronto, it is almost midnight. Ethan changes out his Saudi SIM card for his Canadian. There is a text from Rick.

"Chloe has been discharged," Ethan reads out loud.

"Are you fucking kidding me?" Cate yells. "Less than twenty-four hours after being taken by ambulance to emergency, for attempted suicide?"

"Try to calm down," Ethan says. "Losing it isn't going to help."

Cate takes a deep breath, but she is seething.

"Does Rick say anything else?" Cate asks.

"He says that Chloe convinced the doctor that she would be safe under his custody, and when Rick told them that we were on our way, they agreed," Ethan says as he reads the rest of the text message.

Cate is a ball of nerves. She can't decide if she's more concerned or angry. After they check in, they head to their room and start to unpack. The tension of waiting is thick. It feels like forever, but eventually there is a quiet knock.

"Come in," Ethan says, opening the door.

"I wish you didn't come," is the first thing Chloe says. "As you can see, I'm fine."

It's all Cate can do to hold it together. Rick appears calm, but Cate thinks he looks tired. He has dark bags under his eyes, and his ginger-coloured beard looks like it's been days since he gave it a trim. Chloe looks pale and unkempt and thinner than ever.

"I don't think you can say you're fine twenty-four hours after a suicide attempt," Cate says.

"It wasn't, I wasn't …" Chloe says, tears beginning to form. "I just wanted to escape from my life. As soon as I took the pills, I regretted my decision. I didn't want to die. I made myself throw up and I called Connor."

Chloe does her best to downplay the events. There are more tears.

"I'm going to stay with Rick for a while," says Chloe. She shudders. "I don't want to go back to my apartment, ever. And I made an appointment with Maggie for tomorrow afternoon."

"Well, it's late and we all need some rest," Rick says. "We'll check in with you tomorrow morning."

Rick and Chloe leave. Ethan and Cate fall into bed. Cate feels like she might vomit. Every muscle in her body screams out in pain and her head feels like it is going to explode, but after a while she falls asleep in spite of it all.

In the morning Cate and Ethan discuss the situation. Cate calls the clinic.

"Hi, Maggie?" Cate says. "It's Cate. I know it's last minute, but I wonder if Ethan and I can sit in on the last fifteen minutes of Chloe's session, considering the situation."

"What situation?" asks Maggie. "I don't have a session booked with Chloe. In fact, I haven't seen her since the end of December, when she graduated from the DBT program."

There is a moment of silence. Cate digests the information and looks over at Ethan with a shrug of her shoulders.

"The hospital didn't notify you about Chloe's attempted suicide?" Cate asks.

It is Maggie's turn to be shocked into silence. After a few seconds' delay she responds.

"Attempted suicide?" Maggie stumbles. "No, I wasn't aware. I think we should definitely meet. Let me look at my schedule and get back to you."

Cate waits. The knots in her stomach intensify. She paces the room. Within a few minutes Maggie calls back.

"I can fit you in for one hour tomorrow at two," Maggie says.

Cate hangs up and goes over to sit beside Ethan on the bed.

"Clearly she lied to us," Cate says. "I can't help but wonder what other lies she's told us."

"I'm in total shock," Ethan says. "I almost feel numb."

When Chloe reaches out later, Ethan confronts her. Instead of taking accountability, she deflects. She gets angry with them for interfering. She says she doesn't want to go see Maggie with them, that they can't make her. She tells Ethan he should book their tickets back home. But over the course of the day she comes around to the hotel and ends up changing her mind. She agrees to meet Cate and Ethan at Maggie's office the next day.

Cate and Ethan arrive early. They take a seat in the waiting room. Cate gnaws on her cuticles. Ethan drums his knuckles on the side table. Chloe arrives with her best mask in place, her hair blow-dried, and her makeup applied.

"This is, like, stupid-awkward," Chloe says. "I don't know why I agreed to this."

They sit in strained silence until the receptionist informs them that Maggie is ready to see them. Cate and Ethan sit beside one another on the leather couch, and Chloe plonks down on an armchair.

"Before we start, I request that each of you agree to speak respectfully as you share your feelings," Maggie says. "Do you agree?"

They all nod their heads yes.

"Okay, good," Maggie says. "Who would like to begin?"

"I would," says Cate. "Frankly, I'm shocked and disgusted with how this situation was handled. I feel it was irresponsible for the hospital to discharge Chloe so quickly, with no follow-up plan or communication with you, Maggie, or us, her parents."

"I agree," says Ethan.

"That's because you weren't here," Chloe says. "The psychologist at the hospital did a risk assessment and he felt fine with his decision to discharge me. Because I'm fine."

"Well, I have to wonder if you were totally honest with him," says Cate. "After all, you lied to us about having an appointment with Maggie."

"That's not fair," says Chloe.

"I can't help but wonder if a shortage of medical beds and staff wasn't a part of the problem," says Ethan.

"I don't think it's helpful to try and put the blame on anyone," interrupts Maggie. "That decision was made, and now the question is, how do we move forward?"

"I just want to get on with my life," says Chloe. "I wish my parents hadn't come. I only agreed to this meeting because I feel guilty that they came all this way. They micromanage me and tell me what to do."

"That is incredibly hurtful," says Cate. Tears start to trickle down her cheeks. "We would have to be unfeeling monsters to get an email from Rick saying you attempted to kill yourself and then choose to just wait it out thousands of miles away."

"Not to blame you or anything," says Chloe, "but I did try to tell to you that I felt suicidal."

"Now that's really unfair," says Ethan. "You have said you felt suicidal hundreds, if not thousands of times. How were we supposed to discern whether it was a feeling or something you had a plan to do? How is this our responsibility?"

It continues on like this. The session exhausts Cate. At the end of their scheduled hour, Ethan and Cate's sole responsibility is to encourage Chloe to go the gym with them and invite her for walks. That's the treatment plan, post–attempted suicide. Cate is pissed off. But even more, she is scared out of her mind.

That evening as Ethan and Cate crawl into bed, the front desk calls.

"Sure, send her up," Ethan says.

Chloe storms into the room. She looks like a train wreck, not showered, the hole in her cut-off denim shorts held together with a paper clip, a ball cap on her head.

"I went for my shift at work, but my boss said I've been taken off the schedule for the week," Chloe seethes. "Bad news travels fast. It was probably Connor who ratted me out."

"That doesn't sound reasonable," Cate says. "I'm sure whoever informed your boss did so from a place of concern."

"It's rational for your boss to assume you need a bit of time off," Ethan agrees.

"I didn't come here for you two to side with them," Chloe says. "But I guess I shouldn't be surprised. Thanks for nothing."

Chloe turns on her heels and leaves without a goodbye. A charged energy permeates the room. Cate sleeps fitfully.

In the light of day Ethan and Cate have a heavy conversation and vent their frustrations.

When they had first made their plans, Cate wanted to look for an apartment to rent in Toronto so she could stay and look after Chloe, but now, in light of Chloe's reaction, she's changed her mind. She wants to go back home, to Riyadh, with Ethan, when his compassionate leave expires. Ethan supports Cate's decision 100 percent.

Eventually Cate and Ethan come to terms with what is. They let go of their ideas and expectations and accept Chloe's choices. Cate sits down to write in her journal.

Part of my letting go journey is to accept the things I can't change. I had this crazy, naive notion that my love, and Ethan's love, could be what Chloe needs to feel whole. I was wrong. Just like I was wrong to think Ethan's love could be what I needed to feel whole. The lessons keep getting harder, but the message is clear; we all have our own work, we all have to create our own life story. That doesn't mean loving her isn't an important part of her story. It is. At the end of the day, love is what we have to give. Chloe will decide how to live, or not live. It is Chloe's choice to live or die. Nothing I do, or Ethan does, or anybody does, can stop her if she chooses to end her life.

It's so fucking hard, loving someone who struggles with mental illness.

Chapter 19

*B*ACK IN RIYADH, THE LAST twelve days seem a blur to Cate. Like a really bad dream. She feels in a constant state of pins and needles. The worry never eases up. The feeling is raw and vulnerable. Cate hates living in fear. She plunges herself deeper into her own healing rituals.

His first day back, Ethan returns home from work early, unfit to fly. The doctor gives him two days off and two weeks' worth of sleeping pills. He will have to follow a no-flying restriction when he returns after his two days of rest.

A week after they've been home, Cate wakes up to the sound of Ethan crowing beside her.

"I have something fantastic to share if you're ready," Ethan says.

"If it's fantastic news you've got, I'm ready," Cate says as she rubs her eyes and squints over at him.

"Chloe has sent me an email. She applied for the residential program and was approved. Now she just has to wait for an opening," Ethan says with a whoop. "She even attached the financial agreement."

"I didn't know she had applied," Cate says, suddenly wide awake. "That is incredible news."

Once they are both showered and dressed they call Chloe on FaceTime.

"We are both thrilled with your news," Ethan says.

"Don't get too excited, Papa," Chloe says. She looks drawn and tired. "I'm feeling super anxious. I'm terrified of doing nothing, but I'm even more terrified of committing. I'm not sure the time is right."

"There's likely never a good time," admits Cate. "But the opportunity is now."

"From our end, it doesn't feel like you have anything to lose," adds Ethan.

When they hang up Cate feels the most hopeful she's felt in a very long time.

Chloe calls after dinner.

"There's a spot in the treatment program, starting tomorrow."

"That's great!" Cate says, her voice high. "I'm so proud of you."

"Me too," says Ethan. "This feels like the most courageous decision you could make."

After they hang up, Cate does a little dance. She tilts her head to the heavens and praises God. Cate's optimism is contagious. Ethan joins in on the happy dance and gives Cate a high-five.

The next day Ethan wakes up to a new email from Chloe.

"Dear Papa and Cate, I'm sorry, but I couldn't do it. Rick drove me there and I checked in, but I dropped out this morning. I couldn't tolerate the unhealthy food program. I love you so much, and I know how much you wanted this for me. I'm sorry."

Whoosh, just like that, it all comes undone. Cate feels like she's going to be sick. All the feelings of glorious gratitude she felt the day before are shattered in an instant. Chloe didn't even give it twenty-four hours and Cate is devastated.

"It seems my miracle, so fleetingly granted, wasn't a miracle at all," Cate says to Ethan, a lump in her throat.

"I can't quite take it in," says Ethan. "I was so sure this was it."

"I don't want to accept this," says Cate.

"I know," Ethan says. "But this is where we are, and we have to figure out how to move forward."

Cate knows her best coping tool is to write in her journal. She sits down at the chair in her yoga room and puts her feelings down on paper.

> *Was it just at the beginning of this year that I recommitted to let go of the ties that bind and the fear that controls? I so want to release all expectations and accept the things I can't change. Yet I find myself repeatedly sucked into the drama, into the possibilities and the what-ifs. I'm trying, so hard, but I can't seem to turn off the switch of my mother's protective love, of the advice-giving role that once upon a time was the right thing to do, back when my children really were children and needed that from me. It seems I still have one foot lodged in the past, but at least I've got one pointed in the right direction.*

Cate takes a piece of scrap paper from the pile she
has in the top drawer of her desk. She writes in bold letters:
anger, guilt, frustration, worry, control. She crumples
the paper and sets it in a clay bowl, then lights it afire.
She watches as the words streak across the page and then
disappear into a pile of ashes. She closes her eyes and prays.

Cate and Ethan do their best to carry on. They support one
another over long, difficult discussions, but nothing seems
to resolve and every day is a challenge for both of them.
Cate finds solace in the support and distraction of her tribe.

On Tuesday, tribe is being held at Joan's villa. Cate finds
a sticky note on the front door, "come upstairs." Cate slips
off her shoes and goes up, then down the hall to Joan's yoga
sanctuary. She is the first to arrive.

"Namaste," Joan says, her palms pressed together.

Cate gives Joan a hug and takes a seat on one of the yoga
mats Joan has arranged in a square. There is a centrepiece:
four candles and a silver bowl with sticks of sage, cedar, and
sweetgrass, set out on woven bamboo mat.

After a few minutes Sophia arrives, then Bonnie. Joan
takes her sacred, elk-hide drum from the corner and plays
her instrument, the sound like a heartbeat, thump, thump.
She lights the dried herbs and leads them in a smudging
ceremony.

"Spirits of our ancestors, we ask you to be with us as
this smoke carries away all negativity," Joan says. She
acknowledges the seven sacred directions, and then each
woman takes turns directing the smoke over their bodies
with gentle hand gestures.

"Let's move downstairs for our book study," Joan suggests when the ceremony is complete. "It will be more comfortable."

Once they all take a seat on the overstuffed, grey velvet couches, Joan opens the discussion.

"Let's use my eagle feather to take turns sharing our ideas, like my people do when we hold talking circles," Joan begins. "Does anyone have any thoughts to share on our first chapter of *The Great Work of Your Life*?"

"I related to the nurse who didn't appear to have a clear dharma," says Cate, as she reaches for the feather. "Is my right path my past career as a teacher, or my aspiration to be a writer?"

"I agree with you," says Bonnie, forgetting to request the feather. Just then her phone buzzes. The lines on her forehead crease together as she reaches to check it, then she sets it back down on the coffee table and her face relaxes again. Joan looks mildly annoyed with the interruption.

"Sorry about that," Bonnie says. "I was just about to say that my life path seems to have morphed and changed several times over the years too. I've been an officer in the military, a rock star, a mother, and a university professor. How on earth do you link all those roles together? It makes me think of that song by Meredith Brooks, 'I'm a bitch, I'm a lover,'" Bonnie says as she starts to sing the first few lines.

All four of the ladies nod their heads in unison, able to relate to the lyrics of the song.

"I also loved the metaphor of sitting in a folding chair at a crossroads," says Joan, changing the direction of the conversation, the eagle feather forgotten. "That's how I feel. I'm ready for something new to manifest."

"I'm with you on that one," Sophia says. The consummate yogi, she has moved off the couch to the rug on the floor, stretching her short, strong legs out in front of her and reaching for her toes. "Sometimes I feel overwhelmed and shut down by labels, stuck in the roles I'm expected to play. I'm craving a change."

The conversation is animated. Joan serves iced tea with lemon and homemade chocolate avocado mousse. When Joan wraps up tribe with a closing prayer of gratitude, Cate is in her happy place.

Cate returns home to discover Ethan back from work. She shares the enthusiasm her experience at tribe generated, and he listens attentively.

"I feel ready to become the best version of me," says Cate. "I'm the most inspired I've felt since we got back from Toronto."

"You're the best version of anyone," Ethan says.

"Mr. Charming Pants," Cate says. She moves over to sit beside him on the couch and kisses him. "I appreciate your devotion, but everyone has room to grow, and after everything we've been through, it feels like I still have a lot of work to do."

Cate is scrolling through reader responses to her latest blog when a notice from Dana appears on her screen, "Do you have time to talk?"

"Of course," Cate texts back. "I'll ring you on Messenger."

The connection is weak, even with the video function turned off, but Cate hears Dana loud and clear.

"My guru is a fraud," Dana says. Her voice is thick. "He has sexually assaulted me, Maman. And some of the other women here too. The ashram is a cult."

"Oh my God," Cate says. She slumps forward. "This is absolutely horrible. I'm so devastated for you. How are you coping?"

"Well, I moved out of the ashram into an apartment with my friend Santi, for starters," Dana says.

"It's not easy being a woman, let alone a young, beautiful woman, in this world still so infiltrated with patriarchal entitlement," Cate sighs.

Cate feels sick to her stomach and has an ache in her temple.

"Yeah, I know, right? It's all a long story, Maman," Dana says. "I don't feel like getting into it over the Internet, but honestly I don't know what to do. I feel numb and immobilized. I need my maman. I need your energy and your strength."

Cate wants to scream that she doesn't have enough strength for herself. She doesn't feel ready to take on another trauma, still in recovery from her trip to Toronto. She's so tired of putting out fires, of Dana's history of being drawn into intense situations. But she stays silent, letting Dana vent.

When Ethan gets home from work Cate shares the shocking news.

"It doesn't rain, it doesn't pour, it's a fucking tsunami," Cate says. "I know, it sucks, but Dana needs me, and I want to give her what she's asked for. I want to go," Cate says.

"I understand," Ethan says. "Let's go online and find you a ticket."

As she steps onto the Air India plane, Cate feels like she is stepping backwards in time, several decades. The red carpet is thin and faded, with tears and holes. The upholstery is stained and damaged. Cate takes comfort that she is seated at the front, with a bit of extra legroom, and the airplane isn't booked to capacity. She is in the window seat and the two seats beside her are empty. Cate's smokey-screened personal entertainment system is broken. She reads her book to pass the time.

As the plane approaches the massive, sprawling city of Mumbai, Cate looks out her window at the city spires and modern architecture through a yellow haze of smog. They fly over the slums, where thousands upon thousands of aluminum structures stand row upon row. Tears flow down her cheeks. She is overwhelmed by the poverty and despair. The energy weighs heavy on her like a chain-link shroud.

The heat and humidity radiate in the terminal. Cate removes her abaya and stuffs it into her carry-on, only to realize once she enters the cue that the Indian women are dressed conservatively, clad in colourful, gauzy saris that cover their shoulders. She feels almost naked in her sleeveless dress that falls just below her knees.

Cate has six hours to wait in the Mumbai airport before boarding another plane to Goa. She finds a restaurant and orders a glass of wine and some fries, then logs onto the Internet to reach out to Ethan. They have a short exchange. She scrolls through Facebook and reads emails until it is time to go.

When Cate boards the aircraft she can't help but think of *Airplane Disaster* episodes she's watched with Ethan, where the investigations lead to discoveries of faulty parts in old planes. She pushes the fearful thoughts from her mind and tries to get comfortable in her shabby seat. She is cranky.

The intense air conditioning blasts down on her. She dozes on and off until they land, just over an hour later.

Cate collects her bag from the luggage carousel in the tiny airport and finds her way outside the terminal where she spots her beautiful daughter, a contrasting vision of vulnerability and strength.

"Namaste, Maman," Dana says.

The hot wind blows a welcome kiss across Cate's skin. The energy of India hums around her as she embraces her daughter. She is ready to shower her with all the gentle force of her mother-love.

"Namaste, my beloved daughter."

It is so dark; all Cate can discern of Goa are the thousands of coloured twinkly lights. She smells curry and waste. She hears horns beeping, dogs barking, and chickens squawking as the taxi driver navigates the narrow, dusty roads to Dana's apartment. It is a long drive and Dana has so much to say. Cate listens the best she can, exhausted from head to toe as she is.

The taxi drops them at the creaky iron gate and they each carry one of Cate's cases up the narrow, winding steps, past the resident dog who startles awake and greets them with a bark and a swift wag of his tail.

It is past midnight when Cate and Dana flop onto the twin bed. The fan purrs above and Cate is lulled to sleep. During the night the fan suddenly dies as the power goes out. The heat falls like a heavy wool blanket, suffocating and thick.

"Yes," Dana says with a sleepy voice. "The power goes out sometimes. What to do?"

It feels impossible to breathe, but Cate manages somehow to stay calm. The fan starts up briefly and Cate

pulls the sifted, semi-cooled air deeply into her lungs,
only to have it stop again as suddenly as it began. Eventually
Cate falls asleep, despite her discomfort.

Cate and Dana awaken at the same time, when the sun rises.

"Good morning, Maman," Dana says. "Sorry about the
power outages. I forgot to warn you. Did you manage to get
some sleep?"

"It's all good," Cate says with a soft smile. "I didn't come
here to get rest, I came here to be with you."

In the light of day, Dana gives Cate a tour of the small
apartment she shares with her friend Santi from the ashram.
Silk fabrics in an array of bright colours drape the walls in
the living room. Twinkly lights dangle from the window
frames. There is a large wooden table with an assortment
of paints, paper, books, and incense.

In the tiny kitchen there are no modern conveniences
such as a dishwasher, just one large, deep sink. Dishes are
stacked high in a drying rack. Glass pots with handwritten
labels, "ginger," "garam masala," and "chai," clutter the
countertop.

"Would you like a bowl of oatmeal for breakfast?"
Dana asks.

"That sounds lovely," Cate says. "Just tell me what I can
do to help."

They prepare a simple morning meal and talk easily over
hot cups of creamy, spicy chai tea.

"I was thinking," says Cate. "Perhaps it would be nice
for us to stay in a sanctuary or a retreat for the short time
I'm here? A place with air-conditioning could be quite a nice
treat in this heat."

"That's generous of you to offer," says Dana, "but I don't know what we'll be able to find. Shall we head out on my scooter for a bit of an explore?"

Cate agrees. She grabs her purse and Dana grabs her backpack. The black and white dog that greeted them in the night is lying in the sun on the pathway, and when he jumps up to come over and give Dana a lick, his tail wags.

"Hi, Snoopy, ole boy," Dana says as she gives his head a pat.

Cate loves dogs, but this guy looks a little too mangy for her to consider petting and she hustles past him.

Dana's scooter is parked on the side of the road. Cate is disturbed to discover there are no helmets. She pushes down her fear and discomfort and climbs on behind Dana.

"Hold on," Dana says as she merges onto the crowded, narrow road. She whizzes along, kicking up a cloud of dust. Wild dogs and cows appear out of nowhere to dart dangerously across their path. Cate holds her breath.

Somewhere along the way Dana changes her mind about looking into accommodation. She takes Cate to a quiet little stretch of beach instead.

"I feel like I need some time to talk with you about everything that has happened before we dive into looking for a place," Dana says. She plunks down in the hot sand in her worn and wrinkled fisherman pants. "I feel so betrayed," Dana begins. "I trusted my guru with my most vulnerable self, and he took advantage of his position."

"It's disgusting," says Cate. She struggles to get comfortable, her bare calves burning, but she doesn't want to create a distraction. "I'm just so glad you were able to get out of there."

"Me too," says Dana. "But it has thrown my world into chaos. I don't have enough money to stay in the apartment I'm in for much longer, but I don't know what else to do."

Cate listens while the sun soaks their skin. Dana seems oblivious, apparently accustomed to the heat, but after a while she suddenly switches gears. She gets up and starts to strip down to her bikini.

"I'm going to take a dip in the ocean," says Dana. "Do you want to come in?"

"No, thanks," says Cate. She would love to feel the cool water, but she isn't prepared, without a towel to dry off, and feels uncomfortable leaving her valuables on the beach. "I'll stay here and watch our things."

After Dana dries off they walk to a nearby café. They order mint lemonade and talk some more.

"It's your journey, and your decision," says Cate. "But I think I would want to get as far away from here as possible. Have you thought about returning to Canada?"

"Of course, I've thought about it," says Dana, a bit snippy with her tone. "I don't feel ready to make a decision that huge."

Somehow the day disappears and they never get around to looking at retreats. Dana takes Cate to a restaurant a few kilometres from town. They sit at a rustic table amongst a mishmash of others, smack dab in the sand, only a few feet from the ocean. Dana orders them traditional vegetarian Indian cuisine: eggplant, spinach, and paneer in flavourful curries with rice and naan.

After their meal, Dana drives them back to her apartment. It is another night punctuated by sweltering power outages.

In the morning, Cate walks into the kitchen to find Dana's roommate standing by the sink, stark naked.

"Oops, sorry," Cate says as she turns to go back into Dana's room.

"Oh, hey, hi," Santi says. "You must be Dana's mom; nice to meet you."

Santi walks over. Her small white breasts stand out against her dark skin and seem to stare at Cate like owl eyes in the dark. Santi takes Cate's hand in hers as if they are old friends. Cate is beyond uncomfortable. She decides she will not let the day get away from her again.

After a light breakfast of scrambled eggs with avocado, Cate and Dana clean up their dishes while Santi chats away about some guy she has the hots for.

"Can we please look for a place to stay today?" Cate asks. She dries her plate and stacks it in the cupboard. "I'm too old for another night on a hard mattress without air-conditioning and a series of power outages."

"Yeah, okay, let's head out right away," Dana says, again with the tone. She rolls her eyes and sighs as she pushes into her flip-flops.

The first place they view is the Hotel Lalita, Goa's apparent five-star. Cate is excited when they enter the open-air lobby with signs that indicate there is a spa around the corner, but when they inquire at the desk they are told the hotel is booked to capacity.

"It felt a little too *Lifestyles of the Rich and Famous* for me anyway," says Dana.

Cate bites her tongue. It felt nothing like that to her. They hop on the scooter and Dana takes them to check out a whimsical property called Dreamcatcher. It looks sketchy to Cate, and when she asks about air conditioning the woman at the desk says, "No, no a/c, sorry."

"I know you really want to find something," says Dana. "But I'm feeling totally stressed that you have to make this about your needs. This isn't what I imagined you coming here to be."

"I'm sorry," says Cate. "I'm doing my best."

Dana drives up to a thatched hut where she claims they can get authentic Ayurvedic massages for next to nothing.

The small-statured, ancient-looking Indian woman who is Cate's masseuse leads her to a dark wooden table with no mattress and indicates for her to take off her clothes. Cate undresses to her underwear, but the masseuse gestures for her to remove them as well. Once Cate is naked the old woman hands her a piece of cloth that looks like the garments worn by Japanese sumo wrestlers. Cate ties it clumsily around her waist and climbs up on the hard surface. She tries to relax. The woman pours warm, bordering on hot, coconut oil onto Cate's skin and applies deep pressure massage to her entire body, including her stomach and breasts. Cate is surprised that it doesn't feel inappropriate at all. She drifts in and out of time and almost falls asleep. She hopes that Dana feels soothed too.

Cate gets dressed back in her clothes and combs her oiled hair into a ponytail, then waits on a bench for Dana.

"Do you feel better?" Cate asks when Dana appears.

"Yeah, that was amazing, don't you think? But I'm hungry," Dana answers. "Let's grab a bite to eat at a café I know, just around the corner."

They both order chai tea, which Cate is quickly becoming addicted to. Cate savours the crispy rice flour crepe stuffed with spicy mashed potatoes that Dana recommends. After lunch, Dana is satiated and ready to start back on their mission.

"There's only one place left I can think of," says Dana. Cate hops onto the scooter. She crosses her fingers.

Blue Moon is situated at the edge of a forest, where the river and the ocean converge, a semicircle of white canvas, tent-style casitas, each with a name of a planet. Cate feels hopeful as soon as they walk through the white fence that borders the road.

With a bit of persistence in negotiation with Sunil, the friendly staff member with excellent English who greets them, Cate books the Venus. It is an air-conditioned unit with a backup fan powered by solar energy. Cate fills in one page of personal information, old-fashioned, pen and paper–style, and provides her Visa number for the deposit.

"Let's go and collect our things," Dana says. "I feel really good about this decision."

They can't possibly carry everything on their backs on the scooter, so Dana hails them a tuk-tuk taxi to make the short journey back to Blue Moon.

"I'm going to the beach to meditate," Dana says as soon as they've unloaded all their things inside the tent.

Cate indulges in a large glass of Italian red wine and a bottle of icy cold water she orders from the restaurant that is in the middle of the property. She plunks down on the wooden recliner on their front porch after she retrieves her journal.

> *The cool breeze from the ocean caresses me.*
> *Vibrant, organic, chaotic India challenges me.*
> *My daughter's polar energy, exacerbated by the trauma*
> *of the ashram, her abruptness and criticism, sting*
> *my sensitive nature.*
>
> *I pray that Dana will find a way to integrate the*
> *hard lessons she has learned, while being gentle, loving,*
> *and supportive to herself inside of her vulnerability.*
> *I pray for her to receive insights from God. I pray for*
> *my own courage, to let my daughter find her way,*

*remembering my letting go journey. My purpose
is to love her. I must be strong. I must use the art of
detachment to stay calm when she lashes out, with
the wisdom that it isn't about me, it's about the trauma.
I pray for patience.*

*I pray for the multitudes of women in similar
situations, where spiritual teaching is corrupted
and misused by gurus and other religious people
in positions of power. I pray, I pray.*

Cate is in the middle of it when she feels a tiny pinprick of concern. She sets her journal down on the plastic outdoor table and goes to look for Dana.

Not far away, Cate finds Dana sitting cross-legged on the beach, lightly dusted in sand. She plunks down beside her daughter.

"You look the most grounded I've seen you since I arrived," Cate says.

"I do feel better," Dana says. "I'm sorry I've been a little testy."

"It's okay," Cate says. "I understand."

Cate and Dana order dinner at the on-site restaurant where Cate scored her wine and water earlier. Sunil, who seems to be in charge of all duties, brings them the remainder of the bottle he had opened for Cate earlier.

"Leave it to you to find a good wine in India," Dana says.

Cate orders Mariana Trench, a shrimp specialty on the menu. Dana chooses her usual, spinach paneer. They both indulge in the bananas soaked in rum with ice cream for dessert.

Mother and daughter spend the next few days doing their best to get along. Cate hopes the opportunity to rest and relax will help Dana to recover from the trauma, if only a little. Sometimes they achieve an easy flow, but then some spot of stickiness surfaces as Dana processes emotions in the present that trigger memories from the ashes of the past.

Cate relishes the opportunity to sit beside the Indian Ocean, in contrast to the deserts of Saudi Arabia. Dana finds the ocean energy healing too, and they spend most of their days doing little more than moving from the sand to the water of the ocean.

Cate spreads her towel and stretches out. She watches three crows and a crab as they look for food. The mysteries of the universe seem so simple. She fetches her journal from her tote bag and writes a poem.

> *Three crows dance in the sand, fishing for crabs.*
> *Not fast enough to grasp in hungry beaks.*
> *Patience wanes, a cheeky caw and they depart*
> *on the wings of the wind.*
> *A crab scuttles across the sand, fishing for insects.*
> *An ancient rhythm to his typewriter, zigzag crawl.*
> *His tenacity pays off. He emerges from his hole*
> *with a tasty morsel in his claw.*
> *A woman lies on her sarong in the sand, fishing*
> *for truth.*
> *She closes her eyes and opens her heart.*
> *Serenity descends upon her, filling her soul.*

It's Cate's favourite time of day, just before the sun sets and the moon rises in the sky.

"Let's take our yoga mats to that place where the beach is next to a wall of forest," Dana says.

Cate agrees and they grab their mats. They practice yoga asanas together. Dana leads them in a tantric series.

"Mother Earth," Dana begins. "Show us how to honour and heal our bodies. Help us to relax into each posture with intention, with the support of your age-old sand beneath us."

Cate's body creaks and groans. She is distracted. A dog barks in the distance, crabs scuttle in the sand, and Indian women walk by with their children, their bangles dangling merrily.

The sun sets as they lie in Savasana. Cate hears Dana as she sobs. She reaches across and places her hand on her daughter's. She doesn't say a word. Her intuition tells her that words will spoil the moment. Instead, she prays silently to herself for her daughter to find healing.

Five days from her arrival, Cate leaves Goa in the dark of night. She tries to tiptoe from the room, but Dana stirs.

"Goodbye, Maman," Dana says, sleepy-eyed and groggy. "Thank you so much for coming. I know it hasn't exactly been easy."

"It was an honour," Cate says. She bends over and kisses her daughter on the top of her head, pushing a tendril of her long hair behind her ear. "I love you. You will be in my heart, always, no matter where you are."

A driver arranged through Sunil picks Cate up at the gate and takes her to the airport to begin the long journey home. In the Mumbai airport lounge, Cate reaches out to Ethan. They exchange loving texts with one another. Cate closes her eyes and dreams about being reunited with her husband, her best friend and lover.

Back in Riyadh, Cate checks in every day with Dana to see how she is doing. A week later, Dana tells her she is ready to return to Calgary.

Cate hosts the next tribe. After the ceremony and chapter two discussion, the four women share the recent events in their lives. Bonnie has photos on her phone of the new vacation rental she and Gabe purchased. Joan expresses her dreams for their group to reach out to other women on the compound. Cate tells stories about her time in Goa. Sophia tops everyone, with the amazing news that she is pregnant, expecting a baby boy in October.

Cate is thrilled for Sophia and Quinn. She is excited to soon have the energy of a baby to cuddle and coddle. She is full of hope for the future, that all of her children are going to be okay, that she is going to be okay.

Chapter 20

*T*HE TERMINAL IN RIYADH, AS usual, is thick with people who push carts loaded precariously with taped-up cartons and butt impolitely into lines. Cate and Ethan make their way through the chaos to the check-in desk, ready to begin another five-week Ramadan whirlwind adventure.

This year their five weeks of holiday include a cross-Canada itinerary to connect with family, followed by a stopover in Rome where Cate and Ethan will be joined by Taylor and Becky. The finale is an eleven-day Mediterranean cruise, just the two of them. Cate is hopeful that this trip will be the pick-me-up she needs, that the worst is behind her and the best is yet to come.

After thirty hours of flights and connections, Cate and Ethan arrive in Victoria. Cate feels like a crumpled piece of linen that's been stuffed in the bottom of a dirty hamper for a week. Cate doesn't know where Ethan finds the energy and focus to drive up the Malahat to Celeste and Grayson's home in Cobble Hill, but she's grateful it's him and not her.

It is late when Ethan pulls into the driveway, the street pitch-black, the house quiet. There is a sticky note on the front door. "We've gone to bed. Your room is ready for you."

Cate and Ethan enter the house as stealthily as they can and Ethan carries their luggage down the hall to their room.

"Man, would I love a shower," Ethan whispers, "but I wouldn't want to wake up Oliver at this hour."

"I know," says Cate. "We'll just have to make do until morning."

Early the next day, they are woken by Oliver when he crawls into bed between them.

"Good morning, Grandma," Oliver says. "It's me, your favourite grandson."

"Come here you little cutie-pie," Cate says as she opens her heavy-lidded eyes and pulls Oliver close. "I need one of your super hugs to energize me."

Oliver hugs her, but soon he is impatient to start the day. He squirms and tugs at her hand.

"Come on, Grandma." Oliver hops off the bed. "Let's go play!"

Cate throws on some clean clothes and follows Oliver out to the living room while Ethan heads off for a shower.

"Let's draw pictures," Oliver says, leading Cate to his craft table. "I have a new box of one hundred crayons."

The two of them are busy creating works of art when Ethan walks in, dressed and ready for the day.

"Hi, Grandpa," says Oliver, "Come and see the awesome pictures Grandma and I made."

Oliver lines up on the floor the crayoned stick-people he has drawn. "Now we're going to make a list of all things we're going to do while you're here," Oliver says. He hands Cate a green pencil crayon, his new favourite colour, and a sheet of blank paper. "We're going to 'party every day,' right Grandma?" Oliver sings in an off-key version of the Black Eyed Peas' song.

"Party every day?" says Ethan. "That sounds like a very ambitious plan."

"What does ambitious mean?" asks Oliver.

"It means we better get started," laughs Cate.

That day, "party every day" translates into a trip to the wharf, lunch at the Bakery Café, and the afternoon at Bright Angel Park. Ethan spins Oliver, Cate, and Celeste on the merry-go-round and they dizzy-walk around, then fake crash into the soft grass.

Celeste prepares a special dinner, with cupcakes for dessert. Cate and Ethan give Oliver a present they picked up in the Frankfurt airport on the way.

"Thank you, Grandma and Grandpa," Oliver says as he pulls at the tape and tears at the wrapping paper. "I just love presents!"

"You're welcome," says Cate. "I hope you like it."

Oliver whoops with joy when he discovers a Paw Patrol fire station and Marshall, the spunky Dalmatian. He wants to play with them right away, but Celeste insists it is time for bed. Cate gives him his bath and reads him his stories.

"Can I sleep with Marshall?" Oliver asks with a yawn.

"Yes," agrees Celeste. She tucks his new figurine under the covers with him.

"It was the best 'party every day' ever," says Oliver as he closes his eyes. "I love you so much, Grandma."

The next day Grayson installs Oliver's car seat into Cate and Ethan's rental car for their drive into Duncan.

"Shall we go to the Red Balloon first?" Cate asks as she buckles up her seat belt.

"Yes, please!" says Oliver.

At the toy store, Cate and Oliver decide on a pirate theme. They look for pirate treasure. They find a Lego pirate ship, black balloons with skulls on them, and water pistols.

"I'm so excited for our pirate party, Grandma," says Oliver at the cash register.

"Grandma?" the cashier laughs. "I think you mean Glamma!"

After lunch at Oliver's favourite restaurant they head back home with their loot.

"Mom and Ethan, you've spoiled this little boy way too much," Celeste says, her hands on her hips as Oliver takes all the purchases out of their bags and lays them on the counter. It is clear from the smile that lights up her eyes she isn't upset at all.

Grayson sets up Oliver's outdoor blow-up pool with a slide, and Donna drives up from Victoria to join the party.

"Nana!" Oliver shouts when Donna walks into the back yard. He jumps out of the pool and runs to her with a big, wet hug. "You're just in time, our pirate party just started!"

"Pirates?" says Donna, "Argh, me hearty!"

The mood is festive and everyone goofs off a bit, following Oliver's free-spirited example. They take turns going down the slide and splashing in the pool with Oliver, pretending to be pirates. Cate's sitting in the sun, squinting over at Oliver, hand over her eyes, when she remembers her dream, from before he was born. It's uncanny how much he looks like the boy she envisioned: tall, slim, and tanned with his long blonde hair falling in curly waves to his shoulders.

After a full day of play, dinner, and stories, Oliver practically falls into bed. The adults each pour themselves a glass of wine and retire to the living room.

"That boy of yours is such a hoot," says Cate. "It was hilarious to hear him sing 'party every day' in his pirate drawl."

"It makes my heart full to see you two together," says Celeste. "I'm so glad you're all here."

"Me too," says Donna. "I'm just delighted I was included."

In the morning Celeste asks Ethan and Grayson to look after Oliver so that she can steal a few moments alone with Cate. Cate grinds her teeth. She remembers the last time Celeste requested time alone with her.

Celeste packs a basket with her Goddess cards and crystals, then takes Cate to the part of the ocean they used to walk when Ethan and Cate rented Melissa's home in Mill Bay.

They spread out blankets on the craggy coast that overlooks the ocean and talk about the heaviness between them.

"I'm sorry I've been so hard on you," Celeste says. "I was in a difficult space and I felt so sad that I didn't have you here to support me."

"I understand," says Cate. "I appreciate your honesty. I know how hard it is to raise a child, the pressure and the responsibility. I get it."

Once the air is cleared, Celeste leads them in ceremony. She invokes Goddess to be with them, to guide and protect them. They hold hands and look deep into one another's eyes. They take turns drawing a Goddess card from the deck. Celeste spots a lone horse standing knee deep in the ocean water, and Cate points to a bald eagle overhead. They share sacred space. The hours melt into moments where watches don't exist, the passage of time marked by the beating of their hearts.

Later, in the quiet time before bed, Cate gets out her journal.

> *I have so much to be grateful for. "Party every day" has been so much fun. I love my grandson. It is limitless. I needn't have worried. Our lack of FaceTimes doesn't seem to have altered the closeness of our relationship one iota. All is well.*
>
> *I feel deep gratitude for the sacred time Celeste created. The appearance of the horse and the eagle felt like positive signs to me, of good things to come. I can feel Celeste's anger transforming into acceptance. I think we are going to come out of this stronger and even more connected than we were before.*
>
> *I am grateful for my mom, who has always supported me in my decisions. Her joyful presence brings light and love into my heart.*

After four days, it is time for Cate and Ethan to leave Victoria to fly to Calgary, where they are staying at Michael and Ashley's for three nights. They both have to work and

Sam is in school, but they have a family dinner with Dana planned. Cate has promised Dana some one-on-one time, and Cate has a checkup with Dr. Kensington.

Ethan comes with Cate to her doctor's appointment, where they receive the amazing and somewhat miraculous news that Cate is healed from Lyme disease.

"Thank you so much for everything you've done to support my healing process," Cate says to Dr. Kensington, her voice thick with emotion. "It almost feels too good to be true."

"You did this," says Dr. Kensington, playing down her part. "You should be very proud of yourself for your diligence and perseverance. I know it hasn't been easy."

After her appointment, Cate meets up with Dana at a coffee shop while Ethan runs some errands.

"Hi, Maman," Dana says. "It feels like a lifetime ago since I saw you in Goa." She gives Cate a hug before they grab a table.

"Yes, it does," agrees Cate. "But it's only been two months. How are you managing?"

"I still feel emotional, vulnerable, and overwhelmed a lot," Dana says. "Dad's spiralling again, so that's been hard too"

"I'm sorry to hear that," says Cate, tired of John's negative influence on her daughter, on all their children.

"Yeah, it sucks," Dana continues.

"Well, try not to let that experience derail you, you've been making so much progress," Cate replies.

"Yeah, well, what to do? I'm just taking it one day at a time."

"That sounds very wise," says Cate. "I encourage you to practice some form of self-care every day. And maybe think about spending less time with your dad while you're still feeling vulnerable. I believe you are strong, resilient, and talented and that brighter days are ahead."

When everyone is gathered around the table at Michael and Ashley's for dinner, Cate shares her big news.

"I saw Dr. Kensington this morning," Cate begins. "I'm officially cured from Lyme disease."

"That's the best news I've heard in ages," says Dana with a big whoop.

"I agree, and it deserves a toast," says Michael. "Ethan, will you choose a bottle of champagne from the wine fridge?"

Over dinner there are more stories. When the dishes are cleared away, Dana and Sam entertain everyone with their video production, a super-spy film they made together. Sam sets up Monopoly at the kitchen table. Their antics continue until well past midnight.

"It's long past our bedtimes, especially you, young man," Ashley says to Sam. "Off to bed with you."

"Until next time, desert-dwellers," Sam says. He gives Cate a nose kiss and hugs Ethan.

"I guess I best be on my way," Dana says. She looks so pensive as she heads to the door, Cate feels her heart ache. "I wish you lived closer, Maman, but I appreciate the effort you and Ethan make to keep up our connection. I love you."

"I love you too," says Cate. "And when your life starts to turn around, you'll be so engaged, you won't have time to miss me."

After Dana leaves, Ethan, Cate, and Michael pour themselves more wine and sit down in the living room.

"It makes me so happy to see you thriving, Sis," says Michael. "I've been worried about you, over there in the Middle East, and especially with all the trauma with Chloe and Dana. But I can see you've managed it well and are focused on the good stuff."

"It hasn't been easy," Cate admits. "But when you're in partnership with someone as magnificent as Ethan, it makes it easier." She places her hand gently on Ethan's thigh.

"Well, I'm here for you too, Sis," says Michael. He reaches out his hand to grasp hers. "And for all your kids too."

"I know, and thank you," says Cate. "You've always been so supportive. I really appreciate you."

On the day of their departure, in the quiet of the early morning, Cate gets out her journal.

> *My gratitude cup is spilling over. Pinch me, I'm dreaming. I can hardly believe that I'm healed from Lyme's, even though I hoped as much, with how good I've been feeling. It's been two and half years of an intense regimen, but it was worth every minute of it.*
>
> *Dana has some work ahead of her, but she seems committed. She is going for counselling and likes her new apartment. She started teaching yoga again. I'm sure her finances will be tight, but she can work on a small budget better than anyone I know. Michael, Ashley, and Sam all adore her, and I know they will keep their door open, their arms wide. They are good people, my family. I am blessed.*

Roger and Aubrey fly from Winnipeg to Toronto, the last city on Cate and Ethan's cross-Canada itinerary. They are staying together in an Airbnb in a condominium tower in the heart of the city, close to Julianna's and a short bus ride from Chloe and Rick's apartment.

On Chloe's birthday, Cate makes a reservation for seven at George, a top-rated restaurant located in an old red brick building on the corner of Queen and Church. She reaches out to Rick and Julianna to join the celebrations.

The hostess seats them in the courtyard patio, nestled in a corner partitioned for privacy. The hedge is draped with pale yellow mini-lights, and a tranquil fountain gurgles in the background. The sommelier appears and Julianna requests a bottle of sparkling wine from Nova Scotia. It is dry, crisp, light, and refreshing, a perfect way to begin the festivities.

"To Chloe," says Rick, "who has taught me so much about love. She shares her struggles with courage and vulnerability, and I feel honoured."

"Well said," Julianna agrees. She clinks his glass and continues. "Chloe has taught us all what it means to be a family by choice."

They continue to share stories of Chloe's gifts over an indulgent five-course, chef's prix fixe with wine pairings. They are treated to a bold epicurean menu featuring local food artisans and global wine producers. Throughout the meal the conversation is lively. Julianna entertains with a multitude of stories about her adventures abroad, Roger talks about the good ole days, and Rick tells hilarious stories of intoxicated customer antics at the hotel bar.

When dessert is served, the chef writes "Happy Birthday" in chocolate on Chloe's plate and presents it to her, complete with a candle. Everyone sings "Happy Birthday."

"Make a wish," Cate says.

Chloe closes her eyes, then blows out the candle.

"I feel so spoiled and special," Chloe says, a tear in her eye. "Thank you so much, Papa and Cate, for everything."

In the morning Chloe shows up at the condo bright and early dressed for the weather in shorts and sneakers.

"It's such a beautiful, sunny day, I'd like to take you guys on a walking tour of the area," Chloe says, not long after her arrival.

"I would love that," Aubrey says as she tidies up the last of the breakfast dishes.

"There's a football game on that I want to watch at the pub on the corner," says Roger, not one to go on long walks. "You can drop me off there."

"That actually sounds like a nice change of pace," says Ethan. "I'll join you, Dad."

The ladies drop the boys off at the bar and walk over to pick up Julianna for a two-hour city walk. They take the stairs to Casa Loma.

"I could hardly get up these stairs the last time I was here," Cate marvels. "But this time, it's a breeze."

"It's so wonderful to see you with your energy back," says Chloe. "Did you tell Grandma and Julianna that you are cured of Lyme's?"

"No, she did not," says Julianna. "How could you keep such a thing from us?"

"Last night was Chloe's time to take the stage," says Cate. "I was just waiting for the right time."

Four days later, Cate and Ethan's visit in Toronto comes to an end. Cate feels the same positive energy of gratitude that she felt on Vancouver Island and in Calgary. On the plane to Rome, she writes in her journal.

> *It has been beyond rewarding, this precious time with family and friends. I feel so proud of Chloe. It's like she's a different person since we were here after the crisis, just a few months ago. I'm not being unrealistic; I know she still struggles, and likely always will, but she is taking baby steps, just like Dana. It seems like hitting rock bottom changed something in her. She seems more mature and confident. I heard her telling Aubrey how she hasn't missed a day of work since she started her new job, and it was so lovely to hear her speak of herself with pride. I'm thrilled that she has Rick, who is solid. He loves her and accepts her as she is, and that is a gift worth cherishing.*
>
> *As for Julianna, Roger, and Aubrey, they are consistent. All three of them are wise to the ways of the world, yet somehow, they maintain such positive outlooks on life. With Roger and Aubrey, I know a big part of that is their Catholic faith. Julianna has a deep spirituality too, but more eclectic, like mine. It reminds me that there are many paths to travel on the journey of life, many roads to God.*

Cate and Ethan arrive in Rome having survived the neck-cramping economy class with unpleasant meal service and two crying babies over nine hours of flight.

Outside of the arrivals area, Ethan sees the driver he hired holding up a sign with his name on it and they climb into the car.

It takes forty minutes to drive to the rental they found on Airbnb, in the heart of Rome. Along the way the landscape transforms from barren countryside to tall umbrella trees and thin cedars amongst old brick, stone, and stucco buildings. The houses are painted a colourful palette of pale yellows, oranges, and greens. In the city, the cobblestoned streets are narrow and busy with traffic.

Cate is excited to be in a city of romance, history, and intrigue and even more jazzed to finally meet Taylor's girlfriend, Becky, in person.

The apartment turns out to be clean and modern, almost minimalist. Cate chooses the larger bedroom at the back, which has a view of the open market below, and they unpack their things. Cate has just tucked her last pair of shoes inside the wardrobe when her phone lights up with a message from Taylor, "We're here!"

Cate skips down the steps to greet them at the door. Becky looks ready for the heat, dressed in a colourful, floral sundress that shows off her slim figure, and wearing large, glamorous sunglasses. Tendrils of her thick wavy hair have escaped from her ponytail, softly framing her heart-shaped face.

"Momma!" Taylor says. "We're here, in Rome!" He gives his mom a big hug.

"It's so good to see you," Cate says, then lets go of her son to embrace Becky.

"It feels like I know you so well already," Becky says. "We've had so many FaceTime chats."

Everyone starts to talk at the same time, eager to share their news. Ethan takes Becky's suitcase and carries it up the stairs, then shows them to their room.

Taylor and Becky are hungry after their long journey from London, and there is no food in the apartment, so they set out to explore the neighbourhood. Taylor uses an app on his phone to find a co-op market where they score some staples like wine and cheese, potato chips, and chocolate.

Back at the apartment, Ethan pours everyone a glass of wine and Cate puts out some snacks. They have so much to say, so many stories to tell, they talk non-stop until almost eight o'clock.

"Well, I don't know about anyone else," says Ethan. "But I'm ready for a proper meal."

Out on the streets of their busy neighbourhood, restaurant proprietors aggressively battle for their patronage. They choose a somewhat quiet space in the mercato where the next five days of indulgence in exquisite Italian cuisine begins.

After several hours, they return to the apartment with plans to begin their explorations of Rome the next morning.

Ethan and Cate wake up first. They throw on some clothes and venture to the coffee shop downstairs and purchase espressos to go.

When Taylor and Becky get up a few hours later, the four of them sit down for a discussion over breakfast. They all agree that Vatican City is the first attraction on their long list of must-do's. It is only a short walk down a few streets and under a bridge. They take a selfie by the sign that reads "Via Alla Poesia," to mark the occasion of their first outing in Rome.

"What does *poesia* mean?" Cate asks Becky, who knows Italian, as well as Spanish and French.

"Street of Poetry," Becky answers.

"Even the street names are romantic here," says Ethan.

At the Vatican, Ethan purchases VIP packages. Their guide takes them on an intimate and informative, three-hour tour that includes the museum, the courtyard that overlooks the Pope's gardens, the Sistine Chapel, and St. Peter's Basilica.

After walking for three hours they are past ready for a late lunch, and Becky uses her Italian to find a small pizzeria.

"That was mind-blowing," Cate says as she takes a bite of gooey-mozzarella-cheese-covered pizza. "I can't decide which part I liked best, it was all so incredible."

"I agree," says Becky. "But if I had to choose, the Gallery of Maps mesmerized me with its contrasts of simplicity and complexity."

"I think we can all tick off some big-time bucket list items after that tour," says Taylor.

"And we've only just begun," says Ethan.

Over the next four days, the four of them explore Rome in an intense attempt to pack everything in. Cate finds pause once again to be grateful for her ability to walk without pain in her legs as they traverse from one world-renowned attraction to another. They take in the Pantheon, the Trevi Fountain, the Spanish Steps, the Villa Borghese Gardens, the Coliseum, and Circus Maximus.

Their final night in Rome has them dressed to the nines and off for dinner to the trendy Eitch Borromini museum, restaurant, and hotel.

"Ah, how perfect, it is Mama, Papa, and zee kids!" the host exclaims with passion.

He leads them to the rooftop patio that overlooks grand fountains in the square below. They order pre-dinner cocktails with unusual names like The Diva and The Mexican Mule. The sun dazzles low in the early evening sky, lending a pristine quality to the white and glass elegance of the decor.

"This entire experience has been exquisite from beginning to end," says Cate. "But tonight, we want to acknowledge both of you for your recent graduations from university."

"To Taylor and Becky," Ethan says, lifting his glass into the air.

"You guys have spoiled us so much already, this is really over the top," says Becky.

"Thank you so much," Taylor agrees. "We appreciate your generosity, and even more, your love and support."

When it is time for dinner they are shown to a private dining room with windows that open to the beauty and bustle of the plaza below. Ethan splurges, ordering an expensive Amarone, and they take turns offering up more toasts of gratitude and appreciation. They dine on aromatic, chef-inspired dishes.

Stuffed and a bit tipsy, they laugh and regale one another with more stories on the walk back to the apartment. Before she tucks into bed, Cate gets out her journal.

Pinch me again, I'm still dreaming. Rome has exceeded all my expectations. It has been nothing short of enchanting. But, as Taylor said over dinner, the best part has been how the four of us have connected with such authentic, easy flow.

I notice the many ways my son and I are alike. We share common passions and ideas, values and interests. I guess I should have known that whoever he fell in love with I would fall in love with too, but it doesn't always happen that way. As it is, I couldn't be more thrilled. Becky is as perfect a match for Taylor as I could have fathomed. They challenge one another, neither one of them shy to broach the heavy topics, but they do so with acceptance and tenderness, even when they disagree. My heart is full, my cup is brimming over, spilling onto the floor.

Cate and Ethan check out of the rental shortly after Becky and Taylor catch a taxi to the airport. Ethan has booked a driver to take them to the Port Terminal where they will board the *Celebrity Reflection* cruise ship.

After going through security, Cate and Ethan are issued their Sea Pass cards. They are offered a glass of champagne when they board the ship, then given directions to their stateroom, where Paulino, their attendant, welcomes them with an ear-to-ear grin.

"Welcome to the *Celebrity*," says Paulino. "I'm here to make your stay as comfortable and enjoyable as possible, so please, let me know if you need anything at all."

"Thank you," says Cate, pleased by the warm welcome. His broad Jamaican accent seems to add to his energy of positivity. "It's definitely tight quarters, but with the door that opens onto a balcony, it's bright and cheery."

Once their luggage is delivered, Cate and Ethan head out to explore the ship. A buffet lunch is served in one of the many dining rooms. They are both hungry, so they find a table in the shade on the patio and order a glass of wine.

"I know with absolute certainty that I've never had a vacation this divine in my entire life, and the cruise is only just beginning," Cate says as she looks around in wonder.

"So far it does seem quite impressive," Ethan agrees.

After lunch they set out to continue their exploration of the ship. They stroll along the upper deck where they view the pool and sunbathing lounges, then switch gears to find solace over a glass of red wine in the Cellar Masters. The atmosphere is posh, old-school-study–style, with exposed brick and high-back, burgundy leather chairs.

They dine at the Tuscan Grill and later, when they are back in the privacy of their room, they embrace one another on the fresh, crisp linens, their first time with any privacy in ever so long.

Life on the ship is a continuous contrast. At each port, Cate and Ethan participate in a variety of excursions. When at sea, they use the well-appointed fitness centre, relax by the pool, try their luck at the casino, and generally eat, drink, and get merry.

At the gateway to the French Riviera, they take a taxi to Monte Carlo, where the highlight for them is the Grand Casino. They marvel at the gold-gilded ceiling and elegant architecture. In the main gaming hall there is only one blackjack table, the minimum bet, twenty-five euros.

"Fancy a shot at that price?" Ethan asks.

"What the heck?" says Cate, taking a vacant stool. "It's a once-in-a-lifetime opportunity."

They lose the small amount of money they allocated for gambling quite quickly, but not before two high rollers join in, cashing in a €10,000 chip to bet stacks of €600 a play without blinking an eye. It is all a bit surreal, but Cate thinks to herself, *I could get used to this reality*.

When they dock in Barcelona, Cate and Ethan take a wine and tapas tour that ends with a flamenco dance performance in an intimate theatre in the Gothic quarter. They luck out with front-row seats.

"That gave me goosebumps," Cate says to Ethan. "I feel like I'm starring in an episode of *Fantasy Island*, only we're on a cruise ship and we're not stranded."

"It's really just the fantasy part, then?" Ethan says. "I have an idea for the next episode."

One morning over breakfast on their balcony, Paulino pops in. He spots a butterfly on the ledge.

"You two have good fortune, I see," Paulino says with his contagious smile. "A butterfly on your balcony is a sign of good luck."

It isn't long before Ethan starts to get restless.

"What do you think about heading up to the gym for a workout?" Ethan asks.

"Actually, I'd rather skip the gym to take some quiet time to write in my journal before our tour," says Cate. "Do you mind?"

"Of course not, my love, take all the time you need," Ethan says. He slips into his tan weave shoes. "Since Paulino seems to think good luck is coming our way, I think I'll skip the gym too and head down to the casino to try my luck at blackjack."

Ethan kisses Cate goodbye and Cate fishes out her journal from her nightstand drawer She sits cross-legged on the couch.

> *This time on this blissful cruise, just Ethan and I exploring the world together, has been so delightful. It feels amazing to be living my life for me, without the constant inner turmoil of worry about Dana and Chloe always on my mind. It reminds me how important it is that I continue on my letting go journey and learn how to find a healthy balance. My role as mother is transforming into my role as the crone. Crone. I envision a witch, a gnarly old woman with a crooked nose. I hate how that word sounds. Maybe that's part of my resistance.*
>
> *I still haven't been able to let go of my attachment toward Chloe and Dana's situations. I can't seem to accept their choices and how they live their lives, no matter how hard I try. I remember when I was dating Finn, I realized that accepting isn't about settling, it's about choosing. I choose to allow them their journey, knowing it isn't my responsibility to fix things if they fall apart. I choose to allow myself to feel all my emotions, my grief and my worry. I allow my tears to flow, knowing it is a part of the process, that my tears are holy and healing.*

Cate and Ethan take in another wine and tapas tour in Malaga. They stroll for three hours on a Roman exploration tour in Cartagena. In Ibiza they relax on a casual excursion to Calla Conta Beach.

On the last night on the ship, the captain announces it is an evening chic theme, and Cate decides to go all out. She dresses up in the red gown she bought for the Red and White Ball. Ethan rocks it, James Bond style, in his tuxedo. As they leave the cabin, Paulino emerges from the elevator.

"Lady in red," Paulino sings, then whistles.

"I have to agree with you, Paulino," Ethan says as he takes Cate by the arm. "My wife looks absolutely amazing."

"As this is your last night, I must say farewell," Paulino says.

"Thank you for everything," Ethan says. "We really appreciated your positive energy and the pride you took in your work."

"Thank you for saying so, but I'm only a cleaner," Paulino replies.

"You are much more than that," Cate says. "You are a ray of sunshine. You went above and beyond your duties to provide us with the best service we've ever experienced, and it made a difference."

Tears form in the corner of his eyes. Paulino takes both of their hands in his and thanks them again for their kind-hearted words.

When they return to their cabin after dinner, Ethan pours them each a glass of red wine.

"Let's go sit out on our balcony, one last time," Ethan suggests.

They stare up at the big, black sky, speckled with stars, holding hands. Cate feels like she is glowing as bright as the stars overhead.

"Whether we are on a dream cruise, in Canada, Rome, or Riyadh, it's all beautiful because we're together," Ethan says.

"I love you," Cate says. She takes the last sip and sets her glass down on the table. "And I have an idea for something else we can do on this ship, one last time."

Cate takes Ethan by the hand and leads him back inside.

The next morning, they leave the ship and board a bus that takes them to the airport in Rome. Cate gets out her journal.

> *Ethan pretty much summed it up when he expressed his gratitude for everything we have shared together. I'm feeling as fortunate as it gets. Ethan's love for me may not be the antidote for my healing, but it is the best gift God has blessed me with. Which is saying a lot, because I've been given so much.*
>
> *When we were at the gym a few days ago, an entire fleet of dolphins appeared. They danced with glee in the ship's wake. It felt like when Paulino saw the butterfly, like another sign of good luck. Like the horse and the eagle on Vancouver Island, where it all started.*
>
> *I'm feeling like the luckiest woman alive. It's almost hard to believe that the traumatic events of this spring happened.*
>
> *I'm curious to find out what good things are still to come, just around the corner but out of sight. I know there will be more difficult times too, but I think I've gotten through the hardest of it. I'm feeling hopeful, for Dana and Chloe, for each of my four children, and my grandson too.*
>
> *I still dream of building a retirement home in Panama with Ethan, but who knows if that will come to be. Whatever the future holds, this Ramadan has been larger than life, an experience I will cherish and look back on fondly, with gratitude, forever.*

Chapter 21

CATE AND ETHAN RETURN TO Riyadh, still radiating from their trip of a lifetime. They unpack, do laundry, the little things. It is "same old, same old," but Cate feels like she has a new pair of rose-coloured glasses on. She finds bliss even in the mundane routines of her life.

Cate returns to a healthy schedule that is balanced. She goes to belly dance class and yoga practice. She prays and meditates and uses healing affirmations. She nurtures connection with her loved ones abroad over FaceTime and through emails. She connects deeply with the women in her tribe. She journals and reflects. She pumps up her gratitude practice, making space to be thankful at the beginning and end of each day.

One evening when Cate and Ethan are in the living room, each on one of the couches reading, Ethan surprises Cate.

"I can't seem to stop thinking about the Azura compound," Ethan says.

"Azura? In Panama?" says Cate. "What on earth has made you think about that now?"

"I know, it's kind of crazy," admits Ethan. "We've just had the trip of a lifetime, but something inside me is yearning for a place to settle down, that we can call our own. Wouldn't it be sweet if we had a holiday home to travel to, with no stress around arranging accommodation, where family and friends could come and visit us for a change?"

"It does sound appealing," says Cate. "I think you and I would have a blast building a home together. And you know how much I loved the designs and workmanship of the homes on Azura."

"It's a deal then," says Ethan. "Are you happy for me to send an email? I could let the project developer know we're interested and would like to start drawing up plans during our vacation there in August."

"Okay, I'm in, all the way," says Cate. She glows with happiness. Life really does seem to be taking her in exciting directions.

Cate is in her yoga room, engaged in her practice, when her phone buzzes. She ignores it, because this time is for her. But then it buzzes again, and again. Her intuition starts to tingle. She releases from her pose and picks up her phone.

"Hello?"

"Maman?" Dana says, the word barely a whisper.

"Dana, what's wrong?" Cate asks. Her intuition leaps into full-gear by the anguished sound of Dana's voice.

"It's Dad, he, I…" Dana begins. She stops, then gulps back a huge sob before she can continue. "I just got off the phone with a police officer, he's asked me to come identify a body, Dad's body.

"What?" Cate pauses, stunned into silence. "What do you mean?" She wobbles, then falls to her knees.

"I-I don't know," Dana stammers. "The police just said it was under investigation. Apparently, the cause of death is uncertain.

Cate can hardly compute. She is plunged into the pit. Her vision blurs. Her ears ring. She feels as though she's going into shock. She wants to say something, but she can't form a coherent sentence.

"Maman, are you there?" Dana says. She sounds desperate, like she's coming undone.

"Yes, I'm here my love," Cate says, mustering all her will power to stay strong for her daughter. "I wish I knew what to say, had some words of comfort, but, I don't. It's all so shocking. Do Taylor and Celeste know?"

"No, I called you first," Dana sobs. "It so sucks that you're in Saudi Arabia and Taylor is in London. Even Celeste is too far away. I'm all alone, and it's too much for me to bear."

"I know, it's horrible," Cate says. "I don't think they can make you identify the body if you don't feel comfortable with that. Surely his mother and father can do that."

"Oh, Maman, I've got to go, I see another call coming in," Dana says. "I'll call you back."

After Dana hangs up, the silence lands like a hammer. Cate falls onto her mat and rolls into a ball, her knees pulled into her chest. She lets out a howl. Once released, she can't suck it back in. It isn't just finding out about John's death, although she was completely unprepared for that news. It's about her children and how devastating this will surely be for them.

Ethan returns from the gym and hears Cate sobbing. He drops his keys and runs up the stairs. He sees Cate and walks swiftly over to her, then crouches down to pull her up from the floor.

"My God, Cate, what's wrong?" Ethan asks.

Cate can't answer. She can't find words to speak, what comes out is unintelligible drivel.

"It's okay," Ethan tries to console her. "It's okay, I'm here, but you've got to talk to me. Do I need to call the medical centre?"

"No," Cate manages to say. "Just hold me."

Ethan holds Cate in his arms. She cries until she can't cry anymore. He hands her tissue after tissue. It feels like hours have passed, but in reality, it isn't long before Cate's senses begin to return. She shakes her head, as if waking from a dream, and looks up at Ethan.

"Dana called," Cate says. "The police have found John's body. I, I, I..." Cate stumbles, unable to continue.

"Hush, my love," Ethan says. "You don't have to tell me right now. Just take a few moments to breathe."

"Dana was supposed to call me back, but she didn't and I've tried to call her, but it just goes to voicemail," Cate says. She gets up off the floor with Ethan's help. She almost falls over when she takes her first step. Ethan supports her and they move to their room. Cate shivers and crawls under the covers.

"Try not to worry," Ethan says. "I'm sure Dana will call you as soon as she gets a chance. She's likely overwhelmed herself."

"You're probably right," Cate says. The emotional heaviness overcomes her and she falls asleep, holding her phone.

"Ethan?" Cate calls out. She is disoriented. She was dreaming. Or was it real? She isn't sure.

She looks at her phone, lying on top of the bed covers beside her. "Did Dana call back?"

"No, there's been nothing," Ethan says.

"Dana said she'd call back hours ago. I need to call her. I need to go to Calgary and be with her. But then there's Taylor and Celeste. All three of them must be reeling. I feel so pulled, in every direction, I don't know where to begin."

"Let's just take it one step at a time," says Ethan. "I'm here for you."

Cate tries to call Dana, but she doesn't pick up her phone. She paces the floor and stares into space. She crawls back into bed and sleeps for hours. When she wakes up it is night and Ethan is asleep beside her. She goes to the kitchen and pours herself a glass of water. She takes her journal and her pen and sits down on the couch to write.

> *I should have known the tide was going to turn. That's how it works. If I've learned anything, it's that. The ebb and flow of life, the pattern like a heartbeat on an EKG machine; up, down, up, down. Somehow, I let myself forget. Lest they forget.*
>
> *I don't really know why this has hit me so hard. My mind is racing with questions about what happened. How did he die? It's been so long. I know he was fighting his own demons. Dana has been the only*

one he's spent much time with the last few years,
and even that has been limited to the odd visit here
and there.

Even though there was so much pain and
dysfunction in our relationship, despite it all, there was
a tender side to John. I did love him, once. At least, in
the only way I knew how to love back then. I had my
own challenges, my own share of burdens.

Cate can't focus to write anything more. She sets down
her pen and gets up off the couch. She tells herself to stop
spiralling. These are old emotional response patterns and
Cate knows she can do better. She goes up to her yoga room,
to her prayer cushion, and sits cross-legged. She quiets her
mind. She closes her eyes and goes inward, to her spiritual
centre, where God lives. She prays for strength, courage,
and wisdom. She feels enveloped in soft, purple light. She
feels the energy of God fill her, coursing through her veins
with a power that is palpable.

Several painful, almost unendurable days go by. Cate has
more conversations with Dana and she reaches out to Taylor,
Celeste, and Donna, too. She attempts to move forward by
examining the past. She remembers the time, back when
Celeste wasn't yet two, when she started dating John. When
she saw the wolf at the window and John's severed arm
in a vision. She wonders now, was it a sign of just how deep
his darkness went?

Cate recalls how after she married John, he became so controlling. She remembers the first time she witnessed just how debilitating his depression could be. It was not long after Dana was born. A million memories flood over her.

Cate moves from her bed to the couch. She can't sleep, but she doesn't have the energy to do anything. She stares into space with a vacant look on her face. She doesn't shower or prepare food or walk Fredrick. Her heart urges her to go and be with her children, but she can't make decisions. Ethan has to pick up the pieces.

After two days of inertia, something triggers Cate into action. Her heart tells her that she needs to be with her children, but her head tells her it is too difficult. She worries that it isn't her place, as the ex-wife. She worries that John's family will be angry towards her.

After hours of considering all the possibilities, Cate decides to honour her heart. She doesn't lean on her own understanding, but leans into God. She doesn't have to figure out the details. That will come in time. She prays for the strength to be of service. Not to fix anything, but to love. She gets up off the couch and starts to pack her suitcase.

When Ethan gets home from work later that day, he's barely in the door when Cate appears.

"I need to go and be with them," Cate says.

"I know," Ethan answers.

They go into the office onto the computer and book Cate a flight and accommodation in Calgary. She calls Taylor and Dana, and books them flights to Calgary too.

The night of her departure, Cate is packed and ready to go hours earlier than she needs. She goes into her yoga room with her journal.

I took my first step forward on my healing journey when I hurled myself out of my comfort zone to begin a new life on Vancouver Island. Inside the expansiveness of freedom, I began to discover how to love myself. I found my courage. I started to build my healing tool-kit. I spent time in nature, I journaled, practiced yoga and meditated. I had to re-learn how to listen to my body and my intuition.

Early on I realized there was no destination. What I was searching for was inside me. I learned that acceptance isn't about settling, it's about choosing. Then, when I wasn't looking, I found true love with Ethan. I had to unravel the stickiness of my past with John before I could build a solid foundation to dream upon.

Ethan's love has taught me so much. But I also found out along the way that his angel wing didn't complete me. I had to do my own work. I had to learn how to love and approve of myself unconditionally.

Chloe's battles with mental health, Dana's struggles with stability and my challenges with Lyme disease disrupted my healing process. The move to Riyadh was a huge adjustment too. I had to dig deeper and expand my skill set. I uncovered the importance of detachment as I struggled on my letting go journey. I had to learn to accept what I can't change.

I found strength in the support and wisdom of my sisterhood in Tribe. I chose to let go of the heaviness, guilt, criticism and judgment, to focus on gratitude. I'm not perfect, I never claimed to be, but I am good enough.

Life is a heart-beat. It is an ocean tide that ebbs and flows. If there is one thing I've learned, it is to accept and trust that rhythm. To enjoy the highs and endure the lows. Love is the steady foundation. The healing isn't a place you arrive at, it is a place you discover deep inside you.

It's time to hurl myself back out of my comfort zone. To release all doubts. To find my strength and trust my authentic self. I know it will be hard. But I know how to do hard. I've got the skills and the determination, the love and support. I've got the strength and integrity. I've got this.

Author
Lynda Faye Schmidt

LYNDA FAYE SCHMIDT believes that creating is her life purpose. Whether that manifests in building meaningful relationships, writing poems, blogs, or stories, or simply preparing gorgeous food, she loves to be fully engaged in the process. Lynda writes emotionally impacting, character-driven stories, based on real-life experiences.

Lynda has been honing her craft since she began scribbling poetry in the back of her elementary school exercise books. She has a massive collection of journals, which are her foundational reflective and creative tools.

Lynda earned a Bachelor of Education, majoring in reading and language, at the University of Calgary. As a teacher, she held positions from kindergarten to grade nine. She developed an interest in special needs education early in her career and enrolled in numerous workshops to develop her skills, alongside gaining valuable experience in the field.

As part of her lifelong interest in reading and writing, Lynda has attended writing workshops, was a member of the Writer's Guild of Alberta, completed a creative writing course at Mount Royal College, and finished The Artist's Way online course by Julia Cameron.

In September 2017, Lynda started her blog, Musings of an Emotional Creature, where she writes about topics that inspire, impassion, and ignite her. She writes about everything from travel to life as an expat, relationships, and current events.

Lynda was a contributor for *DQ Living* magazine in Riyadh, Saudi Arabia, from July 2018 to June 2019. In her role as staff contributor, Lynda wrote articles on a variety of topics. "The Way of the Future" covered the ambitious transportation goals of Saudi Vision 2030, including the construction of the new US$22.5 billion metro project. She also wrote a travel article on Bahrain and interviewed two female entrepreneurs: Princess Nourah al Faisal of Nuun Jewels and Sarah Bin Said of Blend Culinary School.

Based on true events, *The Healing* is a work of Women's Fiction / Family Drama that follows Cate Henderson, who, after twenty-six years in an abusive relationship, sets out on a quest to find healing and create a new life.

Lynda believes that solid routines, balanced by open spaces that allow for opportunities, are the foundation for success and happiness. Her days are filled with time spent on her mat, practicing yoga and meditation, reading, writing, taking care of business, and connecting with the people she loves.

Lynda Faye Schmidt is a Canadian expat. She lives in Riyadh, Saudi Arabia, with her husband, David.

With Gratitude...

The daily practice of gratitude has been a foundational tool in shifting my perspective. It has given me space to relax into flow and connect with my creativity. I'm grateful to so many family members and friends. Here, I want to acknowledge the people who were integral in helping to manifest *The Healing*.

David Schmidt, you are my rock; our love is the foundation of everything.

Anne O'Connell, your mentorship and role as a partner in publishing have been life-changing gifts. Your support lifted my writing to new heights.

Krista Wells, the lotus design and cover artwork are stunning.

Grace Laemmler, your interior design is absolutely phenomenal.

Marianne Ward, for your meticulous proofreading.

Danielle O'Brien, your positive energy started the string of serendipitous events.

Anne Pybus, it felt amazing to "blow your socks off."

Anne Marie Horne, it was an honour to bring you "at times to tears, at other times to laughter."

Carol Kujula, your friendship, love, and support as I walk "the path through heartbreak" has been instrumental.

Julia Crouch, your friendship contributed to me finding my resilience and "trust in the journey."

Lynn Lambert, your powerful gifts as a healer were life-changing. Thank you for "diving into the unknown" with me.

Lori Smith, for loving me unconditionally and supporting me always.

CPSIA information can be obtained
at www.ICGtesting.com
Printed in the USA
LVHW030126090421
683894LV00010B/233